the
Hungry Dead

the
Hungry Dead

John Russo

KENSINGTON BOOKS
www.kensingtonbooks.com

KENSINGTON BOOKS are published by

Kensington Publishing Corp.
119 West 40th Street
New York, NY 10018

All Kensington titles, imprints, and distributed lines are available at special quantity discounts for bulk purchases for sales promotion, premiums, fund-raising, educational, or institutional use.

Special book excerpts or customized printings can also be created to fit specific needs. For details, write or phone the office of the Kensington Special Sales Manager: Kensington Publishing Corp., 119 West 40th Street, New York, NY 10018. Attn. Special Sales Department. Phone: 1-800-221-2647.

Kensington and the K logo Reg. U.S. Pat. & TM Off.

ISBN-13: 978-0-7582-8499-0
ISBN-10: 0-7582-8499-3
First Kensington Trade Paperback Printing: October 2013

eISBN-13: 978-0-7582-8500-3
eISBN-10: 0-7582-8500-0
First Kensington Electronic Edition: October 2013

10 9 8 7 6 5 4 3 2 1

Printed in the United States of America

CONTENTS

ESCAPE OF THE LIVING DEAD

PROLOGUE

In the beginning, the most serious question was: How to feed them?

They shunned animal flesh, although the undead were animals themselves, just like all humans living or dead. "Higher animals" versus "lower animals," those were the designations. The undead, for some presently unknown reason, recoiled from the flesh of the so-called "lower animals," no matter how hungry they were. They wouldn't eat it even if they were experimentally starved for a week or more. No, they only liked the flesh of living or recently dead humans.

It was very clear early on, in the laboratory, that these zombies shunned all *nonhuman flesh*—whether living, dead, or near dead. They would not try to make a meal out of a wounded or helpless nonhuman animal of any species, although everyone knew by now that they fiercely pounced upon living or near-dead humans and devoured them like packs of hungry wolves. Even though they were themselves rather slow-moving, their strength was in numbers, and in their ravenous appetites.

But in captivity, when one tried to force-feed them dog meat or horse meat or turkey meat or even more exotic sustenance like rattlesnake or shark meat, no matter what it was mixed with, and no matter if it was marinated, basted, baked, roasted, stir-fried, or deep-fried, it would make them violently ill. It was extremely difficult to control and clean up after them, for they puked and puked, flailing and writhing and banging their heads against the padded walls and the bars of their cells, like crazed crack addicts going cold turkey.

Their value as lab creatures was drastically compromised when they were in such a sick and frenzied state. Dr. Melrose found *that* out in the early stages of the epidemic and the experiments. So did the other scientists. The ones who later viciously castigated him, joining in with the hordes of unenlightened fanatics who smugly, self-righteously proclaimed his ongoing experiments to be "unethical and immoral" and ranted that he was "playing God" and "doing the work of Satan."

Yet many of these same scientists used to wholeheartedly condone marvelous scientific breakthroughs like stem cell therapy, gene-splicing, and cloning. But now it was as if they had crawled back into the Dark Ages. They were acting like ignorant savages, frightened by the rise of the undead and by everything that science, so far, had utterly failed to understand about them.

Dr. Melrose despised these hypocrites and naysayers and came to the realization that he was much braver and farsighted than they were. He was a visionary, and they were not. And he was determined to keep on experimenting with the undead, because if he could solve the mystery of their inability to totally die, he might at the same time unlock the Secret of Eternal Life.

PART ONE

THE OUTBREAK

CHAPTER 1

It was a bright July morning, and the sun had risen an hour earlier, making sparkling diamonds of the dew on the manicured grass between the tombstones.

It should have been a quiet and peaceful cemetery.

But Deputy Bruce Barnes was taking careful aim at a ghoulish creature plodding toward him.

This one was a male, maybe forty-five years old, wearing a tattered gray suit, a dirty, blood-spattered white shirt, and an unknotted necktie that hung loose, outside its vest. Bruce knew that this walking dead man had probably once loved and likely was loved in return. Perhaps, because he was wearing a suit, he could have worked in an office doing some kind of clerical job. Maybe he had been an accountant, a businessman, or a lawyer. But that was all over now. He was yet another unfortunate victim of this horrible epidemic that no one knew how to cure.

Bruce knew that he had to dispatch the undead man with a well-placed shot to his head. He tightened his finger on the trigger of his high-powered rifle, held his breath, and waited for the creature to come closer. He sighted in on it, steadied his aim, and fired, and the creature fell with a heavy thud.

Bruce ejected the spent shell and chambered another round in his lever-action Winchester. Primed to face even more danger, he sensed movement in the leafy shadows of the maple trees on the outer edge of the cemetery. He heard crackling noises of twigs and underbrush, then another of the undead beings stepped out into the open. And when it came into closer view, Bruce saw that it was a huge male—and he shuddered when he realized that the big oaf was munching on the soft biceps of a severed human arm. The arm looked soft, flabby, and stringy, and perhaps relatively easy to bite into. Absorbed in what he was doing, the big ghoulish zombie did not notice, assuming that it was capable of noticing, that he was being watched by somebody with deadly intentions.

Bruce found this particular zombie to be especially scary. The man was not only threateningly huge, but he had a cruel-looking snarl. It was easy to imagine him as a thug of some sort, a mean, brawling behemoth in his previously "normal" life. He was wearing a flannel shirt, bibbed coveralls, and huge clodhoppers, and Bruce guessed his height at over seven feet, his weight at somewhere between three and four hundred pounds. Subduing this guy on a drunk and disorderly, when he was fully alive, would've been a daunting task for Bruce and any other of the three uniformed cops that he worked with on the county police force. But now the big brute was dead and still walking, slowly and painfully with ebbing strains of rigor mortis still partially disabling him—and yet he was even more frightening than he might have been when he was kicking ass in some booze-ridden dive.

Just as Bruce was about to try to bring down the gigantic creature, several more emerged from the surrounding woods. Perhaps they could smell live flesh, for they immediately started shuffling toward Bruce, drooling as if they could already taste him. They were more decayed and dead-looking than most of the ones he had encountered earlier, and there were four of them. He hoped he could squeeze off that many accurate shots before they got to him. He wondered where his fellow cops were. He hoped they didn't get themselves surrounded in some other part of the cemetery, and he cursed himself for impetuously moving ahead at his own pace instead of waiting for them to catch up. He wasn't trying to be a hero; he was just trying to get the job done quickly, and he had thought they'd stay close behind him. But now he might have to pay a terrible price.

Which one should he aim at first?

He decided to keep his rifle trained on the monstrously huge zombie carrying the severed arm, try to take him out quickly, and then go for the others.

Just then a volley of shots rang out.

Two of the zombies menacing Bruce went down, hit in the head with bullets.

The big one in the bibbed coveralls dropped the severed arm and turned back toward the woods. A bullet tore into the dead man's right shoulder, but he kept going, trying to get away. Bruce fired at him and missed. He quickly cocked his Winchester.

More shots rang out as cops and posse members rushed forward, firing their weapons, and several more zombies bit the dust. One of them, a female shot in her torso, reeled but did not fall. Her rasping breath got louder as she kept coming, angry and hungry, wearing an ordinary print housedress, her hair up in curlers. Then a shot right between her eyes brought her down.

Bruce took another hasty shot at the big zombie in the bibbed coveralls, wishing he had a scope on his Winchester, but he didn't, and the bullet went wild. He cocked his lever-action rifle again and was about to take aim when he heard his boss, Sheriff Paul Harkness, yelling from somewhere behind him.

The sheriff was a gruff, big-bellied man with a cigar-smoker's loud, hoarse voice. "Hold your fire!" he barked. "We gotta *collect* a few of these damned things! It's orders from the higher-ups, and we gotta obey!"

Sticking close to the sheriff was another uniformed deputy, Jeff Sanders, who had been Bruce Barnes's sidekick on many a patrol. And following those two lawmen were about a dozen well-armed citizens who had volunteered to be part of the ghoul-hunting posse. They clustered among the tombstones and monuments, catching their breath and waiting for Sheriff Harkness to tell them what to do next.

Bruce was on the verge of firing his rifle again at the big dead ogrelike fellow in the bibbed coveralls, but the sheriff said, "Hold it, Bruce! Stop! Let the doc and his guys try to collect *that* big ugly brute! He might give 'em more than they bargained for! I tried to tell Dr. Melrose we need to kill 'em, not fuckin' experiment on 'em, but he don't wanna listen!"

Bruce really didn't want to ease up on his trigger because the big zombie that he avidly wanted to bring down had momentarily stopped trying to escape and was instead coming back for the severed arm lying in the grass. "I say we kill 'em all!" Bruce said. "Only good zombie is a dead zombie!"

"Listen to me, Bruce," the sheriff said. "The scientists wanna study 'em—find out why they ain't quite as dead as they oughta be."

Bruce shook his head in consternation as he eased up on his trigger finger.

Jeff Sanders put his hand on Bruce's shoulder. "I want to shoot every damn one of them, just like you do," he said. "But orders are orders. You don't wanna get yourself fired."

Bruce knew that his buddy Jeff, ten years younger than he was, was usually even more of a hothead. Dark, handsome, and effortlessly charismatic, Jeff was a ladies' man whether off duty or in uniform, although his habitual flirting didn't seem to ever lead anywhere; it probably could have if he wanted it to, but although he was a flirt, he loved his wife Amy very much, and the bottom line was that he seemed to remain faithful to her. Yet on the job he was often flamboyant or impetuous, sometimes getting both Bruce and himself into unnecessary danger. But at the moment he was trying hard to be the adult in the group and not piss off Sheriff Harkness.

The sheriff yelled over his shoulder. "You guys with the dart guns—c'mon, get up here!"

Four men in white lab uniforms emerged from among the tombstones, wearing white caps and surgical masks and carrying weapons capable of firing the kinds of darts that are used to immobilize wild animals. The sheriff barked at them, "Hurry up! Go get that big guy munching on some poor dude's arm! Don't let him get away!"

The four men advanced timidly toward the big zombie in the bibbed coveralls, and Bruce stared at the bold black letters on the backs of their white coats: MELROSE MEDICAL CENTER. In their temerity about facing an ominously huge zombie feasting on a human arm, they slowed and hung back, and Dr. Harold Melrose, a small, balding man in a dark suit, now came forward, flashing Sheriff Harkness and Deputy Barnes a contemptuous look. Around his neck was a stethoscope, and he wore wire-rimmed spectacles and a prissy little mustache, and to him the sheriff and his deputy were just dumb cops, too obtuse to understand the exigencies of true science, so he hustled past them as if they were as worthless as dirt.

As Melrose's lab technicians got closer to the big foreboding zombie, he dropped the severed arm that was his meal and turned toward the men and scowled at them ferociously. He took a few slow, ponderous steps toward them—and they immediately started firing their paralyzing darts. One dart missed, but the other three struck the big zombie in the leg, chest, and shoulder, and he groaned and fell with an earth-pounding thud, then rolled over, flat on his back.

One of the technicians said, "My dart missed. Lemme have another shot."

Another said, "No, hold off. We're not supposed to finish him. Dr. Melrose wants 'em alive."

"Haw! Alive is exactly what he ain't! Not like you and me anyways."

"That's why the doc wants to find out what makes 'em tick."

Dr. Melrose came on the scene, looked down at the unconscious zombie, and said, "Excellent . . . excellent . . . a fine specimen. Stand back, will you?"

He knelt over the huge specimen, cupped his hand around the bell of his stethoscope, and started to bend forward.

Sheriff Harkness stepped up and barked a stern warning. "I wouldn't get that close if I were you, doc."

Deputy Barnes added, "This is a four-hundred-pound man. You might not have him fully immobilized."

"Nonsense!" Dr. Melrose intoned haughtily. "His eyelids aren't even fluttering. I have to make sure there's a trace of a pulse."

Deputy Jeff Sanders couldn't help scoffing, "What makes you so sure these things even have a *heart*?"

"That's precisely one of the factors I intend to explore," said Dr. Melrose. Then, staring at the sheriff and the deputy, he hit them with a prissy-sounding complaint. "This fellow has been shot in his shoulder. He's damaged goods."

"What do you expect?" Barnes said. "He was coming right at me. I wish I had blown his brains out, or what's left of them. I was trying hard to do exactly that."

"Don't blame you," said Sanders.

But Doc Melrose went on ranting at Bruce Barnes. "You didn't do so well, Mr. Macho Man. You only gave him a flesh wound, a shoulder burn. It may heal or it may not. We can't predict yet how much healing capability they may have. That's one of the very important things we wish to find out."

He crouched and leaned forward, placing the bell of his stethoscope against the big zombie's chest. He listened intently while the other lab men looked on with fear and tension in their faces.

Suddenly the huge zombie that was supposed to be inert lunged at Dr. Melrose and grabbed him by his head. The doc tried to pull away, but he lost the struggle, and the zombie sunk his teeth into the good doctor's throat.

Paul Harkness, Jeff Sanders, and Bruce Barnes jumped around aiming their rifles, trying to get a clear shot to shoot the zombie in his head, but were too scared of hitting the doctor or each other.

The four lab technicians got into different positions close to the big, madly chomping zombie and fired more darts into him, till finally, to everyone's great relief, the zombie slowly let go of his grip on Dr. Melrose's head and fell backward and once more lay still.

Bleeding from his throat, the doctor pulled out a white pocket handkerchief and tried to stanch the flow of blood while he groveled in the grass for his wire-rimmed spectacles and put them back on even though they were bent. His neck wound was a quite terrible one, and it kept bleeding profusely, even after Dr. Melrose decided to lie on his back in the grass and try to calm down, hoping that if he slowed his pulse it would slow the blood flow.

One of the lab men rushed forward and seized the bloody handkerchief, trying to help press it against Melrose's throat wound. The doc was breathing in and out slowly, in great raspy groans.

Deputy Bruce Barnes, a bit panicky now, stepped closer to the doc and put the muzzle of his Winchester a foot away from Dr. Melrose's temple, saying, "He's been bitten. He's gonna turn into one of *them*."

One of them lab men said, "No! Don't shoot Dr. Melrose! Let us take him to the medical center!"

Bruce said, "No way. You smart-fart scientists don't even know what causes this, let alone how to cure it! He's gotta be shot."

"Fuckin' a!" Deputy Sanders said, suddenly blurting out his true belief in no mercy as he drew his own revolver as if he would dispatch the wounded zombie even if Bruce didn't.

But Sheriff Harkness intervened. "Hold your fire, you two! At least for now! He hasn't become one yet, and he won't until he dies."

"He's gonna die right now," the leading lab man said, "if we don't stop arguing over him. We have to get him to the medical center right away!"

Another lab man pleaded, "At least give us a chance to help him pull through. If he doesn't make it . . . well . . . we can do whatever becomes necessary at that time."

"Okay," said the sheriff. "That sorta makes sense. Good luck to you. You're sure gonna need it."

Dismayed by this turn of events, Bruce Barnes grumbled, "Mark my words. Only good zombie is a dead zombie."

And Jeff Sanders said, "Right on!"

Chapter 2

The sky was high in the sky, and the day was made even hotter by the huge fire consuming the bodies of the undead that had been shot in the cemetery. Deputy Jeff Sanders and an armed civilian, Dan Castillo, dragged the inert form of yet another vanquished ghoul from between two large ornate monuments and over to the fire. The dead thing was heavy, even for two strong men grabbing it by its legs and arms, and they grunted as they heaved it onto the fire, then stood back taking a breather as they watched the dead man's clothes start to glow, then incinerate.

"This is definitely the craziest day of my life," Dan said. "I hope I never see another one like it."

"Well, it's not gonna end today," Jeff pronounced. "There're more of 'em around here, that's for sure."

"I think we've got them just about cleaned out," said Dan.

"Just about, but not totally, I don't think," said Jeff. He had been surprised two days ago when he found out that Dan Castillo had joined up with the posse because he had always pegged Dan as the bookish type. They had graduated from high school together, and Dan had entered law school while Jeff was being trained at the police academy. Over the past few years, there had been times when Jeff was unmercifully grilled by Dan in court-

rooms where the defendants were scumbags who'd been arrested. They both said "no hard feelings" afterward and tried to
sincerely mean it, but still they had remained wary while trying
not to start hating each other. At first blush, it was hard for Jeff to
imagine that the suave young lawyer could be an effective ghoul
hunter, but it turned out that he had kept himself fit by playing
tennis and handball and was actually a good shot. He liked to let
off steam by target shooting, not hunting, and he spent quite a lot
of time practicing at a shooting range run by the Evans City
Sportsmen's Club.

"What do you think is going to happen to Dr. Melrose?" Dan
asked.

"Gonna die . . . then come back," Jeff said. "Then he'll have
to be shot in the head by somebody, maybe one of those lab guys
who wanted to try and save him."

"Maybe they don't all die," Dan said.

"Never heard of one who didn't," Jeff scoffed. "Anyone bitten
becomes one of those things. Then they have to be shot or
burned."

"I know that's usually been the case . . ."

"*Always* been the case."

"Yes, as far as we now know," said the lawyer. "But think
about AIDS, Jeff. A disease we totally did not understand, and it
was always a hundred percent fatal. We all thought it was worse
than the bubonic plague. But eventually we found ways to delay
the worst symptoms even if we couldn't defeat it. And now it's
not always a death sentence. Some folks even survive it and go
on to lead normal lives."

"Ain't gonna happen to Dr. Melrose," Jeff said. "He's gonna
turn into one of these thing we're trying to hunt down and kill. I
hope he doesn't get to bite one of his lab guys first, before they
wise up."

"Why do you call them *things* when you know full well they're
human, just like us?"

"Because they're not like *us* anymore. They used to be, but
they're not now. I keep that in mind so I don't choke up when I

have to shoot them. Especially the women and the kids. I hate having to kill them."

"Well, it shows that you're a sensitive person," Dan said respectfully. "I like that quality in you . . . or anybody. You're not just a hard-nosed cop."

"Well, thanks, but you're more hard-nosed than I am when you've got me in front of a jury."

They both laughed, then Dan said, "We better move on and catch up with the sheriff."

"Wait a minute—I hear some noises back there in the woods."

"Just trees rustling."

"Not enough breeze. Something's moving."

"I don't hear anything. I'm moving on. Are you coming?"

"No, not till I check it out."

"Don't go in there by yourself. C'mon, let's catch up with the rest of the guys and get us some hot coffee."

"Something is in those woods, and I'm not letting it stay alive to chomp on somebody. I'm goin' in there."

"Suit yourself. I'd stick with you, but I'm sure you're hearing things, Jeff. I'm sorry, but I'm cutting out."

Dan moved off a ways but then looked back, hoping Jeff would follow. But Jeff didn't. "Don't go in there alone!" Dan shouted, but when he didn't hear any reply from Jeff, he shrugged and reluctantly headed out of the cemetery toward the rendezvous point Sheriff Harkness had previously designated.

Slowly working his way into the wooded area, Jeff's eyes darted around warily, and he stopped and scanned his surroundings. At first he saw and heard nothing, and he thought maybe his buddy Dan was right in arguing that he was making a mountain out of a molehill.

Then suddenly three zombies, two males and a female, came out from within some thick foliage. Both males were wearing shorts and T-shirts that revealed numerous tattoos covering their arms and legs. The female, in a lavender blouse and tight denim shorts, was a shapely teenage girl who probably used to be beautiful, but now her face was hideously ripped and scarred. All three were spattered with the blood and gore of people they must have attacked and devoured.

Startled by them at first, Jeff wheeled and hastily fired, blowing a hole in the young girl's chest. She fell, knocked back by the impact, but started to get up again.

The two male zombies kept on coming.

Jeff took careful aim at the female's head and blew her away. Then he worked his lever-action and swiveled his Winchester onto the closest male zombie.

With a loud rasping groan a fourth zombie suddenly lurched at Jeff from behind, grabbing him by the shoulders and making him drop his rifle. He tried to scramble for the dropped weapon, but now three zombies were upon him, and he had to scratch, punch, and claw at them to avoid being bitten. Pounding a hard blow into the flabby paunch of the zombie who had first grabbed him, he realized its belly was partially rotted and feared that his fist would penetrate into the decayed bowels. But instead the hateful being let out a whoosh of foul-smelling breath and crumpled to the ground, groaning and salivating.

Jeff backed away, yanking his service revolver from its holster. He managed to squeeze off three shots that echoed loudly but went wild as he stumbled backward through the trees.

Emerging into a weed-grown meadow, he found himself immediately in even worse trouble. Six ravenous adult zombies were hovering over the partially devoured remains of a human corpse, and as soon as they saw Jeff, they got to their feet and came at him. He fired his revolver twice, scoring two head shots and a wild miss. But when he pulled the trigger again he got only a click.

Still clutching the empty revolver, he took off running.

The zombies came after him.

He ran toward a small pond and frantically splashed his way in, deeper and deeper. In chest-high water, his hat gone and the rest of his uniform totally soaked, he turned and faced the pursuing zombies. Crazed with fear, he yelled at them, "You damn things!

You're scared of fire—but how about water? I hope you're scared of water too, you ugly bastards!"

Two of the female zombies hung back, at least temporarily, which gave the lawman hope. But four others kept coming mindlessly forward as if the water made no impression on them. Two big males uncaringly, unfeelingly, slipped under the ripples, seemingly to drown—if zombies *could* drown. And maybe they could, because in short order there were bubbles gurgling around them, and then the dead things floated like driftwood on the pond's surface.

But two female zombies kept after Jeff and waded deeper into the water. He clubbed the first one in the head with the butt of his revolver, and then kept on clubbing her again and again till she stopped struggling and floated on the surface like the two others.

When the last remaining zombie lunged at him, Jeff managed to seize her by the throat. Pushing her head under the water, he choked her as hard as he could, terror written all over his face as he yelled at the top of his lungs. *"Die, you bitch! Die! Die! Die! Die!"*

But her evil, twisted face rose up toward him, and with all his strength, he tried to push her back underwater. Then, even though she was being choked, she somehow started talking to him, and he thought he must be going crazy.

"Jeff . . . stop . . . you're hurting me . . ."

He choked her harder, trying to make her last rotten breath bubble out of her.

"Please . . . Jeff . . . you're hurting me . . ."

Suddenly, shimmering, he saw the face of his wife. It wavered like the ripples of the water, then it became clear.

It was Amy, and he was choking her in their bed.

Scared of what he had done, he let go of her, and she fell back, crying and holding her throat.

He covered his own face with his hands, his fingers still tight and sore with the effort of the choking. "Oh, god," he lamented. "Amy . . . I'm so sorry . . . I'm so sorry . . ."

This was not the first time such a thing had happened. It was sixteen years now since the day that Dr. Melrose had been bitten in the cemetery. Jeff's hair was gray now, his face lined and much older looking. He was only forty-one, but he was under the strain of posttraumatic stress disorder. He shook his head dolefully, his hands still covering his face in remorse.

Amy's voice was hoarse from the damage he had done to her with his fingers, and she was overcome with sadness, a sadness tinged with ruefulness because she still loved him. "You say you can't help it, Jeff. But I've stuck with you all this time, through all the counseling, all the rehab and the expensive medication . . ."

"I know . . . I know . . . and I'm sorry, Amy. I understand what you've been through. I understand that it's my fault."

"But you're still flipping out on me, and I have no clue where or when it's liable to happen. I have no idea what sets you off."

"I didn't start having flashbacks until three years ago. And lately it's been coming over me less often. I've been having fewer and fewer nightmares."

"Yes, but it only takes one, like the one you just had, that might kill me. How do I know that next time, or the next, I won't end up dead?"

"I don't think . . . I mean, I always manage to snap out of it in time."

"Always?" Amy said softly. "I'm not so sure I want to keep betting my life on it."

He started to cry. He couldn't help himself. For most of his life, even when he was a child, he had prided himself on his ability to hold back tears, even when others bullied him or said nasty things about him, or when he tried out for plays or other high school activities, such as the football or baseball teams, and didn't make it.

But now he cried. And Amy still loved him enough to wrap her arms tightly around him and try to comfort him.

But he was scared their marriage might be over.

PART TWO

THE MISSION

Chapter 3

Janice Fazio didn't know that she was being followed.

And the person following her didn't know that *he* was being followed also. He felt sure that she was an easy victim. She was obviously headed directly for where he already knew her car was parked. He had already checked it out, and he congratulated himself for his cleverness, his attention to appropriate detail. To his satisfaction, she had left the car in a sparsely lit lot on a murky side street that seldom had a flow of cars or pedestrians.

It was near midnight, and Janice had just left her friend Michelle in a dinky little cocktail lounge on the depressingly quiet main drag of Willard, a slow, boring little town whose sole claim to fame was that it had been a so-called "rescue center" during the zombie epidemic of sixteen years ago.

Big deal. Who really cared about that anymore?

Janice was disappointed in her friend Michelle because Michelle had such poor taste in men, as usual. She had hooked up with a distasteful young man that Janice wanted no parts of. He called himself "Chub." No last name, no first name, just Chub, for God's sake! He had quoits in his earlobes and a face-darkening stubble of black beard that he probably thought made him cool instead of proving that he was too damned lazy to shave. He wore three-quarter-length denim cutoffs with holes sliced in them, no socks, scuffed and dirty sneakers as big as barges, and a limp and faded dirty orange wifebeater shirt with a cartoon of a brown turd on it and big, dripping brown capital letters that said: I GOT MY SHIT TOGETHER. There were amateurish tattoos dotting his hairy, skinny calves, making them look even skinnier and hairier than they actually were.

Chub was the person who was following Janice.

Blake Parsons and Spaz Bentley were the two thugs who were following Chub.

They worked for Dr. Harold Melrose.

Blake and Spaz were two peas in a pod, two thugs in a pack, each feeding off the other's mean attitude and easy disposition toward brutality. Both had rap sheets that included armed robbery, assault with a deadly weapon, manslaughter, and various lesser crimes and misdemeanors. They were big, beefy men with shaved heads, and they carried concealed handguns and leather blackjacks. They each had black teardrops tattooed under their right eyes, prison tattoos that were symbolic of the number of people they had killed. Blake had two teardrop tattoos and Spaz had only one, and Blake often ragged on Spaz that he'd have to hustle to catch up.

They knew that Chub Harris didn't have any teardrop tattoos because he had never done any prison time and had never been punished for any of his rapes and murders. The cops knew he was guilty, but they couldn't prove it. Officially they had him down as only a "person of interest." He had eluded a statewide manhunt for over a year, then he made a minor screwup and the cops got onto him. They wanted to make an arrest, but they needed more evidence. But Blake and Spaz were not under those kinds of constraints.

Chub had the hots for Janice Fazio, not her friend Michelle. He had pretended to be highly interested in Michelle only so he could hover close to Janice and study her. He had blandly and patiently concealed his anger over the obvious fact that she didn't like him. Obvious because she took pains to *make* it obvious. But the smug little bitch was going to get her comeuppance.

As soon as Janice had excused herself with her series of dumb little lies so she could flee from the cocktail lounge and from his unwanted company, Chub had excused himself to go to the men's room—but he never had any intention of returning to the table. Instead he ditched dumb little Michelle and slipped out the back door and into the alley that smelled of rotten garbage. Then he had speedily caught up with Janice, and now she was doomed. He smirked at the thought of it.

Blake Parsons and Spaz Bentley were smirking too. Because they knew that Chub was the one who was doomed.

Doomed to become zombie feed.

The main question in their minds was: How far should they let things go? Should they let Chub have his way with Janice first, and then take him when he was totally unsuspecting and satiated? Or should they save her by pouncing on him before she became aware of any threat to her?

In their philosophical discussions with Dr. Melrose, he had made the point sometimes that it wasn't any of their responsibility to interfere with people's normal destiny. Their mission wasn't to alter history, either personal or political. Whatever was about to happen to Janice Fazio was not set in motion by them; therefore it was not in any way unethical to merely let it happen. They were not under any moral obligation to alter her fate. Ergo, they could not be blamed in any way for letting it unfold naturally.

"Maybe we should phone the good doctor," Blake suggested in a whisper.

"No, it would just annoy him," said Spaz. "He expects us to make the right decisions based on what he's taught us. And, really, we already know the right thing to do, don't we?"

"Yeah, I just wanted to run it by you," said Blake. "What about afterward? Should we make any use of her?"

"Well, if it doesn't get us caught . . ."

"That's what I think," Spaz agreed readily. "It'd be a shame to waste a perfectly usable dead human body."

Meantime, Chub had quickly cut through a path between a poolroom and a beauty parlor and had run through an alley paral-

lel to the main drag so he could outflank Janice Fazio and get into
the parking lot ahead of her. Then, as she approached her little
red Mazda, he was already lurking behind a blue grocery-market
van only two spaces away from her. When she unlocked the
driver's side door and swung it open, he pounced on her. He just ran
at her and delivered a hard body slam. He heard the breath whoosh
out of her. She went down by his sneakers, and he stooped over her
and punched her three or four times in her face. She was out cold
quickly. He picked up her keys and unlocked her trunk. Then he
lifted her limp body and put her in there.

Blake and Spaz watched Chub attack Janice Fazio, a fairly
neat and easy job on his part as planned captures went.

They knew he was going to rape and kill her, probably by slow
strangulation, which was his motif. Usually he would choke to
the point of unconsciousness, then let up till the victim revived,
then choke her again; he would do this six or seven times, till he
ejaculated from the sheer thrill of it. He already had a string of
six victims. Taking him out would be a service to the community,
even to the nation, because he was a killer who liked to travel far
and wide to spread terror.

Blake and Spaz were proud of what they were about to do to
him. He didn't know it, but he had met more than his match.
They were going to do the honorable thing where he was concerned. They were going to take him out. And if Janice Fazio had
to be sacrificed, well then, she was just collateral damage.

The two minions watched Chub load and lock Janice's limp
body into the trunk of her Mazda. Then the ugly little serial
killer picked up her keys from where he had made her drop them
and got behind the wheel and drove away.

Blake and Spaz followed in their van, the blue one with the
fake sign that said OLSEN'S GROCERY MART.

CHAPTER 4

Sheriff Harkness was sitting behind his desk, and Jeff Sanders, looking haggard and sad, was slumped in a chair facing the sheriff. It was a Tuesday, a duty day, and both men were in full uniform.

The sheriff tipped back his hat and said, "Your wife phoned me and told me what happened last night. She doesn't want to press charges."

Shaking his head, Jeff said, "She's too good to me. I don't deserve her."

"Certainly you don't. Not in the condition you're in now. She did say she's been thinking about a divorce."

"Yeah, and I guess I can't blame her."

"Well, I believe I talked her into letting it slide for a while. Amy's a good gal, and she wants to stick by you, but you've been making it too damn tough on her. I think you should put some distance between you and her. It might help a lot if you do that."

"You're saying I ought to move out?"

"I'd like to put you on a little special assignment," the sheriff said. "It might do you some good . . . give you a chance to confront your old demons."

"What are you driving at, Sheriff? You have me stumped. My demons are in my mind. No place else, right?"

Instead of answering right away, Sheriff Harkness pulled out a
pipe and started filling it. "Fucking pipe," he said. "Wish I could
go back to cigars, but the doctor said I'm addicted to them, and
fussing with a pipe and the rigamarole that goes with it might
make me give up tobacco all together. But I'm not sure I buy the
logic in that. Do you?"

"He's trying to use psychology on you," Jeff said. "Reminds
me of my shrink. A hundred bucks an hour, and I'm still a mess."

"Don't be so hard on yourself," the sheriff said. "Speaking of
docs, do you remember Dr. Melrose?"

"Sure. He's the nutty guy who got bitten in the throat."

"Right. And if you ask me, that was worse than what happened to you out in that pond. At least you didn't get bit."

"Well, I wanted to believe that I came through without a
scrape. But I guess I was wrong. I'm a danger to my own wife.
I'm a mental case, just like those soldiers who saw so much and
suffered so much in Iraq and Afghanistan."

The sheriff finished filling his pipe and lighting it, then he said
tentatively, "The special assignment I'm talking about involves
Doc Melrose. He lives way out of town, back in the sticks, you
see . . ."

"He's the only one I ever heard of who pulled through after
being bitten by those dead things. I don't know how he did it.
Some folks swear he made a serum out of the thing's blood."

"He won't tell anyone what kind of medicine he took," said
the sheriff. "Lots of other scientists sure would like to know. Just
in case there's another outbreak like that sometime."

"What does Melrose have to do with this special assignment
you're talking about?"

"We had another disappearance last night," the sheriff said. "A
young woman named Janice Fazio. She works for a dentist here
in Willard, Dr. Patterson."

Surprised, Jeff said, "I know Janice! She's my dental hygienist.
Amy's too. Janice is cute . . . and smart. She was hooked up with

a boyfriend who didn't treat her right, didn't deserve her, and finally she wised up and ditched him. Could he be behind her disappearance?"

"Well, she's gone and so is her car—a red Mazda. The boyfriend has a solid alibi, so it can't be him. But the past year or so, there's been a spate of rumors about strange goings-on around the Melrose Medical Center. And a couple of shady characters who work there were spotted in town late last night."

"Who?"

"Blake Parsons and Spaz Bentley. They both have rap sheets. And they were seen getting out of a van in the same lot where Janice's Mazda was parked. The van had a sign on it that said Olsen's Grocery Mart. I've never heard of it, have you?"

"No."

"Well, no such place seems to exist around here. Anyhow, I can't picture those two mopes bagging groceries. And if they were up to no good, somebody else was probably behind it, because they aren't heavy thinkers."

Jeff said, "Is there any evidence pointing to the doctor?"

"At this point I have to say no. The doc and his kids, they keep to themselves out there in the middle of nowhere. But I have a gut feeling that he ought to be looked at pretty close. I'd like you to nose around."

"Nose around how?"

The sheriff puffed on his pipe a couple of times. Then he said, "I'm talking about sending you in undercover. You maybe could get yourself hired out there, get in tight with Parsons and Bentley, and get the real dope on them. Maybe they'll even start blabbing, if they had anything to do with Janice's disappearance. You might be able to gain their trust if you get in there and play your cards right."

Mulling it over, Jeff said, "We almost shot Doc Melrose sixteen years ago. Looks like maybe we should have."

"Now don't go off at half cock, Jeff. You've got to be clever but careful. If you can get inside of whatever's going down out there, play it cool so they don't catch on to you. Don't try to be a hero. Be a fly on the wall. Just listen and observe. This kind of thing is outside the box, and it could have a beneficial effect on you. It might even turn your whole life around. You've got to get your act together somehow. Otherwise you're gonna lose Amy."

CHAPTER 5

Three days later, Jeff was standing by the side of a rural road with his thumb out, but so far he hadn't seen many cars or trucks, and the few he had seen passed him by without even slowing down.

He had to admit he looked like a pretty rough character, and that was his intention. He was wearing faded jeans, a rumpled flannel shirt, hiking boots, and a backpack. He had a stubble of beard, and all in all appeared hard-bitten and rugged. If he ever got to Doc Melrose's place, he wanted to seem like a drifter looking for any kind of menial work, just so he could get his foot in the door. Somebody without much money or family. Somebody who could easily be taken for granted, and not a person bright or nosy enough to cause trouble.

If he hadn't been on a mission that had him totally preoccupied, he could have appreciated the dazzling fall foliage. With the sun shining through the reds and purples of the changing leaves, it was definitely the kind of day that served as a tourist attraction here in Pennsylvania.

In fact, three such tourists were on their way toward Jeff, and they would soon be plunged into circumstances that would turn out to be momentous for them, even though they had no way to anticipate this.

Albert Mathews was driving slowly on the lonely, twisting, and climbing blacktop road, allowing himself and his wife and son to take in the full effect of the fall foliage. His late-model black Ford had a rooftop luggage rack laden with suitcases and camping gear covered with a blue tarp. Albert and his wife Meg were in their early forties. Their son Stevie was sixteen and always had his MP3 player hooked into his ear, drowning out his parents.

Albert said, "George Washington roamed these hills two hundred years ago, Stevie."

Stevie said, "Huh?"

So Albert yelled louder. "The father of our country fought some big battles right around here!"

"Cripes, you don't need to yell, Dad," Stevie said. He had pulled the sound plug out of his ear for once.

"Well, I'm sorry," said Albert. "I'm so used to talking over that stuff you call music."

"I heard what you said," said Stevie. "You were talkin' about the Revolutionary War."

Turning toward Meg, who was riding in the front passenger seat, Albert said good-naturedly, "I told you these kids don't learn anything in school anymore."

Meg turned and spoke over her shoulder to her son. "Your father was referring to the French and Indian War, not the revolution. French troops were closing in on Washington's troops, and he ordered them to hastily build a fort to try to defend themselves. That's why they named it Fort Necessity. Right, Albert?"

"Right. That's where we're headed, son. It's about eighty miles from here."

Albert, who was a college history teacher, also had written three books on various aspects of the Colonial Period, and his publisher had bought his proposal for yet another book dealing with the defeat of General Braddock, which had taken place near Uniontown, Pennsylvania, not far from Fort Necessity. Albert loved visiting the sites where historical events had actually taken place, and Meg always went along with him with considerable enthusiasm, while to his chagrin, his sixteen-year-old son took little interest.

"An old fort!" Stevie said with teenage disgust. "A pile of sticks! I'd rather be back home hitting the beach."

"Well, the beach and the ocean will still be there when we get home," Meg told him. "So please try to enjoy yourself and learn something about how our country got—Albert, please don't slow down for that man!"

She was referring to the hitchhiker she had just spotted standing at the side of the road a short piece ahead. But in spite of her words of warning, Albert was slowing down to have a closer look at the fellow. "Surely," she said, "you're not going to stop for him. He looks scary."

Albert said, "Well, it crossed my mind, Meg. He might be in some kind of trouble. But I suppose I shouldn't risk it with you and Stevie in the car."

"I should say not!"

All Stevie had to say about it was, "I wish you two would call me Steve or Steven, not Stevie."

But the boy's words went unnoticed as the sedan cruised slowly past Jeff Sanders, who finally lowered his thumb when he realized that yet another car was not going to give him a lift. He stared at the disappearing car as it climbed the next hill. Then he began hoofing it again, glancing over his shoulder now and then, ready to stick his thumb out if he spotted any more approaching vehicles.

Meanwhile, a few miles farther along, the Mathews family pulled off the road into a roadside rest stop with picnic benches. They picked out a place in the shade and set out a Coleman cooler filled with lemonade and started munching on sandwiches and potato chips, and Albert said, "Beautiful out here, isn't it? Unspoiled, that's what I call it. This is Pennsylvania, the Keystone State. It was known as the keystone of the thirteen colonies. The Constitutional Convention was held in Philadelphia, and that's where they have the Liberty Bell."

Stevie said, "Dad, do you ever stop spouting history?"

Meg said, "But that's what your father is, a historian."

"He doesn't have to keep cramming it down my throat."

"Don't talk to me or your father that way! When we get back to New Jersey you are going—"

Her reprimand was interrupted by the approach of a scuffed and banged-up white van. As it slowed down to pull off the asphalt and onto the grassy area close to the picnic bench, the driver poked his head out, eyeing the Mathews family. He was dirty and scraggly, and his ragged beard and greasy shoulder-length hair made his age hard to determine—probably somewhere between twenty to thirty, Meg imagined. The rear side windows of the van were wound up and were so grimy she could not see into them, but she glimpsed movement behind the dirty glass that indicated that the backseat must be occupied. She got more rattled when the van pulled up bumper to bumper behind the car, as if blocking any escape.

The front passenger window wound down, and the driver leaned back, and now Meg could see that there was a strikingly pretty teenage girl in there. This girl was so gorgeous and angelic looking, with perfectly golden hair and such a beautiful face, that she didn't seem to belong on the same planet as the van driver. But she exhaled smoke and handed the van driver a joint, saying, "Here, Hawk." He stuck it between his thick lips and inhaled deeply, his eyes glazed and staring. Then he handed the joint back to the girl as he held in his lungful of smoke.

Apprehensively, Albert, Meg, and Stevie kept their eyes on the van's occupants, wondering how much danger the family might be in. Finally Albert piped up, trying to sound gutsy. "What can we do for you folks?"

Hawk laughed, and an avalanche of smoke gushed out of him. The girl spoke up with a mocking smile on her face. "My name's Tiffany, and this is my new boyfriend, Hawk. Anything we can do for *you*, mister?"

"Back your van away from our bumper so we can get out of here when we're ready," Albert said, summoning courage.

Hawk barked out another laugh.

Tiffany said, "We just wanted to check on you, make sure you aren't broken down or something. Is everything okay here?"

"Sure, everything's fine," said Albert.

Hawk said, "Us'ns thought maybe you could use some help. County cops don't patrol much hereabouts. Nearest town's Willard, about thirty miles over the mountain."

"I know," said Albert. "I've got my road map and GPS. We're just having our lunch break."

Tiffany giggled all of a sudden as a hard-to-see face moved closer to the van's grimy side window. Albert, Meg, and Stevie jumped back with alarm. The "face" was a human skull, pressed against the grimy window, bobbing and leering while the people in the van laughed uproariously.

Giggling, Hawk said, "Sorry if we scared ya. That there skull ain't nothin'. Just Nutso playin' games. He ain't right in his head, but he don't mean no harm to nobody."

The side window wound down, and the skull floated out on the end of a long, hairy, tattooed arm—and two thick fingers were wiggling out of the skull's eye sockets like feelers on an insect.

Hawk said, "It's just an old Injun skull, close to two hundred years old, I reckon. We been excavatin' and dug it up. Nutso likes to play with it."

Appalled by this stupidly callous treatment of a genuine relic, Albert said, "You ought to turn it over to a museum and let the authorities know where you found it so they can explore for more artifacts."

Stevie whispered, "Dad, they're not going to listen to you."

And Meg added, "Just let them be on their way, honey. Please."

The skull floated back in through the window, eye-fingers still wiggling. Sunlight streamed partially into the backseat area, revealing a glimpse of Nutso—a big, moronic oaf with a vacant look in his eyes. Albert, Meg, and Stevie couldn't help staring at him—and also at a second backseat passenger they could suddenly make out in the dim patch of sunshine. It was the hitchhiker that they didn't pick up when they had seen him a few miles back with his thumb out. Now they were more scared of him than ever because of the company he was keeping.

They were relieved when Hawk wound the side window shut, and the van backed out and headed down the road.

Albert said, "Maybe you two should've locked yourselves in the car till they left."

"Oh, sure," said Meg. "Then we just drive off while they beat you to a pulp."

"They gave me the creeps," Albert admitted. "I wonder what that beautiful young girl was doing with them."

Stevie said, "Dad, you're so naive sometimes! Some babes'll go with anybody who can score them some dope."

CHAPTER 6

Tiffany perked up when she asked Jeff Sanders where he was hoping to get to, and he said, "The Melrose Medical Research Center. I'm hoping to get hired there."

"As what?"

"Any kind of work they want to give me. I don't care how menial. I read about Dr. Melrose and the work he does, and I admire him. I'd like to take part any way I can."

"I know some people who work there," Tiffany said.

"Can you put in a plug for me?"

"I don't know. Maybe. I'd have to get to know you better."

She said this slyly, almost like a come-on, and Jeff was taken aback by it. He used to be, if not exactly a womanizer, then something of a flirt. But he certainly didn't want to have to deal with a sexually precocious teenage girl. He wanted to stay focused on his mission and save his relationship with Amy.

However, he wasn't above smoking a joint and guzzling some wine to make these people think he wanted to fit in with them. As the occupants of the van chugged from a half-gallon bottle of cheap red table wine and passed around a joint, the van weaved down the highway through spectacular mountain scenery enhanced by the fall colors. Next to Jeff, Nutso was still playing with the skull, holding it in his lap. He and Hawk and Tiffany were doing a lot of giggling while Jeff often just stared morosely out through the grimy window.

"Those people back at the rest stop were scared of us," he said. "You could see it in their faces." He shrugged and took another swig of wine when Tiffany handed him the bottle, then he passed it to Nutso.

Hawk said, "Why would they be scared? We wouldn't hurt a hair on their heads, now *would* we?"

Jeff said, "They saw me thumbing but were afraid to stop. Everybody's scared of me these days, even my own wife."

Tiffany flashed a sneaky smile and said, "You beat up on her or something?"

"Worse. Worse than that," Jeff admitted.

Then he sunk back gloomily and clammed up.

Hawk said, "Nutso got hisself a lucky strike today. Gonna make hisself twenty bucks. He'll sell that Injun skull to my little brother so he can put blinking turn signals in the eyes and mount it on the back of his Harley."

Nutso giggled, holding the skull up and wiggling his fat, dirty fingers through the eye sockets. Hawk and Tiffany laughed hard, then even harder, and Tiffany stared at Jeff for not laughing along with them. Nutso kept on giggling and staring too. Jeff could see Hawk's eyes staring back at him in the rearview mirror as he drove.

Jeff started to sweat and shake. He tried blinking his eyes and covering his face with his hands. But this didn't chase away the images of the skull with the wiggling finger-eyes staring and laughing.

Jeff let out a groan.

Nutso kept on leering and waving the skull idiotically, spittle dripping from his fat lips.

Suddenly the skull had rotting, oozing flesh on it—it had become a zombie head in Jeff's eyes, and he lunged at it and seized it by the throat, which was really Nutso's thick, hairy wrist. Jeff was in another world now, choking the wrist as hard as he could and yelling, *"Die! Die, die, die!"*

Nutso used his free hand, made it into a big fist, and punched Jeff hard in the forehead, knocking him back.

Dazed, Jeff groaned and panted, sprawled in the backseat.

Hawk barked at him. "Man, you freakin' out? You freakin' out. You gotta get outta my van!"

Jeff just lay there staring into space.

CHAPTER 7

An hour after they had finished their lunch, the Mathews family was back on the road, headed for Fort Necessity which was still seventy miles away, but Albert couldn't wait to get there. "Just being in this part of the country stirs my imagination," he enthused. "It's like stepping back in time. General Braddock got himself killed and his men annihilated because he was used to the way troops marched at each other in open fields in Europe, the way Napoleon fought. He didn't expect to go up against Indians firing bullets and arrows from the dense brush, then charging out to scalp and mutilate him and his soldiers."

Albert shut up suddenly because he saw something curious in the distance. It was Hawk's beat-up white van parked off-kilter, one set of tires down in a ditch.

"My god, they've had an accident!" Meg gasped.

"Cool it, Mom," Stevie said as if he believed himself to be more adult than his parents.

Albert slowed the car and cruised by very slowly, checking the scene out. The van seemed to be utterly abandoned. Albert started to pull over and park.

"Don't you dare stop!" said Meg. "Let's just keep going."

"Meg, be reasonable. If somebody needs help, I wouldn't be

able to live with myself if I just drove off without at least having a look around."

Stevie agreed, saying, "You're right, Dad. Not everybody who looks dangerous *is* dangerous."

Meg warned, "Be careful, Albert!"

He opened the car door and got out, then reached under the driver's seat and grabbed a tire iron. Clutching it, he cautiously approached the van, his eyes darting all around in case someone was lurking somewhere nearby. But he heard and saw no one.

The doors on the passenger side of the van were hanging wide open. Albert warily came nearer.

Meg and Stevie watched apprehensively from the car.

Tire iron at the ready, Albert checked out the front and rear passenger compartments of the van. Finding them vacant, he then went around to the back door and tried the handle.

When he pulled the door open, he had to jump back. Blood splashed at his feet.

Shuddering all over, he stared as the blood continued to drip, and it dawned on him that he was looking at a lumpy pile of blood-soaked sleeping bags. On top of the bags, all bloodied up, was the Indian skull that had been Nutso's plaything.

Gritting his teeth, Albert forced himself to peel back a corner of a sleeping bag, and he found himself confronting the dead, ripped, or chewed-up face of big, dumb Nutso.

He peeled back another corner and saw Hawk's dead face this time—but it was not chewed up at all. Instead there were two puncture marks in Hawk's neck.

Badly shaken, Albert covered the dead faces up, and then backed away from the van, still clutching his tire iron.

"Drop it, Mister!" someone barked at him, and he wheeled around and froze, then started trembling.

Two big, mean-looking men had pistols trained on him.

And another man, back at the car, had a shotgun trained on Meg and Stevie, who stared helplessly at Albert as a feeling of doom crept over them.

CHAPTER 8

The truth was that Dr. Harold Melrose did not know how or why he had been cured. He had taken painkillers, he had applied ointments, such as aloe and vitamins A and E cream, to his neck wound, and he had overdosed on steroids. He had even anointed the wound over and over again with holy water, desperately giving religion a chance, but this had not worked, and in lieu of resorting to an exorcist, he went back to being a full-fledged atheist.

In any event, as luck would have it, he got better. So, in his time of desperation, maybe something he tried had worked. But he didn't know what. Or maybe he had a natural resistance to the ghoul disease. A resistance that other people did not have.

However, in the past sixteen years he had not had any success with experimental "cures" that he kept on trying on his subjects.

He knew, to paraphrase *Hamlet*, that there were more things in heaven and earth than the human mind could thus far comprehend. But that didn't mean that *somebody* wouldn't be able to understand them *someday*. And he wanted to be that somebody. He had utmost faith in his own intelligence, cleverness, and scientific genius, in spite of his many frustrating setbacks.

To date, all of his efforts directed toward rehabilitating the undead had failed. He himself was the only ghoul-bitten person that he knew of who had not turned into one of them. Yet, he was not fully cured. He was carrying a genetic defect that he had unwittingly passed on to his daughters. He had little doubt that a crucial gene of his must have been altered by the ghoul bite sixteen years ago. And he was dedicated to solving the mystery.

His girls, Tiffany and Victoria, both born in years that postdated the year that he was bitten, were now strangely afflicted. Tiffany, the eldest, had been normal in every way until she reached puberty. Then she came down with a rare, almost unheard of disease called porphyria. Dubbed "the vampire disease" back in the Middle Ages, it had lapsed into obscurity over the next few centuries. However, it was responsible for many aspects of the vampire mythology. Sufferers became extremely sensitive to sunlight; they couldn't go out in the daytime without seeing their skin erupt in ugly blisters. Their gums receded from their teeth, making the canines look like fangs. And they actually craved blood, possibly due to the vitamin deficiencies and poor food absorption caused by the disease.

Tiffany was struck with this unfortunate ailment after she reached the usual age of puberty but was late in beginning menstruation. She acquired porphyria when she was fifteen, and it was only after she fought her way through it that she began to menstruate for the first time. In most ways she seemed perfectly normal thereafter. She never got sick anymore, not even a common cold, which in itself was abnormal. To all appearances, she had become splendidly, magnificently healthy.

Except now she craved blood.

Dr. Melrose had little doubt that his youngest daughter, Victoria, who had recently turned fifteen, was going through exactly what her older sister had gone through. And it drove him to despair.

His wife had died of cancer three years ago, and he missed her terribly. He saw her beauty and her personality reflected in his daughters. He wanted to rescue them from the blood-craving aftermath of their strange and frightening disease. But so far he hadn't learned how. And that was one of the major reasons his experiments must continue. He had not given up on his obsession with finding out why the undead could not die. But now he had the additional motive of doing the very best that he could for his beloved daughters, Tiffany and Victoria.

CHAPTER 9

Spaz Bentley pushed a remote-control button disabling the electrical current surging through the chain-link fence and swung the gate open, allowing Blake Parsons to drive through the entrance in the blue van with the fake grocery mart sign. Then Spaz climbed back into the front passenger seat for the short ride to the compound. They pulled up and braked, killed the engine, then hustled around to the back of the vehicle and opened the cargo door. Albert, Meg, and Stevie Mathews were lying on the floor of the van, their hands handcuffed. The dead-faced guy, Hawk, was handcuffed too, but he was also muzzled like a big dangerous dog; otherwise he might have chomped into one or more of the Mathews family. And the doc had said that he wasn't to be fed until he was examined.

Tiffany pushed the rear passenger door open and jumped down onto the gravel.

Spaz and Blake prodded the Mathews folks with their rifle barrels and ordered them to get out pronto.

"Go ahead," Tiffany said. "Take them in and cage them."

The two hired thugs herded Albert, Meg, and Stevie into a barnlike building.

Then Tiffany cooed to Hawk, coaxing him seductively. "Come on, don't be afraid. You can follow me. I won't hurt you."

After a little more coaxing, Hawk stepped down from the van and let Tiffany lead him by his hand. The fang marks on his neck still glistened, oozing a bit of blood.

"That's it, Hawk," Tiffany coaxed softly. "Come on, now . . . come to Tiffany. You're *such* a good boy, Hawk. You'd follow me anywhere, wouldn't you? You know that I gave you your life back. Now come with me. If you behave, we're going to feed you."

Tiffany was used to her strange powers now, and she actually relished them. At first she had hated finding out that, after she had recovered from porphyria, she had developed a blood craving. But she enjoyed it now, not just the taste of human blood, but the fact that along with the craving came a special power. If she bit someone and drank enough of his or her blood to cause death, the victim would arise again as a zombie and would be under her complete control. This made her feel invincible, all-powerful. Hawk was a big man, stupid but strong, and an ordinary woman would be no match for him if he turned brutal. But this cut no ice with Tiffany. She enjoyed dominating big, blustery men like him. And she could do it any time she wanted to.

She hated the underlying stench of the cages in the barnlike building that adjoined her father's laboratory. It was masked by an exorbitant use of bleach and disinfectants, but Tiffany's sense of smell was as strong as a bloodhound's, and the odor of old or dead things came through to her in spite of extraordinary attempts to mask it.

However, she wanted to visit the new captives that Spaz and Blake had brought in two days ago, for she was always curious about people who seemed to lead the ordinary sort of lives that she felt had to be quite boring and useless; in fact, it gratified her to think that because it made her more satisfied with her own circumstances. That's why she had decided to lead Hawk into his cage while they took care of the Mathews family and got them into their new accommodations.

After Hawk was prodded into a cage by himself, still muzzled so he wouldn't, in his hunger, start gnawing into his own arm,

Tiffany went over to the cage that imprisoned the known serial killer Chub Harris. He didn't know it yet, but he was going to become zombie feed. Or maybe he did actually know it by now. Maybe he had figured it out.

"How many women have you raped and killed?" Tiffany asked him.

"What's it to *you*?"

"I like murderers," she said. "They turn me on. If what you have to say pleases me, I could set you free, get you out of here."

"Ha! Why should I believe you?"

"Because my father owns this laboratory."

"Then he's not going to risk letting me go. I might tell on him."

"Tell on him for what?"

"Kidnapping. Holding me against my will."

"Haven't you done that to quite a few women?"

Chub's dry, chapped lips formed a sly, gloating smile, and the lip-stretching smile made one of the chapped places crack open and bleed.

Tiffany looked at the trickle of blood on Chub's lips, but she had absolutely no urge to lick it. Everything about this creep turned her off. She felt that his blood would poison her. Just looking at it made her want to puke.

"I fuck the women's brains out," Chub boasted. "Then I make sure they can't give their filthy pussies to anyone else but me."

"Is that what you did to Janice Fazio?" Tiffany probed, even though she already knew full well what had happened to Janice. Blake and Spaz had let Chub have his fun torturing and raping her, then playing his repetitive strangling game before finally finishing her off. They had watched furtively from a hiding place while Chub dug a shallow grave in the woods. They knew it would be a shallow one because the earth was hard and Chub was so lazy, so they didn't have to wait long before the grisly task was completed. After Janice was dumped in the hole and dirt was shoveled over her, Blake and Spaz had taken Chub down.

"None of your fucking business what I did to Janice," Chub sneered at Tiffany.

"I know what you did. She's buried in the woods behind Willard High School."

"How do *you* know about that?"

"I know everything that goes on around here and everyplace else. I learned a lot from my father. I'm not just some dumb blond bimbo. I'm starting premed school next year. I've been working with my father since I was nine years old. He trusts me more than anyone else."

"Is he screwing you?"

"None of your business."

"You're totally beautiful, blondie. I bet he can't keep his hands off you. But I bet your pussy stinks."

"You're the one who's going to stink real bad when we turn you into zombie feed," Tiffany jeered, then pivoted sharply away from him before he could respond and walked over to the cage that held the sad, terrified Mathews family.

Albert tried to be brave, even though he and his wife and son were helplessly caged. It was almost laughable to Tiffany. "Get away from us!" he blathered at her. "You look sweet and inno-cent, but you're a murderous bitch! You and that other guy!"

"What other guy, dear?" Tiffany said sweetly.

"The other man who was in that van, in the backseat," said Al-bert. "His body wasn't one of the ones I saw—neither his nor yours. One of you must've killed those other two, or both of you did."

"What if Jeff did it and ran away? Or what if he's dead? What if I killed him *and* the other two but didn't leave his body in the back of the van? You're not covering all of the possibilities, Mr. Mathews. Your brain is too addled. You're too stressed out."

"If you're so innocent," Meg interjected, "then why are we caged up here? We're not guilty of anything, and you must know it. So why don't you speak up for us? Why don't you set us free?"

"First of all, nobody in this whole world is totally innocent. We all have secrets. We all have done things we'd be embarrassed about if they were found out. Second of all, I think one of *you* killed Nutso and tried to kill Hawk. They were my friends, but you're trying to pin their murders on me. We're not going to set you free so you can run and tell your lies to the police."

At this, Stevie jumped up and came hurtling at Tiffany, but he was stopped by the bars of the cage. He stood there frustrated, screaming at her, "*Liar! Filthy goddamn liar!* Let me out of here and I'll rip your ugly blond hair out by the roots!"

Tiffany merely smiled at him, gloating in the fact that he was under her power, which was the power of life and death. "Rip my hair out, would you? Wouldn't you rather *fuck* me, Stevie? I'll bet you would. I'll bet your father would too. Are you a *virgin*, Stevie? Do you want to die or stay in a cage here for years and years without ever knowing what it's like to *get laid*? Especially by someone as beautiful and sexy as I am? I could fuck your brains out, Stevie. Yours too, Albert. And I can pleasure a woman just as well, *Meggie*. Wouldn't you like to go to bed with me? *Any* of you . . . or all three of you . . . the excitement might be more than you could take. But you'll never know, will you?"

"Get out of here, you bitch!" Meg screamed at her.

"I was leaving now anyway," Tiffany said haughtily. "Later tonight, after dinner, I'll help my father determine your fate. You should have been nicer to me, but you weren't. But when push comes to shove, I'm a fair and objective person, the way my father taught me to be all my life. So I'll try not to let your poor manners influence my opinion about what should happen to you. Now good evening, you all."

CHAPTER 10

Dr. Melrose tapped on Victoria's bedroom door. She said, "Go away," and he heard her sobbing even though her sobs were muffled by the closed door.

"May I come in?" he persisted.

"I don't want to see anyone."

"Not even your father?"

"Go away, Daddy, please! I'm too ugly to look at."

But he opened the door, peered into the semidarkness, and flipped on the light.

Instantly Victoria screamed and covered her eyes—but in the sudden bathing of light he had already seen her hideous face, all broken out in big, oozing purple blisters. And her legs and arms were horribly blistered too. It was hard for him to remind himself that without the disfiguration she was as beautiful as her sister Tiffany. He believed and hoped that the disfiguration would soon go away, and he had come to reassure her and comfort her with his scientific wisdom.

"Turn out the freaking light!" she yelled at him.

Shakily doing her bidding, he hit the switch and the room was in semidarkness again. Softly he said, "Sorry, sweetheart, I didn't mean to—"

But Victoria snapped at him bitterly, "It's your fault I'm like this! *Your fault!*"

He actually did feel guilty about it, but he said, "The blisters will go away soon. Then you'll be like your sister. She had those kinds of blisters too. But she loves the way she is now. She wouldn't trade it for the world."

"That's easy for *her* to say! She's so beautiful!"

"So are you, sweetheart," the doctor said, leaning over her. "You have porphyria, and it makes your skin very sensitive to the light. It came on when you hit puberty, just like it did with Tiffany, but she got over it quickly, and so will you."

"It's because you got *bitten!*"

"Yes, that's so, but it wasn't my fault. It happened because I was doing the kind of work no one else would do. Other scientists were so scared that they abdicated their sacred duty. I paid the price. I thought I cured myself, but a special gene was passed on to you and your sister. It made both of *you* special. That's the way you must think of it, Vicky. You're very special and very beautiful, and I love you both very much."

CHAPTER 11

When he hadn't had any sort of communication from Jeff Sanders for almost a week, Sheriff Paul Harkness decided he had to make some kind of move. Jeff was supposed to keep in touch by means of a cell phone that he kept hidden in the lining of his backpack. He had actually made several furtive calls, and the sheriff took heart that things seemed to be going as well as could be expected.

On his first surreptitious call, Jeff informed Harkness that he had indeed gotten hired at the Melrose Medical Research Center, but was not yet in a position to learn anything much. Whatever was actually going on was hush-hush, and he wasn't even allowed into certain buildings to clean up. He was employed at minimum wage as a janitor and handyman, but his work was confined to certain areas and everyplace else was off-limits to him. It was made excruciatingly clear to him that if he got caught where he didn't belong, he'd be fired, or maybe worse.

Then, in a second call, Jeff told the sheriff that he suspected Spaz Bentley and Blake Parsons were somehow involved in Janice Fazio's disappearance because of snatches of conversation he had overheard between them when they thought no one was close by. But he had no concrete evidence so far, and he was going to try to break into one of the off-limits buildings on the chance that he

might uncover something. Harkness sternly advised Sanders not to do anything foolish and to abandon his undercover role if he sensed it was getting too dangerous. In his third risky phone call, Jeff sounded half spooked. He said he had failed to get into the off-limits building, and somebody might easily notice that the lock had been tampered with, and he might be toast if he was the only employee out there who might fall under the suspicion of the security guys, Bentley and Parsons. That was the last phone call from Jeff. After that, all communication from him ceased.

Then a burned-out vehicle was found within a couple miles of the Melrose Medical Research Center, a late-model Buick registered to a Mr. Albert Mathews, a college professor from New Jersey. His parents were contacted and said Albert had taken his wife and son on a vacation to Pennsylvania and had not stayed in touch with them, which was highly unusual. It was his habit to phone them every night from wherever they happened to be staying because otherwise he knew they would worry too much. But as of late, they hadn't heard from him.

For the time being, Harkness didn't tell Albert Mathews's parents that his Buick was so totally destroyed by an arson fire that it had had to be identified by the VIN number on a flame-tarnished plate welded onto the burned and twisted frame.

Deeply worried about all these developments, some of which Deputy Jeff Sanders, so deep undercover, couldn't possibly know about, Sheriff Harkness decided to try for a warrant that would enable him to swarm all over the Melrose Medical Research Center with a slew of heavily armed officers, round up everybody in there, and thoroughly search the place before anything incriminating could be gotten rid of. The sheriff was sure that rapid deployment and a fast, hard-hitting raid was exactly what this situation called for. He wanted to use the element of surprise to full advantage. There could be a lot of crazies out there, and maybe some of them would have no hesitation about shooting down lawmen if they were given half a chance.

Sheriff Harkness went before a judge, made the sketchy reports from Jeff sound more weighty than they actually were, and

leaned his argument heavily on the only hard evidence at hand—
the burned-out Buick and its missing occupants. To his great relief, the judge finally agreed with him that there was good reason
to believe that Janice Fazio and some other innocent folks were
being held at the Melrose place against their will, and therefore
there was sufficient justification to issue a warrant that would enable law enforcement to act promptly and forcefully in order to
potentially save lives.

CHAPTER 12

Tiffany entered a small workroom adjacent to her father's laboratory, where Jeff Sanders lay unconscious on a stainless steel gurney. He was stripped nude, and his body was covered with bruises and burns.

Blake Parsons and Spaz Bentley had gotten the truth out of him, so far as he was capable of telling it, by beating him with a rubber hose and burning his flesh with lit cigarettes. Thankfully, he didn't really know much. But that wasn't for lack of trying.

Tiffany was the one who had caught him at his sneaky, traitorous game.

She had a sixth sense about such things.

She had never really believed much of anything he said about himself when he was riding in Hawk's van with her and Hawk and Nutso. The only true and honest thing he had done was to freak out and start seeing zombies where there weren't any. They were in his mind, and he couldn't help it. He must have had a really bad experience with them back when he was younger. Maybe he was somehow a victim of the same outbreak in which her father had gotten bitten.

Suspicious of Jeff at all times, Tiffany had started to keep an eye on him whenever she could. And luckily she had followed him one dark night when he creeped out of his room and worked his way behind the building where the zombie cages were. He had his backpack with him, and he furtively unzipped it and groped around till he pulled out a cell phone. At that very moment, Tiffany got her little .25 automatic out of her purse and aimed it at him. "Drop the phone, Jeff!" she told him sternly. "Drop it or I'll shoot you."

He stared at her, his face taut, then he did as he was told. He dropped the phone in the dirt.

Tiffany said, "You were planning to rat on us, then cut out of here, right, Jeff?"

He stammered, "No. Why should I? I just got hired here."

"And that happened because of me," she confessed. "You didn't know that, did you? I never trusted you, so I wanted you on a short leash. I wanted to give you enough rope to hang yourself, and now you've done so."

"I was only going to call my wife, Amy. I never told you about her. I wanted to find some kind of work here so maybe I'd start making some money and she wouldn't want to end our marriage."

"Liar! I can smell cop all over you! I'll bet some of the numbers you've called plug directly into the sheriff's office."

"No way!"

"It's no use lying to me. I know you're a traitor. Traitors used to be hanged in the old days during wartime, but out here we have our own version of the death penalty. It's called the *living death*, Jeff."

"Well put!" Blake said with a barking laugh. He had just arrived on the scene, and he had his gun drawn. So did his buddy, Spaz. Dr. Melrose was accompanying them, but unarmed, because he didn't need to be. Tiffany turned toward him and said, "Jeffy here remembers the outbreak sixteen years ago all too well, Daddy. He suffers from flashbacks. Funny you two don't remember each other from back then."

"I think I do sort of remember him," said Dr. Melrose. "In fact, I believe he *was* a cop. I never paid much attention to those dolts. They never made any great impression on me."

"I've never laid eyes on you, but I've heard about you," Jeff said. "You're the wacky guy who got himself bitten. I wasn't there, but I was close by, in another part of the cemetery, and we all heard about what happened. We all thought you should've been shot."

"Of course you would think that way. You're the type of person who would have joined the slavering mob who wanted to burn Galileo at the stake. You fear what you don't understand. But I face ignorance bravely and use my intelligence and my scientific curiosity to unlock the secrets that benefit mankind."

"Sure!" Jeff jeered. "Just like Dr. Mengele and all the rest of Hitler's deranged Nazi scientists! They *called* themselves scientists, but they were really a bunch of racist quacks!"

"You *poor* boy!" Dr. Melrose mocked. "You must have had an unfortunate and rather terrifying encounter with some of the undead. I can see that your mind is blown. You're suffering from posttraumatic stress. Maybe you'd like to try to work through your disorder. We can help you reconnect with some of the undead from back then that we still have in our cages."

"You *kept* some of them?" Jeff blurted. "Some of the ones who were infected?"

"We kept some, and we created others," Dr. Melrose admitted, and there was a trace of pride in his voice. "We wanted to keep carrying out our experiments. I was bitten, and I had to try to save my own life. I had to learn more about what may have caused the plague. The government disagreed with me and wanted all experimentation to stop."

Tiffany said, "They wanted to pretend it had never happened, or at least would never happen again."

"I didn't turn into one of the living dead," said Dr. Melrose, "so I came to believe I was completely cured. I think now that I must have had a natural immunity, but it was incomplete. The virus must have hibernated inside my body, like the herpes or syphilis viruses will sometimes do. It came out in a mutated form in my two daughters, around the time they reached puberty. They need to drink human blood. They're not flesh eaters. But

when they take blood from someone, it transforms the victim
into one of the undead, like the ones we keep in our cages."

"You're mad!" Jeff yelled. "You keep them for experiments!
Part of your perversity is that you want to believe these crazy experiments might help you find a cure for your daughters!"

Doc Melrose burst out laughing at this—a maniacal, diabolical
laugh to show that Jeff had missed his point. *"Cure them?"* he
sneered. "Heh-heh! Oh no, not at all! I want to find a way to
make *everybody* like them! Everybody! *Everybody!"*

"It's such a noble goal, Daddy," Tiffany assured him.

He went on rambling at Jeff because he was so proud of himself and he had a captive audience. "I suspect that Tiffany and
Victoria will never die. Yet they have all their faculties—they are
both highly intelligent, and they thoroughly enjoy art, music,
etcetera. They are not like the ones we keep in the cages who
cannot think except for a few basic instincts that animate their
dead brains."

All of this kind of talk brought on another of Jeff's flashbacks
and posttraumatic stress attacks. He totally went bananas. If he
were an ape, he would have been ramming himself at them or at
the bars of his cage and throwing his own feces at them. He was
shaking and cursing and rolling on the ground punching zombies
that weren't even there, and Spaz and Blake stepped back and
enjoyed it for a while, laughing uproariously and kicking Jeff
with the toes of their boots. But finally they tired of the display.
And they got Jeff into handcuffs and took him away to wait till he
came to his senses, so they could interrogate him further. They
had administered enough beatings and cigarette burnings to get
to the bottom of everything he knew. But in their pent-up anger
while they were grilling him, they had unintentionally treated
him far too roughly. Tiffany had ordered them to keep him alive
for the time being, but he kept on ranting and stupidly fighting
back when they tried to handcuff him, and he had another
episode of imaginary zombies, and they hit him too hard over the
head with a blackjack.

Now he was in a coma.

* * *

Tiffany's father was panicked. They all were. They knew now that Jeff Sanders was an undercover cop who had infiltrated his way in here to uncover secrets he wasn't supposed to learn. But luckily Tiffany caught onto him, and she had flushed him out. And the unmasking of him had given her and her father a timely warning that evidence had to be destroyed or cleared out before lawmen arrived in full force.

Tiffany smiled enigmatically now as she looked down at Jeff. His breathing was very raspy and thin. She stroked his damp forehead as if he were someone she cared deeply about. And in a way, she did. She gazed at him almost tenderly. She held his moist hand and stroked his forehead. Then she used her two thumbs to peel back his eyelids so that his two eyeballs seemed to stare straight up at her, unseeingly.

Softly she said, "Can you see me, darling? Can you see me? Because I can see into what's left of your soul."

At that moment, the fangs that had been folded back against the roof of her mouth sprang forward, and she said, "You're such a lovely man, and I'm going to love you to death."

She sank her fangs into Jeff's neck. And trickles of blood flowed as she pulled back. But she bent and drank again. Then she reached for a glass beaker that she had placed on a lab table under a glowing lamp. She brought the rim of the beaker up to the trickle of blood, and the beaker started to fill.

CHAPTER 13

Spaz pulled up just outside the cinder-block building in Hawk's van, and Blake parked behind it in the Jeep in which he and Spaz had ridden four miles to where they had picked up Hawk's van. Now Spaz jumped down from the van, and Blake jumped down from the Jeep. Blake said, "Let's not fool around. Let's get him out and haul him in. There's a kickboxing match on TV tonight."

"Well, we're gonna need help," Spaz griped. "Damned if I wanna rupture myself lifting that sucker."

"Here they come now. They musta heard us pull up."

Two small, wiry men in white lab coats, Morgan Holt and Luke Gentry, two of the same fellows who were on the scene when Dr. Melrose got bitten sixteen years ago, came out through a side door of the cinder-block building and started wheeling a gurney toward the rear of the van. Spaz and Blake came around and opened the cargo door so the two attendants could have a look at the task at hand. Staring bleakly at what was in there and shaking his head in distaste, Morgan said, "No wonder you need us to help you. Sucker looks like three hundred pounds or more!"

Spaz said, "He was close to four hundred when he was alive. Right now there's not as much of him as there used to be."

"How come?" asked Luke.

"No internal organs left," Spaz explained, grinning. "I hit him with two shotgun blasts dead-center, almost cut him in two, and blew away his insides. The middle of him is totally gone. We wrapped the sleeping bag around him so he wouldn't come apart. That would've been a helluva mess."

"He's good for nothing but zombie feed now," said Blake. "We'll feed him to the ones that didn't eat yet."

They hoisted what was left of Nutso's dead body out of the van and onto the gurney. As Luke and Morgan wheeled the gurney toward the building, Blake and Spaz went to their quarters to toss their clothes into a hamper. Then they showered away the blood and gore and kicked back with a couple of stiff drinks while they watched kickboxing.

"Let's take him in through the side door. He's too big, and now his arm's hanging down," said Morgan, and they wheeled the gurney, with some difficulty because of the rough gravel, around the right side of the building where there was a big garage-type door. Luke pressed a button, and with a rasping metallic sound, the door lifted, revealing steel cages of various sizes.

All told there were six cages in this building, which was an adjunct to the main laboratory where most of the experiments were carried out. There was a ramp that led directly from the cage room and into the laboratory so the zombies could be readily transported from one place to another as required.

One of the cages, with a sign on it that said CAGE ONE, was simply a large pen where newly created zombies could be kept en masse till they were categorized. This cage measured fifteen by twenty feet. Right now it contained nineteen inhabitants. DNA samples had been taken from each one, but the results weren't yet analyzed because Dr. Melrose had such a huge workload. DNA analysis was of utmost importance to him due to the fact that obviously there was a genetic factor to the zombie disease, and so there must be some highly unique gene that had aborted the process by which he would have turned into one of the undead, and he desperately wanted to isolate it.

He had plenty of money in US banks and in Swiss bank accounts from selling black market organs of the people he had captured to use as zombie feed or to turn into zombies for his experiments. He could afford to move his facilities to any other part of the country, but he maintained them right here near Willard, close to where the epidemic had started, because he and his parents, grandparents, and many of his ancestors had lived here. The most important DNA he could find in living people or in any of the undead was DNA with components that were a close match to his own. He was searching for a precise match to an anomalous gene that he had found in his own DNA, which he strongly suspected was the anomaly that had given him immunity from the zombie disease and had conferred special powers upon his two daughters.

Cage two was for zombies that Dr. Melrose wanted to separate from the rest because they were set to undergo some special procedure. It measured ten feet by ten feet, and at the moment it was occupied by four zombies on an experimental diet that consisted of corpse meat blended with artificial sweetener, vitamins, and minerals. The doctor was looking to discover a formula that could reduce the need in these ghouls for live human flesh, but so far nothing had worked.

Cage three measured only six feet by six feet, and it was for those unlucky folks who were doomed to become zombie feed, but not right away. Blake and Spaz called it "the pantry," but they were careful not to let Dr. Melrose hear them say that because he had no sense of humor where his work was concerned. He was "deadly serious" about it, but that expression could not have been used to his face either, because he would have deplored it.

Today the occupants of Cage Three were the three members of the Mathews family, Albert, Meg, and Stevie. The parents were all right, but the son, like many teenagers, was a smart mouth, and Dr. Melrose had him gagged after he got tired of being cursed at. He wasn't really sure what to do with the three of them. One choice was to have Tiffany take their blood and turn them into zombies for experimentation. The other choice was to use them for zombie feed, which the doctor had some qualms about, but they were from New Jersey, and to his knowledge he had no relatives from there, and so a link to his own DNA was unlikely. He had to concentrate his investigations on people living or undead who might share some of his own genes, and not waste valuable time on others when the results might be rather fruitless.

Cage four and cage five were isolation cages; in other words, a kind of solitary confinement. Number four held the serial killer, Chub Harris, and number five held the big oaf who called himself Hawk, who was turned into a zombie by Tiffany when she took his blood. Well, she had to have her nourishment, and she shouldn't be looked down upon for this, any more than a tiger should be disparaged for having to kill and eat an impala, a buffalo, or even a human being. The earth's creatures with their built-in inherited qualities could not in any way be blamed for living up to their true nature, which they did not choose and certainly could not control except by denying their instincts in a most painful and debilitating way.

Even the serial killer and rapist, Chub Harris, could not be expected to overcome the festering predilections that had made him that way. He either had a brain defect or a defect in his upbringing that had warped him. He was a freak of nature or nurture and was thus incorrigible; he could not be rehabilitated so as to conform with society's usual standards of behavior. Before assigning Blake Parsons and Spaz Bentley the task of ferreting him out and hunting him down, Dr. Melrose had thoroughly investigated his background in case there might be some redeeming or mitigating factors. But there were none that mattered. He was doomed to go on killing and raping until he was stopped. His birth name was Peter Harris, and he grew up right in Willard, and that was his constant prowling ground. He had a high IQ, but no trace of what is commonly referred to as a "conscience"—a respect for good deeds, a need to give and receive love, and an aversion toward evil.

Pondering how he should make best use of the serial killer in captivity, Dr. Melrose considered the fact that men of Chub's ilk had a single-minded urge toward the violent destruction of others that was not unlike the irrepressible inclinations of the undead. Did that mean that Chub Harris should be kept alive and studied in depth? Or did it mean that he should be immediately used as zombie feed because he was no good for anything else of any intrinsic value? Or, taking yet another tack, did it mean that the serial killer's impressive ability to hunt, track, and capture his victims should be harnessed and turned to good use—in other words, providing he was kept under the watchful eyes of Blake and Spaz, could Chub be trusted to help gather the types of subjects that were constantly needed for the experiments being carried out here in the laboratory?

Dr. Melrose decided that he would discuss this serious matter with Tiffany. She was wise beyond her years, thanks to the aberrant gene she had inherited from him. And Victoria was developing nicely in the same direction. Both his daughters were a wonder to behold, and Dr. Melrose had no doubt that as time went by they would both learn to be even more helpful than they already were. At present, he relied on them for carrying out a great deal of painstaking research, but they needed more math and chemistry to take on the most demanding duties of scientific inquiry. This process would be set in motion as soon as Tiffany began to earn her medical degree, and Victoria was destined to follow in her footsteps. They were both brilliant, as was to be expected in Dr. Melrose's estimation since they had inherited such exceptional qualities from him.

He watched Luke and Morgan wheel in the gurney containing the mortal remains of somebody Tiffany called Nutso, a person he didn't think he needed to know anything much about, because Nutso would soon be zombie feed. Tiffany had already filled Doc Melrose in on this dimwit, who happened to be a cousin to the one called Hawk. This oaf had already been turned into a zombie, thanks to Tiffany. So his past, his family, and his genetics would have to be totally investigated and analyzed, for

he would be an experimental subject. Perhaps he would even reveal DNA with markers similar to those of Dr. Melrose, although
he very much doubted it at this juncture due to the fact that the
oaf *was* an oaf, and the doctor could not imagine that anyone so
oaflike would turn out to be a leaf on his own family tree. But one
never knew, one never knew. Even the most brilliant of people
could give birth to defective children.

Dr. Melrose moved over to cage six and said, "Good day, Barney, how are you?" to one of the cage's long-time occupants. This
fellow was the very zombie who had bitten Dr. Melrose sixteen
years ago. He had been so long in residence here that he was almost like an old friend, and the lab assistants, Luke and Morgan,
had given him the nickname "Barney." Dr. Melrose rather liked
that little touch and eventually found himself using it with easy
familiarity.

Not long after Barney was captured, his background had been
investigated. The initial leverage for the inquiry was furnished by
his driver's license, which happened to be in one of the front pockets of his bibbed coveralls. His real name was Horace Dalrymple,
and he wasn't an indigent barroom brawler, as one would think
upon first impressions, but had been a hard-working dirt-poor
farmer. He had been pulled off his tractor while he was working in
his alfalfa field and had fought off an unknown number of zombies, but one of them had succeeded in biting him, and thus his
fate was sealed. Though bitten, he tried to protect his wife and his
twelve-year-old son, but seeing that he was bitten, they ran away
from him, jumped into an old, battered pickup, and escaped into
Willard. It was a miracle that the same zombies who attacked Barney did not overwhelm his wife and son, but then, the undead
were slow-moving, and there weren't too many of them in that lo-
cale during the beginning stages of the outbreak.

Dr. Melrose had learned many of these details about Barney
and his erstwhile family from newspaper and television inter-
views with the surviving wife and son after the outbreak was
quelled, and had gleaned even more details by assigning Luke
and Morgan the task of furtively prying into the Dalrymples'

past. He had considered uniting the family here in the lab, but he had decided to let Barney's wife and son live out the rest of their lives normally, after reluctantly deciding that they had suffered enough.

Barney showed few signs of age because zombies did not deteriorate much with age as long as they were properly fed. He was as huge and imposing as ever, his diet scrupulously maintained by the attendants and his weight preserved at a pretty steady three hundred and fifty pounds. He was still wearing the flannel shirt, bibbed coveralls, and clodhoppers of sixteen years ago, and every once in a while he was injected with powerful drugs to knock him out so his personal clothing could be disinfected and washed. There was a constant, creeping, underlying stench in the cage room, and the living people could only tolerate so much of it, and so now and then the long-term zombies had to be hosed down and their clothes had to be laundered.

Dr. Melrose firmly believed in treating his zombies humanely. He respected the need to keep them as clean and healthy as possible in order to maintain, not just his experimental integrity, but also his own self-respect.

He wasn't a cruel man, just one who was exceptionally pragmatic and unflinching when it came to the needs of science.

CHAPTER 14

Tiffany entered her sister's bedroom carrying the beaker of blood that she had taken from Jeff Sanders. She felt sad when she saw that Victoria was crying, looking at her hideously blistered face in a handheld mirror.

"Don't worry, Vicky," Tiffany said consolingly. "You're going to be beautiful again. I brought you a nice sweet drink to help clear up those blisters."

Victoria turned to face her older and presently lovelier sister. Her eyes fastened upon the beaker and its contents . . . and she licked her lips, already craving it.

"Yes, sweetheart," said Tiffany. "You instinctively want to drink it, don't you? You understand that it will be good for you."

Victoria reached out quickly and took the beaker in her two hands. She stared at it hungrily, and her tear-filled eyes seemed to brighten a bit.

"Don't be so depressed," Tiffany cajoled. "You'll be better in a few days. When so-called normal people get porphyria they have it all their lives and must never go out in the sunlight. But you and I are different, thanks to the gene we got from Father.

For us, the ugly symptoms eventually go away, and we become far superior to ordinary people."

Heartened by her sister's words, with a faint smile Victoria brought the beaker of Jeff's blood to her lips and drank. And Tiffany cooed to her and stroked her hair as she did so.

CHAPTER 15

Two uniformed sheriff's deputies, Henry Burns and Jesse Halcomb, were on the road in their police cruiser. Henry drove while Jesse smoked a cigarette, which Jesse didn't like because the smoke made him light-headed, sometimes nauseous. But he knew his partner was a nicotine addict, so he tolerated it.

Jesse said, "We make the turn up ahead a piece."

They were looking for the hard to spot weed-grown entrance to a narrow dirt road that would lead them through the woods to the Melrose Medical Research Center, a place that apparently liked to keep itself discreet and well hidden. Sheriff Harkness had sent them out here in advance of the raid he was implementing, in case Jeff Sanders was in trouble and they might be able to do something about it to keep him safe. But the sheriff didn't know what. He just had a premonition that he had to do something that might prevent disaster from happening before the logistics of the raid were properly organized so it could take place.

"What if Jeff *is* still doing okay here, and we blow his cover?" Henry asked. "What'd the sheriff say about that, Jesse?"

"We're just supposed to show up acting like normal nosy lawmen and try to make sure Jeff's okay. If we do stumble into him, he'll be cool enough not to let on he's ever seen us before."

But Henry was skeptical. "That's the way the sheriff's got it doped out, huh?"

"Well, he says if we show up asking questions it ought to even help throw suspicion off Jeff. They won't figure we'd put somebody undercover and still come around ourselves."

"I sure hope he's right," Henry said. "Here's the turnoff."

He humped the cruiser off the main road and onto a narrow stretch of rutted mud and gravel that gave them a bumpy, twisty ride. And in about three hundred yards of this, they came to a cyclone fence, which was topped with barbed wire.

"It's electrified," Jesse said.

"Yeah, I can see that," said his partner.

They both stared at the carcass of a dead, badly charred deer that was sagging against the steel links of the fence as if plastered to it by a jolt of electricity. The two cops weren't about to get out and touch that fence, so Henry laid on the horn in order to hopefully flush somebody out to greet them.

Other than the presence of the dead deer, nothing seemed too spooky. It all seemed very quiet and peaceful in spite of what was rumored to be going on.

When nobody came out to greet them, Henry laid on the horn again. Then he and Jesse got out of the car, and Jesse dropped his cigarette butt and stepped on it. They both looked around, trying to case the place, but there wasn't much to see, just a big house farther back and several outbuildings made of cinder block.

Henry said, "Why did Sheriff Harkness send us out here on a Saturday? Maybe they all take the day off."

"He said a Saturday might be exactly the right time to catch them with their pants down."

Just then, a lovely young woman came walking across the gravel, got up to the fence as the two cops gawked at her admiringly, and said, "I'm Tiffany Melrose. What can I do for you?" She was wearing tight shorts and a T-shirt that showed off her body, and she had an aura of haughtiness about her that did not disguise her disdain for the two lawmen.

"I'm Deputy Burns," Henry said, "and my partner here is Jesse Halcomb. We need to talk with Dr. Melrose. Is he in?"

"Yes," said Tiffany. "He's back in the lab. I was helping him. He's my father. We were in the midst of some critical experiments when we heard your horn blasting away at us. Very disturbing. We must get back to our work, so I hope you won't detain us long. As you can see, this is an electrified fence, but I'll cut off the current."

In her hand she held a remote-control device, and she hit some buttons and then opened the gate, saying, "Follow me, if you will, gentlemen."

She led them through a solid steel side door of one of the cinderblock buildings and into a large, thoroughly equipped chemistry laboratory complete with beakers, flasks, Bunsen burners, microscopes, and other more esoteric and complicated apparatuses that the lawmen were baffled by. Then she disappeared down a long corridor, and they watched her go, wondering what her game was.

Dr. Melrose, a slim and bald little man wearing a neat white lab coat and wire-rimmed eyeglasses, came toward them after putting down a clipboard, and they had no trouble recognizing him from the photos shown to them by Sheriff Harkness. They took note of the scar on his throat, which they knew had been put there sixteen years ago, and it was so faint by now that ordinarily they might not have noticed it.

"What can I do for you, officers?" the doctor inquired in his prissy little voice. "Let's please be expedient. My daughter and I must get back to our important work. We don't get any government grants, you see. We must flounder on our own. And time is money."

"We'll try not to take up too much of your *money* then," Henry said with heavy sarcasm.

Then all of a sudden he made up a story off the top of his head that he hoped might enable him to more directly and cleverly find out whether or not Jeff was still on the premises. Lying through his teeth, he said, "A snitch told us he met a guy named Jeff Sanders who was hitchhiking out on the highway near here, and this guy Jeff is somebody we've been on the lookout for. He's wanted for breaking and entering back in Willard. He tried to burglarize a jewelry store, and the alarm went off and he ran— but we got a good description. Our snitch said he talked about trying to get hired out here. He said it'd be a good place to stay out of sight for a while."

Henry hoped this made-up story would be a good excuse to get to talk with Jeff, under the pretense of grilling him about the phony jewelry store robbery, but Dr. Melrose didn't fall for it. "We don't have anybody new on our payroll," the doctor lied. "And nobody has applied recently. In fact, we haven't seen any strangers in a long time."

Jesse had readily tuned into his partner's line of deception concerning the nonexistent snitch, so he continued ad-libbing the phony story. "You sure about that?" he shot back at Doc Melrose. "Our witness swears your daughter was seen with this Sanders hoodlum. Where'd she disappear to? We want to talk to her, and if we don't like what she has to say, you can bet we'll haul her in for some sharp questioning."

"You can take that to the bank," Henry added meanly.

Rattled, Dr. Melrose fell into the trap and blurted out some things that were partially truthful. "Tiffany went for a ride with some young fellows. We don't know who they were, but I guess one of them could've been this Sanders fellow. They dropped her off here and went on their way. We don't know any more than that."

Both of the cops now knew that Doc Melrose was lying about not knowing Jeff Sanders.. So they were more determined than ever to find out all that they could before they would let the sheriff and his raiding party risk their lives.

"We're gonna have to talk to Tiffany, no way around that," said Jesse. "She might know a whole lot more'n you do, doc. Teenagers often do. So take us to her. Pronto. We're not foolin' around here. We're after a dangerous felon."

"I suppose I'll have to let you speak to her," Dr. Melrose said, his thin mouth twitching. "But she won't be helpful, not because she doesn't want to be, but because she can't be. She doesn't really know anything. But come with me, gentlemen. We have absolutely nothing to hide."

The doctor escorted the two deputies down the long institutional corridor where Tiffany had disappeared, and at the end of it, there was a heavily bolted steel door. The door was bolted from the outside, not the inside, so the bolt wasn't intended to keep people out. It was intended to keep somebody or something *in*. The deputies got immediately more nervous, but they didn't say anything. Dr. Melrose undid the bolt and swung the door open on nothing, it seemed, except murky darkness. Then the lawmen gasped and reeled backward, covering their nostrils.

"Ugh!" Henry blurted. "What's that smell?"

"Something rotten!" Jesse echoed.

"You'll see better when I flip the lights on," Dr. Melrose informed them prissily.

Suddenly the area beyond the steel door was bathed in stark fluorescence, revealing the cage that held Barney and the other long-term zombies.

The two deputies were so taken aback that Blake and Spaz, who had sneaked up behind them, had little trouble plowing into them, ripping their guns out of their holsters, opening the cage door, and shoving them in there. A savage battle ensued as the slavering zombies closed in, Barney taking the lead and shoving some of the others out of his way.

For a time, Jesse and Henry held out and got in some blows, refusing to succumb easily to their fate. For fun, Blake and Spaz had teased them with faint hope of escape by leaving the cell door open, and they punched and clawed at the attacking zombies, trying to reach the opening, even though they were both being bitten in various places on their bodies.

Dr. Melrose watched all this, fascinated, his thin mouth twitching, which seemed to be his way of showing delight in an impending triumph. He knew it was a foregone conclusion that the two deputies would not be able to hold out for long, and with bites all over them and chunks of their flesh torn out, they would be swarmed under.

The hungry flesh eaters would crush them to the floor of the cage and continue tearing at them and devouring them till they were satiated.

Spaz and Blake would watch till the bitter end. They enjoyed this sort of thing more than Dr. Melrose did.

And besides, the doc had important work to do, and he didn't want to neglect it.

He had to finish up some important experiments. Then he had to put himself and his entire enterprise into survival mode. Because there was little doubt that the police would soon be here in full force.

Tiffany came back down the corridor and said, "We've got to get rid of the patrol car they came in, Daddy."

He said, "I know. The keys must be in one of their pockets, but Blake and Spaz can hot-wire it instead of bothering to look for the keys."

Blake heard this and turned around, holding up the cops' guns and asking, "What about these?"

"Hang on to them. I think they will come in handy," said Dr. Melrose. "As a matter of fact, let's hold back on sinking their car into the pond. It might come in handy for a tactical getaway."

PART THREE

THE ESCAPE

CHAPTER 16

Sheriff Harkness had to carry out his raid on the Melrose complex ahead of schedule on an emergency basis because two men he had sent out there as a surveillance team reported that what appeared to be a preparation for an all-out evacuation, or something close to it, was underway under cover of darkness. And the other two men he sent out never came back.

Luckily, the sheriff had insisted on an around the clock surveillance, instructing the two men to spell each other in four-hour shifts and had issued them infrared spy gear including goggles and telescopes. Two nights in a row they had observed trucks and vans being loaded from midnight till dawn with labeled crates of office and laboratory equipment, and also dozens of multisized cardboard boxes that were not labeled but were numbered, probably so their contents could be checked off on a manifest.

The raiding party consisted of a six-man SWAT team and a dozen deputies under the command of Sheriff Harkness. Bruce Barnes was one of the deputies, and he, like everyone else, was worried about the possible fate of Jeff Sanders.

None of these men had any idea what they were going to encounter. But whatever it was, they wanted to get to the bottom of it if it turned out to be something illegal. The sheriff knew that if

Doc Melrose really was orchestrating a pull-out, he might already be one jump ahead of the law. This might turn into a pursuit and BOLO—be on the lookout—instead of a detain and search mission.

This was a chilly October morning, and when the lawmen first arrived just after dawn, the sun had not finished burning off the fog. The grass was dewy, and the dark limbs and wet multicolored leaves of the trees glistened in the first weak rays of sunlight as the mist slowly began to lift.

To the sheriff and his men, it looked like the Melrose compound was deserted. If this was the situation, there would be no shooting. On the other hand, empty labs and offices would probably yield little evidence of any suspicious activity that may have occurred there over the months and years previous.

Sheriff Harkness was armed with a shotgun and a holstered sidearm, and he was also carrying a battery-powered megaphone. His plan was to get on the megaphone and call out to whomever was the honcho in there to shut the current off and immediately open the electrified gate, so he could go in to serve his warrant and hopefully carry out his search without any bothersome interference or, god forbid, foolish gunplay.

But the gate was already wide open.

By means of hand signals and whispers, the sheriff passed along deployment orders and, in a military-style maneuver, the men broke their ranks down into four-man squads that took turns covering each other, while one squad at a time crouched and ran through the open gate and through holes they had made with shears through other parts of the chain-link fence. In a matter of minutes, all the SWAT men and the deputies were deployed inside the compound, their guns trained on the various buildings and doorways, ready to open fire as soon as they were provoked or ordered to do so.

The sheriff pressed a button and spoke into the handheld megaphone, and his gruff voice boomed out all over the compound. "We are the police! We have you surrounded! Come out with your hands up!"

There was no response whatsoever. So the sheriff tried it again. "We are the police! We have you surrounded! Come out with your hands up!"

The sheriff was flanked by Deputy Bruce Barnes, who had performed so well in the outbreak sixteen years ago, and by two other deputies, Jerry Flanagan and Carl Ortiz, officers with just over ten years' service, who were not on the job when the sheriff's first run-in with Dr. Melrose had taken place. But they had no doubt that the stories they had heard about the incident were real. After all, they both had friends and family members who had suffered and died back then.

Wisps of fog still crept among the cinder-block buildings. And here and there the fog was heavier, as if purposely hiding something—at least it seemed that way to some of the lawmen who were creeped out by the place in spite of their need to be brave and alert.

Sheriff Harkness was making up his mind whether to let his voice blare out over the megaphone one more time or whether he should just move forward with a handpicked squad while the rest furnished cover.

But before he made his mind up, three shambling figures emerged from a thick pocket of fog between two of the cinder-block buildings and started shuffling toward the sheriff and the deputies who were flanking Harkness protectively.

"Holy *shit*!" Carl Ortiz cried out.

And Jerry Flanagan took a faltering step backward, as if he had been hit with something. *"Christ! What are they?"* he blurted.

"Zombies!" Bruce Barnes said as calmly as he could. But he was rattled. It seemed like a déjà vu moment to him, and a very scary one at that. "Fucking zombies," he repeated, muttering it to himself.

The three undead beings shuffled toward the sheriff and his flanking deputies, and there was no doubt that they were quite decayed and dead-looking but somehow still "living." One was a red-haired woman in a flower-print housedress, and the two others were middle-aged men wearing olive-green jumpsuits of the type usually worn by workmen, such as carpenters or plumbers.

"Fuck! It's happening all over again!" Bruce cursed.

Sheriff Harkness held back on giving an order to fire. He wanted the undead creatures to get closer first. But suddenly shots rang out anyway, and two of the zombies went down, hit in the head by bullets—the woman and one of the "carpenters." The one still on his feet had been shot in his chest—a big gaping hole appeared there—and he reeled backward and almost fell, but somehow he did not go down. He just kept on coming.

And behind him a half-dozen more zombies appeared, venturing out from behind the buildings.

"Fire at will, men!" the sheriff barked over the megaphone.

A volley of shots rang out immediately, and the "carpenter" zombie who had been shot in his chest took a high-powered shot to his head that splintered his skull and splattered his brain, and what was left of him fell down hard onto the gravel.

Loud gunfire echoed throughout the compound, and several more zombies bit the dust. "There are some over there tryin' to crawl through the hole you guys cut in the fence!" the sheriff shouted to a squad of SWAT men. "Go after 'em! Don't let 'em get away! If they make it into the woods, we might never catch up with 'em!"

The squad moved off, efficiently aiming and firing, and the sheriff watched them kill three more zombies, and he nodded his approval. It seemed to him that the situation was close to being under control—unless there were more zombies inside the buildings.

But things weren't quite over yet, and a female zombie was coming at the sheriff behind his back, and he almost didn't hear her because of the spates of gunfire. At the last second, he wheeled and swung his shotgun into action just in time to shoot the sneaky zombie in the face. She dazedly covered her face with her hands as she sank slowly to her knees, then she toppled sideways.

The sheriff stood over her and saw the damage made by the

shotgun pellets—holes like little BB marks in her partially decayed facial skin, but not a direct hit. She was still breathing, emitting an eerie rasping sound. He drew his .44 Magnum, aimed between her eyes, and dispassionately squeezed off a round. This time she was blown away for good, ghoul brains and gore soaking into the earth.

Breathing hard, Deputy Bruce Barnes came up to the sheriff while he was taking time to reload his Winchester, the same one he was using sixteen years ago. "I think I spotted more of them ducking behind those two tar paper sheds over there," he said. "We better check it out."

"You, Jerry, and Carl come with me," the sheriff responded.

Weapons at the ready, they proceeded around the side of the main cinder-block building and toward the two sheds Bruce had mentioned. Even though they expected to encounter *something,* they were still startled to find three zombies crouched over someone's half-devoured remains. The zombies looked up like pack animals ready to protect a kill. They were chewing and drooling, their faces streaked with blood. They were too satiated and too lethargic to even make much of an attempt to get away.

Without a word, the sheriff and his deputies blasted them down.

Then the lawmen approached closer to the erstwhile feast.

And even though the face was chewed up, they still recognized the dead man.

"Oh god," Jerry said, "that looks like—"

Carl said, "Jeff Sanders."

"It is him," Bruce said, sadly shaking his head. "He must've got himself caught spying, and they *fed him* to these things."

"Then they cleared out," said Sheriff Harkness. "They knew we were coming. That's why none of their vehicles are around. Dollars to doughnuts all the buildings are gonna be empty. Dr. Melrose and his crazy crew are long gone."

Just then a shot rang out, and Carl Ortiz was shot in the chest. He screamed and fell dead as the sheriff and his two remaining deputies took cover behind the tar paper sheds, looking to return fire.

Another shot rang out, and this time the muzzle flash called attention to a sniper on the roof of one of the buildings. He peeped from behind a chimney, and the lawmen cut loose with a heavy volley.

The sniper ducked out of sight. But not without getting spotted long enough to make out that he had a rifle and was wearing a white lab coat.

The sheriff and his two surviving deputies waited tensely with fixed gazes, ready to fire if the sniper peeped up again.

They heard some of the other deputies and SWAT men coming toward them in the distance, drawn to the situation because of the the gunfire now that other areas of the compound were mostly silent.

All of a sudden the sniper peeked around the side of the chimney and squeezed off three rapid rifle rounds.

This drew heavy return fire from the three lawmen.

The sniper screamed and fell behind the chimney, and his rifle dropped and clattered down below him on a brick walkway.

For a long moment, all was still except for the cautious footsteps of the approaching SWAT team and the other deputies.

Then a weak and whimpering voice came from the sniper up on the roof. "I'm hurt bad . . . I'm bleeding . . . I surrender . . . come and get me . . ."

"Damn it. Who the hell *are* you?" Sheriff Harkness shouted.

"Who . . . do you . . . think? I'm . . . Dr. Melrose."

CHAPTER 17

On the morning of the raid against the Melrose Medical Research Center, a young divorcee, Sally Brinkman, and her mother, Marsha, led their horses out of the big barn on their family farm thirty miles south of Willard. The calm, dewy beauty of the sunrise was conducive to relaxing and forgetting their troubles. The morning was a mite chilly, but they both had on warm riding britches and tan leather jackets.

Little did they know it, but this was the calm before the storm. They had no idea of the death and destruction that was about to be visited upon them. Sally smiled as she patted and stroked her horse, Sparky, a three-year-old palomino, and Marsha behaved similarly toward her own mount, Perky, a dark brown mare with a white star-shape on her forehead.

Both women loved their horses and delighted in riding out together to roam and casually inspect the eighty acres that they owned. They mostly grew corn there on part of the acreage with the aid of a tenant on a farm nearby, who was paid for the use of his time and tractor.

Sally was in her late twenties, but she retained the spunky personality that had made her so rebellious and hard for her mother to handle during her teenage years. Marsha understood well these qualities in her daughter because when she was growing up she was the same way. They both had mischievous grins and a perky way of tossing their blond ponytails with a quick jerk of their heads, and sometimes they looked so much alike they almost could be mistaken for sisters. They were sometimes amusingly called "my beautiful hellcats" by Henry Brinkman, husband to Marsha and father of Sally, who came from the house carrying a lunch bucket and heading for a pickup truck parked by the barn. At fifty-seven, he was still lean and physically fit, and Sally thought it was nice to have such a good-looking father. He was handsome in her eyes, even though others might not have thought of him that way because of his craggy, darkly tanned face, thinning gray hair, and deep-set brown eyes that often scrutinized people with a probing no-nonsense stare.

Settling herself into her saddle and stirrups, Sally called out, "Where're you going, Dad?"

"Down to the saloon."

Marsha wasn't saddled up yet, and she half turned with one foot in a stirrup and said, "So early, Henry? You don't have to open till noon."

"I want to finish taking my booze inventory, Marsha, so I can maybe figure out how much was stolen by the bartender I had to fire last week. The damned thief! Such a baby face, you'd almost think he's not even old enough to tend bar, but he was sly enough to be stealing us blind!"

"Don't let it aggravate you so much," Marsha said. "He's not the first bartender you had to can."

She swung herself up into her saddle and got comfortable in her stirrups.

"Too many folks with sticky fingers," Henry groused. "I oughta sell the damn place! But nobody'll buy it 'cause it barely ekes out a profit—thanks to all the chiseling bartenders. That's why I'm so glad you're back helping me out, Sally."

"You know I'll be there right at six, Dad."

"Want me to drive back and pick you up?"

"No need," said Sally. "I can walk over there on a nice day like this. It's not even a mile."

"I know," Henry said. "I still jog to the saloon and back three days a week to try to keep my stomach flat. But right now I'm gonna ride. See you later, honey."

He climbed into his truck, started it up, and pulled out.

Sally and Marsha watched him go, then trotted their horses out of the long driveway and across a field.

Sally said, "Dad keeps finding ways to say how much he needs me. I think he's trying to make me feel better about my divorce."

"Well," said Marsha, "he wants to make sure you know you're welcome to stay here as long as you need to, till you get yourself back on your feet. You do realize that, don't you? Your father and I are both with you all the way. To tell the truth, we never liked the way Michael treated you, but we kept our mouths shut. I have to say we were glad for your sake when you decided to leave him."

"He didn't treat me all that badly, Mom. We just grew apart. He didn't abuse me physically or anything. I wouldn't have let him get away with that. I would've punched him out!" The way she was talking amused both her and her mother, and they both chuckled over it.

"Well, he wouldn't have dared hit you!" Marsha jibed good-naturedly. "After all, he knew you took judo classes!"

"Jujitsu."

"Okay, jujitsu."

"There's a difference, Mom."

"I'm sure there is, honey."

They continued their ride a while longer and got deeper into the field, which was rife with clover, and Sally finally said, "You know . . . my marriage died such a long, slow death. It was really over long before the divorce. When the final papers came last month, I felt relief more than anything else. I'm looking forward to just getting on with my life. I just haven't made up my mind yet which direction to go."

"Take your time, honey, and be sure," Marsha said. "You could always go back to working for those lawyers."

"But I found out I hated paralegal work. It was so boring! I

need to find something more adventurous, or at least more in-
volving. But I don't know what."

Sally had quit her paralegal job as soon as she got pregnant,
and she was looking forward to being a stay at home mom. But
the pregnancy ended with a miscarriage, and somehow that put
the capper on her disappointing marriage to Michael Stotner.
Whereas she had thought he was so debonair and exciting when
she first met him, she had come to dislike his smugness and his
braggadocio. He was a faithful husband, but not a caring or atten-
tive one. He was too much into his exaggerated image of himself
as a hotshot movie producer, even though he only produced TV
spots and sales films of an unremarkable variety; nevertheless he
thought, or wanted to think, that they were impressive.

"You and Dad have been great," Sally told her mom. "But
don't worry too much about me. One thing I've learned is that
nothing in life is absolutely sure."

They rode in silence across the field.

CHAPTER 18

The sheriff ordered his men to make a bonfire out of the zombie corpses, same way it had been done during that other outbreak. They doused the pile with gasoline and touched a torch to it, and instantly it turned into a huge, blazing pyre.

Some distance from the smoke and flames, Sheriff Harkness and Deputy Bruce Barnes stood over Dr. Melrose, who was lying on a gurney near the rear of an ambulance while the two paramedics applied emergency measures, trying to stop the blood flow from the doctor's chest wound and treat him for shock. They knew the irony was that going into shock would slow the blood flow down, but in itself, it would probably kill him. So they had exercised their best judgment, and they felt they were doing the best they could, even though their private opinion was that Melrose deserved to die right here instead of sticking the county for the cost of a long, drawn-out trial.

Melrose went on blathering, even though his voice was getting weaker and weaker. "I'm dying . . . I'm not going to . . . make it . . . to the hospital. It doesn't matter, you see . . . my two daughters . . . will . . . carry on . . . my work. . . ."

Taking in the full meaning of this, the sheriff instantly barked a gruff question.

"What're you driving at, Melrose? Your daughters will carry on what? Where?"

"They're . . . gone . . . you'll never . . . catch them. . . ."

One of the paramedics piped up. "Back off, Sheriff, please! Let us work on him. He's too weak to talk."

Melrose said, "It . . . doesn't matter . . . anymore. . . . I'm done for. . . . I injected myself. When I die . . . shoot me . . . or I'll become . . . one of *them*."

"What the hell're you talkin' about?" the sheriff demanded. "You didn't become one before, why would you become one *now*?"

"*The serum* . . ."

"*What* fuckin' serum?"

"Trying to . . . study them . . . find out why . . . they don't die. The government backed me . . . at first . . . let me capture them . . . and keep them here. But later they wanted . . . to shut me down. But my daughters . . . will carry on . . . in a secret place. . . . You'll never find it. . . . It's under . . . the ground . . ."

Enraged, Sheriff Harkness grabbed the dying doctor and shouted into his face.

"*Where?* Damn you! Tell me where! Do some real good for humanity before you die!"

But Dr. Melrose did not respond. He was a lifeless doll now, his eyes glazed over, staring up at the sun.

Bruce pulled the sheriff back, and they both stared down at Doc Melrose's corpse.

The paramedics looked on in silence. One of them gave a futile wave of his blood-smeared, latex-gloved hand. The other paramedic shrugged and backed away.

The sheriff said to them, "You guys better wash up real good and sterilize yourselves. This nutcase said he injected himself with some kind of wacky serum."

"Shit!" Bruce said. "All we need is for the damn plague to start up all over again!"

The sheriff said, "Somehow we gotta track down Melrose's daughters and put a lid on this thing once and for all."

"How're we gonna find them?" Bruce lamented. "They could be clear across the county by now. We don't even know how they're traveling—plane, bus, or car. We have to run a check, see if there are any vehicles registered to the Melroses. If we could get a license plate number . . ."

"Yeah," said the sheriff. "Phone the station and get somebody busy on it. We gotta put out an all-points bulletin and set up road blocks as quick as we can. Don't forget the train and bus stations, for god's sake!"

CHAPTER 19

A battered old van with the image of a Confederate flag on its front bumper plate pulled into a rest area off a two-lane rural road. Its rear bumper bore two hateful slogans: PROUD TO BE AN AMERICAN NAZI and DEATH TO JEW LOVERS. Drake was driving, and Bones was in the front passenger seat. They were both stoned on crack cocaine, and both had crude swastikas tattooed prison-style on their cheeks and foreheads and daggers with roses tattooed on their biceps with their mothers' names on them.

About a half dozen vehicles of various types were parked at the rest stop, which consisted of one building with toilet facilities and another with soft drink, coffee, bottled water, and candy machines.

Bones and Drake sneeringly gave the once-over to a guy walking a dog and a couple of fat, frumpy women who did their business, got into their car, and drove off.

What made them pull over at this particular rest stop was that they had spotted a trailer-truck logo consisting of the letters M and R inside a painted rose, and underneath the logo, in red letters, it said: M-R ELECTRONICS. And they were always looking to boost stuff they could turn to cash, so they didn't even need to discuss this opportunity when it fell into their laps.

As the two skinheads got out of the van, they stared at the trailer truck with greed in their eyes. But Drake shook his head ruefully and said, "Forget about it, Bones, we ain't gonna hijack that rig all by our lonesome."

Bones said, "Shut up. You got brawn but no brains, Drake. That's why I gotta come up with all the strategy."

"Strategize all you want if it gets your rocks off, but ain't no way we can pull it off without plenty of help."

"We got smarts and we got the element of surprise, don't we? And we got somethin' else."

"All we got is two handguns."

"And a bag of sugar in our grocery bag," Bones said with a sly grin.

"Sugar?" Drake said quizzically. "You shittin' me?"

"Ever put sugar in somebody's gas tank, Drake?"

"I never done it, but I know what it's supposed to do—freezes up the engine and makes it grind to a halt."

"Well, not exactly," said Bones. "My piece of pussy looked it up for me online. Turns out sugar sludgin' up the engine is a buncha horseshit. But what it can do is gunk up the fuel injectors, which is good enough for us, Drake. This big rig here's gotta be loaded with electronic shit we can fence or put to good use. Get me the bag of sugar and keep a lookout while I do the dirty deed."

Drake loitered near a tree where he could seem innocent while Bones unscrewed the fuel cap on the big rig and poured in all the white stuff in the bag. By the time he was finished with this, two truckers came out of the toilets and stopped to buy cans of soda, then headed for the rig.

Bones managed to get the fuel tank capped in time not to get caught. Then he and Drake loitered a short distance away, waiting to see which way the trailer truck would head after it pulled out.

Bones said, "Let's hurry up and take a piss. If we're lucky, their engine will go kaput in a lonely enough spot."

CHAPTER 20

Sally and Marsha rode their horses across a meadow to the edge of a pond where they dismounted and let Sparky and Perky dip their heads and drink.

Sally said, "I should be heading back about now. Dad really wants me to help him today."

"Oh, he can get along by himself," Marsha said with a fond smile, thinking about her husband, "even though he makes doing inventory sound like a major military campaign. He just likes to have you at his side, that's all. Even when you were married, he loved when you and your husband would come to visit us. Remember?"

"Yeah, I could tell," Sally said.

"We both missed you more than we liked to admit," Marsha told her. "So we're glad to have you back, even though the circumstances were nothing we would've wished for."

"I understand, Mom. I really do," said Sally. "Don't worry about me. I'll be okay. I'm determined to get my life back together and move on."

"Spoken like a truly spunky daughter," Marsha said, and they both laughed.

"It's nice to know you believe in me," Sally said. "It helps give me strength."

"You're the one of the strongest women I know," her mother said. "Deep inside, I mean. As a child you were willful—and a handful! But the willfulness morphed into strength. I'm the one who should know. I've lived with you since before you were born."

"Mom, don't pull that one on me," Sally said. "You didn't psych me out while I was still in the womb!"

"But pretty quickly thereafter," Marsha maintained. "Don't forget I have a degree in child psychology."

"Which you never used very much," Sally squelched.

CHAPTER 21

In their beat-up van, Bones and Drake cruised slowly on the wooded rural highway, hoping to spot the big rig disabled and ripe for a hijacking.

Drake grumped, "Ain't gonna work. I don't see a shittin' thing. That bag of sugar didn't do the trick. Maybe somethin' else woulda worked out for us, some wallpaper paste or somethin'."

"Who the hell carries around freakin' wallpaper paste?" Bones jeered. "What really pisses me off is I ain't gonna have no sugar for my coffee if this scheme backfires."

"Or for my Cheerios," Blake interjected. "I like Cheerios, but they gotta be sweet."

"Fuck you and your Cheerios," said Bones, and they both laughed.

Blake kept on driving, only halfheartedly expecting to see a busted-down big rig. But Bones kept peering around intently, staring into clumps of trees and out into fields as far as he could see, and he even tried to see if any grass was mashed down as if a vehicle had careened off the road.

He kept this up for a long while, till finally he let out a whoop. "Ho! What's that over there, Mr. Naysayer?"

"Nothin'," Drake said. "Pure nothin'. Zilch in fact."

"The hell it is! That's a truck track, stupid! Right there off the berm! The fuel lines musta froze up while they were comin' down this hill, and they went outta control."

"And disappeared into thin air?"

"How the hell should I know? They musta skidded back onto the road."

"Then where in the fuck are they, Herr Reich Marshal?"

"Look!" Bones shouted. "Way out in that field! Our fuckin' windshield is so filthy I almost didn't see it."

"I see it now," said Drake, braking and stopping. "A fuckin' telephone pole is cut in two, and the wires are down, man! And there's the rig—jackknifed into a cell tower!"

"Pull off! Let's go lend a hand to the poor unfortunate souls," Bones said with mock sympathy.

Bones took a long-barreled semiautomatic pistol from under the passenger seat, worked the slide to make sure a round was chambered, then screwed on a silencer.

Drake humped the van out into the bumpy field and for part of the distance up a broad swath of power company right-of-way, where he had to circle around the splintered telephone pole and the downed cables, till he finally stopped about about twenty yards from the tractor-trailer rig. He reached under the driver's seat of the van for his pistol, which was the same make and model as the one Bones had, and he screwed on the same kind of silencer.

"Don't show your gun yet," Bones cautioned. "If they're carryin' weapons of their own, they might just blast away at us without askin' any questions. Let's play it sneaky."

They got out of the van, didn't shut the doors so they wouldn't make much noise, and crept toward the cab of the truck with their silencer-equipped pistols tucked in their waistbands under their black leather jackets.

When they got closer, they could hear moaning, which pleased them because they wanted their prey at least partially disabled.

The big rig had crashed head-on into a large cell tower The cab was smashed in, and the windshield was shattered in two head-sized places as if human heads had smacked into those spots. Both doors of the cab were sprung open, but not all the way. The guy on the passenger side was clearly dead, his skull crushed and caked with blood.

The driver was moaning, and these were the moans that Bones and Drake had first heard. "He ain't breathin' very loud," Drake said. "He ain't gonna make it I don't think, but let's make sure." He put his pistol, silencer and all, right up to the driver's temple, and squeezed off a round that made only a little pop.

Bones did the same thing to the other trucker.

"Haw!" Drake scoffed. "You call yourself some kinda brain. How's come you just wasted one of our expensive Teflon bullets on a dead man, Bones?"

"To make absolutely sure, Dummkopf. What'd they preach at us when we trained with the Aryan Brotherhood? Thoroughness. See the job through down to every detail. Don't let yourself take for granted your enemy is out cold or dead. Take the time to make sure—that way he ain't gonna spring up big as life all of a sudden and take you by surprise. Let's get humpin'. We gotta load our van with all the electronic stuff we can manage. Then get our sweet asses outta here."

"Wait a minute. I wanna try somethin'," Drake said, and he yanked out his cell phone and tried to dial a number. "Dead," he said. "Like I thought. This sucker took out the power lines *and* the cell tower, Bones. Anybody we wanna rob ain't gonna have no contact with the outside, and if they got a security system of any kind, it probably ain't gonna work."

"That's good to know," said Bones, "for future reference. But it cuts no ice with what we gotta do right now."

He reached into the cab and yanked the key out of the ignition, then led the way to the back of the trailer truck. He got the big back door unlocked, and as it started to lift, he and Drake started to hear strange nonhuman-sounding voices. And those voices were making sounds of anger and hunger—weird, slavering noises.

Bones and Drake jumped back, startled, and looked at each other momentarily, their eyes widening with sudden terror.

They both knew at once that whatever they tried to do to save themselves would be too late.

Zombies were pouring out of the truck . . . hungry . . . drooling . . .

Perhaps Drake and Bones had heard of Dr. Harold Melrose, or maybe they had read about him when he was in the news so much, sixteen years ago. If so, in their final moments it may have dawned on them that the logo with the rose and the letters *MR* stood for Melrose. And the big rig wasn't really carrying any electronic equipment. Instead it was transporting zombies. Lots of them. Including the huge long-term zombie called Barney, who had always been one of Dr. Melrose's favorites. He wasn't one of the first ones out of the truck though; he was too bulky and slow-moving, and others got out ahead of him, which probably saved his "life."

Drake and Bones managed to shoot some of the first ones out. But at first they failed to use head shots. So the zombies they shot weren't always seriously hurt. They just kept coming.

Three of the zombies came out together, and they even bore a resemblance to one another: a man, a woman, and a teenage boy in neat and clean clothing, as if they were going on a picnic or a trip to the movies. These were newly created zombies, new recruits to the ranks of the undead—and they each had puncture wounds in their necks—and of course Bones and Drake didn't have time to notice this or to even care about it.

Bones shot the teenage boy, Stevie Mathews, in his head, and that was the end of Stevie. He and his parents had been transformed when Tiffany and Victoria Melrose drank their blood last night.

Albert got hit by a bullet that Drake fired, but it was only a flesh wound that grazed his skull.

Meg wasn't hit at all by any of the gunfire. But a zombie next to her got shot in the head and went down, and in her newly zombified state this did not faze her much.

Utterly panicked by the ferociousness of the attack they were under, Bones and Drake belatedly tried to run. But they were choked, pummeled, tackled, and bitten, their legs pulled out from under them.

Then they were swarmed over by hungry ghouls, including Meg and Albert, who took their first satisfying bites of live human flesh.

Bones and Drake kicked and thrashed and screamed at the tops of their lungs, but not for long.

Their screams were overwhelmed by slavering, chomping sounds and then slowly and with utter finality, the screaming faded away forever.

CHAPTER 22

Sheriff Harkness sat behind his desk puffing on his pipe, and Bruce Barnes was in a chair facing him. They were trying to make sense of what they had been through this morning and figure out what had been accomplished, even though the serving of the search warrant hadn't panned out the way they had thought it would. Now they needed to decide what their next moves ought to be.

Mulling it all over, the sheriff said, "Melrose's claim that the *government* backed him at one time was nothin' but poppycock. Probably had a little grain of truth in it, but basically a lie to cover up a guilty conscience."

Bruce said, "I don't believe he *had* a conscience." Seems to me he was a rogue scientist, a loose cannon. It'd be nice to know that the government wasn't involved with a nut like that."

"Well," said Harkness, "when the plague broke out sixteen years ago, he was one of the so-called scientific experts wrackin' their brains tryin' to dope it out and find a cure—but they never came up with anything except cockamamie theories. Meantime pea brains like you and me put an end to it the old-fashioned way—gunned 'em down and burned 'em. Everybody hoped that'd be it—it'd go away like the bubonic plague and never come back. The eggheads were told to stop all their experimenting and dispose of any of what they called 'infectious biological material' that they still had in their labs. I guess the politicians and the big brass were a tad squeamish about using human be- ings like lab animals, even human beings that weren't quite human anymore. They decided it was best to cremate them and hope the plague never came back, even though nobody knew where it had come from in the first place."

"But apparently Melrose wanted to go on," Bruce said. "Why? What do you think he was on to?"

"You got me," said the sheriff. "Probably nothin'. Or maybe somethin'. There's always been a lot of babble in the tabloids about secret laboratories where the army is studyin' zombies, tryin' to figure out why they can't be killed with just a body shot." He chuckled at this. "It'd be a helluva advantage for guys goin' into combat, wouldn't it? But I don't know what good it woulda done Dr. Melrose."

Bruce said, "How did he keep them alive for so long? They would've had to eat, wouldn't they?"

"Well, unfortunately, we know what happened to Jeff Sanders, and he might not have been the only one who was fed to those things. But it's hard for me to picture Dr. Melrose kidnapping and killing people to use them as zombie feed."

"Why not?" Bruce said, with a raising of his eyebrows. "He was the kind of doctor who likes to play God. I read a case study on a nutcase named Doctor Mudd who was getting away with one murder after another back in Chicago in 1893 when the World's Fair was going on there. He was kidnapping people who came to the fair from other parts of the country, killing them, and selling their bodies to a medical college. He was even putting some of the bodies in vats of acid to take all the flesh off, then selling the skeletons."

"Well, there's all kinds of nuts in the world," said the sheriff. "But it's a good thing that not all of them are homicidal 'cause we've got more than enough on our hands as it is." He took an- other thoughtful puff on his pipe, then said, "I had to break it to Amy that Jeff is no longer with us, and she went to pieces so bad.

I don't think she was ever intending to divorce him even though he was so worried about it."

"That's a shame," said Bruce. "Everything about it is a shame. They should've been able to have a good life together."

The sheriff shook his head sadly and said, "I hated to tell Amy how he died, but I couldn't think of a way around it. I asked her to keep the details to herself for now, just say he got killed in the line of duty. I think she'll cooperate. She understands that we have to downplay everything so we don't start a mass panic—at least for the time being. I'm thinking that the zombies we killed at the Melrose place must've been all that he had out there. But we don't really know for sure right now."

Bruce said, "We ought to get in touch with the medical colleges, not just around here, but across the country. Maybe we'll find out Doc Melrose was buying cadavers from them. Maybe that's how he was feeding his so-called *lab specimens*."

"I wouldn't put it past him," said the sheriff. "I wouldn't put *anything* past him."

Bruce said, "It could be that Melrose didn't intentionally kill Jeff. Maybe Jeff stepped into something he didn't understand. He told you he was gonna try to break into one of the buildings out there. If he didn't know what was in there, and one of those zombies jumped him . . ."

"It could've been that way," the sheriff said before Bruce had to finish his grisly thought. "But no matter how it went down, Melrose is responsible. If he was alive, we'd be prosecuting him for Jeff's murder and probably a whole host of other crimes we don't know about right now. Same with his daughters. According to him, they're on the loose somewhere, and we've got to find them."

"It's disappointing that our road block didn't turn up anything," Bruce said. "But all we really had to go on was the possibility of coming across that van we were told about, the one with the sign that said Olsen's Grocery Mart."

Chapter 23

Returning from their morning ride, Sally and her mom halted their horses near the open door to the barn. Marsha said, "You can go in and take your bath. I'll unsaddle the horses."

"You sure, Mom? I've got time to help."

"I don't mind a bit. I want to stay out here in the fresh air for a while before I get started with the laundry."

"All right then. Thanks, Mom."

They both dismounted, and Sally headed for the house, approaching it by means of the long, winding brick walkway. It was the home she had grown up in, and she still felt more comfortable in it than in any other place. For her, it exuded a warmth that was full of childhood memories. It was over a hundred years old, and her mother and father had bought it before she was born, a large, stately, two-story frame house with a railed and pillared front porch that went the entire width of it, and brick chimneys on both ends of the slate-shingled roof. The house was painted white with red trim for the porch banisters and window frames, and it reminded Sally very much of some of the homes she had visited at historical sites going back to colonial or Civil War times. But it was very modern inside as far as the furniture and fixtures were concerned, although the huge stone fireplaces were treasured by her and her family and would never be gotten rid of in spite of the fact that they were seldom used. Gas heating and air-conditioning were just too convenient, and the Brinkman family, like many people, were addicted to it.

As she pulled open the seldom-locked front door and went into the living room, Sally tugged off her riding jacket and dropped it on a leather armchair so she could pick it up on her way out later, after she had had her bath. Then she skipped upstairs to start filling the tub.

Marsha led her horse Perky into a stall, then got her uncinched, unsaddled, and unbridled. She was about to do the same for Sparky when she heard the palomino whinnying and snorting as if something had made him scared. So she hurried out of the barn and was pounced on by a huge beast of a man—or at least she thought it was a man. And it sort of was one! It was the undead behemoth named Barney who had escaped from the big rig that had wrecked into a cell phone tower, thanks to the attempted hijacking by Bones and Drake.

Marsha screamed as Barney seized her roughly and tried to sink his teeth into her neck.

Sparky, tethered to a steel ring in the barn door, whinnied in fear and yanked hard against his reins.

Marsha kicked Barney in his groin and managed to wrench herself out from under his big arms, which of course were exceptionally powerful when he was alive but were not as strong now that he had been undead for a long time. Like all of the undead, his movements were single-minded, but slow and stiff as if still under a semiadvanced stage of rigor mortis.

Marsha whirled and glanced toward the house, thinking to run in that direction, but Barney was coming at her again, blocking her way, so she ran back into the barn.

Sparky whinnied again and reared up violently, tearing loose from his reins. And when the big stallion's hooves came down, they landed partially against Barney's legs, knocking him down. Then Sparky reared up again and trampled on Barney—so hard that maybe Barney would have been killed, especially if the horse had landed his steel-shod hooves on the big zombie's head—but instead of doing that, Sparky ran in panic out into the field.

Barney groaned and slowly pulled himself to his feet. Then he headed into the barn after Marsha. Limping and breathing hoarsly, he passed by the swung-open barn door into a dimly lit, cavernous place of hay bales and animal stalls.

Marsha cowered behind a hay bale.

Barney stopped and looked around, moving his big head slowly and stiffly.

Then three more zombies came into the barn, as if they were a pack of animals who knew the smell of human flesh. One of them was the serial killer named Chub, now zombified, who was so used to hunting humans when he was alive. And perhaps he retained some of his guile and cunning now that he was undead.

The other two zombies were a man and a woman, both dressed in plain clothing, the woman in a blouse and shorts, the man in a T-shirt and faded jeans, and both of them wearing snaeakers. If they were alive they would probably have been wearing warmer clothes because of the October chill. But now they were undead and didn't, or couldn't, care less. Both of them had the greenish flesh often exhibited by corpses, and they were not so much vicious-looking but mute and dumb. And that was somehow scarier than diabolical slyness or fiendish intelligence because they exuded the single-minded intention of not being stopped by anyone or anything until they could tear apart and feast upon a victim. Any victim would do, so long as he or she was still alive.

Marsha risked peeping out from her hiding place, and when she saw around the side of the bale, she gave an involuntary gasp, recognizing that she was now facing not just one zombie, but four! And they were closing in on her, drooling and moaning hungrily.

She darted her eyes around frantically, looking for an avenue of escape. But she was hemmed in by the windowless plank wall of a section of stalls. She grabbed the only thing in sight that she thought might help her defend herself—a two-by-four leaning against a corner.

Perky was whinnying fearfully now—whinnying and whinnying in desperate terror.

The zombies came closer to Marsha. They were slow-moving dead things, but relentless in pursuit, except for Chub, who hung back a little, perhaps instinctively retaining the self-protective, cowardly impulse not to risk himself so readily if he could let others put themselves in danger, then reap the benefits.

Marsha bravely stepped out from behind the bale to give herself room to swing the two-by-four. And when the female zombie got close enough, she swung the lengthy piece of lumber hard against the zombie's kneecaps, knocking her legs out from under her. She went down with a hiss that sounded almost painful, and the male that was right behind her stumbled over her thrashing body.

With another hard swing, Marsha clobbered the stumbling male over his head, cracking his skull, and he grunted and went down like a sack of potatoes.

Marsha swung at Barney, clubbing him in his barrellike chest and knocking him back a step or two, but the impact jarred the two-by-four out of her hands, and when she scrambled for it, the female zombie still thrashing on the ground got hold of the other end of it. They both yanked on it in a tug-of-war. Then Barney pushed Marsha as hard as he could, and she stumbled backward, hitting her head against the side of something hard—she didn't know what.

Then, groggily, she saw that it was the ladder leading up to the loft, and there were streaks of sunlight up there, filled with dancing dust-motes that almost seemed to whisper "salvation." Marsha scrambled up the ladder, hoping desperately that those dead things could not climb.

Anxiously she knelt in shreds of old hay up there in the loft and peered down, then shuddered—because one of the zombies *was* starting to climb! It wasn't Chub, and it wasn't Barney. It was the female.

Marsha tried shaking the ladder to make the female zombie fall, but it wouldn't budge. It was anchored up there by a pair of metal cleats.

Marsha scrambled deeper into the loft, not knowing what she was going to do next to try to save herself.

The female zombie climbed stiffly and laboriously till she reached the point where she could crawl into the loft. Then she raised herself up, turning her head this way and that—and with a victorious scream Marsha plunged a pitchfork into the zombie's chest.

The zombie fell fifteen feet backward and down, pitchfork and all. She lay flat on her back, hissing and writhing, trying to pull the tines of the pitchfork out of her wretched body. The other two zombies stood around staring at this spectacle, awed and backing away from it.

In what seemed to be a state of confusion among the dead beings, Marsha scrambled out of the loft, jumping the final four feet off the ladder, plowing into Chub and knocking him down, then darting for the wide-open sunlit doorway of the barn.

Barney turned, dumbly peering after her.

And just as she got almost to freedom, three more zombies appeared, blocking her way.

She stopped in her tracks, backing up and whimpering, "No . . . no . . ."

Now all the remaining zombies closed in on her from all sides. They clawed at her and pulled her down onto the patch of ground in front of the barn, right where she almost made it to freedom. Their yellowish drooling teeth glimmered in the sunlight.

She struggled for a while, her screams muffled because Barney and Chub pressed their forearms into her throat while the others pinned down her arms and legs.

Six more zombies arrived on the scene, with rasping breath and shuffling footsteps. Two of them started toward the "meal in progress," but the ones who got there first gave them fierce looks, glowering and growling like lions guarding their kill.

The two backed off, then moved with the rest of the newly arrived pack toward the house.

Sally had not heard the sounds of her mother's fight with the marauding ghouls, partly because the barn was a good distance from the house and partly because she was filling the bathtub with loudly gushing water for her bath.

She tested the warmth of the water with her fingertips, sprinkled in some pink, nice-smelling bubble-bath crystals, then she went to her bedroom to get her robe and slippers.

Meanwhile, zombies were starting to surround the house.

Three of them, a male and two females, were standing in the front yard, gazing at the front porch as if contemplating an approach, but for some reason they were hanging back for now.

Two others circled around back, both males. One of them was about twenty-five years old and probably used to look pretty dapper in his blue blazer and tan slacks, which were now wrinkled and torn and smeared with muddy grass stains. The other one was about in his twenties also, but wore a wifebeater undershirt and ragged denim cutoffs, with tattoos all over his legs and arms and rings in his lips and nostrils. In ordinary life they likely would not have hung out together, but they were united in a common goal now that they were undead.

In the upstairs of the house, Sally came down the hall carrying her robe, slippers, and a hair dryer, and went into the bathroom, where the water was still gushing. She set down her slippers, hung her robe on a hook behind the door, laid the hair dryer on the sink counter, and plugged it in. Then she shut the bathroom door and tested the water in the tub again, swirling it around with her hand, maximizing the bubbles, and letting the tub completely fill up before turning off the spigot.

She dried her hands on a little towel on the sink rack, then started to unbutton her blouse, but stopped when she heard footsteps, followed by a bump on the door.

She listened.

More footsteps.

Then *bump . . . bump-bump*.

"Mom?" Sally called out.

She listened at the door.

Then she opened it.

She peeked right and left and saw no one in the hall. But she was startled by some rasping and shuffling noises coming from her bedroom.

"Mom?" she called out once again. Then, "Dad?"

She slowly crossed the hall and went a couple steps into her room—and what she saw caused her to gasp and freeze in her tracks. She caught a horrifying glimpse of an image reflected in her dresser mirror, and her mind was partially paralyzed by what she could not comprehend—a depraved-looking *thing* with the flesh ripped out of his face and maggots crawling in his hair!

She tried to back up and run—but too late—the zombie was already lunging at her. He grabbed her by the throat from behind and pulled her to the floor, almost making her pass out from sheer fright and the rancid odor that instantly overwhelmed her. She landed with a bone-wrenching thud, her body twisted and her legs half under the bed. The putrid zombie was kneeling over her head, trying to choke her and get close enough to take a bite out of her face.

When he was almost biting into her cheek, she grabbed his long, greasy, maggot-ridden hair—her fingers slippery with crushed maggots—and pulled hard, slamming his forehead against the steel bed frame . . . once . . . twice . . . three times. It made him loosen his grip on her throat, and she managed to slide her feet out from under the bed, kicking hard at the zombie's body and punching her fist into his Adam's apple. He reeled and spluttered, emitting a rasping, choking sound, and Sally scrambled to her feet.

But the zombie came after her, growling and drooling.

She ran into the bathroom, then tried to slam the door shut and lock it, but the zombie barged in on her before she could slam the bolt home. He clawed at her, and she backed herself into a corner.

She groped frantically, trying to grab on to something she could use to defend herself. Soap, a soap dish, and bottles of shampoo and conditioner clattered to the floor. Still groping, Sally latched onto the hair dryer, but in his wild, mindless thrashing the zombie knocked it out of her hand, and it landed in the sink. She had the crazy thought that she could've held on to it if her hands weren't still slippery from those filthy maggots.

The zombie was on her once again, seizing her by her shoulders in a life and death wrestling match, a grapple in which Sally's goal was not only to get away but to somehow avoid being bitten. Like everyone else, she had heard plenty of stories of what had gone on around here sixteen years ago, and it was clear in her mind now exactly what she was facing. She and the flesh-hungry zombie had hold of each other's clothing and were pulling and twisting.

Then the zombie stepped on a wet bar of soap.

His legs whooshed out from under him, and Sally used his own weight and momentum against him, as she had learned in her jujitsu classes, to spin and shove him down, splashing him backward into the bathtub.

He grunted and groaned, his dead, stiff hands slipping on the walls of the tub as he tried to pull himself up, still growling viciously at Sally.

He managed to sit up, got one foot out of the tub and onto the floor, and started to arise . . .

Sally backed into the corner again. Then her eyes fell upon the hair dryer. She snatched it up and turned it on.

The zombie was halfway up now.

She dropped the hair dryer into the tub, and electricity sparked and sizzled.

The zombie screamed—a horrid sound that was not quite like anything human. He fell all the way back into the tub, and the current zapped through him.

As he burned up, Sally bravely—and she knew *crazily*—took a fleeting moment to run hot water over her maggoty hands and dry them on her jeans. Then she stepped gingerly around the electrocuted zombie who was still sizzling and burning, and ran from the bathroom.

But now two more zombies were in the hall.

At first, they seemed as stunned to see *her* as she was to see *them*. They hissed and reeled back, but then they came at her.

She couldn't make it to the stairs because they were blocking the way. So she pivoted, ran into her room, and slammed the door, bolting it just in time. Hastily, breathing hard and scared out of her wits, she pushed her nightstand against the door, sending the telephone, lamp, and other stuff flying to the floor.

The two zombies were now pounding at her locked door, and it was starting to give way under the frenzied onslaught. It was the kind of door with a largely hollow, wood-framed interior, built for privacy rather than strength. A hard-punching fist could crash all the way through it. And the screws that were holding the bolt were starting to rip loose.

Sally ran to a window, unlocked it, and opened it as wide as it would go. Then she knocked out the screen.

From under her bed she pulled out a cardboard box containing a rope and hook device that could be used in emergencies as a fire-escape ladder. Desperately she fumbled with it because the ropes and the hardware were unusable and all tangled up.

The screws holding the bolt popped, and the bedroom door started to open as it was pushed against the nightstand she had put in place there.

Sally finally got the hook and rope device untangled, ran to the opened widow, set the hooks in place on the lower window jamb, and dropped the rope with its knotted rungs out the window and down the side of the house. But it fell about six feet shy of the ground.

By this time, there was a zombie jam-up at the bedroom door, three or four of them trying to get in all at once and mindlessly impeding their own progress.

Sally hoisted herself out the window and scrambled with her feet to catch hold of a ropy rung of the ladder. She slipped and almost fell thirty feet, but managed to hang on with her hands clinging to a shoulder-wrenching grip on the ropes, and then she started to descend. At the end of the dangling rope ladder, she had to let go, and it was a long hard drop. Her knees crumbled as her boots struck the ground, and she fell to the turf. But she quickly bounced back up, shaken and yet amazed that she hadn't broken any bones.

She ran for the barn, calling out to her mother. "Mom! Mom! Where are you?"

She stopped short, frozen in horror, when she came upon the pack of zombies slavering over her mother's remains. She let out a scream. And some of the zombies got up and started to come after her.

She ran out into the field. But she saw more zombies out there, so she abruptly changed direction and cut toward the woods. In among the trees she ran past a party of zombies who seemed to be heading in the direction she had come from, but they were so slow that she got past them, skirting about ten yards around them, and she ran and ran till she came to the pond in the clearing where earlier she and her mother had watered their horses.

To her surprise, Sparky was standing by the pond, panting hard, his reins hanging down to the ground, and she gasped out his name. The palomino snorted, eyeing her warily, greatly disturbed by all that had happened. She could tell he was very edgy, and she feared he might panic and take off again.

"Easy now, boy, easy," she murmured softly. "Easy, Sparky. You know I'm your old buddy now . . . and you know I need you . . ."

The horse shied and backed away, but then stood still again and snorted.

Sally eased close enough to take hold of the reins, and then she mounted, somewhat surprised that in his agitated state Sparky still let her. She settled into the saddle and petted him, soothing him as best she could, saying, "Come on, Sparky, we have to get out of here, boy. Let's go find Daddy."

They trotted out of the clearing toward a wooded path.

Soon Sally got Sparky into a slow trot.

But around a twisting bend in the path, two zombies stepped out from the foliage, making the palomino whinny and rear up, almost dropping Sally. It was all she could do to hang on to the reins.

Sparky clobbered one zombie with his slashing hooves, and Sally beat at the other, using the long leather reins as a whip. That zombie, a teenage girl with wild, tangled red hair, a scarred and bloody face, and big yellowish teeth, backed off under the whipping Sally was giving her. And Sally spurred her horse, trampling over the downed one—a gray-haired zombified old man—while the redheaded teenage one grabbed on to one of Sally's legs and one of her saddle straps. She dragged the undead creature along, spurring Sparky faster and whipping the zombie's face some more with the reins, till finally she dropped off.

Sally kept going, riding Sparky hard.

CHAPTER 24

Henry Brinkman's roadhouse had a large neon sign that said HENRY'S HIDEAWAY. Out back was a woodshed, a Dumpster, and a garage-sized toolshed. Henry's pickup truck and an older model car were the only vehicles in the gravel parking lot.

Inside, there was a dance floor, a jukebox, mounted animal heads spaced around the walls, and a black-powder musket displayed over a large stone fireplace. All the chairs and stools were stacked upside down on the square oaken tables and the Formica-topped bar because the place was not open for business yet. Henry was finishing up his inventory, counting and itemizing the liquor bottles on the tiers of glass shelves behind the bar. He picked the bottles up one at a time, turned them in the dim bar light so he could read the labels, and made notations on a yellow legal pad.

Smokey, a grizzled tobacco chewer in his late sixties, poked his head through the kitchen aperture across from the waitress station at the far end of the bar and said in his crackly, squeaky voice, "Damned if I ain't short of buns again. How'm I supposed to serve people their dogs and burgers? I can cook 'em up, but for sure I gotta put 'em *on* somethin'."

"I gave you the money to buy buns," Henry accused. "What'd you do? Drink it all up again?"

Moving his chew to one side of his mouth, Smokey said, "You ain't never *gimme* no money!"

Henry laughed. "How the hell would you *know*, old man? You were drunk at the time. Your head was screwed on crooked, and your wisdom teeth didn't have any wisdom at all in them. And your head ain't screwed on too tight right now neither."

The two of them argued like this all the time, and Henry never thought of firing Smokey because he got a kick out of him and because folks liked the old codger, and he did a good job in many ways as a short-order cook, general handyman, and substitute bartender. He was a fixture around the place, having been here through three owners, and Henry had inherited him.

Smokey scratched his grizzled head and mumbled, "Well, ya never . . . I mean . . . did ya?"

"You ain't too sure, are you? Relax, you old fart. I told you I'd buy the buns, and I did. They're in my pickup. I forgot to bring them in."

"I'll go get 'em."

"Here are the keys."

Henry tossed the truck keys onto the counter, and Smokey ducked back from the aperture after he snatched them up. He went out the back door of the roadhouse, which was the kitchen exit, and he wedged the door open so he wouldn't have to struggle with it when his hands were full. Then, as an afterthought, he ducked back inside for some big, bulging garbage bags and took them out to the Dumpster and tossed them in.

He spat tobacco juice into some weeds by the Dumpster, then headed for the pickup truck, going all the way around to the front of the roadhouse where Henry had parked it. He unlocked the passenger door and saw that the bags of buns were there, on the floor between the seat and the dash. He stooped to pick them up.

That was when two zombies pounced on him.

He never had a chance.

The zombies were two big, heavily bearded males, both wearing green workmen's jumpsuits like the kind worn by roofers or plumbers. They looked like they had done lots of heavy work before they became undead.

They slammed Henry against the pickup truck, and he dropped the bags of buns. Dragging him down, they trampled uncaringly all over the buns, mashing them to pulp. One of the zombies was choking Smokey and biting his face. The old man's chaw of tobacco oozed out of his mouth, and his tongue protruded, dripping and brown. He was able to kick and thrash for a while, but then his struggles ceased.

The zombie who was biting his face pulled back momentarily, his mouth and chin a bloody smear.

The other zombie lifted Smokey's limp, dead arm and bared his teeth and licked his lips in anticipation.

Meanwhile, inside the saloon, Henry Brinkman was taking upturned chairs down from tabletops in preparation for opening time. He slid a chair roughly into place, then turned around, exasperated, hands on hips. "Smokey!" he called out. "I could sure use some help in here!"

He listened but heard only silence. Then he strode quickly around the bar, through the kitchen, and out onto the slab of porch at the back door, where he stopped and looked left and right.

"Smokey," he called once again. "Finish your chew and stop lollygagging! We gotta open up in ten minutes!"

No answer.

Henry stepped down off the stoop. He still didn't see the old man, so he moved farther out into the back lot.

And when Henry's back was turned, a large male zombie in a blue short-sleeved shirt and tie shuffled in through the open kitchen door.

Close to his truck now, Henry was puzzled and annoyed to see the passenger door open and the keys lying on the ground. He snatched up the keys, slammed the door shut, spun around, and took a few steps.

Then he froze—because he saw the two jump-suited zombies crouched over Smokey's dead body, tearing him apart. And more zombies were coming out of the surrounding woods—at least eight or nine of them.

Henry spun, gravel flying under his work boots as he ran back across the front lot and in through the kitchen door. He tried to pull it shut behind him, but forgot about the wedge, so that the door wouldn't budge at first, till he kicked the wedge aside, cursing at it.

Then he slammed the door shut and bolted it. It was a heavy steel door with a dead bolt, and Henry tugged hard on it a few times to make sure it was secure, then he turned around and flattened himself against it, breathing hard. He tried to think what to do next. He knew exactly what he was dealing with. The plague had started again. He didn't know why, but it was clearly happening all over again. Thoughts of his wife and daughter slammed into his brain: *Did they know about it? Were they in danger?* He made a move toward the phone out in the bar—

But before he could get to it he heard a heavy rasping sound, and the zombie that he was unaware of—who had entered when his back was turned and the kitchen door was open—now shuffled into the kitchen again, from the main barroom.

Henry was frozen for a long moment, just staring at the undead creature. Then he turned toward the steel door he had just bolted—but he realized futilely that even if he had time to escape from the one in here, there were even more of them outside. And he had locked himself against the danger from outside only to be confronted with unexpected danger from right here in his own kitchen.

The zombie snarled and came toward Henry, and he scrabbled for a butcher knife on the kitchen counter.

The undead being came forward in spite of the knife, too mindless to recognize any threat to itself.

When the zombie lunged at him, Henry plunged his knife into the thing's solar plexus and jumped back from a spurt of blackened blood.

The zombie reeled backward and almost fell because it stumbled over a mop and bucket. But it didn't go down. Pulling itself up by clutching with its stiff, dead hands on the countertop, it stared at the knife buried in its belly.

Then with both zombified hands it slowly pulled the knife out and dropped it onto the floor.

But Henry had time to snatch up a cleaver, and when the zombie came at him again, he delivered a series of hard whacks, hacking into its chest, then its face.

This time the zombie went down, and Henry stepped on him with his boot and hacked and hacked at the thing's head.

Finally the thing seemed totally dead, not "living dead" anymore, and Henry stared down at it, relieved. But then he had the chilling thought that maybe it was just immobilized and not totally finished off—because its eyeballs were twitching, even with the cleaver embedded deep in its skull.

Henry turned toward the bolted steel door. Cautiously he unbolted it and opened it just a sliver so he could peek out. He didn't see any zombies close by, so he opened it wider—and then he saw some, in a cluster by the Dumpster—but they were far enough back that he decided he could risk dragging the "dead" zombie outside.

He grabbed the thing's ankles and dragged it out onto the stoop. Then he quickly reached back to a shelf just inside the door and grabbed a can of lighter fluid and a box of wooden matches.

At this point, the zombies by the Dumpster started to come forward, moving stiffly, emitting heavy, rasping breaths.

Henry doused the vanquished zombie's upper body with lighter fluid and pulled the cleaver, which he thought might still come in handy, out of the zombie's head and tossed it back onto the floor of the kitchen. The zombie's eyes were still twitching when Henry struck a match and set it on fire. With only the upper part of the creature burning at first, he could still grab hold of the ankles, and as the surrounding zombies backed away in fear of the flames, he dragged the burning zombie down off the stoop and farther away from the building. Then he squirted more lighter fluid all over the thing, and the blaze really got going.

Henry backed away toward the kitchen entrance.

Just then he heard hoofbeats on gravel, and his daughter Sally came galloping toward him from the other side of the lot. She pulled Sparky up short, and the zombies moved toward them.

Henry yelled, "Sally! Get inside quick!"

With a frightened glance, she took in all the elements of danger and grisliness here—about two dozen "live" zombies and one who was burning.

"C'mon, Sally," Henry yelled again. "Or else they'll get you!"

She jumped down from the saddle, smacked Sparky on his rump hard, and shouted, "Go, Sparky! *Go!*" The big stallion whinnied, then galloped across the lot and into the woods, knocking down two zombies as he fled.

Henry pulled his daughter into the kitchen and slammed and bolted the steel door once again. Sobbing, Sally threw herself into her father's arms. She choked out her grief, her voice muffled against his chest. "Oh, Dad . . . Mom didn't make it . . . what are we gonna do?"

Just then the lights in the place blinked a couple of times . . . off . . . then on . . . then off permanently. The roadhouse was windowless except for two grimy windows in the kitchen that let in twin slashes of murky, rudimentary light, and that was all the light that was left after the sudden loss of electrical power.

CHAPTER 25

Darkness came early in the fall, and at dusk two big Harley motorcycles roared down the two-lane highway and out into the field where Drake and Bones caused the big rig to wreck and afterward unwittingly released a horde of zombies. The men on the motorcycles were two skinheads named Slam and Bearcat, both wearing dark glasses, black Nazi helmets, and leathers and chains, the leathers adorned with swastikas and SS insignia. Bearcat's biker chick, Honeybear, was hanging on to him from behind, her nice firm ass in the saddle and her shapely legs straddling it. She was a stunner in her red halter and red hot pants—the epitome of a blond, beautiful "Aryan" woman.

When they got out to where Drake's van and the wrecked trailer truck were, they all dismounted and looked around, taking everything in.

Bearcat said, "How the hell'd you spot Drake's ride way out here, Slam? Him and Bones were s'posed to meet us at the junkyard."

"Well, I figgered somethin' weird musta happened to 'em on their hijackin' gig, so when I didn't see hide nor hair of 'em around the junkyard shack, I remembered the road they said they was on when they was trackin' the rig full of electronics. I checked out all the side roads one at a time. Took me an hour at least, and I almost gave up. This was the last place I was gonna look."

Slam and Bearcat walked around, kicking at the tall grass, and suddenly Bearcat stooped and picked up a gun with a silencer. "Hey, looky here!" he called out.

He pulled back the slide and a live round ejected. So he popped out the clip.

"Still loaded?" Slam said.

"Five rounds left in the clip."

Honeybear sounded off then. "Hey, I found another one!"

She held up the other pistol with a silencer and worked the slide and popped out the clip. Bearcat came over to her, took the clip, and stared at it. "This one's half full too," he said. "Bones and Drake always kept nine rounds in the clip plus one in the chamber, so they musta run into some big trouble."

Slam said, "Let me have that one, Honeybear," and took the pistol she had found away from her. Bearcat gave him the clip, and he shoved it home with a metallic click.

Bearcat thought for a while. Then he said, "If they had their silencers on, they were up to somethin' and thought they had the upper hand. But it musta backfired on them. Let's have another look around."

Honeybear was already doing that. She worked her way around the van, then let out a little shriek. She was staring down at Drake's mangled, chewed-up remains as Bearcat and Slam came up beside her. "Ugh!" she said. "Is that Drake?"

"Yeah, what's left of him," Bearcat answered. "I can't believe it."

Slam said, "What in the world coulda done this to him? We better—"

Just then they heard a rasping, groaning sound—and the skinhead named Bones, mangled and partially devoured, emerged from the surrounding woods. One side of his face was eaten away, and his left arm was missing, ripped off like a drumstick from a roast chicken, with stringy vessels and fibers hanging down from the socket. His body cavity had also been chewed out, exposing coils of white intestine. And he was coming straight toward his former skinhead pals, almost as if he expected to be welcomed by them.

Slam and Honeybear backed away, terrified, but Bearcat stood his ground.

Slam yelled, "C'mon, Bearcat! Let's get the hell outta here!"

The Bones zombie came closer.

"Gotta finish him off," Bones declared. "He can't do it for hisself, and he wouldn't wanna live like that if he had a choice, Slam."

Gritting his teeth, Bearcat waited for Bones to get so close he couldn't miss, then got into a firing crouch and took careful two-handed aim and pumped two rapid-fire bullets into Bones's brain. The big, heavy, grotesquely mutilated Bones zombie went down like a ton of bricks.

Bearcat headed for his Harley, climbed on, and kick-started it. Honeybear hopped on behind him.

Slam kick-started his bike too, and the three of them roared back across the bumpy field, then careened onto the road and sped away.

CHAPTER 26

There was a full moon now, and Henry's Hideaway was surrounded by clusters of zombies, about thirty or forty of them in all. They milled around, staring at the place, knowing there was succulent human flesh inside.

In the barroom, which was dimly lit by lantern and candlelight, Henry and Sally were discussing their desperate situation. She got up from her stool and paced in front of the lit fireplace while he remained sitting on a bentwood chair turned backward.

Both of them were overwhelmed with issues of survival while they were also trying to deal with Marsha Brinkman's death. This involved memories that kept churning up in their hearts and minds, plus unspoken fears of what kind of fate, if any, might have been waiting for her beyond her known fate. In other words, was she going to become one of *them*? This fear was stronger in Henry than in Sally because she had had no direct experience of the phenomenon sixteen years ago, while her father had gone out as part of a volunteer posse to rescue people and gun down and burn the undead creatures that were menacing them. He had actually seen a ghoul-bitten person come back to "life" when that person to all intents and purposes shouldn't have been able to move anymore, let alone sit up and try to attack him. That was the third ghoul of seven that he had shot during his six days as a posse member.

Sally said, "We've gotta keep our spirits up, Dad. Mom wouldn't want us to give up."

"That's one thing we know for sure," her father agreed. "But I'm glad to hear you say it. I know I can count on you to keep your cool. If we get out of this alive, there'll be time to grieve afterward."

And he knew he would have plenty of grieving to do. His marriage had had its ups and downs, like all marriages, but although their love for each other had gone through many changes over the years, the basis for it had remained solid. And they had been united in their love and their deep sense of pride in their only daughter.

Henry had worked for twenty-three years running his own construction business, putting in bathrooms, porches, patios, awnings, and other home improvements for people, and he had never stopped using his own hands as well as those of his laborers. He hammered, welded, and poured concrete right along with them, and as a result of all the hard physical work, he was in great shape for his age, and he had the energy and the vitality of a much younger man.

Four years ago, he had sold his business to one of his best workers and had made a bit of money on the sale, and his investments had done well enough over the years that he could afford to buy the roadhouse. He wanted to keep on working, but with a lot less pressure. And up until today he had been content with the way things had turned out for him, and he was glad he was in a position to help his daughter get through her divorce and build a better future for herself.

But now they might not have a future if they couldn't fight their way out of this awful predicament they were in. Henry inwardly thought of himself as a strong and courageous man in most circumstances, even stronger and more courageous than most people, but losing Marsha was already such a terrible blow that he didn't think he would want to live anymore if he also lost his daughter.

But there was no time for despondency. Sally interrupted his thoughts, saying, "If we can get to your truck . . . or even Smokey's car . . ."

"His car doesn't even start half the time without jumper cables," Henry told her. "We'd better forget that old clunker—we might get stuck in it, surrounded by those things. It's my truck or nothing. But I think maybe we should just sit tight and and hope the power comes back on and we can get some news."

"About what?"

"About how *bad* it is out there, Sally."

"We already know how bad it is. We're *surrounded* by those things."

"Well, about what to *do* then. Last time, the county set up rescue stations and armed patrols."

"I was only ten years old, but I read about it and heard about it, a lot. Some of the people who didn't try to make it to rescue stations were overrun. I don't think the power is going to come back on either. Somebody was probably attacked and crashed into a transformer pole or something."

"So if it's happening all over," Henry said, "if there are armies of those things everywhere, where would we go to, even if we could make it to my truck?"

"Oh God, I don't know!" Sally blurted in despair. She momentarily stopped pacing in front of the fireplace and confronted her father with a tough question. "What makes this happen, Dad? They never found out the first time, did they?"

Henry thought about it, then said, "I think it's like a cancer."

"But cancer cells are *alive*," Sally said. "These are people who're supposed to be dead but *aren't*. Right?"

Henry said, "Cancer is a part of us and yet isn't part of us. It destroys us, and in the process it destroys itself. When we die, it dies."

"But people with cancer can't infect other people," Sally said. "Those beings out there *can*, Dad."

"Maybe they're inhabited by some alien force."

Sally thought about this for a moment or two. "Like from outer space?"

"Maybe," Henry said. "Some kind of entity we know nothing about. It inhabits the bodies of our dead and turns them against us."

"That's so sickening to think about," said Sally. "I don't think I can go out there, make a break for it, I mean, if it's just the two of us."

"We may end up having no choice," Henry told her.

"Yeah. I know," she agreed dolefully.

"We have only two windows, the ones in the kitchen, boarded up, and both of the doors are thick steel with heavy dead bolts. We can probably remain safe here for quite a while."

"Probably," Sally said doubtfully.

"Well, honey, we're sort of short of weapons," Henry said. "All we've got are a couple of butcher knives and a meat cleaver."

"We could have our own electricity," Sally pointed out, "if we could make it to the shed and turn on the generator."

"Yeah, but what good would that do?" said Henry.

"I don't know," Sally answered dispiritedly.

Suddenly she brightened up and reached toward the black-powder rifle above the mantel. "Hey, how about this, Dad? Got any bullets for it?"

She took the musket down and hefted it in her hands.

"It takes lead balls and black powder," Henry said. "And flint, or caps, I forget which. The instruction book and all that stuff are in a box under the sink—if it's still there. I haven't looked for a long time."

"Let's look!" Sally said.

"All right, but even if you could make it work, that old gun only shoots one lead ball at a time, and it takes forever to prime and reload, so it's not like you could use it to shoot your way through those things. You'd be better off with just a torch. They're afraid of fire, and they burn easily. We learned that last time."

"Maybe we could go up on the roof and pick some of them off one at a time," Sally said. "Maybe if we dropped a few, the rest would back off . . . and hopefully even go away."

Henry got to his feet to go and look for black gunpowder, lead balls, flints, and bore-cleaning solvent. But he stopped and said, "They don't have much fear in them—they're too mindless. As for the roof, how're we gonna get the ladder out of the shed and climb up there without those things swarming all over us?"

"I don't exactly know," Sally said. "But if we could get up there, at least we could have a look around and see if there might be some way to make it to your truck. So let's look for the bullets and stuff."

CHAPTER 27

Jed Terance, a rugged thirty-five-year-old telephone company lineman, shinnied up a telephone pole, wearing hobnailed boots and a harness strap for safety. He also wore a wide leather belt with a leather pouch full of tools, a plaid flannel shirt, denim jeans and jacket, and a cap with the logo of the Willard Power Company. His SUV bearing the same logo was parked near the base of the pole.

As he climbed higher, he gazed at a line of telephone poles laden with wires that stretched one after another through the grassy, hilly right-of-way. His job was to figure out where the break was that had caused a power outage.

When he got himself situated up there, he scraped off insulation, then used his test meter. It registered zero. He muttered to himself, "No wonder the parochial school doesn't have any power."

Meanwhile three zombies came out of the woods, approached Jed's van, and silently stared up at him, hungering for live human flesh. He was so high up that he didn't hear their approach and was totally unaware of their presence.

But Jed's dog, a golden lab named Casey, was sleeping on the passenger seat of the SUV, and his ears pricked up, and he awakened when he smelled the approaching ghouls. He started barking and jumping all around in the cab.

The three zombies picked up rocks and started smashing at the SUV's windows.

Startled by all the commotion, Jed quickly started shinnying down the pole.

The side windows of the SUV were pulverized, and zombie hands were reaching for the dog. Casey managed to bite into a ghoulish hand, snarling viciously and hanging on. Refusing to let go, when the ghoul pulled away, Casey was yanked out of the vehicle through the shattered window.

Casey and the ghoul both tumbled to the ground.

Jed yelled in panic, "Casey!"

One of the ghouls smashed a rock at Casey's head. The dog howled. The ghoul smashed him with the rock again and again. His head a bloody mess, the dog died.

Jed was down from the pole now, his harness strap dangling from his waist. He pulled the best weapons he had on him—a big screwdriver and a claw hammer—from his leather tool pouch. Consumed with rage over the death of his dog, he advanced upon the three flesh-hungry zombies.

He tried to bash one of them in the head with his hammer, but he missed, dealing only a glancing blow to the dead creature's shoulder. The other two started closing in, and Jed knew he was in big trouble. He felt like a gazelle being circled and hemmed in by hungry coyotes.

He jabbed his screwdriver at one of the zombie's eyes, and that one backed away. But the other two, drooling and hissing, were unfazed. They hovered right by the SUV, blocking the doors.

Since the SUV was his only means of escape, Jed came at those two zombies, swinging his hammer and jabbing with his screwdriver. But then the third one sneaked up and tackled him from behind. He fell, dropping his screwdriver but somehow managing to hang on to his claw hammer. He thrashed and struggled, trying to get back up, but the zombie who tackled him was lying heavily across his legs. He tried to crawl away as best he could, dragging the zombie with him, and now the zombie had him by the ankles. But Jed was stronger, so he managed to get halfway up, and then he smashed his hammer down on top of the clutching zombie's head. That zombie was done for, its dead eyes staring straight up into the sun and its cracked head oozing black blood.

But the other two zombies fell on Jed, pushing him all the way down to the ground and knocking his hammer out of his hand. They bit into him, tearing bloody chunks of flesh out of his face and neck. In the midst of this attack, five or six more hungry zombies shuffled out of the woods. They were more than anxious to help devour Jed, and they readily joined in. He died a slow, horrible death, terribly weakened by blood loss, and at the end, when he succumbed, he was almost glad it was over, and he came to reluctantly accept his own hideous fate.

After the zombies satiated themselves on Jed's remains, some of them wandered into the woods till they stumbled onto the grounds of Saint Willard's Catholic Church and Elementary School, which was already surrounded by more than a dozen ghouls. Some of them carried dismembered, partially devoured body parts, and one of them, an obese, greasy-haired female about sixty years old, in a dress as big as a tent, sat under a tree, gnawing on a hand and forearm. The meat of it had been mostly stripped away, down to the nearly naked bones, which were held together by only a few stringy ligaments. The greedy zombie burped. She used her big yellowish teeth to pull off one last string of flesh from the arm bone. Then she dropped the bone onto the ground.

Father Ed Hastings, the pastor of the church and principal of the school, stared in despair from one of the boarded-up windows. His little domain had been under siege since about two hours after the pack of zombies was inadvertently released from the big rig that wrecked in the nearby field. First the power went out, then the cell phones. But first, before he even knew about the zombies, Father Ed had put in a call to the Willard Power Company. Of course he didn't know that the lineman had been killed and devoured just a little while ago, and he was still entertaining a desperate hope that the electricity would come back on and the county police would arrive—but he didn't even know if or how they could be aware of his situation.

Father Ed's church and parochial school were combined in one small building, not in the kind of large stone edifice that might be found in a highly populated town or city. Instead it was a modest wood-frame building doing double duty and serving poor country folk. The evenly spaced windows were tall and narrow, of ordinary glass, not stained glass, and most of them had already been smashed in, the glass shattered, the windows hastily boarded up against the onslaught, which so far had not occurred in full force.

The priest, a nun, and a teacher's aide were holed up in there with two dozen children age six to twelve. After a thirteen-year-old boy had been killed and devoured while going outside to fetch logs for the potbellied stove, the survivors in the little schoolroom had panicked—they had seen the boy being mauled and ripped apart by five or six ghoulish marauders. Father Ed had rallied them and had gotten everyone to work, barricading the windows with wood torn from broken-up desks and benches. Still desperate to make the place more secure, he had a hammer and nails and was trying to hold a chunk of desk in place over a window frame and pound a nail in at the same time. He turned and called out to twelve-year-old Annie Kimble. "Annie, will you give me a hand, please?"

Annie, a bright and winsome child, jumped up and helped hold the board in place while Father Ed drove in some nails. He felt that he should keep all the children as fully occupied as possible with their own defense because it would help them feel useful, even hopeful, and might chase away some of their fear.

Janice Kimble, the volunteer teacher's aide, was Annie's mom, and the teacher of the one-room school was Sister Hillary. They were both capable and resourceful and adept at handling children. Bertie Samuels, a spoiled, pampered nine-year-old, was being coddled in Sister Hillary's lap, his perpetual tears of anguish soaking into her black skirt. He kept bawling for his daddy, as if Daddy could somehow get there through an army of ravenous ghouls.

Father Ed nearly got sick when he peered through the boarded-up windows and saw the zombies feasting on gory body parts. He kept praying that someone would come and save the children. And he kept telling God to do with him as He would. He hoped that his own life and the lives of the other adults would not have to be sacrificed for the sake of the young Catholic students, but if it came to that, he wanted to believe that he could be as willing to accept his fate as were the Christians of Roman times, martyrs who had to uphold their faith by dying in the pagan arena under the fangs and claws of wild beasts.

CHAPTER 28

Blake Parsons and Spaz Bentley had installed a GPS tracking device on the undercarriage of the big rig, so when it didn't show up at their prearranged rendezvous point, a truck stop fifty miles from Willard, they had a rough idea of where it might have gotten detained. The GPS signal went on the blink somewhere south of Willard, but not fifty miles south, so they could tell that the rig never got very far, and they circled back to try to find it.

"I hope the fuckin' fuzz didn't pull it over," Spaz said.

"If they did, we're fucked," Blake said. He noticed that when Spaz grimaced or squinted into the sun while he was driving, his single teardrop tattoo wrinkled up in a strange way, and Blake guessed that his two teardrops must do the same. He figured he would check it out sometime by squinting at himself in a mirror. He was vain about his teardrops and knew that their mere presence helped him intimidate people. He had thought about getting another one tattooed on his cheek just for the hell of it, but the first two were legit and adding a third one would be a kind of dishonesty that he didn't want to commit, even though most kinds of dishonesty were right up his alley.

The two thugs were riding in that same blue van with the Olsen's Grocery Mart sign on it because they didn't know the county cops were wise to it. They knew the route that the big rig was supposed to take, and that's what they followed when they did their backtracking. So it was pretty easy for them to find where the rig had gone off the road and where it had wrecked out in the field.

There they found the partially devoured remains of the two drivers, Luke and Morgan, whom they had known formerly as Dr. Melrose's lab assistants. They had been relied upon to get the big rig and its cargo to the doc's secret lab. But now they were dead and horribly mutilated, their abdominal cavities hollowed out and practically devoid of internal organs. Spaz and Blake knew very well that the undead considered the entrails to be a delicacy, probably because they were easier to chew on than the tougher organs like hearts and livers. Once enough organs were gone, even if the head and body remained mostly intact, it had never been known for a person thus devoured to be still able to rise again.

Spaz and Blake wordlessly drew their guns, sharply scanned everything around them, and spotted nothing and nobody. They knew that the zombies had somehow gotten loose and devoured the two truckers, but they had no idea how.

"Look! Up ahead!" Spaz cried out suddenly.

He had spotted three or four zombies disappearing into the woods.

"Let's track 'em!" Blake said. "We might be able to recapture 'em somehow!"

"Right on, we have our zombie nooses," Spaz enthused.

"Haw!" Blake guffawed, because he knew that his buddy enjoyed using the "nooses" whenever he could. They were the kind of tool that dog catchers used to capture and restrain mad dogs—long leather-clad poles with leather loops at the ends that could be put around a dog's head like a lariat, then cinched tight. Spaz and Blake had innovated the use of them in Doc Melrose's laboratory as an efficient way to pull zombies out of the cages or back in, or to wherever the doc needed them and for whatever purpose. So they ran back to the van and got their zombie nooses.

They lost some time doing this, but were able to catch up with and track the slow-moving zombies till they ended up in the gravel lot of Saint Willard's Catholic Church and Elementary School.

Quickly casing the place, Blake and Spaz saw the priest and some of the children staring in utter fear from behind boarded-up windows.

"Shit! We can't capture all those zombies!" Blake said. "What're we gonna do, Spaz?"

"We gotta help those kids."

"How?"

"The law probably doesn't even know they're in danger. Nobody is comin' to save them, but they probably hope somebody is. It's gotta be us, Blake."

"You sayin' we should risk our lives for a buncha fuckin' *kids?*"

But in spite of his cursing and his wanting to always be a tough guy, Spaz was already weakening. When they were doing jail time, like almost all prisoners, they hated the ones who were in there for raping and killing children. Guys who had murdered, robbed, and even raped adults male and female despised the ones who committed those same crimes against kids. They were labeled "Short Eyes" because when they were outside the prison walls their eyes were always cast downward, checking out and lusting after little kids. Sometimes the authorities knowingly and on purpose had the worst of the Short Eyes, especially those that didn't get the death sentence they deserved, put into the general prison population so the lifers could take care of them in the way that the court system failed to do. Not too many of the Short Eyes lasted to serve out their time, and both Spaz and Blake had participated in some of this kind of rough justice.

"The school is Saint Willard's," Spaz said. "A drinkin' buddy of mine has a boy and girl on the honor roll in there, and I gave 'em candy and potato chips, and they actually liked me. I can't let 'em die. I'll have nightmares about what those zombies'll do to 'em. If you don't feel the way I do, you can take off, Blake. Don't leave me though. Wait by the van."

"Aw, fuck, I'm not gonna wimp out on you, man. I guess this is our chance to help some little kids while they're still alive. But how're we gonna handle this?"

"First we gotta go back for more ammo for our handguns. Gotta get our rifles and shotguns too," Spaz said. "And maybe we make some Molotov cocktails outta the empty beer bottles in that case we didn't toss."

"Sounds like a plan," Blake said, trying to summon a vestige of desire to actually do some good in the world. He knew that if he hadn't seen that there were children in there, he would have let all those people die. And he wondered if he was being a sap not to still do it anyhow.

They got themselves ready, and while they were doing so, they laid out a scheme.

First they trundled their rifles, pistols, ammo, and the beer case of gasoline-filled bottles with cloth wicks through the patch of woods and onto the perimeter of the church and school. Then they split up, each taking some Molotov cocktails plus their firearms and ammo to opposite corners of the gravel lot.

They moved quickly and quietly so as not to alarm the hungrily milling zombies too much. Then they each lighted the cloth fuses one at a time and tossed four flaming cocktails apiece into the clusters of zombies that were nearest to them, and those unlucky zombies went up in flames, staggering and moaning and falling down in separate pyres.

Then they opened fire, an all-out fusillade.

They scurried and fired, scurried and fired.

Maybe it was easier than they imagined it would be. They were expert shooters, and they scored plenty of head shots on the first try.

They caught glimpses of children and adults watching their attack on the zombies through the boarded-up windows. They even heard cheers from the people inside.

At last there were no zombies still standing, and they held their fire.

"Time to cut and run!" Blake yelled.

"Yeah, buddy!"

They hotfooted it out of there before any of the people inside could dare open the barricaded door. They didn't want to be thanked. They didn't want to be appreciated, or worse, recognized.

In case they might be surprised by any roving zombies they had not gotten to deal with, they kept their guns at the ready as they backtracked on foot through the woods and made it back to their van. They put their weapons in the cab, then got in and peeled out of there.

But their luck ran out almost as soon as they got back onto the main road.

Deputies Jerry Flanagan and Bruce Barnes, cruising in their patrol car, spotted the blue van and saw the sign on it: OLSEN'S GROCERY MART. So they turned on their siren and pursued. While Jerry drove, Bruce used the police-band radio to call for backup, and they found themselves in a hellishly dangerous high-speed chase.

A roadblock was set up, and Blake and Spaz tried to crash it.

Their van overturned, and Bruce and Jerry almost crashed right into it. But they were able to screech the patrol car to a stop, scramble out of it, and take up firing positions using the car and its wide-open doors as a shield.

Though Blake had a bloody head gash, and Spaz had a busted knee and a twisted, obviously broken left arm, they somehow got out of the overturned van and started firing at the cops. They kept coming, out in the open, as if they thought they were invincible—or as if they wanted to die and get it over with.

Bruce and Jerry and the four other cops whose vehicles formed the roadblock had no chance to call for the two men to drop their weapons and put their hands up. The thugs were running at them, guns blazing.

Trying to remain calm under fire, Bruce Barnes squeezed off two well-placed rounds, one in Spaz Bentley's chest and one in his head, and Spaz fell dead in the dust.

Screaming like a banzai warrior, Blake Parsons managed to kill a patrolman who had a wife and two kids and had only been on the job less than a year. Then Jerry blasted Blake down with two bullets in the groin and one in the chest.

After the two thugs were confirmed dead and the dead patrolman's body was covered up with a blanket, Bruce phoned a report in to Sheriff Harkness, who by this time had gotten into his uniform and was ready to hustle out of his house as fast as he could to join in the pursuit of the blue van or back up the roadblock team. "There's a lot of carnage here, Sheriff," Bruce said. "It's all over. But you'll want to be here to take charge of crime-scene control and the collection of evidence."

"I guess there was no chance of taking the bastards alive," the sheriff said.

"No, I'm sorry," said Bruce. "They came out firing. I'm tempted to say it was suicide by cop. Can't say what was in their heads. But if they wanted to die, they didn't need to shoot one of us."

"Bastards like that don't give a shit," Harkness said. "Don't really give a shit about anybody or anything. Too bad we couldn't know in advance how they were gonna turn out, so we could smother them in their cradles."

"I agree with you," Bruce said. "But I'm not like Dr. Melrose. I don't have any wish to play God, at least I don't think I do." But even as he said this, he knew that he sometimes had to fight the urge to administer quick and sure punishment to some of the people he had to arrest.

He also knew that the sheriff had wanted Spaz and Blake to be taken alive so they could be questioned, but things didn't turn out that way. But it wasn't his fault that there had never been a chance to get a handle on the whereabouts of Tiffany and Victoria Melrose.

CHAPTER 29

Henry and Sally were trying to figure out how to load the musket from over the fireplace when they were jolted by the noise of motorcycles.

Slam, Bearcat, and Honeybear roared into the lot on their Harleys, churning up clouds of dust and gravel, then whirling and spinning on the bikes, shooting down zombies in the bright moonlight. Slam and Bearcat yeehawed and fired their pistols while Honeybear hung on, giggling.

Then they wheeled up to the front door of the roadhouse, jumped off their bikes, and started pounding and yelling.

Inside, Henry and Sally were rooted in their tracks, frightened.

Bearcat yelled, "Let us in! We're *people*!"

By this time, two live zombies had managed to shuffle up close to him and Slam, who whirled and took both zombies down with perfectly planted head shots. Both zombies fell heavily.

Then the steel door unbolted and Honeybear went in first, past a wary Henry Brinkman. Bearcat and Slam pushed past him immediately, pushing their motorcycles inside with them and knocking aside tables and chairs in the process.

Henry shut the steel door and rebolted it, noticing that Slam was staring at Sally in a way that looked kind of hungry and lecherous. Sally was obviously scared and nervous, standing there still cradling the black-powder rifle.

Bearcat said, faking a heavy drawl, "By golly, Miss Molly, does that weepon work agin' them goldern Injuns out there?"

Slam and Honeybear tittered and guffawed.

To Henry and Sally, Bearcat said, "My name be Bearcat, and this here's muh saddle-sore sidekick, Slam, and muh soul mate name of Honeybear. Who be you folks?"

"I'm Henry Brinkman. I own this place. This is my daughter Sally. We've already been through a lot, and we're glad you fellows are armed and can help us defend ourselves."

Still drawling excessively, Bearcat intoned, "Yuh mean y'all ain't got no weepons?"

Slam let out a bark of laughter.

Sally moved closer to her father. Eyeing the newcomers, she bit her lip. Henry fidgeted nervously. They were both realizing that they may have stepped out of the frying pan and into the fire where these new arrivals were concerned.

Slam said, "Ahm hongry, Bearcat. What say we ask the purty leetle lady o' the house here to cook us up some vittles?"

"Why shore, Slam," said Bearcat, continuing the charade. "We'll git ourselves all refreshed and revitalized with some hot vittles and strong spirits, then mebbe we'll feel like venturin' outside agin and gunnin' down a passle more o' them thar Injuns."

Honeybear giggled at this.

Slam drawled, "These here newfangled Injuns is a dern sight more troublesome than the ol' kind, ya noticed that, Bearcat? They hanker to take a lot more from a feller than jest his scalp."

"They're powerful uppity 'n persnickety all right, 'n they shore ain't a mite perticular over which part 'o ya they git. They'll gobble up innards jest as well as legs 'n thighs."

Slam and Bearcat cracked up over this.

Grimacing in distaste, Sally spun on her heels, leaned the black-powder musket in a corner, and headed for the kitchen.

Slam stepped in front of her. "Hey, where you be headed, gal?"

"To the kitchen to cook some burgers and fries," she said sharply. "That's what you want, isn't it?"

"I wants that much, sure 'nough. But it might not be *all* I wants from a purty leetle gal like you."

"Well, it's all you're getting," Sally snapped back.

And Slam made a move toward her—till Henry confronted him, saying, "Look here, my daughter's a decent young lady, and I'd appreciate it if you'd treat her with more respect." He said this in a no-nonsense voice, not kowtowing, but holding back in light of the fact that these were obviously very rough and unscrupulous men, and right now they had the advantage.

Slam's eyes went wide in a pose of exaggerated and mean-spirited amusement.

"Whale, tar 'n feather me 'n call me a banty rooster! I'd shore like to take time to court yer purty leetle offspring good 'n proper like, Mista Henry—but we is in whachoo might call a despert sitchamitation, with a pack 'o flesh-thirsty Injuns out thar that don't want us to live to see sunup. People has a tendency to wanna do what comes natcherly under sech terrible circumstances. Right, Honeybear?"

"You mean like me and Bearcat," she said coyly.

"Right on, babe," Slam said, dropping his exaggerated drawl. "You was all bent outta shape at first, but now you're so tight with us you don't wanna split no more. Same thing happened to whatsername, that rich bitch that was captured 'n brainwashed by them freakin' commie radicals back in the seventies."

Since he had dropped out of his drawl, Bearcat did likewise for this part of the conversation, which was "serious" to them because it had to do with "commies"—who were the archenemies of Hitler and thus anathema to these skinheads also. "You're talkin' about the so-called Symbionese Liberation Army, Slam. Buncha white chicks, blacks, 'n lezzies all humpin' each other. They were all gunned down 'n burned by the pigs in Los Angeles."

"Pigs'd love to do the same to us," Slam said. "They don't

realize their chains're bein' pulled by the pinko traitors in the gov'ment who want this country to go commie."

Honeybear said, "Don't get yourself on a rant, Slam. Right now we're not facing commies. We're facing zombies. That's what we've gotta protect ourselves from."

"*And* from the pigs!" said Bearcat. " 'Cause if they come here to shoot 'n burn up the zombies, they're gonna shoot 'n burn *us* up too, no doubt about it!"

Henry muted the sharp look he almost threw at these intruders whom he had at first regarded as saviors. They had arrived shooting down the undead creatures that had the roadhouse surrounded, but they weren't saviors at all—they were clearly outlaws.

They were probably as indifferent about shooting innocent people as they were about gunning down zombies. They didn't even have enough sense to be scared of the undead. They treated it all as a lark, a perfectly fine adventure as long as they got what they wanted. And Henry knew that at any instant one of the men might want Sally. And if push came to shove, what was he going to do about it? What *could* he do? He was unarmed, and he was in the presence of three strangers with ominous intentions.

CHAPTER 30

After the shoot-out that killed the young policeman as well as the two perps, Sheriff Paul Harkinson and Deputy Bruce Barnes badly needed to unwind, so they were in a homey little coffee shop on the main street of Willard, two blocks from the county police headquarters. For privacy they had chosen a high-backed wooden booth in a corner, even though at the moment they were the only customers. Harkness was sipping coffee and munching on a cream-filled doughnut while Bruce was talking on his cell phone.

"But it rang thirteen times, Linda! If you'd keep decent hours, you wouldn't be dead to the world so late in the day!" He listened briefly, then got even more exasperated.

"Don't you sass me! I just wanted to let you know I'm okay, but I'll be working late. Will you make sure to eat something besides junk food?" He listened again, then jabbed the off button and plunked the phone on the table.

Harkness said, "Your daughter givin' you some crap, huh?"

"They talk about sweet sixteen! Well, she's more like snotty sixteen!"

Bruce sipped his coffee, then bit into his frosted doughnut as if biting someone's head off.

"Don't let her give you heartburn," the sheriff said. "Kids today got a lot to deal with, and it makes 'em a little wacky, you know?"

"Tell me about it!" Bruce said. "Linda's got natural good looks, but she tries to make herself ugly. Rings in her nose and eyebrows, hair chopped up like it was done with an ax, and dyed purple. Weird tattoos on her legs and arms, and I don't want to know where else. Ginny is no help—she's a bigger mess than my daughter is!"

Sheriff Harkness nodded his head in empathy. He knew that Bruce was speaking the truth about his ex-wife, Virginia, who used to be a beautiful, dependable woman but was not that way any longer. She got hooked on painkillers while trying to recover from a car accident that had left her with debilitating back and knee pain and crippling fits of clinical depression. From oxycodone she had gone on to Percocet and crack cocaine. Bruce had tried valiantly to hang on to the marriage and had suffered through Virginia's failed attempts at rehab and her myriad of promises, crying jags, and false hopes, till finally he couldn't take it anymore. They had been divorced for over a year now, and though he had gained custody, Virginia's inroads into Linda's life were still a threat. He couldn't keep them entirely apart, and when Linda was with her mother, Virginia's lazy, self-pitying lifestyle seemed like "carefree fun" to Linda's addled teenage brain. To top it off, Bruce was paying a thousand dollars a month in alimony to Virginia because the court had ruled that the failed marriage had left her dependent upon him and unable to take care of herself; therefore, according to the court, her well-being was still largely his responsibility. This seemed grossly unfair to Bruce—and also to the sheriff, if truth be told. Bruce had argued that *he* was being punished because *she* had made herself into a drug addict, but the ruling still went against him. In spite of all this, he was struggling valiantly to get by on a policeman's less than lucrative salary and to cope with all the hazards of being a single parent.

Harkness said, "Today's society is sick. People who wanna be good parents are fightin' an uphill battle against drugs, booze, and sex."

"Yeah," Bruce agreed with a sigh. "I'm pretty sure Linda is sexually active. I tried talking with her about love and commitment, but she called me a dinosaur and laughed in my face."

"Well, maybe she'll turn out okay somehow," the sheriff ventured.

But Bruce went on worrying. "I know she's tried marijuana. I just hope to God she's not into anything worse."

"You can't watch over her all the time, Bruce. You're just gonna have to let her make some mistakes and hope they ain't the really bad kind. This is harder for us cops than for most parents 'cause we have a tendency to sorta be control freaks. We wanna save people from themselves and keep 'em in line."

"I shouldn't be crying on your shoulder," said Bruce, "when we've got bigger fish to fry."

The sheriff nodded in agreement and said, "Right now we've got us a situation we not only can't control, we don't even know what to do next—unless we get some kind of lead."

"Do you think a general epidemic is gonna break out?" Bruce asked.

"Probably not," Harkness said, dolefully mulling it over. "We don't know where Melrose's daughters may be headed, but we know it's to a secret lab someplace. As long as their cargo doesn't get loose, I don't think we're lookin' at the same kind of thing we had sixteen years ago. But I'd like to put an end to whatever they might be up to before we all go to hell in a handbasket."

CHAPTER 31

In the murky candlelight of the Hideaway, Bearcat and Slam sat at a round oaken table guzzling vodka straight from the bottle and wolfing down burgers and fries. Henry stood behind the bar where he could keep a close eye on his daughter through the serving window. She was still in the kitchen cooking up more food, and Honeybear was in there with her.

Bearcat suddenly barked, "Hey, Henry, you got a basement in this joint?"

"No, it's built on a slab."

"Where the hell do you store stuff?" Slam demanded.

"In my shed out back," Henry said. "I have a generator in there, if we could get to it." He wouldn't mind having some light in his place, if for no other reason than it would make it easier for him to monitor the hoods' movements. And it would give them fewer dark, shadowy places from which to lurk and then pounce on his daughter.

"Hmmm . . . what else you got in that shed?" Bearcat mused.

"Like what?" Henry asked him.

"Like copper cable. Or better yet, fencing wire or barbed wire."

"What for?"

"For me to know and you to find out."

"There is some copper cable," Henry admitted, trying not to lose his temper, for fear it would give Bearcat and Slam all the provocation they would need to start beating on him or raping Sally. "I guess about a hundred feet of it, for when I use the Weedwacker. None of the other kind of wire though. I never had any use for it."

Slam said, "Why don't you have a cell phone or at least a portable radio?"

"I do have a cell phone," said Henry, "but it's not getting a signal. I imagine a tower is down. I thought about having a radio in here, but my customers never want to hear anything but the jukebox or the TV."

"Well, what good is the generator to us right now?" Slam asked gruffly. "It ain't gonna help us pull in any stations if the cable is out."

"It'd give us power for the refrigerator and the electric lights," said Henry.

"Fuck that!" Bearcat barked. "I got my own ideas what I wanna use the generator for!"

"There's a radio in my pickup," Henry said. "If you want to risk going out there to listen to it."

Bearcat said, "What we need is a shortwave radio so's we can listen to the police bands."

Henry shook his head despairingly. "Power's out. Phones are out. I wish we had some kind of communication with the outside world."

"Why?" Bearcat said sneeringly.

"So we'd know exactly what's happening," said Henry. "How widespread *is* this thing? What are the authorities doing about it? And what do they advise *us* to do?"

Slam and Bearcat both snickered. Then Slam said, "*Piss* on the authorities! Me and Bearcat has permanently *run afoul* of 'em as the sayin' goes. Like I tol' ya, they find *us* here, we're as good as zombie meat."

"*If* they find us," Bearcat said. "Which they might not do right away, if all the communications is down."

"They might think we'uns is poor innocent lambs!" Slam blurted drunkenly, and it sent him and Bearcat into paroxysms of laughter.

Finally Bearcat said soberly to everyone within hearing distance, "Don't believe it if anyone tells you we're hard men. We're just misunderstood. We try to do good, but no good deed goes unpunished. Right, Slam?"

"Right on, Bearcat," Slam said, continuing the charade.

For the past week they had been trying to distance themselves from a horrendous crime they had committed in a suburb of Pittsburgh. It was a home invasion gone bad, but in their own minds they were not to blame—it was the fault of the victims. If the man of the house, Jonas Silverberg, hadn't tried to be brave and snotty, he'd still be alive to talk about it, and so would his wife and his two sons who had to die because of his own foolishness. Honeybear had met the Silverbergs in her square previous life as a nine-to-five receptionist for an insurance agent. She had filled out some of the computerized forms pertaining to their homeowners' policy, which revealed that they were temporarily keeping cash and jewelry at their house that was worth an estimated twenty-five thousand dollars. The fact that they happened to be Jewish made them perfect targets for her new skinhead buddies, and she figured she'd really get in good with them by handing them the Silverbergs on a silver platter. In fact she put it that way—"the Silverbergs on a silver platter"—when she told Slam and Bearcat all that she knew about them, including their home address, their work schedules, and their days off. The two skinheads chortled when she made an even bigger joke out of it, saying, "From now on we'll call them the Platterbergs."

"You gotta get us in there," Slam said. "They ain't gonna open the door to *us*. We look too fuckin' suspicious."

"Don't be stupid," Bearcat countered. "They know who Honeybear is. Cops'll track us all down through her. We gotta go in with masks on."

"That means a nighttime job," said Slam. "We bust our way

in, and they won't know what hit 'em. Honeybear can stay in the car, and be our lookout and getaway driver."

They pulled off the home invasion on a Tuesday, a couple hours after midnight, because Bearcat said it was best to rob people in the wee hours when they were all in bed, so nobody comes home and surprises you. Honeybear stayed outside in the car, ready to gas it and take off. Wearing red bandanas for masks, Slam and Bearcat kicked the Silverbergs' back door in, charged upstairs into the master bedroom, got the parents under control at gunpoint, and then rounded up the two kids. They tied and gagged the whole family except for the mother because they wanted her to lead them to the cash and jewelry, which Honeybear had told them was in a safe, and they wanted Mrs. Silverberg's hands to be free to work the combination. But she wouldn't talk, and she wouldn't budge. All she did was cry. So they took Jonas Silverberg's gag off and told him he better do what he was told or they would rape and kill his wife. That's when he called them "despicable assholes" and Slam pistol-whipped him, and Mrs. Silverberg jumped into the tussle, and in the flurry Slam's mask came off—so Slam shot her. Now the whole family had to be killed because they could describe Slam, and if the cops got Slam, they would immediately figure out that his accomplices were probably Bearcat and Honeybear. The two skinheads didn't want to keep on shooting people, for fear that the noise would attract attention, so they got knives from the kitchen, herded Mr. Silverberg and his kids down into the family room, and slit their throats. The bodies weren't discovered for two days, but the license plate number and the make of Honeybear's car were memorized by a woman walking her dog in the quiet of the night, and the three renegades had to go on the lam. They ditched and torched the car, but that didn't do much to take the heat off them.

Highly pissed because they hadn't glommed onto any of the cash and jewelry, Bearcat gave Honeybear a good beating as soon as they got themselves holed up in a fleabag motel. He felt that everything that went wrong was either the Silverbergs' fault or else Honeybear's fault for setting up such a bum job.

When Bearcat took a desperate chance on getting in touch with Drake and Bones, and Drake bragged about the big rig they were going to hijack, full of equipment from an outfit called M-R Electronics, it seemed like salvation—a chance to come up smelling like a rose, just like the rose in the emblem on the truck. But once again Bearcat had gotten drunk on the smell of somebody else's cork. The big rig and its promise of electronic gear was nothing but fool's gold. He had hoped that the cargo could be fenced for a ton of cash. But whoever heard of fencing a truckload of zombies?

CHAPTER 32

Flipping a greasy burger on the grill, Sally said, "What did those two guys mean when they talked about you? You didn't willingly join up with them?"

"Hell, no, not at first," Honeybear said. "I was Little Miss Goody Two-shoes, with a prim little job at an insurance agency—till Bearcat and Slam bopped in and robbed the joint with two other guys named Drake and Bones. They gagged me and tied my wrists and dragged me with them in the back of a van while they held up a couple more places! I was scared out of my wits. I wanted to make them like me so they wouldn't kill me, and I figured if I gave myself to them it wouldn't be as bad as being raped. Thinking about it like that, I got turned on in a weird way. There was a side of me that liked the things they did. They didn't take any crap from anybody, they weren't part of the rat race that I had always despised, and they showered me with the money and stuff that they stole."

Sally was subtly trying to engage Honeybear in meaningful conversation, in hopes that she might make a connection with her and maybe turn her into at least a partial ally. In an attempt to draw the girl out, Sally said, "They say that even bad guys have their good side. Do you think that's true of Slam and Bearcat?"

"Well, to them I'm their ideal blond, blue-eyed Aryan woman.

No man that I ever went to bed with in my old life had me up on that kind of pedestal. Or any other kind of pedestal whatsoever."

"You're flattered by that?"

"I am, in a way. I admit it."

Sally blinked and raised her eyebrows, then went back to pressing the sizzling burger patties with her spatula. Through the serving window, which provided her with a view out to the bar, she saw Slam gleefully pushing buttons on the dead, unlit juke-box, pretending to be selecting music. As if he were the record he had just played, he started singing a rock song badly off-key and dancing drunkenly by himself, hugging a bottle of vodka. Then Sally's father went by, eyeing Slam warily and carrying a little cardboard box over to the table where Bearcat was still sitting.

"You find the stuff?" Bearcat demanded.

Henry said, "Lead balls, black powder, and extra flints."

"How about wadding?"

"It's in the box with the other stuff."

"Bring me the weapon," Bearcat ordered.

Still dancing and stumbling around hugging the vodka bottle, Slam called out, "Why you wanna piss around with it, Bearcat? It holds only one shot at a time, and what if it blows up in your face?"

Henry fetched the black-powder musket and handed it to Bearcat, who hefted it fondly. "I know what I'm doin'," he said confidently. "My grandpap had one of these. I just wanna see what it'll look like to blow them zombies' faces off with a big fat lead ball."

With a loud clatter, he spilled the contents of the cardboard box out onto the tabletop.

CHAPTER 33

Victoria looked beautiful, Tiffany thought, as they sped along a country road in their father's vintage Pontiac, a black 1967 Grand Prix. She was proud of her fifteen-year-old sister, who had the stunningly voluptuous good looks of someone three or four years older. She could definitely be an outstanding seductress. She should have no trouble taking blood from any man or woman she chose. By working together, Tiffany thought, she and her sister could seed the world with subservient creatures under their own control, or with vastly superior ones who might share their own attributes.

Now that Victoria had fully recovered from porphyria, she was angelically gorgeous. All of her oozing purple blisters had disappeared, much as a pimply teenager magically outgrows the embarrassing acne that overrides her natural beauty and emerges in the full blossom of her sexuality and her femininity.

"I'm hungry," Victoria said, not at all whiningly, but as a straight-forward statement of fact.

"I understand, dear," Tiffany responded warmly. "We'll have to get you fed. It's a vital priority."

The fact of the matter was that once a pubescent female recovered fully from that ugly disease, she would always become ravenously hungry, and this inordinate hunger would last ten days or more. It demanded to be fed. And its need was not ordinary food, but human blood.

That's why the two sisters were driving on a country road instead of an interstate. They were looking for an isolated victim. Someone they could feed off and then kill.

Someone whose body might not be found for a long time after they were gone. Someone whose body might not ever be found if they could take the time to hide it or dispose of it well.

CHAPTER 34

With the power out to the roadhouse's neon sign and interior lights, it would have been pitch-black were it not for the full moon in the night sky. Zombies milled about in the parking lot, breathing huskily and hungrily.

Some of them hovered in the shadows, back by the Dumpster or among the trees, making munching or bone-cracking sounds. They were consuming parts of the old man, Smokey, who had been killed by them in the early part of the day.

They looked up from their feasting when they heard heavy footsteps on gravel, as if they were afraid of a superior force that might come to steal their meal from them.

They started and cowered when they saw the huge zombie named Barney coming slowly, ploddingly toward them from someplace beyond the shed.

Other zombies followed behind Barney as if somehow he had become their leader. The pack of followers included the zombi-fied serial killer, Chub Harris, who looked the worse for wear now that he had been undead for about twenty-four hours. His eyes were yellowish and his skin was a putrid gray. The quoits in his earlobes had been ripped out, and the loose flaps of ear skin hung down like ropy strings of dead flesh.

Chub and his companions had found their way here from the

Brinkmans' farm, and now they were in search of another food supply.

The one called Barney, perhaps because of exploratory treatments he had received while under the care of Dr. Melrose, seemed to possess a bit more of a functioning brain than did some of his followers. He was also better fortified, thanks to the regular "meals" he had consumed over the years while he was in the doc's care.

He stopped and stared at the roadhouse, the shed, and the Dumpster, moving his big head slowly and stiffly, taking it all in. Then he picked up one of the whitewashed stones that bordered the gravel parking lot.

CHAPTER 35

"Hey, you wenches gonna bring us more burgers or not?" Bearcat demanded from out in the bar area.

"Yeah!" Slam shouted. "We want 'em today, not next week!"

"Hold your pants on!" Honeybear yelled from the kitchen, where she and Sally were cooking more food for the rapacious skinheads.

"I'll beat the pants off *you* if you get smart with me!" Bearcat roared back at her.

Sally said to Honeybear, "Well, I guess these ones are brown enough. Here, bring the platter over. I don't want those two beasts to start pounding on you."

"I hope they get trichinosis," Honeybear muttered.

Sally worked a well-done patty onto the spatula, and Honeybear reached toward it with the platter.

A loud crash of glass shattering.

Sally and Honeybear both gasped and jumped back, and Honeybear dropped the glass platter, which broke into sharp shards when it hit the floor.

More shattering glass.

The whitewashed stone picked up by Barney was doing the smashing and shattering, wielded in his big, partially decayed hands. He succeeded in smashing a hole through one of the boarded-up kitchen windows, then pounded what was left of it to bits. Then his zombie hands poked through.

Another crash!

Bloody, greenish hands started poking through the other window, clawing and grasping, not caring if any of the dead skin was torn or gashed.

Then a heavy thud against the door! And more thuds!

The zombies were clubbing and pounding at the front and back doors!

"Omigod!" Honeybear cried. "They smell the food cooking!"

Sally contradicted her. "No, they smell *us*!"

Henry, who was closest to the kitchen, came running in, followed by Bearcat and Slam. Slam had his pistol drawn.

Bearcat's pistol was still in his belt. He was carrying the black-powder musket, and even as he ran into the kitchen he was using the ramrod to jam home a lead ball and wadding.

The two skinheads each manned a window. They grabbed kitchen knives and whacked at the hands poking through till the zombies backed off. Then Slam poked the barrel of his pistol through and fired.

"Shit! Missed her!" he said. "I'm too goddamn drunk! Got her in the chest though!"

The zombie he had shot, a gray-haired old woman, had a gaping hole in her chest, and she was staggering from the impact, but it hadn't felled her.

Slam fired again, hitting her between the eyes, and her dead breath whooshed out of her and she went down.

Bearcat took careful aim with his old-fashioned musket, squeezed the trigger, and blew a male zombie's head off.

"Whoa!" he cried exuberantly. "This thing is somethin' else, man! Blew his head clean off! Nothin' left but the neck! I oughta load up again!"

Slam said, "Too goddamn much time, Bearcat! We need rapid fire, man!"

Bearcat leaned the musket in a corner and drew his pistol, but he held his fire when he returned to one of the windows. Through the glass-shattered spaces between the nailed-up boards, he and Slam could see that the zombies outside were just milling around, as if with a degree of uncertainty.

The one called Barney (although the people inside the roadhouse had no way of knowing his name) had backed off, due to a rudimentary sense of self-preservation. The noisy, dangerous bullets and flaming muzzles had scared him somewhat, giving him pause, and the other zombies around him instinctively followed suit.

The pounding and thudding at the steel doors, both front and back, was still continuing, but for the time being the doors seemed to be holding.

Bearcat said, "We gotta get outta here. We can't afford to diddle around. Gotta get to that shed and grab the generator and cable." To Sally, he said, "You're goin' with us, babe, whether you like it or not."

It was the last thing Sally wanted, and the mere thought of it spiked her fear to the breaking point. "No!" she said. "Don't you see? They don't seem to be able to get in here! This might be the safest place we could possibly be!"

"I agree," Henry said, backing up his daughter and not wanting her to be alone and in the clutches of the desperadoes. "We're staying put. Whoever wants to can go."

Bearcat and Slam snickered uproariously.

"Nice try, dude!" Slam said mockingly.

"You crack me up, Mista Henry," Bearcat intoned in his phony southern drawl. "No way're we leavin' you 'n purty leetle Sally to rat on us when the pigs show up."

He grabbed Henry by the throat and put the barrel of his pistol right up under Henry's chin.

"Leave him alone!" Sally cried. "He won't tell on you! Neither will I! We don't even have much to tell—all you did was save us from those zombies out there. We'll say you were heroes."

Slam stepped up to her and prodded his pistol hard into her ribs, saying, "You're comin' with us, gal, so relax and enjoy it!"

Meanwhile the pounding on the doors was getting louder and louder.

Bearcat threatened Henry more menacingly. "Gimme yer car keys and shed keys pronto, dude! Be nice now, if you don't want us to waste you and your daughter!"

Grimacing from the pain of the gun barrel pushed up against the soft underside of his chin, Henry fumbled in his pocket for a ring of keys and handed it over.

Slam said, "Gotta make torches to hold 'em off before we wheel our bikes out there."

Honeybear grinned slyly as she said, "Torches would be good, but I know what'd be even better."

Realizing what she was driving at, Bearcat's and Slam's eyes immediately lit up with sadistic glee, and Slam said, "Zombie feed!"

Bearcat said, "Right on! You're elected, Henry. Betcha you feel too honored for words."

CHAPTER 36

Sheriff Paul Harkness became aware of the fact that some of Melrose's zombies were loose in Willard County when Father Ed Hastings, pastor of Saint Willard's Catholic Church, made it out to a two-lane road and flagged down a patrol car. At first the two cops who picked the priest up didn't want to believe his story. But finally they called it in to the sheriff, who ordered them to bring Father Hastings to his office, then proceed to the church and school, where they would meet up with backup patrols, ambulances, and paramedics—precautionary measures in case the children and adults left at the school were still in any danger.

By the time all this got underway, it was around nine o'clock in the evening, on the same day of the raid on the Melrose Medical Center. Power lines and cell towers were still out of commission in that part of the county, and the full depth of the crisis was largely unknown to the sheriff and other authorities.

Under questioning, Father Hastings said that he had left Sister Hillary, Janice Kimble, little Annie Kimble, and the rest of the kids barricaded inside his one-room school, while he had hiked through the woods till he got onto the road and flagged down the patrol car. "I came across a lineman's vehicle—a Jeep," he said. "Its windows were smashed out, and I think I saw part of the lineman's remains out there in the weeds. It was sickening.

The creatures who attacked him must've been some of the same ones who caught us all alone and unsuspecting."

"You're lucky you made it," Sheriff Harkness said. "How did you get through?"

Father Hastings then described how he and his flock had been rescued by two armed men who appeared out of nowhere and gunned down and torched a bunch of the zombies. "Never saw them before in my life," he said dolefully. "They must've been sent by a guardian angel. Whoever they were, they were the answer to our prayers."

"I wonder . . ." Bruce Barnes said musingly. During most of the sheriff's questioning, he had been sitting to one side of Harkness's desk, saying next to nothing.

"What?" the sheriff asked him.

"I was going to say something, but I better not," Bruce said. "I just wonder who those two saviors might've been."

"You don't think?" the sheriff said, catching the drift suddenly.

"Maybe they had some good in them," Bruce said, shaking his head at the notion.

"We may never know," said the sheriff. "But we can't waste our time wondering. We've got to get a posse together and see exactly what is going on out there. It's gonna take helicopters, paramedics, civilian volunteers, the whole works. Just like last time."

"Just like sixteen years ago," said Bruce. "I'd better phone my daughter, tell her I won't be home till God knows when."

"It's definitely happening all over again," said Father Hastings. "I'll hope and pray for you. And for the poor innocents I left back at the church and school. If I'm the only one who survives this tragedy, I'll never forgive myself."

CHAPTER 37

For a long while, some of the zombies kept pounding on the steel doors of the roadhouse, while others just milled around. But most of them had rather short, brain-damaged attention spans. So they started to lose interest eventually and began to back off. Their incessant pounding dwindled down to a few bangs and thuds, weakened, and finally stopped. But the most persistent of the zombies still hovered close to the doors.

The big long-dead one named Barney took up a watchful position at the edge of the gravel lot.

Suddenly the front door banged open, knocking two zombies back, and out came Bearcat with a pistol in his right hand and his big left hand dragging Henry Brinkman by his rope-tied wrists. Slam followed them out with a gun and a torch, menacing the closest zombies to him, making them step back. One of the dead creatures caught fire and backed off, flailing at his burning clothes.

Bearcat shot a young male zombie in the face. Henry stumbled and almost fell down because his ankles were hobbled with a short length of rope. Bearcat yanked him by his wrist ropes to keep him on his feet.

Slam covered Bearcat with gun and torch as Bearcat dragged

Henry farther out into the gravel lot. Now they were on the side of the lot opposite Henry's pickup, Smokey's car, and Henry's shed.

Honeybear watched all this through a slightly ajar front door, her eyes agleam with anticipation of Henry's fate at the hands of the hungry zombies. Behind her, Sally was already tied and gagged, slumped on the floor by the fireplace, helpless.

Wanting a better view of Henry so she could watch the zombies ripping him apart, Honeybear got brave enough to step out and gawk around, but when a zombie started coming toward her, she back-stepped into the roadhouse and slammed and locked the steel door.

Leaving Henry hobbled and at the mercy of the merciless zombies, who immediately started closing in on him, Slam and Bearcat ran toward the shed. In half-panicky excitement, Slam fumbled trying to get the key in the lock, and Bearcat yelled, "Stand back, Slam!"

He aimed his pistol at the lock and blew it apart.

By this time two big, drooling male zombies were almost upon the two skinheads, but they wheeled and blasted both of the zombies down with head shots.

Then Slam stepped into the shed, waving his torch around and scoping out a lawn tractor, a stepladder, shovels, picks, and assorted junk—and a generator and cable.

"You see it, Slam?" Bearcat yelled.

"Yeah! Got it, Bearcat!"

"Let's hoof it, man!"

Henry was trying to hobble as best as he could away from some pursuing zombies, and because they were so slow-moving, he was having some temporary success. But his luck could not possibly hold out because more of them were now stirred up by the smell of live human flesh, and they were starting to come after him. Zombies were closing in on him from all sides, and he backed against the Dumpster. He reached back over his head, pulled himself up with his roped hands so he could swing his hobbled feet freely, and kicked the nearest zombie in its ugly, decayed face. It fell backward, knocking into another zombie and toppling them both.

Henry quickly turned and got a handhold on the top of the six-foot-high steel Dumpster, his legs and boots scrabbling against its slippery sides. Then, with great effort, he managed to pull himself up, swing his legs over, and land on top of the Dumpster's corrugated steel lid.

Just in time, he skedaddled out of reach of grasping zombie hands. Then he stared at the undead creatures trying to claw at him and pull him down. Frightened, sitting on his rump, he tried desperately to stay out of reach of the living dead, and he drew his legs up tight because some of the zombies were trying to grab him by the ankles. To his partial relief, they made no attempt to climb up after him. Apparently they were unable to do it—or unable to *think* to do it.

He spotted an empty wine bottle someone must have tossed on top of the Dumpster, picked it up, and smashed it. Maybe he could have used it to slash at the zombies. But instead he wedged the neck of the broken bottle between his knees, its sharp, jagged edge pointing up, and he started sawing through the rope that bound his wrists.

At the same time he could hear Bearcat yelling from the front of the roadhouse.

"Honeybear! Open up! It's us!"

The front door was opened by Honeybear while Slam stood by, facing out into the lot with his waving torch.

Honeybear asked, "Did you get the generator?"

Bearcat said, "It's in the back of the pickup already! C'mon, hurry up! We gotta wheel the bikes out!"

He pushed past Honeybear, yanked the bound and gagged Sally to her feet, and dragged her through the doorway, where Slam pulled her along then hoisted her like a sack of potatoes into the bed of the pickup with the generator and cable.

Slam and Bearcat wheeled around just in time to blast down two more zombies and set another one on fire—and the flames caused another cluster to back off. Then the two skinheads hoofed it back inside the roadhouse and wheeled out their motorcycles, with Honeybear's help. She kick-started one bike and Bearcat kick-started the other, and Slam jumped into the cab of the pickup and fired up the engine. Then they all headed out of the gravel lot.

But before Honeybear's bike got up to speed she was clothes-lined by big, dead Barney, who stepped from behind a tree and yanked her down, a choke hold around her neck.

Her motorcycle crashed into a tree and burst into flames.

Bearcat glanced over his shoulder at this dismal turn of events, then gassed his bike hard and peeled out, right behind the pickup, and both vehicles zoomed down the road.

Henry was still trapped on top of the Dumpster with the zombies groping and grabbing at him. He finally finished sawing through his wrist ropes with the broken bottleneck, and when his hands were free of their bindings, he was able to untie the ropes hobbling his ankles.

He stood up in the center of the Dumpster, well away from the groping dead hands, and saw a cluster of zombies moving toward Honeybear, who had now become zombie feed. Henry shuddered, knowing this was the exact fate that had been intended for him.

Big old Barney was crouched over Honeybear's body, and other zombies were coming to join him in his "feast." One of these was Chub Harris, in life a serial rapist and killer of women, and now that he was undead, his zombified brain still took a heightened, though primitively muted, delight in feeding upon a voluptuous young woman. His perverted sex drive was gone, but his urge to destroy and consume Honeybear was much more powerful than those urges in the other zombies.

Henry was seized with revulsion and a sudden burst of wild anger. "Damn you!" he shouted at the top of his lungs. "Damn you all to hell!"

He snatched up the broken bottleneck and, crouching, jabbed

it hard into the face of the nearest zombie, who in life had been a portly middle-aged lady. The jaggedly sharp point plunged deep into her eyeball, and she reeled backward, her hands clutching at the source of her "pain," but the sharp glass stayed embedded, and she died.

The zombies near the Dumpster shambled past the fallen one without the least concern, for their sole interest had now become the feast provided by Honeybear's young, fresh corpse. They didn't want to miss out on their share.

All of this ghastliness was revealed to Henry Brinkman in the flickering flames of the wrecked motorcycle at the outer edge of the lot. He saw that the impromptu feast had created a diversion that might benefit him, and his eyes moved from the cluster of feasting zombies toward the area of the gravel lot where Smokey's old battered car was still parked. A few zombies were between him and the car, but the area was not so infested that he could not take a chance, so he jumped down from the Dumpster and made a run for it.

His gravel-spewing run across the lot attracted the attention of quite a few zombies, and they came after him. He snatched up a heavy whitewashed bordering stone and smashed a huge zombified oaf in the face—this was Barney, in his bibbed overalls, but of course Henry did not know the oaf's name. Barney was knocked back by Henry's blow, but otherwise was unfazed, while Henry kept running, barely eluding the grasp of two other pursuing zombies and throwing a body block into a third one, who went flying over Henry's back and landed in the gravel face first.

Desperately, Henry yanked at the door of Smokey's car, and it sprung open on noisy hinges. He dived inside and managed to slam the door shut and lock it before more zombies were upon him. Luckily, the key was in the ignition. But Henry knew that the clunker did not always start.

He twisted the key.

Nothing happened.

Zombies were now surrounding the car, pounding and clawing

at the windows as Henry frantically kept twisting the ignition key.

Two of the zombies picked up stones. They smashed at the windows. At first, although the glass showed cracks, it did not shatter completely. But the zombies kept on hammering, like mindless cretins. Finally the two side windows shattered and stones and shards of glass came flying through. Henry ducked and got his hands up over his face, but one of the stones glanced off his head. His forehead bleeding, he blinked his eyes groggily.

Zombie hands reached in for him. The living dead were clawing and drooling, their breathing heavy and raspy.

Henry shook his head, trying to overcome the wooziness. Slowly, painfully, he reached for the ignition key again and gave it another try.

Nothing happened.

He jumped back—because in order to fool with the key and get his foot on the gas pedal he had to put himself dangerously close to the shattered driver's side window where zombie hands could easily reach in and grab at him.

He spied a heavy metal flashlight sticking out from under the seat, and he clutched it hard and used it to smash at the nearest zombie hand. Then he jiggled and twisted the key again, in utter desperation.

Success! The engine coughed and sputtered to life.

But then it died.

Henry tried again . . . and again.

Finally the engine caught hold and kept on running, but with an ominous rattling sound. The zombies were still trying to reach in and pull Henry out of the car. And the engine must have been burning oil because there was a thick cloud of black smoke pouring from the exhaust.

Henry nevertheless put the car into gear and stepped on the gas—cautiously at first—and when the engine did not die he hit the gas pedal harder. Some of the zombies tried to hang on, their arms halfway through the holes in the shattered windows, but

Henry gunned it, running over two of the undead on the far side of the lot, and by the time he humped out onto the road, the rest of the zombies dropped off.

He headed Smokey's clunker down the road, in the same direction taken by the pickup and the motorcycle driven by Bearcat and Slam.

CHAPTER 38

The weak headlights on the old clunker flashed now and then on a zombie or two lurking along the wooded road, but as he got farther and farther away from his roadhouse, Henry encountered no more of the undead creatures. He breathed a sigh of relief and kept driving while he tugged a handkerchief out of his pants pocket and blotted at his bleeding forehead.

At that moment the car rounded a sharp bend and someone—or something—stepped out in front of him, giving him no time to determine if it was living or living dead. He jerked hard on the steering wheel. A tie-rod snapped with a loud ping, and the car swerved out of control, braking and squealing and finally crashing into a tree.

Rocked by the crash, Henry stayed slumped over the wheel for a long time, and if anyone had seen him at that moment, he would have been thought dead. But no, he started to move. He could hear that the engine was no longer running, even though the headlights were still on. The door on the driver's side was sprung open wide.

Henry was stunned when he saw that the "person" he had swerved to miss was turning toward him and moving in his direction—and as it got closer he saw that it truly was one of the undead. He yanked hard on the sprung door, but he couldn't get it to close. And the zombie kept coming closer.

Henry punched at the headlight switch, dimming the lights so they wouldn't drain the battery, then he jiggled and twisted the ignition key, but the engine refused to start. He tried once more to shut the sprung door, but it wouldn't budge. Summoning his courage, he shakily got out of the car and frantically looked around for some sort of a weapon. His eyes fell on a broken tree branch in the road, and he snatched it up just in time, for the zombie was now upon him. This one in life had been a thirty-year-old account executive for an ad agency, and he was still wearing a three-piece pinstriped suit that probably had been his normal work attire.

Henry rammed the jagged end of the broken branch into the zombie's chest, knocking the creature back but not felling it. He swung the branch at it a couple of times, landing some glancing blows, but the zombie still wouldn't back off. Suddenly Henry swung his club at its knees, knocking its legs out from under it, and it fell hard onto the asphalt. Then it tried to crawl away, but Henry hit it in the head and face again and again.

Finally the creature lay still, and Henry stood over it for long seconds, breathing hard. He dropped his club right there.

He went back to the car, got inside, and tried once more to make it start. Nothing doing.

He remembered the heavy metal flashlight he had used earlier to smash at the zombie hands that were groping at him, and he picked it up and clicked it on. Surprise! It worked, emitting a bright beam.

He yanked the key from the ignition and, flashlight in hand, came around and unlocked the trunk, casting the beam on a pile of Smokey's junk: balled-up grease-stained clothing, crumpled-up road maps, empty whisky bottles, and more. Henry rooted in this mess, found a toolbox, and opened it. He tossed aside a lot of tools he felt would be useless to him, then selected a large, heavy screwdriver with a ten-inch shaft and a big, thick plastic handle.

He hefted it like a knife and tested it by making stabbing motions. Then he tucked it under his belt.

He went back to the body of the vanquished zombie in the pinstriped suit and picked up the club he had used to do it in.

Then, utilizing the glow of the flashlight beam, he started hiking down the road.

CHAPTER 39

Slam used a long stick to poke in a small fire and fish out what was left of the generator cable. Bearcat watched him and said, "Insulation burned off pretty good?"

Slam said, "Yeah, man. *Ow!* It's too hot to handle!" He yanked his fingers away from the flame-discolored copper.

Bearcat laughed and said, "Don't waste our drinkin' water. Piss on it to cool it off. We gotta get it rigged before some of those things smell us out. Here they come! Shit! Hurry up!"

Sally stared fearfully at the approaching zombies. She was bound and gagged, slumped against a tree, the flames of the small fire flickering on her worried, scared-looking face. The pickup and motorcycle were parked nearby, and sleeping bags for Bearcat and Slam were spread on the ground, not far from the fire. The trees in close proximity to the makeshift campsite were widely spaced apart, but farther back they were more dense and more threatening.

Bearcat drew his pistol as he eyed five or six zombies that had emerged from the dark foliage.

Slam hurriedly unzipped and peed on the hot copper cable, making it steam and hiss.

CHAPTER 40

Henry kept walking down the middle of the dark road, shining his flashlight. He kept looking left and right, in case any zombies stepped out from the tall weeds near the edge of the asphalt.

Suddenly a zombie came at him—a thirtysomething woman, short and round, about five-and-a-half feet tall and weighing around two-fifty. Her fat thighs were squeezed into large-sized jeans, and her arms were like sausages swelling out the short sleeves of a faded print blouse.

Henry backed up a couple of steps and pulled his long-shafted screwdriver out from under his belt. When the fat undead woman was only a foot away from him, he shined his flashlight in her eyes. Henry already knew that the undead were afraid of fire, and he was hoping that bright light scared them too. The woman tried to block the beam with her slow, clumsy hands. And when she raised her hands, half blinded, Henry clubbed her in her throat, and she gurgled and fell. She thudded onto the pavement, and Henry dropped his club and rammed his screwdriver blade deep into her right eye.

He stood back, the screwdriver still embedded, and watched, panting, as the thing flailed for a while and became still. Then he put his foot on her neck and pulled the screwdriver out of her eye socket.

He wiped the shaft on a tuft of grass at the side of the road.

CHAPTER 41

Bearcat and Slam hurriedly strung the bare copper cable from tree to tree, encircling their campsite, and protecting all their belongings including the pickup and the motorcycle.

The zombies that had come out of the woods were getting really close now, moving stiffly and slowly, but rasping and drooling hungrily and menacingly.

One end of the cable was already connected to the generator terminal, and Bearcat let Slam pull the other end over to him, then he knelt and connected it, saying, "I sure hope this damn thing starts!"

Sally hoped the same thing. She had already been in terror of the two men, and now a pack of zombies had been added to the mix. Her eyes wide and darting, she wondered if she'd rather be raped and then shot, or ripped apart and devoured.

Bearcat yanked on the starter pulley, but nothing happened. He yanked again. And again. The motor backfired.

"*Fuck!*" Slam swore. "Let's just lock ourselves in the pickup, Bearcat! We can let 'em feed on Sally here! Maybe that'd satisfy 'em enough."

"Thought you wanted her to satisfy *you*. Anyhow, I got a powerful fuckin' urge to electrocute some of them things!"

He yanked on the pulley cable one more time, and the generator came to life with a satisfying purr.

Bearcat and Slam stood back, hefting their pistols and watching the zombies come ever closer. Sally watched too, hoping that what the men hoped would protect them, would actually do so.

Suddenly a loud *pfffft!* And they whirled to see a zombie behind them—a young undead boy that they had not noticed as he snuck up on them, then touched the hot wire. The boy was jerking and sizzling and erupting into flames, just like the one Sally electrocuted earlier in the bathtub.

Then a second and a third zombie hit the wire, and they too went up in sparks and flames.

The three electrocuted zombies tumbled and burned on the ground. And the rest of the zombies murmured and rasped, backing away.

Bearcat chortled triumphantly, tucking his pistol back in his belt.

Slam yelled, "They're leavin', Bearcat! You're a freakin' genius, by God!"

Chapter 42

Sally woke up before the two men did and tried to think how she might be able to escape, even though she was still tied and gagged, with a ragged quilt thrown over her. She scanned the campsite, hearing birds chirping—which sounded extraordinary somehow, in the face of her situation—not to mention the purring generator sound that she hoped would continue to protect her. Evidence of its protection the night before was in the burned-up corpses lying outside the wire.

Bearcat and Slam were snoring in their sleeping bags.

And a big male zombie in a sweater and slacks was stepping out of the woods.

Sally hoped it wouldn't come any closer.

She didn't want to wake Bearcat and Slam, for fear that one or both of them would rape her, now that they felt protected by the cable and generator. They might figure they had plenty of time to "enjoy" themselves.

The zombie kept coming closer. Soon it was almost on top of her.

But the electrified cable would protect her. Wouldn't it? *Wouldn't it?*

The generator sputtered . . . kept on running for a few seconds . . . then died.

The zombie came closer.

Sally wanted to scream, but her mouth was dry from fear, and the squeak that came out was stifled by the gag.

The zombie reached for her—and fell over the "dead" cable.

It fell hard. Pulled itself up. Then, grunting and drooling, it rolled next to Slam in his sleeping bag.

Slam and Bearcat started to wake up—but too late for Slam, for the zombie was biting into his arm.

Slam screamed, and Bearcat yanked his pistol out and shot the zombie in its face. It reeled back and fell on its side, lying still.

Slam cried, "Oh, damn, damn, *damn! I'm bit!*"

"Shoulda kept your leather jacket on," Bearcat pontificated.

"Fuck you, you don't have yours on!" Slam cried. "Too fuckin' hot in the fuckin' sleeping bag!" Blood was pouring from his left forearm, and there were ugly teeth marks. Slam yanked his pistol from inside his sleeping bag, gripping it tightly in his right hand, and looked around as if he expected more zombies to come at him—but none were in sight.

Bearcat said, "You're gonna turn into one of them *things*, Slam!"

"*No!* I don't believe it! C'mere, have a look. How bad is it?"

Bearcat leaned in to have a look, and Slam cracked the barrel of his pistol down hard on Bearcat's wrist. Bearcat dropped his gun, and Slam said, "Back away, Bearcat! You ain't gonna shoot *me!* I'm gonna waste *you* first!"

Bearcat said, "What the hell's got into you? You already brain-dead?"

"See what I mean?" Slam answered. "You always treated me like your flunky, but you're scared of me now—what I might turn into. You'd waste me soon as my back was turned, like Bones and Drake."

Bearcat tried to sound very sincere as he said, "Naw, man, they was already turned, and you ain't. I'll get you to a doctor, man. I know one who'll keep his mouth shut."

"Thanks, but no thanks," Slam told him. "So long, Bearcat, it's been nice knowin' ya."

He fired twice in rapid succession, shooting Bearcat in the chest and head.

Bearcat gasped and fell dead.

Sally shrunk back in fear as Slam came over to her.

Then she thought she heard helicopter sounds in the distance somewhere, so faint that she wasn't really sure at first that she really had heard them. And Slam didn't even seem to notice. He was too preoccupied with his bleeding, zombie-bitten arm.

He said, "I'm gonna take your gag off, gal. But if you start screamin', I'm gonna drill ya. Understand me?"

She nodded, wide-eyed, and he untied the gag and dropped it onto the ground as he jammed his pistol up under Sally's throat. He said menacingly, "I gotta get this wound treated. You tell me where or I'll kill ya."

She heard the helicopter sounds getting louder, but still Slam gave no hint he had heard them. She told him, "The hospital is—"

"No!" he barked. "I don't want no hospital! The cops'd love to get their paws on me. Shit! You hear that helicopter. It might even be them!"

Sally said, "There's a first-aid kit at my house. Iodine and bandages. It's not far."

Slam pulled out a large switchblade knife and flicked the blade out.

Sally gulped and swallowed hard. She was afraid he was going to slit her throat now that he knew where to get the bandages and stuff.

But he said, "I'm gonna cut your hands and feet loose. And you better not try anything funny, bitch!"

She watched as he sliced through the ropes around her wrists and ankles, then she rubbed her wrists and moved her fingers, which had become stiff and sore.

Slam said, "Pick that bandana up! I want you to turn it into a tourniquet. Fasten it around my arm, a few inches above the teeth marks."

Hesitantly, Sally obeyed, asking, "Right here?"

"No, a little farther up, about six inches. I'm hopin' this thing can be treated like a snakebite. Tourniquet might stop the poison from gettin' up to my brain."

Sally doubted it but said nothing. She wanted Slam to maintain hope, because if he admitted he was surely going to die, he might take her with him.

"Hurry up!" he commanded. "Tie it tight."

She did the best she could.

Then Slam said, "Let's go. Get in the truck. You're gonna drive. You better be a good little nurse and try to pull off some kinda miracle on me, 'cause if I don't shoot you before I die, I'll chomp on you afterward. No doubt in my mind about *that!*"

CHAPTER 43

Whirring blades were very loud and up close as a helicopter descended. Large white letters on its sleek black body said COUNTY POLICE. And it landed in the field where the Melrose big rig wrecked and Bones and Drake became zombie feed as the result of their foredoomed attempt to hijack the rig's cargo.

A police car was moving across the field and toward the scene of the zombie escape. Deputy Bruce Barnes was driving and Sheriff Paul Harkness was in the front passenger seat.

Two cops armed with rifles and handguns jumped down from the helicopter, its blades still whirring.

Bruce killed the car engine, and he and Harkness got out and started walking toward the van and the jackknifed trailer.

Two zombies, a man and a woman, came out from behind the van once driven by Drake and Bones. The police didn't know it, but these two zombies were Albert and Meg Mathews, still accompanying each other in their undead state, as if they had some dim memory of being man and wife. They had wandered back to the trailer that had been their traveling prison, instinctually hoping that since food had been there once, they might find some there again.

The two chopper cops held their fire till they were sure that the two beings confronting them were not alive in the normal sense of the word. Then they took aim and fired.

The male and the female zombies—Albert and Meg—had what was left of their brains blasted out of them, and they both fell dead in the field.

The cops advanced closer to the empty van and the jackknifed big rig. They found the remains of the truckers who were shot in the head by Drake and Bones, their bodies having been dragged down out of the cab and partially devoured.

Harkness said, "I don't know how these folks got here at the same time or why. But it's pretty clear what they were attacked by."

Bruce Barnes stared up at the logo on the big rig, and a glimmer of realization spread over his face. He said, "Look at that logo, Sheriff."

Harkness said, "What of it? An *M* and an *R*."

"With a rose," Bruce added.

Then Harkness got it. "Hmmm... Doc Melrose had a twisted sense of humor, didn't he? If that trailer truck was full of zombies, and all of them got loose, folks that live around here are in some deep trouble, like Father Hastings said." He turned to the two chopper cops. "How long ago'd you guys spot the wreckage?"

One of the cops said, "Two hours ago, when we called it in."

Bruce Barnes said, "We're less than thirty-five miles from the Melrose Medical Center, so the zombies musta got loose early yesterday, and if some of them have been on the move since then . . ."

"Yeah," said Harkness. "We're gonna have to comb this whole area." To the chopper cops, he said, "Why don't you two guys get back in your helicopter and see what you can spot? Meantime me and my deputy will start calling up more men."

"Right, Sheriff," said one of the chopper cops. "We spot anything weird, we'll radio." He and his partner headed for the chopper.

The sheriff said, "C'mon, Bruce, let's scout the perimeter, make sure some of those things aren't gonna pop out at us while our backs're turned."

The chopper lifted into the air, and Sheriff Harkness and Deputy Barnes, with their guns drawn, moved toward the edge of the field, peering into the surrounding foliage.

A sudden noise made Bruce whirl, pointing his gun.

Henry Brinkman, dirty and disheveled, and with blood caked on his forehead, stepped out from behind a tree. Not knowing if he was alive or undead, Bruce yelled, "Halt!"

Henry said, "No! Don't shoot!" He dropped his club and screwdriver to show that he was peaceable.

Bruce did not immediately relax but remained in a tense firing stance. He said, "Who are you, man? I damn near blasted you down."

Sheriff Harkness came up to them, backing Bruce up by keeping his pistol trained on Henry.

Henry started to explain himself, saying, "I'm Henry Brinkman. I live near here. I own the Hideaway saloon. Two thugs took my daughter and left me to die. They thought those things would finish me, but I got away. I don't remember much after that. I must've passed out in the woods."

Eyeing Henry warily, the sheriff said, "Were you bitten? Tell me the truth, man."

"No . . . I almost ran down one of them, and the car hit a tree. My head smacked the windshield. I was okay, I thought, just a little groggy, and I started walking down the road. But maybe I got a concussion or something . . . everything got blurry, and I don't remember what I did next."

The sheriff and Bruce Barnes glanced at each other, both trying to decide how much of Henry's story could be believed.

Henry said, "It all started when my wife and daughter were attacked at my house. My wife, Marsha, was killed, but Sally made it to the saloon. Then we were attacked *there*—not just by those dead things, but by the crazy idiots that kidnapped Sally. If we don't rescue her somehow, they're gonna kill her. They think killing's fun."

Sheriff Harkness said, "Come with us, Henry. Show us the way to your house. We'll start there. First though, Bruce, call up more men, even some volunteers, like last time. We don't know yet how widespread this thing is, so maybe we're gonna need a lot of help getting it under control."

Henry asked, "You got a gun you can lend me, Sheriff? I wanna be one of your volunteers right here and now. I've got experience with this too. I killed some of them sixteen years ago."

CHAPTER 44

Driving her father's pickup, Sally pulled into her own driveway, where two zombies happened to be lurking.

Slam barked, "Run the damned things over! It'll save me ammo, and I won't have to deal with 'em later!"

Sally was almost glad to do it because these two undead beings might have been some of the ones who killed her mother. She gritted her teeth, plowed into them, and ran the tires over them. One of their head was crushed, and he was definitely finished. But the other one was crawling, even with its lower body crushed and twisted.

Slam jumped down from the pickup, took out his switchblade, and forced the narrow sharp blade in at the base of the creature's skull and up into the brain. It stopped squirming and lay still as Slam wiped his blade in the grass.

Sally stayed behind the wheel, watching, till Slam ran over to her, yelling and waving his knife and gun. "What the hell you waitin' for, gal? Get out!"

She jumped down from the cab, and he prodded her with the barrel of his gun, pushing her toward the house.

A few zombies were milling around in the yard. Slam eyed them, then ignored them and pushed Sally up onto the porch.

The front door was wide open. He warned, "Don't get too far ahead of me, babe. If I get the idea you're gonna try to run out the back door or somethin', I'm gonna drill ya."

He stepped in behind her, into an empty but totally trashed living room. Taking this in, he turned, closed the front door, and bolted it, then prodded Sally with his knife, saying, "This wouldn't feel too good in your kidneys, would it? So don't cross me. Nice and slow, go and lock the back door if it needs it."

They found the back door wide open just like the front one, and Sally shut it and bolted it.

Slam muttered, "Gotta do somethin' about this bite. Can't waste any more time, whether we're alone in here or not. If some of them things are in here, I guess I'm just gonna have to shoot 'em. Where're the bandages, the first-aid stuff?"

"Upstairs in the bathroom, but . . ."

"But what? You freakin' out on me? You keepin' somethin' from me, babe?"

"No . . . no . . . it'll be okay. It's just that something is up there that I don't want to look at."

"What? An unflushed commode?" He giggled half dementedly at his poor attempt at a joke, then he wiped his brow, which was suddenly pouring perspiration, and said, "Shit! I'm startin' to lose it. I can't think straight all of a sudden. I got a bad fever. You better not screw me up, babe, I'm warnin' ya. You seen the way I done Bearcat, and he was my best buddy, not a useless piece of fluff like you. Now, go on, get up there!"

He pushed her toward the stairs, and they both went up.

Entering the bathroom, they found the remains of the electrocuted zombie still in the tub, its shredded flesh tarry and oozing, smelling like a watery cremation. Sally averted her eyes and pulled open a drawer beneath the sink. She pulled out a first-aid kit, a loose roll of gauze, surgical tape, bandages, and ointments, and set it all on the sink cabinet.

Slam was still bossing her around, and he said, "Loosen the tourniquet for me, babe. I'm gettin' delirious, maybe 'cause of the lack of circulation. Don't want it to go to gangrene. And I wanna make it bleed more—shoulda done that when it first happened, but we hadda get the hell outta there."

Sally untied and loosened the tourniquet. Slam's arm around the wound was turning an ugly greenish purple. "Ugh!" he said. "Never seen anythin' like that. Did you?"

She shook her head no and dropped the tourniquet into a wastebasket. "What'd you toss it fer?" Slam immediately demanded. "I'm gonna need it again."

"It's filthy. I can make a nice clean one if you cut up a washcloth."

"Good thinkin', babe."

Sucking in his lips to steel himself against the pain, he cut into his wound, producing a lavish flow of blood and letting it pour into the sink. "Goddamn, that hurts!" he moaned. "Gotta just let it bleed a spell. Then we'll put on a clean tourniquet, like you said, and hope for the best."

At this point, Sally was on the same page with Slam in not wanting him to turn into a zombie. Much as she hated to show him any mercy, she had to do it in order to save her own skin. Nevertheless, an eerie thought struck her, and she gave him a funny look as she flushed his blood down the sink. He picked up on this and said, somewhat shakily, "What? What's the matter? Why'd you look at me that way?"

Making unabashed eye contact with him, Sally said, "You killed a zombie with that knife. Maybe you just made your infection worse."

"Oh, shit!" he swore. "I *told* ya I ain't thinkin' straight! But what could be worse than the bite, hey? You got a snakebite kit?"

"Yes, but the antivenin's out of date."

"Don't be so fuckin' stupid! I don't need no antivenin—a zombie ain't a snake. Get the kit out and gimme the rubber thing that'll suck out poison. You better hope it works 'cause if it don't, I'm gonna make you do it with them luscious lips of yers."

Sally grimaced, got out the snakebite kit, and found the rubber suction cup. No way did she want to put her lips on Slam's wound.

Meantime, unbeknownst to her, a helicopter was circling above her father's roadhouse. A dozen or so zombies were still clustered around the place, even though the live humans were long gone.

A squad of Sheriff Harkness's posse men trudged toward the zombies from the two-lane road. When they got close enough, they started shooting, aiming for head shots.

Crouching and firing, the men soon advanced into the area by the Dumpster and the wrecked and burned motorcycle. They took note of Honeybear's devoured remains, but they didn't stop to take a close look. They just kept firing their weapons.

They got off a few shots at big old Barney, but he managed to escape into the woods along with a half dozen or more of his zombie followers.

Slam and Sally were still in the bathroom. She removed the snakebite suction device from his wound, rinsed it off, then swabbed the swollen purplish wound with alcohol. She eyed the pistol that was tucked in his belt, but she didn't dare make a try for it. He still clutched his switchblade knife in his right hand, a constant menace in case she might make a wrong move.

"Whoa!" he yiped, sucking in his breath. "That burns like a motherfucker!"

She said, "Hopefully it'll burn out whatever poison is still in you."

She proceeded to bandage his wound with cotton, gauze, and surgical tape.

His eyes went shut for a second, and he weaved woozily. Sally took note of this while pretending not to. She opened a drawer, pulled out a clean white washcloth, and held it toward Slam, stretching its upper edges taut between her hands.

He looked shaky and was pouring sweat. When he spoke, he

slurred his words, and his thoughts seemed slow and discon-
nected. "I . . . am . . . really spaced. Whatcha . . . holdin' that up
fer?"

"For you to cut off a strip. I think we should apply a clean,
fresh tourniquet, don't you, Slam?"

He nodded his head slowly, took his knife, and rinsed it under
the tap.

"I was . . . thinkin' about Bearcat," he mused. "Almost like
dreamin' about him. . . . I hated to off the dude . . . me and him
had . . . some really great times. He was the one . . . got me into
the Aryan Brotherhood. First time . . . I ever felt . . . like I belonged . . . to anything. If it weren't fer folks . . . like us . . . there
wouldn't be no more . . . white people by and by."

His brain was so spacey that he continued rinsing the knife for
a long, long time, all the way through his reminiscences. Sally
couldn't help eyeing the knife, wondering how she might get
hold of it. She tried for it, saying, "Why don't you let me have
that? I'll wipe it down with alcohol for you."

But he wasn't as spaced out as she hoped. "Haw!" he spat. "Nice
try, bitch! My head . . . might be a tenny-weeny bit fogged . . . right
now . . . but that don't . . . mean I lost all my . . . fuckin' marbles."

"Well," Sally said, "you're gonna have to cut me a strip of this
washcloth with it, whether it's sterile enough or not."

She held up the washcloth again, purposely chest high so that
he had to reach up with the knife, his arm bent at an awkward
angle. He started slicing—and all of a sudden she pushed hard
against the blade with the washcloth, forcing the knife against his
throat.

And at the same time she kneed him in the groin as hard as
she could.

He doubled up in agony and dropped his knife—it clattered
on the tile floor.

Sally ran out of the bathroom toward the stairs.

The cut she made into Slam's throat was deep but not fatal,
even though it bled a lot. He slowly straightened up and pulled
himself together, drawing his gun.

Sally hit the landing and darted toward the kitchen doorway, but suddenly stopped short.

A zombie confronted her! It must have been in the house all along, and now it was facing her, drooling. She pivoted and yanked open another door, one that led down into the basement.

Slam came after her from upstairs, more woozy and sweaty than ever, but still pointing his gun ahead of himself, ready to shoot.

She slammed the basement door shut.

Reaching the landing that led to the kitchen, Slam poked his head around the corner—and the zombie that had confronted Sally pounced on Slam from behind and sank his teeth into Slam's trapezius. Both Slam and the zombie fell, crashing onto the living room floor.

Slam rolled and got his gun up. Lying on his back, he fired and missed. The slug plowed into a wall. The zombie rasped and drooled, lunging toward Slam, but he managed to get his gun up in time and shot the zombie in its face, knocking it back.

It fell dead.

Slam got to his feet, his legs wobbly. He was now dripping blood not only from the knife wound in his neck but also from the fresh zombie bite in his trapezius. But he had seen where Sally had gone, so he pulled open the door to the basement. Weaving, he started down the semidark stairs, holding on to the railing, sweeping the muzzle of his pistol ahead of him as he descended, but seeing nothing to shoot at.

Sally had run into the laundry room, where she hurriedly unhooked the hot-water hose from the washer. She turned the hot-water spigot on all the way, then flattened herself against the concrete-block wall and waited for the gush of water to turn to steam.

At the foot of the basement stairs, Slam heard the water running and headed toward the gushing noise. He prowled through the cluttered basement and rounded the corner of the laundry area, crying, "Haw! *Gotcha*, bitch!"

He poked his gun toward Sally even before he actually could

see her—and she sprayed him in the face with steaming hot
water! He backed up, screaming loudly from the scalding pain,
and she stayed with him and kept on hosing him in the face.

He dropped his pistol, his face red, blistering and peeling.

But Sally went too many steps forward with the hose, and it
pulled off the spigot. The hot steaming water now gushed harm-
lessly into the stationary tub.

Slam, with his ugly blistered face, sneered hideously at Sally
and stopped backing away from her.

She dove for his dropped pistol, but he stepped on it before
she could grab it, then kicked her in the face. She scrambled to
her feet and ran as he stooped slowly to pick the pistol up.

She dashed into the garage.

He came after her, dripping blood and looking weaker than
ever.

She hit the button for the garage-door opener, and the door
started to lift with an agonizingly slow, grinding sound. She
couldn't wait to get out of there, and when the door had only
risen a couple of feet, she stooped to duck under it—

That's when Slam fired at her, and the bullet tore into her
shoulder, its impact knocking her down onto the concrete. She
rolled just in time to make Slam's second shot miss, then he fired
again but got only a click.

The grinding pulleys stopped, and the garage door came to a
halt all the way up.

Sally was on her feet again now, but she didn't manage to dart
outside, for Slam was upon her, choking her and pressing her
against a concrete-block wall. Because of her shoulder wound she
wasn't much of a match for him even in his weakened state. His
sweaty, blistering, and peeling face was inches from hers as she
tried to pull his hands away by digging her nails into them before
he could strangle her to death. He started banging her head
against the wall and knocked her hands loose—and one of her
groping hands hit against something that made a metallic clatter.
She was almost losing consciousness by now, but she recognized

the feel of what her hand had struck, and she reached out for it as far as she could stretch and got a grip on its handle.

It was a sickle, hanging on a tool rack that also held dangling rakes, brooms, and shovels.

Sally pulled it off the rack and swung it hard, like an uppercut to Slam's solar plexus, plunging the long curved blade deep into his stomach. He screamed and reeled this way and that, letting go of Sally's throat and trying to pull the sickle out, but his hands got slippery with his own blood, and he slowly sank to his knees, fell onto his side, and rolled over . . . dead.

Sally sagged against the concrete-block wall, panting and holding her throat, which bore the sore, reddened imprint of Slam's fingers. She struggled to pull herself together, and gradually her breathing slowed and she stopped trembling. But a sudden groan made her jump, and her eyes darted to Slam's body.

His eyes were open . . . his hands were twitching . . . he was now one of the undead.

With the sickle blade still in him, he started to slowly get to his feet.

Sally screamed and ran out through the wide-open garage door—

And the zombie called Barney stepped right into her path. His flabby lips were grimacing and drooling, and he lunged at her even as zombified Slam staggered toward her from behind.

And there was even more jeopardy now, for there were about a dozen zombies all around the house. Their breath rasping hideously, they all started to close in on Sally in their demented desire for live human flesh.

Sally backed away from Barney, but this put her closer to Slam. He was coming at her, sickle and all. She jerked this way and that, trying to see a way out, but there was no place to run— the zombies had her hemmed in. One of them hung back a little, as if waiting for the others to take all the risks; this was Chub Harris, the one who in life was a serial rapist and killer of women.

Sally thought she was done for. But then a shot rang out—

BLAM!—and Chub was blasted in the back of his head. He reeled and staggered and sank to the earth as a second shot was fired, and Slam took the slug right between his eyes.

The shooter was Henry Brinkman, and when Sally saw him she yelled, "Daddy!" He ran toward her, a smoking rifle in his hands, as another volley of shots was fired.

Sally became aware of the whirring of a police helicopter, circling overhead, and at the same time Sheriff Harkness and Deputy Barnes came toward her, leading a group of armed civilians. They tried to blast down Barney, the big zombie in bibbed coveralls, but he ducked into the surrounding woods.

Henry took Sally into his arms.

The posse men kept firing at any zombies they spotted.

And from the circling helicopter, cops were strafing the living dead with machine-gun fire. They even tossed a couple of grenades when they saw several zombies together in a close grouping.

Sally clung to her father and cried into his shoulder.

Both their faces were wet with tears.

CHAPTER 45

There was a full moon in the night sky.

A pile of zombie corpses was starkly lit by the moonlight.

Posse men were carrying more zombie bodies, tossing them on the pile.

Henry Brinkman, a rifle slung over his shoulder, came forward with a large can of gasoline.

Sheriff Harkness stood by, watching, smoking his pipe. He said, "I told ya to take a break, Henry. We could have handled all this. You've been through enough."

Henry said, "I want to do this part, Sheriff. Wanna see it for myself. One of these, if not all of them, probably helped kill my wife."

Two posse men heaved yet another zombie body onto the pile, and one of them said, "That's all of them, Sheriff Harkness. All we could find."

"Douse 'em then," said Harkness.

Henry doused the pile of corpses with gasoline, moving around and around the pile. Then Harkness said, "Okay, light 'em!"

A posse man used a torch to set the pile of bodies ablaze. The flames leaped toward the sky, making a huge pyre.

The sheriff said, "May they rest in peace."
And Henry said, "Amen."

Standing back by the front porch of her home, Sally watched the burning pyre, the glow of the flames flickering on her face. Her bullet-wonded shoulder was bandaged, and her arm was in a sling. She felt worn out and sad. She averted her eyes from the pile of burning bodies, and for a long moment she lowered her head.

Suddenly she heard a scuffling noise, and she looked up, afraid.

But it was Bruce Barnes.

And to her surprise he was leading her horse into the front yard.

"Look who I found," he said to her.

She murmured, "Sparky," and allowed herself to feel some joy. She smiled and came down off the porch to pet her horse and make sure he was okay. "I thought for sure he was dead," she said. "Thanks for finding him, Bruce."

"Well, it was hardly any trouble," he said shyly. "I was out there near the trees, and he came right toward me. I think he was headed home and would've made it all by himself."

"You're too modest, Bruce. I'm sure you deserve some of the credit, and I'm giving it to you whether you like it or not. Sparky doesn't come to just anybody, I can assure you of that."

"Well . . . thanks."

They both fell silent. Both petted the horse.

Sally said, "Good boy, Sparky. I'm glad to have you back."

Bruce worked up the nerve to say, "I'd like to come back here and see you sometime, Sally. If you wouldn't mind."

"I guess that'd be okay," she told him. "If we're still here, that is. My dad is talking about selling the saloon, and I don't blame him after what's happened. He might want to sell everything and move away. Me too."

"Where would you go?"

"Maybe a complete change. Maybe move back to town. I could still keep Sparky. Pay somebody a stable fee."

Bruce said, "I live in town with my daughter. I'm divorced. It's a long story. But I'd sure like to see you again."

"We'll see," Sally told him.

CHAPTER 46

In the moonlight, Barney lumbered along the two-lane blacktop.

Two soft shots pierced the silence of the night—*Pfft! Pfft!*—sounding a bit softer than the suppressed sounds of Bearcat's and Slam's silencer-equipped pistols.

Barney's addled brain was stunned and confused all of a sudden, even more stunned and confused than usual.

He had been struck by two darts of the sort used by zoologists to anaesthetize wild beasts.

The darts had been fired by two men in dark clothing. They watched Barney fall unconscious, then they slung their dart-firing rifles over their shoulders and picked up a stretcher. With great difficulty because of his enormous weight, they loaded Barney's massive frame onto the stretcher and carried the stretcher and the inert zombie over to a white van parked a short distance away with its back doors open.

After loading Barney into the van, they slammed its doors shut and got into the cab.

Then they drove away.

CHAPTER 47

In the gaudy central pavilion of an upscale suburban mall, two lovely young girls browsed the storefronts, window-shopping.

Victoria's ugly purple blisters were totally gone by now, and there was no evidence that they had ever existed. Her skin was clear and radiant, and she was every bit as beautiful as her sister Tiffany.

They approached a kiosk where two handsome teenage boys were fingering through racks of T-shirts silk-screened with images from various monster movies.

Tiffany said, "Oh, there you are, Benny! And this must be Mark."

Mark said, "Right on."

Victoria said, "Cool."

Tiffany said, "This is my sister, Victoria. You can call her Vicky. She's your blind date, Mark."

Lighting up in the presence of Victoria's awesome beauty, Mark said, "I never been on a blind date before, but maybe now I'm gonna try it more often."

Victoria smiled coyly and said, "I guess that's a compliment."

Tiffany patted her on her arm and said, "My kid sister used to believe she would always be an ugly duckling. And now she's become . . . well . . . something even better than a swan."

At this, the two sisters flashed each other secret smiles.

Benny noticed this and complainingly he said, "I can't follow you half the time, Tiffany. Why do you even wanna go out with me? You sound too smart. Almost snooty sometimes."

Tiffany said, "I already told you. You have something I especially need."

The two sisters chuckled over this, but the boys didn't get it.

Benny said, "So what're we gonna do? See a movie?"

Victoria said, "I don't care."

Marks said, "I don't care either." He was trying hard to seem blasé, but he was already dreaming of getting into the sack with this hot little beauty. He reached out and took her hand.

The four teenagers strolled happily through the mall . . . very normal-looking to anyone who took notice of them.

Victoria said, "I was thinking maybe I'd like to take a walk through a cemetery tonight. There's supposed to be a full moon."

Mark laughed and jostled her with his elbow. "What're you tellin' me, babe? You a werewolf or something?"

"Not exactly . . . no," said Victoria.

Benny said, "Whaddaya mean, not *exactly?*"

Mark said, "Yeah."

"Well, Benny boy," said Tiffany, "that's for us to know and you to find out. Right, Vicky?"

"Uh-huh."

The two pretty sisters led the two handsome boys out of the mall and toward the fate that awaited them.

MIDNIGHT

For my mother and dad

Special thanks to Al Zuckerman and Sandy Bragg, whose suggestions concerning this and other of my books have been most helpful

Man is capable of perpetrating the worst barbarities imaginable in the name of holy science, holy religion or holy truth.
—Morgan Drey, *The Appeal of Witchcraft*

PROLOGUE

From the dirt road, they heard the demon screaming in pain and rage. It was trapped! It was out in the field like the other one.

"Run! *Run!*" Mama cried. "Don't be afraid—I'm right behind you!" She hurried along on her thin legs, a stout club of birchwood in her hand.

Luke and Abraham, ages fourteen and twelve, each had shovels. They were leading the way, running real fast.

Cynthia, at ten the youngest, could hardly keep up. But she had said the prayers which had enticed the demon to their trap. She was thrilled and proud of herself. And scared, too.

Behind her, Cyrus giggled. He was almost sixteen, but not smart. He huffed and puffed, trying to make his fat legs churn up distance.

The family scurried down off the shoulder of the dirt road and out into the weed-grown field where the creature was screaming. They broke through a thicket of tall weeds and saw the thing in the middle of the gas company's right-of-way that cut a broad swath down the side of the mountain and across the field.

"It looks like Jimmy Peterson's sister," Abraham blurted.

But it wasn't, of course. It was a demon.

"They can *look* like anything," Mama cautioned. "Don't you

dare get too close, Luke! Hit it with your shovel!" She stood back, brandishing her club.

The trapped thing wailed and screamed hideously. The steel jaws of the trap had bitten down hard, chomping clean through to white leg bone. There was plenty of blood. The thing couldn't get away because of the heavy steel chain and peg that had the trap anchored to the ground. Luke and Abraham always drove the pegs deep.

"*Hit* it!" Mama yelled encouragingly.

The demon stopped wailing momentarily and cowered, looking surprisingly like Jimmy Peterson's little sister. The same reddish hair and freckles. But the eyes gave away the secret—they were a beast's green eyes, wild and flashing.

Luke stepped forward boldly and swung his shovel with all his might with both hands. The demon had started screaming again, but it stopped. The edge of Luke's shovel blade had split open its face and skull.

"Hooray!" Abraham shouted as the demon reeled and thudded to the earth. He ran up and both he and Luke smashed at the thing with their shovels again and again. It sounded like beating a rug. Once in a while the shovels hit each other, making a loud clang. Luke and Abraham chopped at the creature's head, legs, and body. When they got done it was a bloody mess. Its red hair was matted in blood.

"You did real good," Mama said afterward. "Now Cyrus can make a coffin and we'll have a funeral."

"Why did it look like Jimmy Peterson's sister?" Cynthia asked, as Luke and Abraham stood back a few feet, breathing hard, looking down at their gruesome handiwork.

Mama got angry. "I *told* you, they can take any form they want to—a rabbit or a possum, or even a human being. It's our job not to be taken in—if they're sent to us, we have to destroy them."

Cyrus borrowed Luke's shovel and, looking to Mama for approval, hit the dead thing one more time on its shattered head.

CHAPTER 1

Nancy Johnson let the heavy door of the church swing shut behind her, dipped her fingers in holy water, and made a careful sign of the cross. She was seventeen, blonde, and pretty, and panicked over the thought of going to confession. For two years she had lived in sin, committing mortal sins of the flesh with her boyfriend. Several months ago she had broken up with him and the wounds of the breakup were beginning to heal, and she wanted to cleanse her soul. She had already vowed never to give in to another boy till she was married. She had done it out of love, but he had ditched her for someone else, leaving her to get over the agony and the shame.

Nancy was a small-town girl, with a history of regular attendance at mass and frequent acceptance of the sacraments. She had graduated from the local parochial school, which only went up through eighth grade, then had enrolled in the public high school but continued to take the required catechism lessons once a week in the basement of the church. She was not fanatically religious, but to the extent that she was, she felt she had fallen short of worthy ideals better lived up to by priests and nuns. She had a guilt complex. Her healthy sex drive often made her secretly wish for the day she could be married so her indulgence would no longer be considered sinful.

As she advanced down the aisle of the church with its high vaulted ceiling and looming crucifix, she felt humble, even intimidated. The place of worship had an aura of piety and holiness. The statues of Jesus, Mary, and Joseph were shrouded in purple for the Lenten season and would be unveiled on Easter Sunday to celebrate the rising of Christ from the dead.

A few old ladies in black dresses and babushkas knelt in the pews. Not many people came to confession on hot Saturday afternoons. Nancy had been banking on this because she didn't want to stand in line. She wanted to get the ordeal over with before she lost her nerve.

During the past two years she had gone to confession ten times without telling the priest that she was having carnal relations with her boyfriend. And each of the ten times she had taken communion at mass the following day, accepting the sacrament while not in a state of grace, which was the most horrible mortal sin a person could commit: sacrilege. She had been afraid to tell the priest that she had given in to sex. And she had gone to the rail for communion, anyway, because her mother always went to mass with her and would have known something was funny if her daughter stopped taking the sacrament.

Nancy genuflected, squeezed between two pews, and lowered a padded kneeler to the floor as her knees bent to meet it. She prayed, reading from the chapter on preparation for confession in her missal. "Oh, my God, grant me light to be truly sorry for my sins. To think that I have offended Thee after being forgiven so many times! I lay the rest of my life at Thy feet. Let it atone for my past. Mary, Mother of God, help me to make a good confession."

Leaving the pew, she entered the confessional and shut the door softly. Her knees found the kneeler in the dark. There was a cloth-covered aperture through which the priest on the other side of the compartment would be able to hear her voice, and she hoped he would not recognize it. Father Flaherty had said in catechism class that God helped him and all other priests never to remember a confession or a confessor. But Nancy did not lean too close to the aperture, for fear he could see through it. "Bless me, Father, for I have sinned. It is two years since my last good confession."

Father Flaherty's voice came back so loudly that Nancy just knew everybody in the church could hear. "Speak up! I can't hear you. Come closer to the screen."

She inched closer, then repeated herself.

"You say it's been *two years* since your last good confession?" Father's voice was shocked, incredulous.

"Yes, Father," Nancy meekly admitted. Her throat was dry, her tongue thick, her voice low and hoarse. She perspired profusely.

"Let me get this straight, young lady. Do you mean to tell me that during the past two years you just haven't been to confession, or do you mean that you made bad confessions during this time?"

"I made bad confessions, Father."

There was a lengthy silence that Nancy was sure the priest needed to recover from being stunned. Then: "These bad confessions—how many did you say there were?"

"Ten, Father."

"How do you mean they were bad? Did you fail to tell some sin you were guilty of?"

"Yes, Father."

"And why in the world did you do that?"

"I don't know. I was afraid."

"What sin were you afraid to tell?"

"Having carnal relations with my boyfriend, Father."

"I see. Is he Catholic?"

"He was, Father. But we broke up."

"It was undoubtedly the best thing that could have happened. You were living in sin with him. Do you realize that?"

"Yes, Father."

"And yet you fail to tell this mortal sin in confession so that you might receive forgiveness. Does that make good sense to you? You realize, surely, that this kind of sin is grievous enough to send you into eternal damnation."

"Yes, Father."

"Would you rather go to hell for all eternity than suffer a bit of embarrassment here in the confessional?"

"No, Father."

"All right." Father Flaherty sucked in his breath, then delivered the question Nancy dreaded most: "Did you afterward go to communion with these mortal sins on your soul?"

"Yes. I'm sorry, Father."

"Oh, my gosh! Do you mean to *tell* me that you existed in a state of mortal sin for two years? That during this time you defiled the sacrament ten times—just because you were ashamed to confess your sins?"

"Yes, Father."

The priest let out a long sigh of exasperation. "You have committed the grievous sin of sacrilege ten times by making false confessions. And you have each time committed the worse sacrilege of accepting our Lord's body and blood while in the state of mortal sin. This is one of the most awful sins a Catholic can commit. Do you realize that you can burn in hell forever for this one sin? Do you understand that for a period of two years the power of sanctifying grace was absent from your soul? If you had died at any time during those two years, you would right at this instant be burning in hell. Your immortal soul would have descended directly into the arms of Satan."

"I know, Father. And I'm sorry."

"What other sins have you committed? Go on with your confession. And make it a good one, young lady."

Telling the rest of it was almost easy, compared with the magnitude of what Nancy had just been through. She finally said, "That is all, Father."

The priest replied, "Now make a good act of contrition. And for your penance say ten rosaries. Ask Jesus to help you avoid temptation. And come to mass and make *good* confessions and take communion more often."

"I will, Father." Nancy could hear the priest praying in Latin behind the screen while she said her act of contrition in English. "Oh, my God, I am heartily sorry for having offended Thee, and I detest all my sins because I dread the loss of heaven and the pains of hell, but most of all because I have offended Thee, my God, Who art all good and deserving of all my love. I firmly resolve, with the help of Thy grace, to confess my sins, to do penance, and to amend my life. Amen."

She waited for Father Flaherty's Latin to come to an end so she could receive her final blessing. "In the Name of the Father and of the Son and of the Holy Spirit. Amen. May God bless you."

"Thank you, Father."

Still smarting from embarrassment, Nancy stepped out of the church into gusting spring air that soon evaporated the perspiration on her brow. She began to feel greatly relieved, and she raised her arms over her head to let the breeze dry and cool her underarms. Across the street from the church, she cut through a grassy field on her way home. The sunlight felt good and she enjoyed the blue sky and the freshness all around her, and she knew it had been a long time since she had felt so happy and clean.

She looked at her watch: ten minutes to one. Her stepfather ought to be home by the time she got there, and he had promised to let her use his car to go shopping. A local policeman, Bert Johnson was off duty at noon on Saturdays, but he usually would stop for a few drinks after work. Nancy decided that if he wasn't home yet she'd take a shower, wash and dry her hair, and call up her girl friend Patty. Maybe Patty would want to go to the mall, too.

As she walked, her stride unusually light and carefree, Nancy began saying her rosaries.

Chapter 2

Bert Johnson, Nancy's stepfather, drank by himself at the long, dimly lit bar. The only other customers in the place were two drunks playing the bowling machine, the old-fashioned kind with balls instead of pucks. Bert was so wound up in his own thoughts that the drunks' curses, niggling arguments, and braying, booze-thickened laughter did not bother him. Neither did the roll and thunder of their bowling. Bert was nursing his fifth double bourbon and draft chaser.

An outburst of exceptional raucousness caught his attention, and half turning, he saw out of the corner of his eye that the one drunk had sneaked up behind his buddy, who was in the act of launching a ball, and pulled his pants down. The ball went ricocheting down the gutter as the bowler, too stupefied to react, straightened up slowly, muttering to himself, his stained and tattered underwear and fat fish-belly-white buttocks quivering in the fluorescence of the bowling machine.

"Hey!" Sleepy, the bartender, yelled. "Don't you two clowns know there's a *policeman* in here? You want to get busted for indecent exposure?"

"What's so all-fire indecent about it?" the drunk pulling his pants up slurred indignantly. "My ass is as decent as any *you* ever seen! I ain't got nothin' I ain't proud of."

"How do you like *that?*" Sleepy said to Bert. "Why is it most of my customers are refugees from the loony farm?"

Bert didn't answer. Instead, he drained his shot and chaser. This was his way of letting Sleepy know he didn't want conversation. Taking the hint the bartender refilled the bourbon and the beer and moved on down to the far end of the bar to keep a close eye on the bowlers. Sleepy kept a baseball bat under the set of shelves near where he stood and was fully prepared to charge out and use it if it looked like the two drunks were going to get rambunctious enough to maybe break something.

Bert Johnson, contemplating his reflection in the mirror behind the bar, ran his thick stubby fingers through his thinning brown hair. His policeman's cap was parked on the barstool beside him. The weight of his service revolver and nightstick pulled down on his gunbelt, making his paunch uncomfortable. He hitched up his belt and trousers, lifting his wide rear end off the stool a few inches till this maneuver was accomplished. He averted his eyes from the mirror because his appearance disturbed him—he was no longer young, no longer decent looking, no longer in good physical condition. His nose, always a trifle large for his face. now had some broken capillaries from drinking too much. He was well aware that he ought to cut down, but he could not find the incentive to do so.

He was disgusted with his marriage. His wife, Harriet, almost youthfully attractive and desirable when he married her six years ago, had immediately started showing her age and put on thirty or forty pounds. Bert felt that she had somehow cheated him by not obliging herself to remain sexually appealing. He would not have married her in the first place if he had known he could not continue to be proud of her appearance and stimulated by her. Not that sex was everything; but more and more, a saying Bert had heard once seemed to be true—that when a marriage went bad, it went bad in bed. Did Harriet love him or not? He wasn't sure. Maybe all she ever really cared about was trapping a man—someone to take care of her and her daughter so she could relax and let herself go to pot.

Bert liked to think he was still young—only forty-five. Plenty of life in him yet, for the right woman. A woman who could make *him* feel like taking care of himself again.

Still and all, he didn't want a divorce; in fact he was rather frightened of the prospect. He didn't want Harriet to leave him. He had been lonely and sexually frustrated through most of the years preceding his courtship with her. Up to age thirty-nine he had never been married, had not dated much, had never felt really free to make a life for himself till his father passed away. Crippled by a steel mill accident, the old man had needed him badly. And how could Bert have expected any woman he might have married to accept a seventy-year-old invalid as part of the package? So Bert had waited, devoting himself to being a good, hard-working cop, and watching the good things in life pass him by. His marriage to Harriet had seemed like a fresh beginning, almost too good to be true. The status of "married man" pleased Bert, even though it was starting to go sour. He had been much less happy before. If only Harriet would do something about herself!

In his stepdaughter, Nancy, Bert could see the youth and sensuality that once had belonged to Harriet. Sometimes his eyes stayed on her too long when she paraded through the house wearing a skimpy pair of shorts and a flimsy T-shirt with no bra. Maybe she did it to tease him; he didn't think so, but he wasn't sure. He had to remind himself to look upon her as his daughter, not as a sexy young girl. He was ashamed to admit, even to himself, that he sometimes felt these unmentionable stirrings toward her.

With a tingle of excitement in his groin, Bert mulled over an incident that had happened last night while he was on duty. An anonymous caller had phoned police headquarters to report a car parked behind the high school, and Bert's squad car had been dispatched to check out a possible attempt at vandalism or breaking and entering.

"Probably just a couple of teen-agers screwing," Al McCoy, Bert's partner, had said.

But still they had to be careful and take the usual precautions. And so, driving slowly up the road to where the school was, Bert killed the headlights and pulled the car off the shoulder and he and Al got out. They proceeded on foot, flashlights ready and weapons drawn, knowing they had a good chance of catching the perpetrators redhanded.

Thinking about it now, Bert was almost ready to admit to himself that both he and Al probably secretly wanted to catch some pretty young thing with her pants down.

When they got up close to the target vehicle, a late-model Chevy with the front windows wound down on a warm evening, they could see the chassis rocking and could hear the undeniable sounds of lovemaking coming from inside.

Bert didn't know why he and Al didn't simply holster their service revolvers and slink on out of there, leaving the kids alone. They obviously weren't trying to break into the school; they already had what they had come for.

As if under some kind of compulsion, Bert and Al sneaked up on the car, till Al was looking in on the passenger's side, Bert on the driver's side. For a long time they both just stood watching . . . the nakedly entwined bodies clearly illuminated by moonlight, totally unaware that they were no longer alone.

All at once, as if on signal, Al and Bert turned on their flashlights. The boy jumped and hollered, immediately losing his erection as he turned over. The girl screamed. She was a good looker with long black hair and large, firm breasts, no more than fifteen or sixteen years old. The boy scrambled for his clothes, got a piece of her red slacks over his groin, but she couldn't grab hold of anything and tried to hide her body behind his. She had stopped screaming and just stared wide-eyed as a frightened doe, and Bert couldn't take his eyes off the nipple that wasn't hidden behind the boy's naked back.

"Cops!" the boy scoffed, an attempt at bravado. "What in the hell do you *want?*" He was older than the girl, maybe in his early twenties, and was making a show of regaining his cool. He even had the gall to start pulling his pants on, the flashlights helping him to see what he was doing, but also putting pretty good illumination on his girl friend.

"Billy! For God's *sake!*" she blurted, because his body was no longer protecting hers from view.

Al and Bert kept ogling her.

"We weren't doing anything wrong. You have to let us go," the boy in the car said.

"Cool as a cucumber, ain't you?" Al drawled sarcastically. "You ever hear of corruptin' the morals of a minor? I oughta smack you one in the teeth with this flashlight—teach you to mind who you're talkin' to."

"Get dressed—*both* of you!" Bert snapped. His mouth was dry and he was nervous. Ashamed of himself, he realized he had the beginning of an erection. He kept his light trained on the occupants of the car, ostensibly so they could find their clothes. The girl's breasts hung ripe and full when she bent to pick up her blouse, and Bert saw how good her thighs were as she slithered into her panties and slacks.

When the two were dressed, Al kept his flashlight on them while he delivered a stern lecture about how the girl was obviously a minor. And what would her parents do if she and her boyfriend got booked for disporting themselves lewdly in a public place? Not to mention a possible jail sentence for the boy for corrupting the morals of a minor. She started to cry, while he remained morosely silent, conveying the impression that he was not repentant but dragged.

Bert kept thinking about the girl's body.

"We could of screwed her," Al said after the young couple drove off.

Bert turned the key in the ignition of the squad car.

"We could of *had* her," Al insisted, "if we wasn't such square, honest cops. We could of got some for not turnin' her in."

Annoyed, Bert said, "Her boyfriend never would've stood still for a shakedown like that."

"You think not? What's *he* care? It's no skin off his ass. I didn't get the idea he was in love with her. Know what I mean?"

"Let's drop it, huh?"

"Okay, okay," Al replied testily. "I'm just sayin' we passed up a good opportunity to get laid."

"She had a fine body," Bert admitted wistfully.

"Damn right," Al said. "I could stand a shot at somethin' young and fine. Doin' it with my fat old lady is about as much fun as shovin' it into a cud-chewin' complacent cow."

Bert thought of Harriet . . . and Nancy.

CHAPTER 3

Sliding her hand along the smooth, curved mahogany railing, Cynthia mounted the stairs to her Mama's room. She knocked and entered. As usual, Mama was in her rocking chair.

"It's getting on toward Easter," Cynthia said. "Time for our congregation to be gathering. There'll be almost two hundred of them this time—some from as far away as California."

Mama never spoke much anymore, but Cynthia could read her thoughts and knew she was pleased. So many people coming to the services!

Cynthia told her Mama, "Luke and Abraham have the chapel all spic and span. Cyrus is making coffins. Some of the people who've been here for services before will bring food and do the cooking. Don't you fret; you don't have to do any of the hard work. We'll do it like you taught us."

But Mama seemed worried, so to cheer her up Cynthia said, "We'll have three young girls for the midnight rituals. Luke and Abraham already have one captured. We'll get two more by Easter Sunday."

This seemed to gladden Mama some. "Wish Papa could be here," Cynthia almost told her, but she refrained from mentioning it out loud. Instead, she smiled and said, "Lots of interesting people going to be here for the services."

Cynthia still missed Papa occassionally, but Mama didn't like to talk about him anymore, since ten years ago when he ran away.

"Everything is right on schedule, Mama," Cynthia said. "No cause for you to worry."

CHAPTER 4

In bra and panties, Nancy Johnson sat cross-legged on her bed, talking with her girl friend Patty over the telephone. She had taken her shower and was now brushing her hair, cradling the phone between shoulder and chin to leave her hands free. It did not bother her that her radio was blaring rock music from a top-forty station. She liked being home alone so she could do these sorts of things without being yelled at; her mother would have told her to turn off the radio or hang up the phone, one or the other, if she didn't want to go into adulthood wearing a hearing aid. Patty had just confided that a certain boy she was interested in had finally asked her to the prom.

"He *did?* Oh, I'm so happy for you! I told you he'd get up the nerve eventually. I saw the way he kept staring at you in home room. He's really *shy*. I bet the two of you will hit it off."

"But I'm the opposite of shy," Patty protested, obviously considering shyness an undesirable quality.

"I know," said Nancy. "Your outgoing personality is the perfect balance for Bob's shyness. Don't you know what I mean? Opposites attract."

"Yeah, I guess so," Patty said, perking up.

Nancy had got done brushing her hair and was appraising her body in the mirror, turning this way and that, wondering if her breasts were large enough and whether her legs were too thin. Meantime, Patty was explaining that she was sorry she'd have to pass up the shopping trip to the mall because her mother had outlined a program of chores. "On Saturday, too!" Patty lamented.

Just then Nancy's doorbell rang.

"Hang on a minute, Patty, I think I hear my stepfather at the door."

Laying the telephone receiver down on the bed, Nancy tugged on her nightgown and went to the front door—as the bell rang again and again, insistently. When she flung the door wide open, Bert Johnson was out on the porch leering at her, grabbing onto the doorframe so he wouldn't fall down. Nancy stepped back, frowning, seeing immediately that he was drunk, giving him room to enter without staggering into her.

"Hello, Daddy," she said.

In a brazen and slurring voice, Bert Johnson blurted, *"Good* morning, sweetheart! How's about a big warm smooch for your old man, huh?"

Startled, Nancy stared at him. He had often been drunk in her presence, but this business about a smooch was definitely out of character. Her stepfather had always maintained an almost cold aloofness toward her, not ever really taking the place of her real father, so this sudden change in him was alarming, although Nancy didn't specifically know why. But she knew enough to begin to get scared.

Lunging forward, he stumbled into her and hung onto her shoulders to support himself, pressing her against the wall. "Daddy!" she gasped, getting a face full of the liquor on his breath.

He pushed himself away from her, keeping her trapped between his two extended arms. His voice was low, husky, almost pleading. "You don't need to call me Daddy all the time, Nancy. I'm only your stepfather, and we both know it. There's no blood between us. So there's nothin' wrong with bein' nice to me once in a while. How's about a little kiss, huh?" But he perked up suddenly, looking around, listening. "Where's your mother?" he whispered warily.

Ducking under his arms, Nancy backed away from him toward her room. "She went to the beauty parlor to get her hair done, remember? You said I could use your car today to go shopping. Can I?" With these questions, she hoped to divert his attention away from her. She trembled, seeing a gleam in his eyes which she did not like.

Tossing his policeman's cap onto a settee in the hallway, he lunged at her, grabbing her by the wrist and pulling her to him in a drunken embrace. "Sure I'll give you the car, honey. Now, where's my big hug and kiss? How's about it, huh? I won't bite you." She averted her face and he kissed her wetly on the cheek. She was afraid to push him away, for she sensed that outright rejection might make him turn angry and violent. Maybe she could talk her way out of this.

"Daddy . . . you're hurting me. Please, let me go. My girl friend Patty is on the phone. She's waiting for me to get back on the line. I told her you were ringing the doorbell."

He loosened his grip and she squirmed away from him and hastened into her bedroom, shutting the door. She took a deep breath, pulling herself together. Then she picked up the telephone receiver, which she had left lying on the bed.

"Patty, I'm back. Patty? Are you there? Ooh—darn it! Why'd she have to hang up?"

Bert Johnson slumped on the settee in the hall, a few feet from Nancy's bedroom. He felt guilty and ashamed and erotically aroused all at the same time. The worse thing for him would be if his pass at his stepdaughter went nowhere. She could hold it over him, maybe even tell her mother. And Harriet would divorce him. Damn it. That little tease! She had been flaunting herself at him, walking around the house so provocatively all the time— and now that she had goaded him into making his move, she pretended to be scared. What did she want—to be coaxed?

When Nancy cradled the phone, she looked anxiously toward her closed bedroom door. As she got up with the idea of sliding the bolt shut, the door banged open, making her jump back, and her stepfather entered, gazing at her boldly. He had removed his shirt and was now naked to the waist, his fat belly hanging over his wide black policeman's belt.

"Come here, now, Nancy, honey . . . show Bert some of the lovin' he don't get from your mother."

"Daddy, leave me alone!" Nancy backed away, thinking maybe she should have stood her ground; perhaps a show of strength and determination would have controlled him. But she wasn't thinking clearly at all.

"Just let me look at you," he pleaded. "I won't lay a hand on your body, I promise. Take your nightgown off for me. Let me see what you really look like. We don't need to go any further than just looking . . . unless you want to."

"But . . . you can't be in your right mind. You don't know what you're saying. You're my *stepfather!* Get out of my room right now! Or I'll tell my mother when she comes home."

"Come on, now . . . I know you have to put up a show of resistance, to keep your self-respect. But you can't tell me you're a virgin. I heard you and your boyfriend one night out on the porch."

"Get out of my *room!*"

Nancy cowered as he lurched for her, his hands reaching for her breasts. She managed to sidestep him at the last instant and slapped him in the face with all her might. He stopped in his tracks, glowering at her, breathing hoarsely. With a sudden savage movement, he ripped at her, tearing open her nightgown. She started sobbing as he seized her shoulders and spun her around roughly, stripping the flimsy garment off her and flinging it to the floor.

She couldn't believe this was happening. She stood there crying while he ogled her near-nakedness.

He got her in a bearhug, pressing his heavy drunken kisses upon her. He fumbled at her bra, and because he could not hold her so tightly while he was thus occupied, she struggled and squirmed, almost managing to get loose. But his knee shoved

into her between her legs; he used his superior strength to push
her down onto the bed. She tried to kick and squirm, but his
massive weight bore down on her, taking her breath away. Straddling her, he got his thick hands on her breasts. His right hand
moved downward, caressing her torso and hips as he worked her
panties down off her legs. He was so caught up in what he was
doing, he failed to stop Nancy from getting her hands on the
portable radio lying behind her on the pillow, still blasting rock
music. Clutching the radio, she swung it as hard as she could
down onto the top of her stepfather's balding head. He grunted
in pain and surprise. Then his face sagged as he collapsed,
unconscious.

Disheveled and scared out of her wits, Nancy extricated herself from beneath him. She pulled up her panties and, glimpsing
her bare breasts in the mirror, hastily snatched her bra off the
floor and put it back on.

For a moment, she was afraid she might have killed her stepfather with the blow on the head, so she picked up his arm, felt
for the pulse in his wrist, then let the arm drop. His knuckles
smacked the floor and his arm dangled over the edge of the bed.
He began to snore. Nancy looked down at him disbelievingly,
full of anxiety mixed with relief.

What would he be like when he came to? How would Nancy
and her mother and he ever go on living together in the same
house?

Backing around the bed, she went to her closet, rummaged,
and pulled out a suitcase. Pushing bottles of makeup and her
large jewelry box out of the way, she made room for the suitcase
on top of her dresser, then began opening drawers and going
through them, filling the suitcase with clothes and other belongings.

Bert Johnson, lying flat on his back, continued to snore loudly.

Nancy felt frightened, worried, alone—shut out rudely and
suddenly from a world she had believed to be reasonably comfortable, loving, and safe. She knew she had to leave home. But
she had no clear idea of where to run.

CHAPTER 5

Cynthia remembered when they first started using the traps. From the time she first saw them, she was fascinated with their gadgetry, although they did not belong to her but to her brothers, Luke and Abraham. Cyrus, her oldest brother, was too addle-brained to be allowed to play with anything so dangerous; for some reason, though, he was very good at making little wooden coffins to bury birds and mice. Luke and Abraham had three traps each, given to .them by Uncle Sal.

Cynthia recalled the serrated steel teeth set with a strong hook and spring, the fiat metal lever where the bait was put, and the steel chain and peg that kept the trap anchored. It started before the traps, though, really. It started with Mama and the things she taught Cynthia and her brothers from the time they were babies, when the whole family lived up above the shop where Mama sold magical herbs, potions, amulets, and books to strange people who came from as far away as New York and Philadelphia. Papa was still with the family then and took them all to visit Uncle Sal and Aunt Edna on holidays.

Cynthia sat with her legs tucked under her in the back seat of the car. She had on a pink starched dress, her shiny black hair combed and brushed. She could see the back of Papa's head and try to imagine the thoughts that were going on there. She could see the left side of Mama's rouged face and part of her left shoulder. If she stood up on the car seat, and Mama didn't catch her, she could see more, could glue her eyes to the snaky, white unraveling road line or watch white guardposts rushing by in endless cable-linked procession until her eyes got sore and she had to sit down before Mama yelled at her.

"You stay in your seat, Cynthia! If we hit a hard bump or Papa has to make a quick stop, you'll go flying right out the window."

Such a thing seemed unlikely. Especially with the window closed. But Mama must be right, or why would people come from so far away to have her sell them magic things or read their fortunes?

Cynthia and her three brothers, crammed together in the back seat of the sedan, looked at each other and giggled. Luke, all pink-cheeked and polished with his yellow hair plastered down, had on a sailor suit with long pants and a real starched-white sailor's cap. Abraham was wearing a soldier suit with short pants, which made him mad when Papa bought it for him—he had never seen a soldier with short pants—but he felt better when Papa showed him the hat that came with the outfit, a realistic officer's cap with a shiny black beak and imitation gold braid. Cyrus was big and chubby for his age, and he was wearing green trousers like the kind bus drivers wear, a white short-sleeved shirt, and gray suspenders—and he dressed that way most of the time and looked kind of funny because Mama could never find regular clothes to fit him.

Cynthia thought of her Easter basket, which Mama had made her leave at home. "You're not going to spoil your appetite, young lady. Aunt Edna and Uncle Sal will have plenty of sweet stuff for you." Luke and Abraham had to leave their baskets home, too. But Cyrus was allowed to bring his with him, which was a laugh because his candy was nearly all gone. The pink, crinkly straw was a mess, stained with melted chocolate and jelly beans. Cyrus had saved a few of the yellow marshmallow rabbits to eat last because he liked them best, as did Cynthia; real gooey and soft, they stretched and snapped apart between your teeth, then melted like powdered sugar on your tongue.

"The Easter celebration originally had nothing whatsoever to do with Jesus," Mama had said. "It was a pagan rite of spring. Rabbits and eggs are symbols of fertility, of giving birth—thus, the Easter bunny delivering eggs. Understand, children?"

Cynthia didn't, not when she was seven years old. Maybe Luke and Abraham understood more. To Cyrus it, meant absolutely nothing; all he understood about Easter was biting the head off a marshmallow rabbit.

When they had been piling into the car, some of their school friends had been starting off for church. "Why don't *we* go to church?" Cynthia had asked.

"Because we don't believe in it," Mama had replied. "We believe in things that are much older than the church, and a great deal more powerful. Church is for weaklings. It's not for us, as it wasn't for your grandfather or great-grandfather, either."

"*Tell* us about Grandpa," Luke begged at one point during the long car ride.

"Well, he was a Cunning Man," Mama began, "as was his father, before him."

"What's *that?*" Cynthia piped up, though they had all heard the explanation many times before.

"A Cunning Man is a witch doctor," Mama explained. "The word 'cunning' means wise, sly, crafty. So Grandpa Barnes was a wise man. In the village where he lived, in England, he was known as a magician. He could do wonderful and sometimes very frightening things that made the people's hair stand on end. He was feared and respected. But he had followers . . . his own congregation, so to speak. His magic wasn't the fake kind that you see on television, it was *real*—it came from his knowledge of demons."

"What're they?" one of the children asked.

"They live in hell," Mama said. "They work for Satan, or for whoever knows how to summon them with magic."

"Did Grandpa know how?"

"The people said he did. They said he could make people die by compelling them to do so."

Cynthia didn't understand "compelling," but it sounded horrible.

"You shouldn't fill the kids' minds with this kind of stuff," Papa interjected.

"But it's all *true*," Mama insisted. "Besides, it's no worse than the Hansel and Gretel stories—people getting pushed into ovens and all."

"I disagree," Papa stated flatly.

To show him that she would talk about whatever she wanted to, Mama stubbornly told still more stories about Grandpa Luke Barnes and his father, Abraham Barnes, both Cunning Men, for whom Cynthia's brothers, Luke and Abraham, were named. The Cunning Men could, according to Mama, fly through the air under their own power and could pass invisibly through walls. They knew how to foretell the future, locate buried or stolen treasure, and cure sick people or animals merely by touching them and reciting magical spells.

Cynthia and her brothers listened with solemn, rapt attention to these awesome stories. Many of them they had heard before, but they always enjoyed having them repeated. They particularly liked hearing Mama tell about Grandpa Barnes' battle with a witch from a neighboring village in England. This old woman had caused Grandpa to come down with a severe case of arthritis. With the aid of certain ancient charms and talismans known only to him, Grandpa consulted his magic mirror. The identity of the enemy witch was revealed in the mirror, and Grandpa knew what to do; he followed her home one night over a dark path in the woods and carefully stabbed each of her footprints with a brand-new knife over which he had recited a special prayer to a demon. The demon made the witch fall dead on her own threshold, and Grandpa's arthritis was cured.

"Poppycock," Papa scoffed. He was wearing his gray sharkskin suit with the peppermint necktie. He smelled like after-shave lotion, the kind he had once dabbed on Cynthia's face to let her feel how much it burned. His stiffly starched white shirt collar had rubbed the back of his neck red, and his hair was edged in the neat arc of a fresh haircut around his ears. White skin showed in places through his thinning black hair. Cynthia found herself noticing everything about him because he was home so seldom; most of the time he was away on long business trips, and then he would show up finally with presents, like the pink dress for Cynthia, Abraham's and Luke's soldier and sailor suits, and Mama's earrings.

"Sheldon, don't you dare make fun of my ancestors," Mama said. "I believe firmly that their spirits are with us, protecting this family."

"You don't believe in religion, but you believe in *that* nonsense," Papa grumped. "Don't blame me if the children grow up to be a pack of superstitious fools. Why don't you save the spiel for your customers? It's all right in its proper place, when you're making a buck out of it."

Mama did not deign to reply to this, but her silent anger permeated the closed-in car. She had ordered all the windows to be **kept** tightly wound shut so the wind wouldn't mess up her new permanent; only a finger-thick crack was allowed in Cyrus' window so he wouldn't get carsick. Mama looked nice, wearing the navy-blue suit Papa had bought her for her birthday. Her lips were red, her cheeks rosy—not pale like when she talked to customers or ironed clothes. Cynthia could see one of her white earrings and her pearl necklace fastened with a tiny hook and chain behind her neck, and the big white Easter flower almost hidden by her shoulder. Her perfume, like the flower, smelled sticky-sweet in the hot, stuffy car.

"Children, listen to me," she said when her anger subsided. "Don't forget to wish Aunt Edna and Uncle Sal a happy Easter. They'll have some presents for you, I'm sure. You must remember to say thank you. We taught you some manners—don't be afraid to use them. You, too, Cyrus."

Papa parked the car in Uncle Sal's long gravel driveway and

the whole family got out, Mama helping Cyrus with his Easter basket. Looking up at the house, a large and stately building of red brick with a wide veranda and tall white pillars in front, Cynthia was awed and impressed by it, as usual. It was a real Southern mansion. According to Uncle Sal, the man who owned this place prior to the Civil War also owned slaves; then later he became the overseer and landlord of all the sharecroppers and tenant farmers in the valley. Most of the farms were inactive now, although people still lived 'round about, sometimes putting in small gardens for their own use, but mostly earning a living from the nearby coal mines. Uncle Sal wasn't a farmer or a miner; he was an artist who had come here for peace and quiet. There was an old country church on his property, a hundred yards or so from the house, which had once been the Sunday come-to-meeting place for all the farmers in the valley who worked, played, and prayed under the wing of their overseer. Now the hundred-year-old church was Uncle Sal's studio, where he churned out oil paintings of the Good Old Days to be sold to art galleries, department stores, and other customers on commission.

Cynthia loved to go into the church to look at Uncle Sal's work, and she hoped she would be allowed to later. But they always had to go to the house to eat first. She noticed how the gravel stones scampered away as she walked on them or else bounced up and put marks on her white Easter shoes. Mama grabbed her hand and pulled her along angrily, as if it was her fault, while Cyrus waddled in front without a care in the world, swinging his Easter basket. Luke and Abraham, in their soldier and sailor outfits, walked smartly behind Papa, stiffly aware that they were members of the military. Papa rapped his knuckles on the screen door and, without waiting to be admitted, led the way through the living room and into the steamy, good-smelling kitchen.

Aunt Edna came running excitedly from the dining room. "Happy Easter!" she shrieked, letting out a big, silly laugh and pushing her eyeglasses back up the bridge of her nose. Her white apron was stained with gravy and cherry juice. Cynthia and the boys immediately began thinking of cherry pie, while Mama and Aunt Edna hugged and kissed like they always did on holidays.

Uncle Sal had followed behind Aunt Edna to shake hands with Papa. "Let the two sisters smooch each other for a while," he said in his gruff manner, smiling. "Want a shot of bourbon, Shelly?"

Papa said, "No, not right now, Sal. Happy Easter. I'll take a beer, though, if you have one."

"Happy Easter, Cindy! What did the Easter bunny bring you?" Stooping over, Aunt Edna hugged Cynthia' so hard it hurt, then turned her loose with a big "Um!" and planted a rough, watery kiss on her cheek. Then she did the same to the boys, which embarrassed them, except for Cyrus, who didn't know any better. The kiss made Cynthia's cheek cold and wet, but she was ashamed to let her aunt see her wipe it off, so she simply waited for it to dry.

Uncle Sal shook hands with all the boys. To Cyrus he said, "That's a real good-looking basket you have there, kid, but the candy's all gone. You're a regular sweet tooth."

Cyrus held the basket out, so Sal bent over, pretended to select and eat a jelly bean. "Oh, boy, that was good!"

Uncle Sal growled, rubbing his stomach and grinning to make Cyrus feel good. Uncle Sal was a small, trim man with a ragged brown mustache. Around the house he always wore a pair of the paint-daubed blue jeans that he wore in the studio. His manner was gruff, cheerful, and informal, and the children liked him.

"I have some special goodies for you kids," beamed Aunt Edna. "I'll show them to you now, but you have to promise not to touch them till after supper so you won't spoil your appetites. Do I have your word of honor?"

"Yes, Aunt Edna! We promise!"

"Cross your hearts."

They did so, getting fun out of it.

"Okay," said Aunt Edna. "You're going to have a real surprise."

"Yeah, kids," said Uncle Sal, laughing. "We have some pregnant rabbits for you."

"Sal!" Aunt Edna chided. "Watch how you talk around the children."

"Nothing wrong with being pregnant," Sal countered. "How do you think they came into the world in the first place?"

Mama said, "It's all right, Sal. I didn't raise them to be frightened of sex."

"Yeah, but you're scaring them silly with your crazy witch stories," Papa complained, pouring beer into a glass.

Mama glowered at him, but he didn't seem to notice.

Aunt Edna had turned to the kitchen cabinet and opened the doors so she could reach to the highest shelf. She brought out a large flat tray and held it so Cynthia and the boys could have a look. The tray contained four gingerbread bunnies with white button eyes and frosted whiskers, and each bunny had a hard-boiled egg for a stomach. The children eyed their pregnant rabbits with amusement, then squinted at each other and laughed and giggled.

"Thank you, Aunt Edna! Thank you, Uncle Sal!"

Cyrus was the only one who forgot to say thank you. His mouth hanging open, he kept ogling the pregnant rabbits as if he half-expected them to get up and run away.

"*I* don't want any thanks, kids!" Uncle Sal exclaimed. "I don't do any of the baking around here; I just bring home the dough." He winked and all the adults laughed, but the children didn't get it.

Aunt Edna's holiday meal was lavish and delicious. As on all holidays and special occasions, each of the children was permitted to have a shotglass of home made wine as an appetizer. Cynthia sipped hers cautiously, but, even so, her eyes watered and her throat burned, but she continued to sip it a little at a time till she got sort of used to it, and when it was gone her cheeks glowed and her belly felt warm and good. Luke and Abraham were able to drink theirs faster, almost like grown-ups. Then Aunt Edna served mashed potatoes and gravy and thick slabs of juicy turkey; pickles, celery, olives, and radishes; hot buttered cornbread, green beans, cole slaw, and root beer. And the grand finale—cherry pie topped with vanilla ice cream.

Cynthia and her brothers, all sitting on one side of the large dining table, leaned back and compared bellies. "Look at all of you!" said Uncle Sal. "Swelled up like four little basketballs! I think I'll take you outside and dribble you. You first, Cynthia!"

"I bet you couldn't dribble Cyrus," Cynthia said. The grown-ups thought this was cute and got a laugh out of it. Cyrus smiled lopsidedly, aware somehow that he had become an object of attention.

"This one's going to be the brains of the family," Uncle Sal pronounced, meaning Cynthia, and she glowed inwardly, embarrassed yet pleased by the compliment.

"Now, Uncle Sal and I have got more surprises for you," announced Aunt Edna. She trotted up the stairs and stayed away for a few minutes, which seemed, to Cynthia and the boys, like an excruciatingly long time. But at last her high heels clicked into the room and she was laden with packages, one for each child.

Cyrus opened his first, and his present turned out to be a big toy shovel with a long wooden handle and shiny steel blade: a good shovel, one you could actually dig with, not one that would bend or break easily. Cyrus smiled his lopsided smile.

The boxes given to Abraham and Luke were quite large, and when opened were found to contain three steel traps for each boy, given to them by Uncle Sal, who had not forgotten his last year's promise to teach them how to set bait and trap wild animals like rabbits, raccoons, and possums. "Maybe you'll even catch the Easter bunny—who knows!"

Cynthia laughed. Luke and Abraham were thrilled, even though at first they may have been a trifle disappointed that they were considered too young to be given BB guns. Luke was ten and Abraham was eight.

Cynthia opened her package and found a shovel just like Cyrus'. She liked to get toys instead of dresses all the time and

loved her Aunt Edna and Uncle Sal for understanding this. Immediately, her head was filled with visions of using her new
shovel to dig a pirate cave such as the one she had seen in her
first-grade reading book. Or, better yet—if Mama would teach
her some magic, maybe she could find some buried treasure, like
Grandpa Barnes, the Cunning Man.

"Is there such a thing as a Cunning Girl?" Cynthia asked. "Because I'd like to be one when I grow up."

Everybody laughed except Papa.

"It would be called a Cunning Woman," Mama told Cynthia.
"And you can't just simply decide to become one—you have to
be born with the magic in you. It would have to come to you
through me and Grandpa."

Papa began shouting. "Damn it, Meredith! If you keep on filling the kids' heads with that garbage, you're going to turn them
into a tribe of lunatics!" He slammed his fist on the table so hard
that the cups and saucers jumped and rattled.

Everybody was momentarily stunned to silence, even Mama,
because Papa seldom showed such a violent outburst of temper.

The children couldn't understand what all the fuss was about.
They couldn't help being thrilled and excited, even a little
pleased, that they had had a man like Grandpa Barnes, so famous
and powerful, and even possibly evil, in their very own family. It
made them feel special, in a way. It gave them something to
share and be proud of. And in their secret dreams they entertained obscure but enticing visions of worldly delights, fame, and
riches that might lie in store for them someday, if they could truly
inherit the powers of the Cunning Man and have a congregation
of their own.

When Cynthia was nine years old, Papa went away on business and did oot come back. For a long time Mama would talk
about his letters, making lighthearted small talk about what was
supposedly in them, even though no letters actually came.

Mama began spending more and more time in the back room
of her shop, poring over rare and expensive grimoires, books of

magic, covering subjects such as divination, conjuration, and necromancy—the art of communicating with the dead. Something bad had happened to Papa, and the family knew it.

There was very little money coming in. People no longer wanted to come to Mama's shop after finding out that they had to wait impatiently at the counter or browse through the place unserved while Mama stayed in the back room, totally absorbed in her books. She began to hoard herbs, potions, occult works and ritualistic paraphernalia that might have been sold at a good profit. Papa had insurance, but it could not be collected until he was proven deceased or legally declared so at the end of seven years.

Sometimes when the children came home from school, or when they got up in the morning, the house would be full of the heavy, yet sweet, smell of incense mixed with candle smoke. Mama paid less attention to their meals, their grooming, and her own housekeeping. They had few friends at school or in the neighborhood. Other kids started picking on Cyrus with increased frequency, intensity, and nastiness. His sister or one of his brothers had to walk him to the bus stop each morning to see that he got off safely to his special school, and he had to be met again at the bus stop in the afternoon.

Desperate to help their mother in some way, Cynthia, Luke, and Abraham began working in the store after school and on weekends. This was partly because they didn't know what else to do with themselves; they felt like outcasts, rejected by the community. Many people referred to them as "the witch's kids" and either secretly feared them or openly made fun of them.

Working in the store, Cynthia began to read books on sorcery, spell-casting, and magic. She learned that a Cunning Man, like Grandpa Barnes had been, was in reality a white witch, with the ability to combat the power of Satan. But in the end, Grandpa Barnes had been overcome by a witch practicing black magic, as opposed to his own kind. According to Mama, in his old age he succumbed to a stroke, the product of an evil spell cast on him by a rival witch who had gotten a lock of his hair. He knew it was no use to struggle, for the rival witch had stronger magic, and he predicted the time of his own death down to the very hour and minute. Did this not mean, Cynthia pondered, that black magic must be stronger than the other kind?

She hated her father for leaving Mama. But she loved him, too, and wished he would return. Many a night she cried herself to sleep, hoping to see him bending over her in the morning, laden with the usual armloads of presents. Not having been raised in the ways of the church, Cynthia found herself "praying" to Grandpa Barnes to bring Papa back to her. The Cunning Man appeared to her once in a dream, but when she tried to talk to him he vanished and she awakened. Repeatedly dwelling upon the meaning of this, turning it over and over in her young mind, she was struck by a realization of what Grandpa must be trying to tell her—that he was not strong enough to help her and her own spiritual resources were not sufficiently developed to stay in communication with him.

Every time she had the opportunity, Cynthia studied her mother's library of modern and ancient witch's lore, much of it seeming weird and incomprehensible to her at first. But it began to flesh itself out with meaning, to become more meaningful and real to her than her daily chores. Because she herself was distracted, Mama did not notice her daughter's intense absorption in matters that did not concern the average nine-year-old. In the shop Meredith would hobble past Cynthia, eyes straight ahead, as if her mind was far off somewhere, her arms laden with tomes she was taking to the back room to study alone, while Cynthia engaged in her own studies behind the counter.

Neither mother nor daughter paid much attention to customers anymore, or seemingly to each other, as their lives went on amid an array of herbs, potions, amulets, Tarot cards, altar cloths, grimoires, and other such equipment. Luke or Abraham waited on the few people who came into the place, and played gin rummy, pinochle or double solitaire between customers. Cyrus was easy to handle; he could remain busy for hours, doing the same things with the same objects, over and over. His favorite playthings were such items as voodoo charms and witches' bottles from the merchandise in the store.

Late one evening at about midnight Cynthia was awakened by the odor of incense and flickering shadows cast by candlelight spilling into her room. Propping herself up on her elbows, she heard Mama's voice coming from somewhere in the house but could not make out the words. She tiptoed down the hall and saw what Mama was doing. Then she went to the boys' room and awakened them, her forefinger touched to her lips.

The children gathered around Mama at the dining table. She looked up at them but said not a word. To them she seemed uncannily serene, preoccupied, yet intense and commanding; her demeanor filled them with an unfamiliar solemnity and awe. She was wearing a black robe cinched at the waist with a gold cord, and around her forehead was a wide black ribbon with a name inscribed upon it in shimmering gold letters: TETRAGRAMMATON. From her reading, Cynthia knew this was the usually unspoken name of the Spirit of the Universe.

The dining table was a large round one, and over it, centered, Mama had draped a black cloth with a magic circle printed on it in gold, inscribed with mystical symbols and formulae. Inside the magic circle next to an ornamental copper incense burner there was an iron retort, or witch's bottle, supported on a ringstand over a lit candle, so that the substance being heated bubbled and seethed, transmitting its vapors throughout the semi-darkened dining room. The stench of urine, or something like it, was recognizable despite the efforts to overwhelm it with incense.

Cynthia realized that the words Mama was reciting came from *Lemegeton*, a medieval grimoire, the text of which lay open before Meredith at the dining table, which was now an altar.

"I conjure thee, Sheldon, my husband, the father of my children, that thou forthright appear and show thyself unto me before this circle, without delay.

"I conjure thee by Him to all creatures are obedient, whether alive or dead, and by this ineffable Name, Tetragrammaton Jehovah, which being heard the elements are overturned, the air is shaken, the sea runs black, the fire is quenched, and the earth trembles.

"I invoke and command thee, O Spirit, to come from whichever place in the world thou art. And give answer to my questions, answers that shall be true and reasonable. Come, then, in visible form, and speak that I may understand thy words!

"Come, visibly, before this circle, obedient in every way to my desires! By these holy rites, I conjure and exorcise thee, distressed Spirit, to present thyself here and reveal unto me the cause of thy calamity, where thou art now in being, and where thou wilt hereafter be.

"If thou dost not come, or disobey in any way, I will curse thee, and will cause thee to be stripped of all blessings and powers, and consigned to the bottomless Pit, where thou wilt remain until the Day of Judgment!

"I will cause thee to be bound to the Waters of Everlasting Flame, Fire, and Brimstone!

"Come, then, Sheldon, spirit of my husband, and appear before this circle, to obey me utterly!"

The children kept their heads bowed, afraid of what might happen—and yet desirous of seeing it. They wanted their magic to succeed in bringing a spirit into their midst. From time to time the smoke and the candlelight played tricks on their eyes so that something seemed about to happen. They thought they saw forms moving in the shadows. Cynthia was sure for a moment that her mother's magic was working. But eventually for the boys the excitement of anticipation wore off, their eyes began to go shut, their heads to nod. Cynthia, however, remained wide awake long after her brothers had crept away to bed, their mother not venturing to stop them.

"Why didn't it work?" Cynthia inquired at last.

Mama replied somberly, in a soft, persuasive timbre. "It may not work the way we would like it to. Magic does not always succeed completely, because there are sometimes strong forces to overcome. But if we have succeeded partially, if Papa's spirit is trying to reach us, we may get a sign. He might be trying to break through sinister, evil forces that are surrounding this family."

"Why would they pick on *us?*" Cynthia asked, frightened.

"I don't know," Mama replied. "Perhaps it has something to do with Grandpa Barnes. Perhaps the witch who killed him put a curse on him and his descendants."

Three days later, on a Sunday, Aunt Edna and Uncle Sal were killed in a fiery automobile accident. They were on their way to visit Meredith and the children, having made arrangements for the occasion two days before by telephone. During the course of the call they had tactfully expressed their worries about the state of Meredith's emotional health and her ability to "cope with things." But an enormous tractor-trailer truck lost its brakes behind them on a steep, winding grade and pounded down on them, unable to stop, crushing their small foreign car like an accordian against a sheer rock wall. The driver of the rig and Edna and Sal were incinerated in the violent explosion which followed the impact.

It was not lost on Cynthia and her family, attending the closed-casket funeral, that Edna and Sal had been virtually cremated: the exact punishment ordered by Meredith to be brought down on the spirit of her husband if he failed to appear. Was this retribution?

One week after the burial, Meredith was summoned by her relatives' attorney to a disclosure of their last will and testament. All their property, money, and worldly goods were now hers, which amounted to the mansion eighty miles away, its contents and surrounding fifty-five acres, the chapel on the grounds, Sal's unsold paintings, contracts, and royalties, a savings account containing fourteen thousand dollars, and insurance policies totalling seventy-five thousand dollars.

In succeeding weeks, the decision was made to leave the town and the shop, for which they were paying rent, and go to live in Uncle Sal's and Aunt Edna's house.

Her inheritances, and the financial security that came along with them, enabled Meredith to give herself completely to the occult. She could live off the insurance and the savings until the expiration of the seven years when her husband would be declared legally dead. Then she would get more insurance money, and Social Security.

The family name had been Brewster, assumed when Meredith married Sheldon. But with the move to the mansion, Meredith began telling the children their last name was now Barnes, her maiden name while she was growing up in England, the daughter of Luke Barnes, the Cunning Man. "It's a name to be proud of," Meredith said. "In reclaiming it for ourselves, we lay claim to Grandpa's heritage, his powers."

Mama had discovered a trunk full of the Cunning Man's books and magical equipment in the attic. The stuff must have been shipped over from England when he died, and Edna had never let on that she had gotten hold of it. Maybe she had been ashamed of it—she and Sal had often accused Meredith of being superstitious. In any case, it was quite an exciting find, and it occupied Meredith and Cynthia for days on end, as they read through everything and then discussed their discoveries. There were many diaries and notebooks kept in the Cunning Man's own hand. Both mother and daughter, by this time, were deeply intrigued by witchcraft—its origins and possibilities. Luke and Abraham were in awe of it and were believers in its potential power, but they were content to allow Mama and Cynthia to become the experts.

Cyrus, who was fifteen at the time of the move, seemed to blossom in the country. It was as if the rural atmosphere—the outdoors and the absence of strangers in large numbers to nag and tease him—formed a more hospitable environment for his uncomplicated mental processes and abilities. He began to look more healthy and strong, if not more intelligent. He liked to pick flowers or catch butterflies. He never harmed the butterflies, always letting them go. One morning he found a dead bird and cried over it till Cynthia, trying to appease him, came up with the idea of having a funeral for it. She found a few scraps of wood and showed Cyrus how to make a small coffin. They went into the chapel, which had been Uncle Sal's studio, and made up a few prayers, which they recited. Then outside, in the small cemetery that had been the family plot of the overseer who had owned the place back before the Civil War, Cyrus and Cynthia dug a hole, tied two sticks together to make an upside-down cross, and had a burial ceremony that mimicked a Satanic one Cynthia had read about. After that, Cyrus was always looking for dead birds or mice that the cat had killed. He took to making small coffins in advance or saving shoeboxes to have in a pinch. Cynthia always helped him by reciting prayers and incantations over the tiny graves he dug.

None of the children was supervised. Meredith spent long hours upstairs in her room reading or feeling sorry for herself over the loss of her husband. She never ate much anymore and didn't cook, either; the family subsisted on sandwiches, canned goods, and sometimes fresh fruit bought at the country store up the road or picked from fruit trees in the surrounding woods. Meredith began to look gaunt, sickly, even jaundiced, but the children grew accustomed to her deteriorated appearance. Without discussing it in so many words, Meredith and Cynthia both knew that they intended to tryout some of the things they had learned from Grandpa Barnes' notebooks. Nothing had been attempted since the day Mama had invoked Papa's spirit—with disastrous results.

One day, to amuse themselves, Luke and Abraham rummaged around and brought out the traps Uncle Sal had given them for Easter two years ago. They jauntily made a foray into the woods to set the traps and could hardly sleep all night waiting for dawn so they could get up and go see. Cynthia and Cyrus went along, too. One by one the six traps were checked, but they were all empty. Luke angrily kicked a clod of dirt, while Abraham hung his head and looked dejected.

"What kind of bait did you use?" Cynthia asked.

"Bread. We wet it and made dough balls," said Abraham.

"Huh! Who taught you to do that?"

"Nobody. I mean, I know you can use a dough ball to catch fish."

They all laughed, even Cyrus.

"I guess there ain't too many fish swimmin' through these here woods," Luke admitted.

"Why don't you use a carrot?" Cynthia suggested. "Then you might catch a rabbit."

"Yeah, at least we know what rabbits eat," Abraham agreed.

"One rabbit caught, and each of us could take a lucky rabbit's foot!" Luke exclaimed in gleeful anticipation.

After the change in bait, for three more mornings all the children went out and checked the traps, only to find them empty. This was all the more frustrating because most of the time when they were on their way to the traps they would see plenty of rabbits and other game scampering around in the fields. Luke threw rocks at the animals, but he never hit one.

"Shit! Wonder what these rabbits around here *eat?*" Abraham grumped.

"Lettuce, maybe," offered Cynthia.

"Gonna try it one more time with carrots," Luke pronounced determinedly.

"Why don't you let me work a spell for you?" Cynthia blurted.

They all stared at her. She knelt by the last trap they had checked, and with a stick she drew a magic circle around it. Then she got some dew on her fingers and sprinkled in on the fresh bait. Bowing her head, still kneeling, she said the following words, paraphrasing something she had read in one of Grandpa Barnes' notebooks: "May the dewy tears of Almighty Tetragrammaion, Lord of Creation, anoint the tools of the hunter. May the Spirit of the Hunt bring food to our table. Amen."

"We're not gonna *eat* the rabbit, are we?" Abraham said.

Cynthia got up, brushing dirt from her jeans. "*That* doesn't matter, silly. The important thing is the charm. Tomorrow we'll see if it really works."

They went around repeating the ceremony over each trap, and

for the boys it got a little boring. But Cynthia was intensely excited, more so than she let on, for this could be a test of her power. Mama had told her that she could be the Chosen One of the family, because at birth a caul—a portion of her amniotic membrane (whatever *that* was)—had remained covering her forehead, and according to tradition among white witches, this was a sure sign of tremendous psychic powers to be vested in one so blessed. Mama had dried this membrane and kept it locked in her cedar chest, and she said that it must remain with the family forever and never be allowed to fall into strange hands, for the loss of it would bring dreadful results.

The next day they caught a rabbit. When they spotted it struggling in the trap, they all ran up and stopped short, out of breath, staring at it. They had run up whooping joyously, but up close it wasn't a very pretty sight. The animal was weak from loss of blood; the mauled grass around it was streaked red. The rabbit's leg was bitten or gnawed down to the white bone, and still it remained locked in the steel jaws of the trap, vainly trying to pull free.

"Poor thing," Cynthia said. But an inner part of her was thrilled because the rabbit had been caught as the result of her magic.

For long moments the boys were speechless, in shock.

"Fun'ral," Cyrus mumbled. Tears were rolling down his chubby cheeks.

"What're we gonna *do* with it?" Abraham asked.

Nobody knew. It was one thing to dream about catching a rabbit, but it was quite another thing to watch it die. Luke picked up a stick and hit the animal, trying to end its suffering. But the blow did not suffice; the rabbit crawled in circles for a while, then resumed pulling against the steel chain.

"Maybe we should let it go!" Cynthia blurted before Luke could strike another blow.

"Naw, it's gonna die. Might as well put it out of its misery."

He swung the stick—thump!—down on the quivering ball of fur, then thumped it again and again, till it stopped quivering.

Then he squatted, so he wouldn't get blood on his trousers, and unlocked the jaws of the trap.

They all stood over the dead rabbit, looking at it in awe of its death.

"Gimme your pocketknife," Luke said to Abraham.

"What're you gonna do?" Abraham asked apprehensively as he handed the knife over.

"Skin it."

"You're kidding!"

"Nope."

Luke unclasped the long blade of the knife and stood over the dead rabbit, looking down on it. "I ain't chicken," he said, as much to bolster his own courage as to convince the others.

"Wait!" Cynthia called out. "He's *my* rabbit as much as yours! I want some of his blood!"

"What *for?*"

"For magic."

Luke and Abraham waited while their sister went home to get a witch's bottle, and Cyrus went along with her to fetch a shoebox. Filled with lurid fascination mingled with queasiness and fear, the others watched while Luke sliced the rabbit's jugular vein and drained some blood into Cynthia's bottle. She wiped off the bottle with Kleenex, corked it, and put it safely in her pocket. Then, with nobody like Uncle Sal around to act as teacher, Luke made a horrible mess of his attempt to skin the rabbit, and in the end they put the bloody, mangled pieces— pelt, bones, and carcass—into the shoebox.

In the little cemetery by the chapel, Cyrus used his toy shovel to dig a grave.

After the burial, and the placing of an upside-down cross on the mound of earth, Cynthia knelt and recited: "Almighty Tetragrammaton, we beg you to accept this sacrifice which we now offer to you, so that we may receive your blessings. We ask you to bless our deeds, that we perform in your Almighty Name. Consecrate the blood you have given us this day, that it may further your holy work. For we ask only to serve you, for ever and ever. Amen."

Mama heard about the incident in all its gory detail that evening after supper. She seemed in good spirits and listened keenly, though the children kept interrupting each other to get it all told. It was one of those rare occasions when Meredith had troubled herself to cook a full meal, including a cake for dessert (made from a boxed mix).

She said, "The power is in you, then, Cynthia, as I had suspected. Grandpa Barnes has chosen you as his receptor, the bearer of his blood lineage. If you prayed over the trap and consecrated it, then whoever you found in it the next morning was your enemy."

"A *rabbit?*" Abraham blurted.

Mama shot him a cold, withering look. "Evil spirits, demons, can assume *any* shape," she instructed in stern, serious tones. "It is not uncommon for them to take the guise of a rabbit. Though they may appear quite harmless outwardly, this is only a devil's trick, and you must protect yourself by destroying them. It's the only way to counteract the evil power inside them."

In the following weeks the Barnes children redoubled their efforts in setting traps and torturing, maiming, and killing the animals that were sent to them. These were mostly squirrels, raccoons, possums, and rabbits, with an occasional stray dog or cat. It became a challenge to see who could devise the most ingenious, painful ways of dealing with these enemies. The children grew callous about performing amputations and decapitations, searing live flesh with fire, gouging or poking out eyes and mutilating genitals. No amount of cruelty was too extreme for the evil spirits embodied by these apparently harmless creatures. Luke and Abraham did most of the killing, while Cynthia presided over the ritual aspects of their activities and Cyrus did the burying.

And one day the inevitable happened: a human being was caught. At least it *looked* like a human being.

The children heard the creature's screams as they walked along the dusty road, about a hundred yards from their house. They stopped in their tracks, listened, and knew that the screaming was coming from out in the field where they had set several of the largest traps. This was truly frightening: potentially the largest thing they had yet caught. Afraid of what they might find, they took their time about heading into the field. Cynthia began praying to Tetragrammaton to protect them. All of a sudden Luke took off running, out toward the middle of the field, having first grabbed Cyrus' shovel out of his hand. Whatever it was they had caught, it was behind some tall weeds. Luke went crashing through the weeds, Cyrus huffing and puffing behind.

Luke was standing over the body of a boy. There was a lot of blood. The steel jaws of the trap had nearly severed the boy's leg, and Luke had apparently split his skull open with Cyrus' shovel.

"Is he . . . is he *dead?*" Abraham managed to gasp out.

Luke was still breathing hard. "Don't know." He took a rapid series of deep breaths. "No. I guess not. Look! He's still breathing!"

Luke raised the shovel over his head to hit the boy one more time.

"Wait! That's Jimmy Peterson!" Cynthia said.

They all came around to look at the boy's face, trying to see his features through the smeary mask of fresh blood. Jimmy Peterson was the son of the man who operated the country store, several miles up the road. The Barnes family didn't have any love for the Petersons; both father and son, and even Jimmy's little sister, liked to poke fun at Cyrus whenever they saw him, calling him "dum-dum" or "weirdo." Luke had fought with Jimmy once, and Jimmy had won by giving Luke a bloody nose.

"It's him, all right," Abraham said.

Cyrus nodded his head, his eyes wide.

"Wonder how long he's been caught," Abraham mused.

"But it ain't *really* him, is it?" Luke said.

"Don't make no difference anymore," Abraham intoned in a near-whisper. "He done stopped breathin'."

They all looked and saw that the boy was dead.

"We all know that it's not really him," Cynthia said with assuredness. "And now that he's not alive anymore, he doesn't even look like Jimmy."

"True," Abraham agreed.

"He must have been sent to us like the others."

So they dug a grave and buried him, like any of the animals they had caught before—except instead of using the cemetery on their property, they dug a hole in the woods—and Cynthia recited incantations over his grave. His remains were buried deep and out of sight forever, except for a bottle of blood which Cynthia needed, and one of his front teeth—a dead man's tooth—which, according to a passage in a medieval grimoire she had read, was absolutely indispensable to the working of certain powerful spells. In fact, in one of his diaries Grandpa Barnes had written that no magic at all could be entirely dependable without the vital ingredient of a dead man's tooth.

When the children got back to the house for lunch, they told Mama what they had done. Luke started it by saying, "We caught something big today. And we took care of it, like you said."

A few weeks later, the second demon in the guise of a human was caught in a trap out in the same field. This one looked like Jimmy Peterson's sister. For a while it almost tricked them into not killing it. But Mama was behind them this time, and she wasn't fooled—she broke the demon's spell.

"Hit it!" she yelled. "I *told* you, they can take any form they want to! *Hit* it, Luke! Don't let it get the upper hand on you!"

The demon screamed and screamed, till Luke's shovel blade smacked into its face and skull. It fell down, and Abraham and Luke both kept beating it for a long time.

When it was dead, it didn't look like Jimmy Peterson's little sister anymore.

Copying Luke and Abraham, Cyrus took up the shovel and hit it, too.

"You did real good," said Mama. "Now Cyrus can make a coffin and we'll have a funeral."

When the thing was buried, Cynthia said the prayer over its grave: "Almighty Tetragrammaton, we ask thee to help us in the destruction of our enemies, as thou has done today. We pledge ourselves to thee, and will continue to be thy faithful servants. Whomsoever thou send to us, we shall destroy, knowing it is thy will. Amen."

CHAPTER 6

Nancy was afraid of the boys who had picked her up in their van. They both seemed a little wild. Or maybe they were just trying to impress her. They said they were fraternity brothers from some college in Massachusetts—and they were going to Fort Lauderdale for Easter. Thousands of kids would be swarming on the beaches, "having a ball"—according to Tom Riley and Hank Bennet. Tom, the driver, was sort of good looking, with light brown hair parted in the middle, long, sharply etched sideburns, and a touch of acne around his mouth and chin. His buddy, Hank, was a tall, lanky black, with a wary look in his eye and a protruding Adam's apple.

Nancy didn't say much, hoping they'd understand that she was not as free and easy as some girls. It was impossible to carry on any extended conversation, anyway, with the tape deck in the van blasting Rolling Stones music. Nancy liked her music loud, but the volume in the vehicle was so excessive she could envision the cilia in her ears bending like waves of grass in a strong wind; she had read you could permanently impair your hearing that way.

For better than an hour she had stood hitchhiking at an intersection near the outskirts of town. Cars kept passing her by, and each time she was terrified one might contain her mother or her stepfather. She kept her thumb out, looking awkward and feeling that way, for she had never hitchhiked before. Her suitcase was at her feet by the curb, along with her guitar in a leather case.

"Out of sight! You play guitar!" Tom had exclaimed when Nancy first climbed aboard.

She played clarinet in the band at school, but she didn't take any pride in it; instead, she prided herself on her folk singing. A few weeks ago she had entered the annual talent contest for seniors, singing a ballad about true love versus sexual love, self-consciously taking the edge off the understanding and sense of pathos in her voice, afraid of letting students and faculty know that she had personal experience with the song's subject matter. Still, she had won second prize. It meant more to her than her good grades or anything else she had achieved in high school. There was a message in the folk ballad she hoped had penetrated to her ex-boyfriend.

Where was she going to go, and what would she do with herself? Standing on the corner with her thumb out, she wanted to break down crying. By running away from home, she'd miss out on graduation. Could she get a diploma later? She didn't know. She had an older sister, Terri, who had gone off on her own to California a few years back to try to become an actress, and now she was working with a repertory theater group in San Francisco. Nancy supposed she should try to get to the Coast, too, to dump her troubles in her sister's lap and hope Terri wouldn't send her back home. She didn't want to face her stepfather ever again. But she was a minor, under eighteen. Couldn't the authorities make her go back to her mother if they caught up with her before her eighteenth birthday? If so, she would have to tell what had happened, and if her version was believed, she'd be responsible for wrecking her mother's marriage.

With these thoughts tormenting her, she was startled to see that a late-model green Cadillac had pulled over to the curb, and a man leaning across from the driver's side was pressing a button, making the window wind down. He was a fat, balding, middle-aged man in a plaid business suit who reminded her of her stepfather. "How far you goin', honey?" he called out, his voice low and hoarse, as if he had smoked too many cigarettes.

"C-California," Nancy replied uncertainly.

"That's quite a long trip. What sort of arrangements might we make if I agree to take you as far as six hundred miles of it?"

"What do you mean?"

"Don't play *coy* with me, young stuff. I'll make it simple for you. Three hundred miles today; then we share a motel room. Tomorrow another three hundred miles, another motel room . . . and we kiss each other good-bye in the morning with no hard feelings. That way your conscience is clear; you've paid your way. I'm only going as far as Detroit, but you'll be a good chunk closer to where you want to go. You headed for LA. or Frisco?"

"F-Frisco. "

"Better put some flowers in your hair," the man joked, chuckling coarsely.

"Mister, you better get out of here or I'll call a cop!" Nancy threatened. Then she added, ironically: "My stepfather is on the police force!"

The man sneered. "You smart young slut! If I had hair down to my ass and beads around my neck, you'd jump in here in heat and tear your clothes off!" He hit the gas pedal hard and peeled out, leaving Nancy alone by the curb, backing away, shaken.

Down the block in their van, Tom and Hank were stopped at a red light. Looking in the rearview mirror, Tom said, "Hey, Hank—the young chick is still back there on the corner. The guy in the Cadillac didn't pick her up. I'm going back for her."

"For Chrissakes! Forget it, Tom! There'll be plenty of chicks in Lauderdale. She'll probably tear open her blouse and threaten to yell rape to the nearest cop if we don't hand her all the money we got in our wallets."

"You worry too much. She's probably just a nice young chick who needs a lift. I—"

"C'mon, white boy," chided Hank sarcastically. "Don't be so *naïve*. Most of the time if a fine-looking piece like that has to go begging for something, it means she's in some kind of trouble—

either that, or she *is* trouble. Why you want to mess up a good vacation?"

The light changed to green and Tom executed an abrupt right turn instead of going straight ahead. Hank looked dismayed, but Tom ignored him, saying, "If *we* don't pick her up, she's liable to get picked up by some creep."

"All right, you're the driver. But I sure hope you ain't doin' somethin' *dumb.*"

As the van rounded the block, Nancy was standing once more with her thumb out, more timidly than before. Tom smiled brightly when he saw her there. Instead of stopping by the curb, he pulled into the lot behind her so she'd be on his side of the vehicle and he could talk to her without being obstructed by Hank.

"Hi!" Tom called out above the blare of music. "Need a lift?"

Warily, Nancy asked, "Didn't you go around the block once before?"

Tom grinned. "Yeah. I wanted to pick you up the first time. But you appeared to have your problem solved."

"Oh, sure, all my problems would've been solved for good. All I had to do was let that man take me to a motel. Is that what you're after, too?"

Angrily, Hank scoffed, "I told you, Tom—the chick's nothing but *trouble.*"

But Tom persisted, talking to Nancy with sincerity. "Look, me and Hank, we're not creeps. We give you a ride, you don't owe us anything. I'd hate to see you get picked up by a lunatic, that's all. We're heading down to Lauderdale."

"I wanted to go to my sister's place in California," said Nancy, wavering.

"Okay, let her *go,*" Hank blurted.

"Wait a minute!" Tom argued. Keeping his eyes on Nancy, he said, "Why don't you come down to Florida with us? Have a really good time for a few days. Lots of college kids down there. After Easter you should easily be able to catch a ride west with someone your own age."

"What makes you think so?"

"Kids'll be going back to college to finish out the term. A good many of them make the jaunt to Lauderdale from schools in the Midwest, and so on. You'll be able to check out a potential ride for a few days on a personal level—make sure it's somebody safe."

"Well . . ." Nancy hesitated, biting her lip, telling herself that if these two boys were decent, being with them was probably better than being totally on her own.

"Come on," Tom said, persuading her.

She made up her mind and got into the van.

Bert Johnson sat at the kitchen table over a cup of black coffee, while his wife prattled on and on about her experience at the hairdresser's. What she was saying made little impression on him. He was too worried about where Nancy might be and what she might do next. He should never have gone after her, whether she was leading him on or not. He had let the booze get hold of him. Now he could lose his marriage, his job, and his reputation—if Nancy opened her mouth about what had happened. Bert was wearing a small bandage on top of his forehead over the spot where his stepdaughter had clouted him with her portable radio, and he hoped the excuse he had ready would suffice when his wife asked about it.

Looking at herself in a mirror in the hallway, Harriet said, "So he cut my hair shoulder length, styled it a little differently, and frosted it less than last time. It's not as light as Nancy's, though. Where did you say she went? I had the impression she wanted to take your car to the mall."

"As far as I know, she *did* go to the mall," Bert said. "She wasn't here when I got home. One of her girl friends must have picked her up early."

Harriet went to the breakfast counter and poured herself a cup of coffee. "Probably she went with Patty. She's not dating anyone new, is she?"

Bert shrugged. "How in the world should I know? I can't pretend to keep track of that wild crowd she hangs around with sometimes."

Mrs. Johnson brought her cup of coffee to the table and sat down across from her husband. Putting in double cream and two sugars, she said, "I don't think Nancy and her crowd are particularly wild. In fact, they're pretty nice compared to many teenagers nowadays."

"Don't worry, they know what it's all about," Bert said, grimacing. "Some of them could teach you and me a wrinkle or two."

"Bert, whatever do you *mean?*" Harriet purred, the implied meanings in her husband's tone having aroused her sense of curiosity and scandal.

"Don't ask me to tell you, Harriet."

As he intended, this caused her to crease her brow and pout worriedly.

"Nancy isn't everything you think she is," he said, as if confessing it reluctantly.

"I think you had better explain yourself," she challenged.

"Well . . . I've been debating for a long time whether I ought to say anything. But I suppose it's best that you know. She pretends to be very sweet and innocent when you're around, but it's only an act. She's been flaunting her little body at me, rubbing up against me whenever she gets an excuse, and I've been trying to avoid her because I have no idea what her game is. I think she wants to break you and me up."

While he was talking, Harriet's expression had gone to disbelief and shock, and for a long moment she stared at her husband, stunned, not able to find words to express herself. Her voice came out finally in a near-whisper. "Bert . . . are you saying what I think you're saying—that Nancy has tried to seduce you?"

Skillfully, he backed off from his accusations, rendering them more believable. "I don't think she wants it to go that far. Maybe she's just testing her sex appeal . . . or something . . . in a juvenile way. I have no doubt that she's still a virgin."

Harriet drew in a deep breath. Then: "I happen to know that

she's not. She was heartbroken when her boyfriend dumped her . . . and I happened to overhear one of her phone conversations that made it pretty clear she had given herself to him."

Bert shook his head sadly.

"She won't confide in me," Harriet said. "I have to learn everything by accident. Not that I expected her to remain a virgin—she's too pretty. And this isn't the nineteenth century. Sex is out in the open, and our children grow up too fast, way too fast. What was I supposed to do with Nancy, keep her locked in her room?"

"I'm afraid it's too late for that already," Bert lamented. "It could be that she resents the fact I'm not her real father. Maybe she wants to destroy me—and get back at you, too, Harriet, at the same time."

"Bert, you must be imagining things! I'm not going to believe this nonsense for one minute. After all, Nancy is my daughter— my flesh and blood."

"All right, Harriet, if it makes you feel better to bury your head in the sand. Why do you suppose I've had to start hitting the bottle again? It's because of your daughter. Till now I couldn't bring myself to break it to you. It's such a terrible thing to have to face. So I've been trying to shield you from it . . . and doing my best to stay away from her. I was even glad that she wasn't here when I got home."

Harriet did not reply, her mind in turmoil. Could it be that Nancy was actually the way Bert described? Harriet had been hurt deeply by her first husband, because she had closed her eyes to his infidelities in the face of evidence, intuitive and otherwise, that should have convinced her something was wrong. She was always too trusting, too ready to accept people at face value, especially those close to her; she expected from them the same honesty that she gave. After her divorce, she had learned not to be disappointed by the worst in people when it finally came to light. But her own daughter? The idea of Nancy doing the things Bert said was repugnant, unreal, no matter how hard Harriet tried to allow for the possibility that it might be true. Because of being a working mother for so many years, Harriet didn't feel that she understood her daughter as well as she should.

If push came to shove, who should she believe—Nancy or Bert? She didn't want to lose Bert. Before he came into the picture, loneliness and penny-pinching had taken their toll on Harriet's confidence and self-respect. Bert represented companionship and security for her old age. Offspring couldn't be depended upon; look at Terri, off on her own in California already, and maybe a letter from her once every six months—unless she found herself needing money, and then she suddenly knew how to write. This was the first installment on the reward for working hard to raise two daughters all those years, without a husband and father in the house.

Well, Harriet thought, she'd have to talk to Nancy about this and get her side of the story. Perhaps it was all an innocent misunderstanding of some sort. Looking up at her husband, Harriet noticed his bandage and inquired solicitously, "Bert, did you get hurt on duty last night?"

Glad that she had thought of it herself, Bert used her lead to follow through on the excuse he had planned all along. "I had a run-in with a punk who was drunk and disorderly. Not too serious of an incident, really. Al and I got the cuffs on him and hauled him in."

"Did Al get hurt, too?"

"Are you kidding? Does Al ever have bad luck? Not a scratch on him, as usual."

She reached out and put her hand on his. "Bert . . . you and I haven't had much of a sex life lately. Could it be because of what you've been going through with Nancy?"

From the moment this explanation had occurred to her, she had clutched at it, willing to believe in it rather than blame herself for a failure in the bedroom.

Bert pressed her fingers in his and gazed at her balefully. "What do *you* think? I love you, honey, and I don't want to lose you. One of these days Nancy might come to you with some wild stories, trying to put the blame on me. I just want you to be aware of my side of it first, so nothing can ever come between us. Naturally, we have to give Nancy love and understanding. But the important thing is for you and me to stick together."

Overcome by Bert's sincerity, Harriet's eyes smarted and a tear rolled down her cheek. Even if Bert was partially to blame for this crisis, she didn't want to lose either him or her daughter.

By this time Nancy, Tom, and Hank had crossed the Pennsylvania border into West Virginia. Hank was smoking a cigarette. Nancy was sitting rather morosely in the back seat of the van, still overcome by her troubles, although Tom had been trying to cheer her up. Reaching to the dash to turn down the volume, he commented happily, "Dig all these mountains without a trace of green on them yet, except for a scattering of pine—I love it! Tonight we'll be camping in the Blue Ridge Mountains, maybe on the Shenandoah River. Do you know the song 'Shenandoah,' Nancy? Maybe you can sing it for us. Then the next day or the day after we'll all see the scenery turn greener and greener . . . the farther south we go . . . all the way to good old Florida."

"Goin' where the weather suits my clothes," Hank drawled.

"I'm staying in my bathing suit the whole time!" Tom said exuberantly.

"Say somethin'," said Hank, turning to peer inquisitively at Nancy. "We give you a ride and you put a damper on things."

"I'm just tired," she apologized.

"Man, how tired you gonna be by the time we go another thousand miles?" Hank challenged.

"I'm hungry," said Tom, changing the subject.

The speed limit slowed to thirty-five; they had come into a rural hamlet in southern West Virginia. Hank turned the rock music up loud as the three youths sized up the town they were cruising through. The place was called Cherry Hill—one more in a succession of colorfully named West Virginia towns like Man, Cabin Creek, Hundred, and Nitro. Cherry Hill had a large general store, a feed store, several rough-looking saloons, and a place that sold mining equipment. People walking on the narrow main street all seemed to be dressed as farmers, miners, or hunters. Parked outside the saloons and stores were several pickup trucks with racks full of rifles and shotguns mounted in their rear windows.

"Wow! What a haven for rednecks!" Tom said. "We better watch ourselves here, Hank."

"Why?"

"Some of these hicks would just as soon blow us away as look at us."

"You been seein' too many movies. My parents came up from Tennessee. They said the South ain't nowhere near as mean as it's portrayed."

"Still, I don't think we should try anything," Tom said, and Nancy's ears perked up as she wondered what he had in mind.

Hank told Tom, "Sometimes you're a chicken-shit, you know that? Nothing out of line ever happens in a one-horse town like this. If you're smart and you got balls, you can get away with damn near anything."

Made extremely apprehensive by this kind of talk, Nancy asked, "What would you want to get away with, Hank?"

Glancing at her sideways, he said, "Anything. I mean—" He caught himself and fell silent for a moment, then said to Tom, "You gotta realize some of these hick places don't even keep their deputies on duty after midnight."

"What *is* this all about?" Nancy demanded.

Haltingly, Tom explained, afraid of the impression his explanation might make on Nancy. "I might as well tell you, as long as you're going to be riding with us. Me and Hank . . . well . . . we're not exactly what you could call rich. Hank has a football scholarship, but it doesn't pay his full tuition, and I have to struggle by on what my parents give me, plus what I earn waiting on tables in the fraternity dining room. So we sat down and figured out a careful budget before we left campus. If we paid for our gas, we wouldn't have enough money to buy food, and if we bought food, then we wouldn't have money to pay for gas. So we made up our minds we'd just have to steal groceries all the way from Massachusetts to Florida. That's how we've been makin' it. If you don't want to stick with us now that you know, we'll let you out and you can hitch another ride."

"After you talked me into going to Florida instead of California!" Nancy complained in exasperation.

"How much bread you got on you?" Hank inquired sharply.

"Uh . . . fourteen dollars."

"Certainly not enough to feed yourself all the way to Frisco."

"Nope. But . . ."

"Then you have to steal," Tom concluded. "And if you *have* to, then it isn't a sin."

To Tom, Hank said, "Did you spot any lawmen so far?"

"Uh-uh."

Nancy slumped in her seat, wrestling with the moral implications of what had been discussed. She was just beginning to like Tom and Hank and feel safe with them. And now this. She had little doubt, though, that it was only one of a series of scary adjustments she'd have to make now that she had left home.

"Here's a nice grocery store made to order," Hank said, showing how much he relished the discovery by emitting a low, throaty chuckle. He was pointing at a chain food-store on the righthand side of the road, and Tom pulled over and parked the van with the engine running.

"You could help us pull this off," Hank said to Nancy.

"You don't have to if you don't want to," Tom stated emphatically, turning to face her after flashing a glance at Hank.

"But if you stick with us without doin' your share, you're gonna be eatin' stolen food, anyway," Hank pointed out.

A few minutes later, Hank and Nancy entered the grocery store, sauntering past the checkout counters. She wheeled the shopping cart down an aisle to begin shopping. "Let's make this a real spree," Hank said with a mischievous grin, then started tossing items into the cart. Joining in the lark after a moment of panicky hesitation, Nancy soon got caught up in the swing of things, and it was strangely liberating. She and Hank piled their cart high with anything and everything they could grab off the shelves—meat, cereal, cocoa, eggs, butter, bread, cheese, condiments, potato chips, pretzels—whatever struck their fancy. They found themselves laughing uproariously and tossing things back and forth to each other as they sped down the aisles weaving around regular customers who stood and gawked.

The cart filled, Hank and Nancy wheeled over to the check-out counter. The woman behind the checkout counter, a prim-looking old biddy, checked, tallied, and bagged their selections, ringing them up and holding out her hand for money. "Just a minute, I want to return this cart," Nancy said.

Meanwhile, Hank had picked up two armloads of groceries and was already moving toward the exit. Wheeling her way through the checkout aisle, Nancy pushed the empty cart into an area where it would temporarily obstruct pursuit by the woman behind the counter, then snatched up the remaining bag of groceries and ran behind Hank out through the automatic door and toward the van, which Tom had kept waiting outside, doors open and engine still running. The woman screamed and hollered for the store manager as Nancy and Hank made their escape.

They piled into the van on the run, strewing stolen groceries all over the back of the vehicle. The van lurched out and began speeding away. But immediately a siren started wailing—a police car was in pursuit.

"Gas it!" Hank yelled.

Nancy cowered in the back seat, trying belatedly to get her seat belt fastened.

Hitting sixty miles per hour, the van left the outskirts of Cherry Hill, attempting to outrace the police siren.

They were on a rare straight section of two-lane blacktop, heading into sharp curves. Nancy screamed and Hank yelled, "Look out!" because Tom was going too fast to make it. But he didn't attempt the curves. Instead, he careened off, humping and bumping into a farmer's field. A dirt road ran through the field and Tom got on it and there were fewer bone-jarring bumps. The police car still followed, some distance behind. When Tom caught sight of it in the rearview mirror, it spurred him to go faster. The dirt road had a hard-packed surface, but there were plenty of bends and twists. Still, Tom barely slowed down. Whoever was driving the police car was more cautious, for the police were not in such close pursuit as they had been before.

The road wound through a valley of poor, rundown farms, few and far between. In a blur, Nancy watched unpainted barns and farmhouses flashing by every once in a while among the trees, foliage, collapsed fences, and branches that sometimes whipped against her window because the road was so narrow and Tom kept swerving from one side to the other in his effort to go fast and still control the vehicle. Every once in a while there would be a narrow turn-off, but they'd shoot past it too quickly to do anything about it. Finally, Tom took a chance and slowed down. When a turn-off came up, he took it, hoping to lose the cops. As soon as he was around the bend, he gunned it, hoping they wouldn't be able to spot his dust. In a little while the sound of the siren seemed farther away. Tom kept driving as fast as possible for a few more minutes. Finally, he slowed to normal speed, looked over at Hank, and burst out laughing. Hank and Nancy laughed, too. The laugh felt cleaner and fresher than anything Nancy had experienced in her life. Was this the joy of thievery? The hard-driving chase had been terribly frightening. But now that they had gotten away clean, a sense of exhilaration set in. They laughed their heads off, not wanting to stop. As they began to recover, Tom turned to Hank, momentarily taking his eyes off the road.

"Wow! What a rush! I'd love to have been with you two in the store. I—"

"Tom! Look out!"

As Nancy screamed, Tom swerved the van to narrowly avoid hitting a man at the edge of the dirt road. The man, large and brawny in farmers' bibbed coveralls, had stepped out into the van's path, and he was carrying some sort of long, bulky bundle wrapped in a soiled blanket. As the van swerved, the man ducked back into the cover of woods from whence he came. He continued to stare stolidly after the van, still supporting the bundle in his arms.

In the van, Tom said, "Damn! I almost hit that guy! Whew!" Perspiring, he wiped the back of his hand across his forehead.

"He was carrying something," Hank said. "Did you see that?"

Tom chuckled nervously. "I was lucky I saw him at all. Thanks for yelling, Nancy."

She ran her tongue over dry lips, then spoke in hushed, anxious tones. "There was something creepy about him. I got a look at his face and he seemed to be grinning, even when it looked like you were surely going to run him over. I swear, he had some kind of strange smile on his face. And I think I saw a shoe sticking out from under his blanket." She shuddered from her imaginings.

Hank turned around and laughed at her. "Naw! He was just a big farmer with a bundle. You're shook up, girl. Your mind's playing tricks on you. Soon as we find a good place to camp, we'll smoke some grass to loosen you up."

Nancy stared out the side window, mulling this over. She had tried marijuana once, with no results; she had failed to get high. She wasn't particularly against trying it again. But in the company of two strange boys? How loose might they expect her to get?

The man with the bundle watched the van going away, stirring up dust, disappearing around a thickly wooded bend in the distance. Then he stepped ploddingly back into the middle of the road. He was a broad, beefy man with a leering smile on his face. A corner of the soiled blanket fell away from his large bundle, revealing the lower part of a bare leg, and one foot wearing a red high-heeled shoe. The man continued to stare down the road, in the direction of where the van disappeared. Blood ran down the calf of the dangling leg and dripped off the tip of the red shoe.

CHAPTER 7

They parked the van in a field by a stream and camped for the night. They went through the bags full of stolen groceries, delighted with the pile of goodies now that they had a chance to really look it over. "We won't have to steal anything for another few days," Hank said. Nancy was glad to hear it, and she helped Tom separate out the perishables, like milk, eggs, and cheese, and pack them into a Coleman ice chest in the back of the van. In the last waning half-hour of dusk, the two boys gathered dry twigs and fallen timber and built a small campfire. Then all three had a supper of ham-and-cheese sandwiches and hot cocoa.

Afterward, Hank rolled several joints, lit one, and passed it to Nancy without a word as he held in his drag. She didn't feel like arguing, so she took it and inhaled deeply. Noticing her slight hesitation, Tom said, "You ever smoke grass before?"

Still holding in the smoke, she nodded her head yes as she handed Tom the joint. She didn't tell him that she had not succeeded in getting high and didn't expect to this time. Tom dragged on the joint, then passed it to Hank and it kept going around till it was finished. Then Hank lit another one and passed it. "This is real good dope," Tom said sagely.

Nancy giggled wildly and realized with a shock that she was stoned.

Tom and Hank looked at her knowingly and laughed, too.

"It's so nice to relax around the fire at home after a hard day of shopping and being chased by creditors," Hank said, and his comment seemed hilarious.

The threesome laughed and laughed. Tom exploded a lungful of smoke that his laughing forced out of him, as he once more handed the second joint to Nancy. It was so short it burned her fingers.

"Gimme the roach," Hank said. And taking an alligator clip from his pocket, he used it as a roachholder so they could continue smoking the thing down to nothing. When it was too small to hold between his lips, Hank held the glowing remnant next to his nostrils and sniffed the hot vapors. Then he lit the third joint and handed it to Nancy. Really stoned now, and enjoying the euphoria of total abandon, she continued to take drags every time the joint came her way.

"I got the hungries," Hank said, his eyes crinkling in the orange glow of the campfire as he rubbed his stomach and giggled.

All three were ravenously hungry because of the marijuana, and they went into the back of the van and brought out crackers, jelly, peanut butter, apples, bananas, potato chips, and pretzels—and root beer to wash it all down. For a long time they ate, trying the peanut butter and jelly on crackers, potato chips, pretzels, apple slices, and chunks of banana. Because they were stoned, it was all wildly delicious.

Every once in a while Tom or Hank tossed a log on the fire.

"Beats the hell out of bein' back on campus," Hank said. "When we get back it'll be time to start crammin' for finals."

"Oh, what a bummer!" moaned Tom. "Did you have to remind me, Hank? Huh?"

"What's your major?" Nancy asked.

"Psychology," Tom told her. "Let's change the subject. Sing something for us, why don't you?"

Feeling uninhibited, Nancy got out her guitar and sang a black spiritual, "All My Trials." Tom thought she sang wonderfully and enjoyed watching the seriousness and the emotion in her young face; he was beginning to be attracted to her romantically. Hank noticed this, and for some reason it irked him; he and Tom had set out for Lauderdale to have a ball, not get hung up on one chick. If Tom lost his head over this girl, as he was giving every evidence of doing, it was clear to Hank that their trip would be much less of an enjoyable adventure; Hank would be on his own, unpaired, looking for strangers on the beach to get to know and get involved with. And they would mostly be *white* strangers. Although he told himself to stay cool, Hank couldn't help but feel that in some unplanned, accidental, and unforeseen way his buddy, Tom, was in danger of copping out on him.

Strumming on her guitar, Nancy finished the last chorus of the spiritual:

> If religion was a thing that money could buy,
> The rich would live and the poor would die,
> All my trials, Lord, soon be over,
> All my trials, Lord, soon be over,
> All my trials, Lord, soon be over.

Letting her voice trail off with the concluding chords, she leaned her guitar against a tree and sat back self-consciously, wondering what they had thought of her singing. She was pretty sure Tom liked it, but she had no idea about Hank.

"Nancy . . . you sing nice," Tom complimented.

She smiled and thanked him, feeling pleased with herself.

"I don't think you got much right to be singin' a *slave* song," Hank jeered angrily.

"Come on, Hank!" Tom snapped back. "Don't start getting paranoid on us."

Hank eyed Tom coldly, lighting up a regular cigarette instead of another joint. "Who's paranoid? Not me. I just said I don't think a white girl ought to be a singin' a slave song, that's all." He made a great show of being calm and aloof by laying his head back and slowly blowing a chorus of smoke rings. "Black people paid their dues in that area, not whites. A white chick like Nancy can't have the *least* idea of the feelin's behind the black spirituals that deal with slavery."

Tom shook his head in disagreement. "That's pure bullshit, Hank. What's gotten into you? Every time something's eating you that you don't want to be up front with, you cover it with silly-ass rhetoric. Next you'll be telling me an Italian can't sing an Irish ballad."

"You don't like me, do you?" Nancy said to Hank.

Hank looked over at her. With an air of having made a very shrewd deduction, he told her, "It dawned on me that you got to be runnin' away from home. And if so, me and poor, innocent Tom are accessories. How old are you?"

"Nineteen." But she immediately gave up on the lie. "No, I'm seventeen . . . almost eighteen."

"Sure you ain't sixteen, or *fif*teen?"

"Leave her alone, dammit, Hank!" Tom shouted.

"Shut up, white boy. One of us has to have the sense to find out how much hot water we may be in. You ever hear of the Mann Act?"

"Come off it!"

"Transportin' a minor across state lines. Better think about it, Tom. We could have the F.B.I. on our asses."

"Bullshit, Hank! I know you want to get into law school, but you're not there yet. Now come off it." To Nancy, Tom said, "Hank gets mean sometimes when he's stoned, but it doesn't last, so don't worry about it."

But Nancy wanted to speak for herself. "If you're uptight about me, Hank, you don't need to keep me around. I wouldn't want to be a burden to you. We can go our separate ways in the morning." But she didn't get through it without crying; a tear rolled down her cheek, glistening in the firelight.

Tom came to Nancy and put his arm around her. "Hank doesn't mean it, Nancy, honest. Dammit, Hank, tell her you don't mean it. Now you've gone and made her feel bad."

"I *do* mean it. We hardly know this chick. I warned you she'd be trouble."

Crying, Nancy got to her feet and headed off into the woods by herself, picking her way along the path by moonlight.

Tom jumped to his feet, too. "You're the one who's trouble, Hank. I wish you'd learn to keep your big mouth shut. Tomorrow when you're not stoned you won't even remember what a hassle you caused."

Chasing after Nancy, Tom found her sitting by herself at the edge of the stream. He stopped behind her, a few feet away, looking down at her. She did not turn around to face him. "Mind if I sit with you?" he asked.

She flipped a pebble out into the water, watching it splash and ripple. Since she still hadn't said anything, Tom took a few steps toward her and laid a comforting hand on her shoulder. "Wouldn't it help if you told someone your problem?"

"What makes you think I've got one?" she blurted defiantly.

"If you haven't got one, there's no need to talk about it," he admitted. Then he sat down beside her. She kept staring straight ahead. Tom told her, "I just want you to know, Hank really isn't a bad guy. He'll let you stay with us, you'll see. Everything will be okay in the morning."

"I don't want to be a burden," Nancy said quietly but determinedly. "I just want to get to my sister's house in California. And I'd rather not come between you and your friend. You'll get along better without me."

"That's not true at all," Tom insisted. "You've been helpful and . . . and . . . fun to be with. I *want* you to stay with us, Nancy."

She didn't know what to say. Despite efforts to the contrary, she had started crying again. Tom opened his mouth to tell her not to cry, and at that moment both he and Nancy heard a noise from back in the woods which caused them both to whirl around.

Tom shouted, "Hank! Is that you?"

There were more sounds, of someone tramping through the brush, and suddenly the footsteps stopped. Tom and Nancy listened, getting a bit frightened. Tom called out once again: "Hank! *Hank!* Is that *you?*"

No one answered. On their feet now, Tom and Nancy peered

all around. The moonlight could not penetrate some of the denser patches of woods. They strained their eyes to see into the foliage, from where the footstep sounds had seemingly come. Just when it appeared that the surrounding woods had fallen completely and permanently silent, a low, throaty chortle came from somewhere and Nancy jumped and grabbed onto Tom.

"Probably some kind of animal," he said, trying to be reassuring. "A hyena, maybe, if they have them around here. Or else Hank's playing tricks. Come on, Nancy, let's get back to the campfire and turn in. We'll want to be on the road early tomorrow, and I hope you'll decide to still travel with us. I like having you around. I mean it."

Feeling scared and needing the comfort of his nearness, Nancy allowed him to escort her back along the path in the moonlight, away from the stream.

Peering from behind some branches, the man in bibbed coveralls watched them go, grinning. He liked the girl real well. She was very pretty, and he couldn't wait to look at her up close and touch her and feel her long blonde hair.

Bert and Harriet Johnson were up late worrying about Nancy—for different reasons. It was almost time for Bert to go out on the midnight shift, so he was in his uniform. Harriet was in pajamas and bathrobe. She had waited until after the eleven o'clock news, then had placed a few phone calls to Nancy's friends with unsatisfactory results; no one could shed any light on her whereabouts.

When Bert picked up his lunch bucket and came over to kiss Harriet good-bye, she said, "Something happened between you and my daughter, didn't it? You've been lying to me, Bert, and I want to know why. Why didn't Nancy come home?"

Believing firmly that righteous anger was his best defense, Bert exploded: "How the hell should *I* know? I told you the kid isn't as innocent as you make her out to be. She could be out carrying on someplace."

"It's not like her to stay out *this* late without phoning. I'm worried about her and I think you know something you're not telling."

Bert looked hurt and insulted. "For Chrissakes! You've got a fantastic imagination! I've got to get down to the station. I'll check the blotter when I get there, if it'll make you feel any better. If anything's happened to Nancy that the police know about, I'll get the information. By the time I call you, she'll probably be safe in bed."

"I certainly hope so," said Harriet, relenting.

Bert kissed her good-bye and went out, slamming the door.

Harriet went to the liquor cabinet, poured herself a good stiff drink of bourbon, and gulped half of it down. She carried the remainder with her into the bedroom, where she sat on the edge of the bed, feeling wrung out. It looked as if she might have to choose between her daughter and her husband, and she didn't feel capable. She had never been a strong person, and this sort of emotional strain was too much for her. She downed the rest of the bourbon, set the glass on the nightstand, and noticed a bottle of sleeping pills there. Snatching up the bottle immediately, she shook out some capsules and swallowed them, then lay on her back on top of the covers, a night-light burning in the bedroom.

She was jarred out of the drug-induced sleep by the ringing of the phone. She groped for it and answered groggily: "Hello? Nancy?"

The voice on the other end of the line said, "This is your husband, Bert."

"Oh, Bert," Harriet said, coming to her senses, "have you any news?"

He said, "I just heard from Nancy. She says she's at one of her girl friend's houses. She's staying over."

"Which girl friend?"

"I don't know. She must've said, but I don't remember. Guess I didn't catch it. You do feel relieved, though, don't you, honey?"

"Yes, of course. But why didn't she call me at home?"

"She said she *tried* to call. Claimed she must've dialed the wrong number. But I think that was just an excuse, to make us think she tried to get in touch earlier. She was probably in the middle of something—you know how teen-agers are—and never even thought about phoning till late."

"Oh, I suppose so. Bert . . . thanks for letting me know. I'm sorry I was angry with you."

"No problem. Good-bye now, honey. See you in the morning."

Bert hung up the pay phone, satisfied that his lies had worked to confuse the issue, at the very least. If Nancy had run away from home—which is what he suspected, for he had found her suitcase and some of her belongings missing—then tomorrow when she still didn't show up he'd say that obviously her phone call of this evening had been a trick designed to throw him and her mother off the track. In the meantime Harriet would calm down and stop badgering him. If Nancy was merely staying with her girl friend, and had phoned him about it as he had indicated, then how could something bad have happened between them? Bert's only problem would be if Nancy chickened out and came back home, but by then he'd have strengthened his position and sown so much confusion that Harriet wouldn't know who to believe.

Bert hoped Nancy would stay away for good. That way his position would be safest. When he thought about what he had done he felt ashamed, threatened, and frightened. If Nancy ever brought charges, even if he were acquitted, the scandal and gossip would be enough to wreck him.

Not long after sunrise, Nancy awakened at the campsite. She had spent the night curled up in a sleeping bag Tom had loaned her. The morning was cold and damp, the nylon bag wet with dew. Tom and Hank were still asleep in their sleeping bags, not far from the now-dead campfire.

Nancy eased herself out of her bag and moved quietly away from the campsite, alone. She walked along the path for quite a ways, till she got to the edge of the stream where she and Tom were last night. She hunkered by the stream, contemplating her reflection in the water. Her hair was matted and damp; she wished she had brought a comb, brush, and towel along so she could wash her face and fix her hair. She still hadn't made up her mind whether to stay with Tom and Hank or chance it on her own. In a pensive, indecisive mood, she picked up a few pebbles and dropped them into the stream, letting them fall out of her hand slowly, one by one.

Back at the campsite, Tom and Hank were still sound asleep in their sleeping bags. They did not hear the footsteps sneaking up on them through the woods. Finally, both Tom and Hank were prodded in the ribs by heavy brown boots—and they jumped up, startled, to see gun barrels staring them in the face. They had been jarred out of slumber by two sheriff's deputies brandishing service revolvers.

"Hold it, fellows!" one of the deputies barked. "Don't make any foolish moves. Keep your hands visible."

The second one said, "If either of you tries to reach into his sleeping bag for a gun, I won't wait to find out what you're reaching for. I'll just shoot."

In a shaky voice, Tom asked, "What's this all about, Officer?" In the back of his mind he figured it must have something to do with the stolen groceries.

"Shut up!" the man covering Tom snapped, pointing his pistol at Tom's face.

The other deputy suddenly gave Hank a savage kick in the ribs. The boy screamed and writhed in agony, imprisoned in his sleeping bag, while both deputies chuckled. "A bug in a rug!" one of them sneered, and they both went on laughing. Tom stared up at them, wide-eyed and frightened. The deputy standing over him was tall and powerfully built, his tight lips and piercing black eyes set hard and mean. The second deputy was shorter and more wiry, with a perpetual scowl on his face. Both wore tan uniforms with heavy brown boots and wide-brimmed hats. The tall one had sergeant's stripes on his sleeve; the other was a corporal.

"Where's the girl?" the corporal demanded harshly. "You killed her, didn't you?"

"Filthy sadistic scum!" the sergeant added.

The short, wiry corporal lashed out with his boot, dealing Tom a kick to his ribs. Tom yelled in pain and terror as Hank continued to moan softly, staring up at the deputies in scared bewilderment.

The sergeant planted his boot squarely on Tom's chest and aimed his gun between Tom's eyes. Tom whimpered, still hurting badly from the kick in the ribs. "Shut up, goddamn you!" the deputy warned. "Stop making a spectacle of yourself, or I swear I'll blow your brains to bloody pieces!"

The corporal chuckled softly. "Maybe they think they can pin us with a police brutality rap. Niggers especially take the cake in that department, *don't* they?" Emphasizing his point, he prodded Hank with his boot in the sore spot where he had kicked him.

"These filthy scum don't deserve humane treatment," said the sergeant. His foot still on Tom's chest, he applied pressure, demanding: "What did you do with the girl, you maniac? Where'd you hide her body?" He stepped up onto Tom, putting all his weight on the boot that was pressing into the boy's chest. Tom gritted his teeth to stop from crying out but let loose a slight whimper despite his efforts, making the sergeant angry. "Don't you scream, I told you! I'll blow your fuckin' brains out!" He jammed his revolver up against Tom's forehead, threatening to pull the trigger.

Grinning meaningfully, the corporal said, "Maybe we ought to drag them back in the woods one at a time, and question them separately."

"Good idea. Which one should be first? Eeny, meeny, miny . . ." He waved the barrel of his weapon back and forth from Tom to Hank. "Catch a . . . nigger . . . by the . . ."

"Wait!" Hank cried. "Can't we talk about this? We didn't kill anybody. There was a girl *with* us, but she must've cut out in the middle of the night."

Through his pain, Tom said, "All we're guilty of is stealing a few bags of groceries."

The corporal chortled exuberantly. "Oh-ho! A confession!

Trying to. get off lightly by admitting to a lighter offense, no doubt. Well, it won't work. We've heard that ploy before, right, sergeant?"

The sergeant pursed his lips thoughtfully. He said, "I'm tired of playing games with you two. We *know* you're guilty. Your van was spotted near the place where that poor girl was found raped and stabbed to death. You can't lie your way out of it. We have to make you pay, and we don't much care if we bring you in alive or dead."

"We're entitled to a trial," Hank insisted. "We're *innocent*!" He knew why they were picking on him, he thought, but it didn't make any sense for them to be so down on Tom.

The short, wiry one gestured with his revolver. "Get your asses up out of those sleeping bags—pronto! Which one are we going to question first, sergeant?"

Tom pleaded, talking desperately: "No! I just remembered— we saw a big heavy man in farmers' bibbed coveralls. I almost ran him down; he was standing right in the road. He was carrying a heavy bundle—it could've been a body. It *must've* been one. Is he the one who turned us in? If so, you can see he was trying to divert suspicion from himself. My father's a lawyer back in Boston. He—"

But neither deputy apparently believed Tom's story, for they both started chuckling. The chuckling turned into derisive laughter as Tom and Hank crawled out of their sleeping bags and stood in front of the dead campfire looking hurt and helpless.

Nancy, who had come back from the stream, was hiding behind some bushes about fifty yards away, observing what was going on. At first she had been alarmed by noises of scuffling and arguing coming from the direction of the campsite. Then when she saw the two policemen, she was afraid they were out to arrest her and bring her home. So she stayed in concealment, hoping to learn more about the situation. To her amazement, she saw Tom and Hank being handcuffed.

The corporal seized Hank's handcuffed wrists and yanked him in an about-face. Hank trembled, feeling totally at these unreasonable men's mercy and reaching a point of panic. All at once he started to run, trying with all his energy to get away. The corporal crouched, sighted, and fired twice. Hank crumpled and hit the turf, sliding on his chest and face, then lying very still.

Tom yelled, "You killed him, you stupid redneck! You didn't need to do that! We're innocent! *Innocent,* goddamn you!"

His face was a mask of rage and anguished helplessness, and bitter tears rolled down Tom's cheeks. He made a move to go to Hank, but the sergeant made him stay in one place by jabbing him severely with his revolver.

Standing over Hank's body, the corporal gave a long glance back at Tom, a faint wry smile on his face. Then he took careful aim at Hank's head and squeezed the trigger. The loud report all but blotted out Tom's scream. Then there was silence.

After a moment the corporal said, "I warned the spade he could get his head blown off. But he had to try me. Serves him right, the young punk."

Dazed and rapidly going to pieces, Tom mumbled, "You must be crazy . . . crazy . . ."

"Come off it!" the sergeant barked in his loudest tone yet. "Your buddy was resisting arrest. You want to try the same? I guarantee you you'll end up the same way, too. You ready to confess to raping and killing that girl? I knew her and her family, see. I'm willing to go to any lengths to bring in her killers. People in this county will turn their heads to any irregularities, as long as they feel they got justice."

Practically screaming, Tom said, "But I tell you I'm innocent! What proof could you possibly have? This is all so cockeyed, I don't understand it. Let me call a lawyer. *Please!* One innocent life has already been lost."

Still watching from her hiding place, Nancy was terribly frightened. Rooted there by fear, she was not about to show herself. She wanted to do something to help Tom, but she was powerless, at a total loss. And she hadn't heard enough of what was said to really understand the situation.

The corporal came over to Tom and jammed his gun into the

boy's abdomen. "You ready to confess, or do we have to beat it out of you?"

Tom's dilemma was beyond his comprehension. He spoke weakly, in. a near-whisper. "You might as well kill me, too. That's what you're going to do, aren't you?"

The sergeant replied sternly. "Well, we know you're guilty, so actual confession is merely a formality. The fact that your partner tried to run doesn't make *you* look very innocent. Me and the corporal like to save the taxpayers money every place we can."

"Yep," agreed the corporal. Again he prodded Tom with his gun. He jammed the weapon hard, over and over, into the boy's ribs, making him cry out painfully. "Why don't you run, too?" he suggested diabolically. "How much of this kind of treatment could you take before you decide to run?"

The sergeant pointed his revolver at Tom, saying to the corporal, "Step aside. Gimme a clear shot."

Tom trembled and closed his eyes. Without further ado, the sergeant pulled the trigger, shooting Tom in the chest. As the boy sagged and fell, the sergeant fired again . . . then again. Tom lay on the ground not far from Hank, both bodies bloody messes.

From her hiding place, Nancy screamed and started running in total hysterical panic. Both deputies wheeled and spotted her simultaneously. The corporal instantly crouched and aimed, ready to fire. But the sergeant stopped him, shouting, "No! Take the girl alive! We want *her* alive! Don't get carried away now! After her!"

The two deputies started running, trying to catch up with Nancy. She plunged into the woods on the far side of the clearing, running and running for all she was worth. The two deputies kept coming after her, at a steady trot, as if they were not particularly worried that there was any real chance of her getting away. They kept plodding after her relentlessly, waiting for her to tire herself out. Every time she looked back they appeared to be just over her shoulder; she couldn't seem to lose them, though she tried to put her last ounce of energy into it, out of fear and desperation.

Nancy broke out of the patch of woods onto a dirt road, a section of the one the van had traversed yesterday. She ran down the
road, looking behind her now and then to see how close her pur-
suers were, screaming for help now and then and looking frantically for someplace to hide.

When the two deputies got out onto the road, Nancy seemed
to have gained on them, but she had merely disappeared around
a bend. For a moment this confused them as to which way she
may have gone, and they halted, peering up and down. Then, realizing she couldn't have gone right or she'd be visible on the
straightaway, they took off running to their left, toward the bend
in the dirt road. They put on speed, loping along, making up lost
distance. Both men were now breathing hard, but their pace was
still relentless.

Nancy spotted a red brick house with white columns, set far
back off the road. She ran across the vast lawn and up onto the
veranda and beat fiercely on the front door and tried to open it.
But it was locked. She yelled and yelled for someone to come
and let her in. No one answered. She ran around the side of the
house and up the steps of the back porch. In a panic, she yanked
at the door, which was stuck, but it finally gave way and swung
open. Nancy dashed into the house, slamming the door behind
her and locking it with a sliding brass bolt.

She found herself in the kitchen. She looked all around,
breathing hard, amazed at its vastness, taking in at a glance the
enormous Colonial fireplace. Then her eyes fell on a huge mahogany highboy filling one corner of the kitchen. Taking quick
strides toward the piece of furniture, she pulled open a drawer
and in her haste overturned it. Silverware clattered out onto the
floor, making a tremendous racket, hurting Nancy as it struck her
on the legs and feet. She dropped the drawer with a loud, resounding crash. Nancy stooped and rummaged feverishly among
the silverware on the floor—but to her dismay there were no
knives, only forks and spoons. This was as odd at it was
disappointing. She needed something with which to defend herself.

Pivoting sharply, she headed for the front of the house, crossing the threshold of a large, elegant dining room—only to be brought up short upon seeing a young woman in a white dress sitting at the dining table, engaged in a game of solitaire. This strange young lady, about Nancy's age, with comely features and black hair worn in a tight bun, laid a playing card face up on the table and gazed at Nancy placidly.

Nancy stammered, "I . . . uh . . . thought nobody was home. I was calling for help. Why didn't you hear me? Do you have a telephone?"

The young woman did not reply to any of this, as Nancy's momentum carried her into the room.

"Are you deaf?" Nancy wondered out loud. Still getting no reply, she darted her eyes beyond the woman at the card game and saw into the next· room and immediately let out an ear-shattering scream. In frozen horror she stared into the living room, where two mangled corpses were hanging from the cross-beamed ceiling. The bodies were those of men, clothed only in bloody underwear. Each corpse had four or five knives protruding from various parts of the anatomy, which explained the absence of knives in the kitchen.

Because she was so horror-struck by the sight of the dangling bodies, at first Nancy didn't see that the demented man in bibbed coveralls was in the living room, also, standing just behind and to the right of the corpses. He had in his hand a large butcher knife, which he was sharpening on a whetstone. He smiled at Nancy as she continued screaming, terror rooting her in her tracks.

The young woman at the dining table played another card, calmly laying it face up, red on black, as if nothing of unusual interest was going on around her.

Nancy bolted and ran, the man with the butcher knife taking a step or two after her. She unbolted the kitchen door and ran out into the backyard—straight into the arms of the two deputies, who instantly pounced upon her, wrestling her to the ground and pinning her arms behind her back. While the deputies were busy subduing Nancy, a hand reached out and pulled the kitchen door shut and the man with the butcher knife did not come out of the house.

Hauled to her feet by the two deputies, Nancy struggled and babbled hysterically. "Ohh! Please . . . let me go! I . . . you killed my friends—both innocent! The *real* murderers are in *there*!" She stared at the closed door of the house, her eyes flashing wildly.

"Well, now," said the sergeant, "let's have a look. Got to investigate . . . see if this young lady is telling the truth."

He and the other deputy began dragging Nancy up onto the back porch. She screamed and dug her heels into the ground, trying with all her might to resist their pulling her along. "No! Please!" she cried. "I don't want to go in there!"

The corporal said to the sergeant, "She's stark-raving mad, I'm afraid. Doesn't want to come along with us and prove her innocence. Maybe she's lying."

The two deputies pushed open the back door and dragged Nancy into the house. She fought back, grabbing onto the doorframe, but they methodically punched her hands loose. Finally, they knocked her down and pulled her across the floor by her ankles—through the dining room, where the young woman playing cards looked up disinterestedly—and into the living room, where the two corpses hung from the rafters.

The man in bibbed coveralls chortled, watching the girl he had spied on yesterday being dragged helplessly over the living room carpet. At the far end of the large room were three wire cages, of the sort used to cage and transport show dogs. In one of the cages was a young woman, wild and disheveled looking in her underwear, who cowered in her cage as Nancy was being dragged across the floor. The other two cages were empty.

The man in bibbed coveralls, still chortling, moved to one of the empty cages and opened the door for the two deputies, who were maneuvering Nancy into position. As she lay flat on her back in front of the opened cage, one of the men—the corporal—straddled her and laughed and started pulling off her jacket and blouse. When she resisted, he slapped her face. The man in bibbed coveralls looked on, leering and chortling, swishing his sharp butcher knife through the air above Nancy's head.

The other girl cowered and cried in her cage while Nancy was being beaten and undressed down to her bra and panties, the three men flinging her garments around the living room. The undressing completed, Nancy was forced into a cage and the wire door was locked. The man in bibbed coveralls pranced insanely around the cage, laughing and grinning, prodding Nancy from one side to the other by jabbing at her with his long-bladed knife. She alternately screamed and cowered, trying to avoid being stabbed. For a time the two deputies enjoyed this game, elbowing each other in the ribs with amusement.

But at last the sergeant spoke up: "Enough! *Enough*, Cyrus! Look at the mess you made in here!" He pointed disapprovingly at the hanged bodies. "We have got to get this house cleaned up. Mama doesn't like it like this. You know she's got a bug for keeping things tidy."

The two deputies pushed the man in bibbed coveralls ahead of them out of the room, and, fear-ridden, Nancy watched them go. For the first time she noticed the holes in the backs of the deputies' shirts, streaked with dried blood, and she knew for sure now that the real deputies were hanging from the ceiling. She shuddered. Her situation was hopeless. She had fallen into the hands of a quartet of homicidal maniacs. In her agony she broke down sobbing, throwing herself down onto a ragged, musty quilt on the bottom of her cage, and in a while, due to exhaustion and shock, she lost consciousness. Her last thoughts were of Hank and Tom.

The girl in the other cage watched her sleep.

In the next room, Luke Barnes, still in his deputy's uniform, stood before his sister, Cynthia. She was nineteen now. It had been ten years since they had killed their first demon. Cynthia, eerily pretty and pale, her pallid complexion accentuated by her bun of coal-black hair, looked up from her game of solitaire.

Luke said, "Sister, you've. got to help us straighten up the house. For Mama's sake. Or else Mama is going to be mad."

Cynthia eyed her brother sternly. "You had better go up and talk to her, Luke. You know darn well she's going to chastise you for killing that other girl ahead of time. Mama told us we're supposed to have three, for the Easter services."

"I'll have another by Good Friday," Luke promised. "I'm not about to let the whole congregation down."

"But now we've got to go out and catch us another one," Cynthia complained. "And catching them is the dangerous part—people are liable to get wise. You and Cyrus and Abraham know that. How many times did Mama tell you?"

Chagrined, Luke said, "I'll go up and talk to Mama soon as the living room is cleaned up. We're not in any trouble yet. Mama won't yell at me for no reason—you wait and see."

When Nancy came to, opening her eyes slowly and recoiling from the shock of her surroundings, she found the girl in the other cage looking at her piteously. "My name is Gwen Davis," the other girl whispered. "They killed my sister."

Gwen stifled a sob. She was about twenty-five years old, probably attractive, if not so beaten up and scared. Her brown hair was plaited into two pigtails that made her look girlish, so that you had to look closely to get an idea of her true age. One of the pigtails was tied with red ribbon, but the other ribbon had been lost, no doubt in a struggle with her captors, and the ribbonless pigtail was coming undone.

"The two deputies . . . the *real* ones," Gwen said, "maybe could've saved us . . . but they're hanging from the rafters. You and I have to pull together . . . figure a way to get out of here . . . before they kill *us.*"

"How are we going to do that?" Nancy said hopelessly, and she started to sob, burying herself in the ragged quilt on the bottom of her cage.

Luke, Abraham, and Cyrus clomped into the room. Nancy kept her head and eyes buried and continued to cry softly while they went about the business of cutting down the bodies and getting them out of there. Luke and Abraham were in jeans now.

Luke backed his pickup truck out of the garage and kept it parked in the driveway with the engine idling. Abraham and Cyrus came out the front door carrying the body of one of the slain deputies, wrapped in a blanket, and heaved it into the bed of the truck. In a little while, after going back into the house, they came out with the second body, also wrapped up, and laid it into the truck, too. Abraham and Cyrus then squeezed into the cab of the pickup truck and Luke backed it out of the driveway.

Cynthia came out on the porch and watched the truck go, churning up dust, then went back into the house, shutting the front door behind her. She started cleaning up the living room, every now and then glancing at Nancy and Gwen.

"Let us go," Gwen tried.

But Cynthia only chuckled.

"But you're a young girl like us," Gwen said. "Surely you must have some feelings for what we're going through. How can you condone torture and . . . imprisonment?"

Cynthia came over to Gwen's cage. Gwen looked up at her, thinking how young and pretty she was, her figure so lithe and girlish; it just didn't seem possible that she could be as evil and perverted as her brothers—except for the intense gleam of her black eyes, which leant her face a scary kind of radiance despite the paleness of her complexion. Looking down at Gwen, she said, "I'm not like *you*. Don't ever try to tell me that. I have special powers. A congregation of my own. They believe in me. You'll see for yourself, come Friday at midnight, when the services start."

"What if I believed in you, too?" Gwen asked. "Could I be part of your congregation?" She was hoping to continue a dialogue that might cause Cynthia to waver and perhaps think about letting her and Nancy go.

"It is too late for you to be saved," said Cynthia. "A false profession of faith will not fool me."

The pickup truck pulled into the camping area where Tom Riley and Hank Bennet had been shot to death. The white van was still parked there, the sleeping bags strewn all around. Luke, Cyrus, and Abraham got out of their truck and laid the bodies of the two slain deputies on the ground, on top of the cold embers of the campfire.

"Good place for a burning," said Luke. "Nice and secluded. They couldn't have picked it better for us."

"Burn 'em and bury what's left," said Abraham. "Start diggin' a hole big enough to hide the leftovers, Cyrus!"

Luke and Abraham dragged over the bodies of Tom and Hank, making a pile of corpses. They covered the pile with blankets, sleeping bags, and miscellaneous gear from the van. The deputies' uniforms were thrown on the pile, too. At last Luke poured a can of gasoline over it all, then struck a match and started a bonfire, a funeral pyre. The faces of the three brothers— Luke, Cyrus, and Abraham—were highlighted weirdly by the roaring flames.

CHAPTER 8

Cynthia lay in bed reading from a book entitled *The Appeal of Witchcraft,* by Dr. Morgan Drey, a professor of anthropology at New York City College:

It is no accident that the devil is portrayed in medieval woodcuts as a cloven-hooved beast with his tongue in the shape of a triple penis. Sadism is a sexual perversion. And a belief in witchcraft is the horrid sickness of a sexually repressed society. The inquisitor and the witch are both perverted by the belief, by the insistence by church and state that witches do indeed exist as agents of the devil and need to be rooted out, punished, and destroyed.

The individual becomes either witch or witchhunter because it gives him an outlet for his perversions. In saying 'I am a witch,' one gives license to oneself to indulge in lascivious, erotic practices running to the obscenity of sadism; in saying 'I will persecute witches,' one gives oneself license to treat the witches sadistically. In either case, human beings torture, maim, and kill each other in an orgy of righteousness and unrighteousness, holiness and unholiness, till the two sides of the coin become one: both witch and inquisitor, operating within the witchcraft mystique, or matrix, give vent to impulses which *are* sadistic.

This duality of holiness transmuted to unholiness was personified by Gilles de Rais, the soldier-protector and rumored lover of Joan of Arc. In 1429, when their mystical triumphs on the battlefields had resulted in the coronation of Charles VII, Joan was revered as a saint and Gilles was made a Marshal of France. He was only twenty-five years of age, had inherited enormous wealth, possessed a love of books, music, and poetry, and was extremely handsome and famous. In the language of today, Gilles 'had everything going for him.' He went home from the wars with the intention of leading a life of genteel beauty, luxury, and good works.

But in 1431, through treachery, Joan of Arc was condemned as a witch and burned at the stake. This event, coupled with several other key disappointments in Gilles' life, seems to have torn his brain loose from the moorings of sanity. He left his wife and renounced all future sexual intercourse with women. Withdrawing to his castle, he surrounded himself with an army of soldiers, sycophants, homosexuals and perverts, He began to squander his wealth by traveling around the countryside with a sumptuously armed and outfitted entourage and by sponsoring lavish public entertainments which rivaled some of those staged by the fabled Roman emperors.

Gilles, in fact, felt an admiration and kinship with the most depraved and corrupt of the Romans—Nero and Caligula. He pored over prized books in his vast library which were filled with woodcuts elaborately depicting the emperors' excesses of lasciviousness, brutality and torture.

As Gilles' coffers were being depleted by his profligate life-style, he hired a sorcerer and alchemist, Francesco Prelati, to aid him in transforming lead into gold. Many medieval alchemists used their "art" as a pretext for debauchery and perversion, and Prelati was no exception. He convinced Gilles, after a few futile experiments, that no real progress would be forthcoming without making a pact with the Devil.

Gilles lured a young boy to his castle, raped him, then tore out his eyes, mutilated his genitals, and ripped out his heart and lungs. Gilles used the boy to vent his sexual appetites, and Prelati used the blood and organs in alchemical experiments. Thus began a period of eight years in which Gilles, goaded by Prelati, raped, tortured, mutilated, and dismembered literally hundreds of children. When he was finally arrested and sentenced to be hanged and burned, and the prosecutor asked him the reason for his hideous crimes, he replied: "Truly I had none, but the gratification of my passions." This was an amazingly candid admission by Gilles, who would be expected to rationalize his behavior by telling himself that the young boys had to be killed, anyway, for the all-important purpose of turning lead into gold.

Most of the time aberrant behavior needs an excuse, a justification. Religious fanaticism gives birth to witchcraft by encouraging a deep-rooted fear of a very real Devil who walks the earth and possesses living persons. It was once said that: Nothing is so healthy for religion as a strong, unshakable belief in Satan.

What priest today wouldn't secretly love to meet Satan in person—to be confronted with incontrovertible proof that the Prince of Hell *does* exist and therefore the lifelong devotion to a priestly calling has not been a futile waste of energy?

Having come to the end of a chapter, Cynthia laid down the book and thought about the author, Dr. Morgan Drey, whom she had met at her store in Greenwich Village. He had come in to purchase books for research and artifacts he could photograph to illustrate *The Appeal of Witchcraft*. When the manuscript was published some months later, he had returned to present her with an

autographed copy and ask her to let him take her to dinner. She
surprised herself by saying yes.

She had not opened the store to get involved with non-believers.
It had been her idea to go to New York and run a place of her own,
specializing in the sale of witches' paraphernalia, potions and
herbs—much like Mama's old store—so that she could meet other
people with beliefs similar to her own. She did not care to meet
skeptics like Morgan Drey. She wanted to use the store as a way of
building her own congregation. Over a period of four years, she had
been successful in developing a conclave of almost two hundred
witches from various parts of the United States. Each year the services took place at midnight on Good Friday, Holy Saturday and
Easter Sunday. Special rites, pulled off at considerable risk, were
looked forward to by all. Some of the members of the congregation
were gaining followers of their own and conducting services
regularly in other states and cities. But the services in the chapel on
the Barnes family estate were by far the grandest and most daring.

Morgan Drey had interviewed Cynthia for his book. She had
been open with him, except where self-protection made discre-
tion imperative, and had even told him, rather proudly, about
her own congregation and the annual services conducted under
her leadership. Over a sip of wine in the Italian restaurant where
he had taken her, he chuckled good-naturedly. "Surely you
don't really believe in all this," he told her. "I can realize that
you have to maintain avidly that you do, for the benefit of your
customers. But you can tell *me* the truth. What are your private
feelings?"

Her eyes met his across the table. He was a goodlooking, if
scholarly, man in his late twenties. His forehead was high, and
Cynthia knew this was a mark of intelligence. He had light brown
hair, deepset inquisitive blue eyes, and a scrupulously trimmed
goatee and mustache.

"My private beliefs are as I have said," Cynthia told him. "I
believe in my powers."

"*What* powers?" he challenged. "What proof do you have that
you've ever worked any extraordinary magic?"

She clenched her teeth, her eyes flashing with annoyance. "I cannot tell you," she said, haughtily angered.

"You mean there is nothing," he persisted.

"I mean I can't tell you," she uttered coldly. "These matters are not to be discussed lightly with a nonbeliever. "

"You know, you're very pretty when you get worked up," he said, changing the subject and continuing to stare at her intently.

She knew intuitively that he liked her, and more—he wanted to get involved with her romantically; this was pleasing, but also frightening. He reached out and took her hand, but she drew it away as if it had been burned, and her cheeks flushed red from embarrassment.

"What's the matter?" he said, startled.

"Nothing. I—"

"Are you afraid of men?"

"No."

"Do you have a boyfriend . . . a fiancé?"

"Certainly not."

"What do you mean, certainly not? As if the mere idea were out of the realm of possibility?"

She did not answer. He had her unsettled.

"You had better be careful, Cynthia," he warned. "Or else these beliefs of yours will become a horrid obsession. You're much too young and pretty not to have a normal life—one free of anxiety and repression. You need to fall in love someday and have children."

"*Never,*" she said fervently. "I have other things to do which are more important."

"Let me see you again," he pleaded. "I'm attracted to you. I'd like a chance to change your mind, to show you another way of thinking. That mother of yours—I know you love her, but she has given you some warped ideas. And 1 believe you have a hostility toward men because you were deserted by your father ten years ago and you've never gotten over it."

His words shook small tremors of self-doubt in Cynthia, making her angry. How dare he! What gave him the nerve to be so impertinent? She would never allow him to undermine her confidence, her commitment. Her congregation was proof of her sanctity. They worshipped her because she had inherited tremendous spiritual gifts from her grandfather and great-grandfather. She had the power of the caul, the mark of Tetragrammaton, who had chosen her to be even greater than her ancestors, the Cunning Men.

"I would appreciate it if you would never come to my store again," she told Morgan Drey.

He immediately looked hurt, baffled, his usual aura of self-assuredness gone. She had succeeded in wounding him, instead of the other way around. The triumph was hers. She smiled at him to make his pain worse. She had to get him out of her life so she could go on leading her congregation. He was a stupid and dangerous non-believer. She did not need him. There were others who cherished her for the proper reasons. When she needed a man, or *men*, she could choose from among those who had the truest, deepest, most violent ability to please her.

What did Morgan Drey know? His book was nonsense, full of theoretical babbling. What would he think if he saw the rituals in person? He would go starkraving *mad*, his pitiful imaginings dwarfed to ridiculous pettiness by the real thing.

An extraordinary idea occurred to Cynthia: What if she could convert him? The possibility was titillating. She knew he was attracted to her; maybe there were reasons he didn't want to admit. Perhaps he wasn't as skeptical as he seemed to be. His writings about Gilles de Rais, Jack the Ripper, and the Marquis de Sade might be an outlet for a side of himself he barely understood, a potential yearning to be set free. Skeptics made the most passionate converts once they were shown the way to the actual, rather than the vicarious, indulgence of their passions. Judging from his writing, Morgan Drey seemed particularly fascinated by Elisabeth Bathory, the sixteenth-century Hungarian countess who kept hundreds of young girls chained in the dungeons beneath her castle, so she could periodically renew her own vigor and beauty by slitting the young girls' veins and bathing in their blood. What would Morgan think if he knew that some of the countess' practices would form the basis for rituals of Cynthia's devising which would commence in two days, on Good Friday, when the entire congregation had arrived?

She laid down his book and closed her eyes, shutting him out of her mind. She wondered about the girls downstairs, who were going to be unwilling contributors to her rituals. What sort of lives did they lead? Did they have boyfriends? Lovers? Were their sexual preferences normal, or bizzare?

From across the hall she could hear the muffled tones of Luke's voice droning on, talking to Mama behind her closed bedroom door: "Mama . . . I hope you've gotten it out of your head that I'm to blame for doing wrong. We didn't mean for that girl to die . . . but she went and hurt Cyrus pretty bad. And you always said he had a delicate temper. It was the girl's fault. Me and Abraham . . . we're gonna catch another girl tomorrow. We got us a van that don't belong to us . . . nobody can trace it to us. Tomorrow morning we'll take it out on the road, and we'll find us another girl, I promise. Maybe it'll be somebody young and pretty . . . maybe a virgin. Don't you worry now. Me and Abraham . . . we ain't goin' to disappoint the congregation."

Mama didn't say anything. She just sat in her rocking chair, looking out the window. Luke didn't know if she was angry at him or not. Hoping that he had his mother's approval and understanding, even though she didn't voice it, he backed sheepishly out of the bedroom and shut the door. Then he went down the hall to his own room and started getting undressed for bed.

Downstairs in their cages, Nancy and Gwen were talking, keeping their voices low.

Gwen tried to remain calm while explaining how she had been trapped. "My sister and I were driving by, exploring the back roads, and . . ."—she stifled a sob—". . . and Sally . . . she liked to hunt for old cemeteries . . . the older the better . . . to take pictures and make tombstone rubbings. Right away she noticed the family graveyard out back, across the field, so she wanted to stop and look. But she wouldn't dare go out there without asking permission. We got out of the car and went up on the porch to knock, and the door banged open all of a sudden and the three brothers jumped us. It was awful . . . awful! I didn't do a good job of fighting back . . . I was in shock or something. Sally bit and scratched and they had a hard time with her. She kicked Cyrus, the big crazy one, between the legs—and he roared like a wounded bear . . . and then he stabbed her . . . again and again. I was half out of my mind, already in my cage. I—" Gwen buried her face in her hands and broke down crying.

Nancy trembled, not knowing how to comfort the older girl. She said, "I'm sorry, Gwen. Please . . . maybe you shouldn't talk about it anymore."

But Gwen went on, as if she had to get it all out of her system. She was thinking it out as she talked, trying to get it all straight in her mind, reciting details that refused to yield to reason or under-standing. "The two deputies stopped here. I could hear them talking out on the front porch. They said they had been chasing a white van that had gone speeding away from a grocery store in town. But Luke must've been afraid and suspicious. The deputies said they had wrecked their car in the chase. Luke of-fered them some hot coffee, and he brought a fresh potful out onto the porch. I wanted to scream . . . but Abraham had a gun on me. The coffee must've been drugged, because in a little while the deputies were dragged in here, tied up with rope . . . uncon-scious. They were tortured and stabbed to death . . . and I had to watch. But most of the time I shut my eyes. I guess I babbled and raved and pounded my bare fists on the cage. . . ." Gwen held up her hands, which were bruised and swollen and scraped raw.

"Oh, God!" Nancy moaned. "*Why?* Why is all this happen-ing?"

"There's no reason for it," Gwen said soberly. "I keep remem-bering my grandfather telling me to never forget man is capable of the worst imaginable acts of cruelty. He was in a Nazi concen-tration camp during World War Two. But at least that was war-time. What excuse is there for what's happening to us now?"

Nancy was silent, coming face to face with a guilt she had just realized—she and Hank and Tom were partially to blame for the deputies' deaths, because the chase never would have happened were it not for the theft of the groceries from the store. Oh, what a lark it had seemed to be! And getting away had been the best part. They had thought themselves so terribly clever, never suspecting that the deputies weren't able to give pursuit anymore because they had wrecked their squad car. As these realizations struck home, silent, remorseful tears rolled down Nancy's cheeks. *"Damn* my stepfather," she said suddenly.

Gwen hunched forward, peering through the wire cages, her eyes bright with desperation. "We have to try to escape! We have to try to get out of here. They'll kill us. The whole family is crazy. They think they're vampires or witches or something."

"Shh!" Nancy whispered, afraid Gwen was talking so loudly that she'd be overheard.

But Gwen went on, barely lowering her volume. "I've been locked up in this cage for two days . . . I've heard them talking . . . planning . . . diabolical things that would send chills up your spine. Their mother is in charge of whatever they're going to do . . . only I've never seen her. She lives upstairs. She's a witch, or they think she is. They're preparing for a Black Mass . . . an insane ritual of some sort. And you and I and some other poor girl are intended to be human sacrifices."

Nancy didn't want to hear what Gwen was saying. It didn't make sense. It couldn't be happening. It overwhelmed the senses, numbing a person's intellect, a person's physical and emotional resources, till the ability to struggle for survival was lost in a nightmarish vortex of futility and despair. Nancy had sunk back against the rear of her cage; the fight had gone, out of her; she was hopelessly disconsolate and almost ready to die. She even felt she probably deserved it, because of her guilt over the way the two deputies had died.

"May the Lord have mercy on them," she mumbled under her breath. "And on Hank and Tom."

Pressing her face against the wire mesh of her cage, Gwen

whispered insistently, "I tell you, Nancy, we have got to try to get out of here. Don't give up on me—*please*. If you and I lose hope, we'll be done for. We've got to think our way out of this somehow."

Nancy spoke through her tears. "But what can we do, Gwen? It's useless . . . useless . . . in these cages. At least if we were locked up in a room—but this way we don't have a chance of trying to escape." She continued sobbing.

"Look, you've got to pull yourself together," Gwen said. "It's not as hopeless as you think. In the morning Luke and Abraham will unlock the cages to give us food and march us out into the field to go to the toilet. If I get a chance, I'm going to try something."

"You're not going to make a run for it?" Nancy asked, panic-stricken, remembering how Hank and Tom had been gunned down.

"No. Something else. I'll seduce one of the brothers if I can . . . or both of them, if I have to. And I'll kill them if they let me get my hands on a gun."

Nancy mulled it over, terrified of the risks. "What can I do?" she asked timidly.

"You'll have to create a diversion and do your part. Be ready to use a club or a rock—whatever you can grab."

"I'm scared, Gwen," Nancy whispered weakly.

"I am, too," said the older girl. "But what else can we do? If you have a better suggestion, I'm willing to listen."

"Maybe somebody will come for us."

"Who?"

"Somebody looking for the two deputies."

"We can't count on it. How would they know to look here? Look, Nancy—try to get some sleep. Be strong tomorrow, and be brave. They'll try not to kill us if they can help it. We have a value to them. They want us for their crazy rituals. And somehow I don't figure we ought to stick around."

Nancy and Gwen wrapped themselves up in the ragged, dirty quilts on the bottoms of their cages. Silently, saying each word with slow, careful enunciation in the privacy of her mind, Nancy prayed till exhaustion overcame her and she dozed, tossing fitfully and crying out once or twice in her sleep.

Gwen lay wide awake, staring up at the white ceiling through wire mesh. The room was brightly lit. Their captors didn't trust leaving them alone in the dark. Gwen tried not to think about her sister Sally . . . not to dwell on the horrors she had already been through. By an effort of will, she concentrated on her own survival, and in this her aged grandfather was an inspiration. She recalled much of what he had told her of the Nazi death factories; these experiences, once so terrifying but remote, now had a meaning for her that she never suspected would come to pass. She wanted to be as strong as her grandfather. He had not been saved by prayers, he always maintained, but by his own ingenuity and a hefty measure of good luck; those who remembered how to pray and nothing else, died. Gwen did not pray. She concentrated on summoning energy and determination within herself for the escape attempt which must be made.

It helped to remember how much she had to live for, which was something she had only recently come to realize. And that made it all the more ironic, if she should die, a victim of someone's homicidal whim.

It had taken her a year to begin to get over her divorce. Her ex-husband, Warren, was a metallurgical engineer for Wheeling Steel Corporation. On the job he was capable and effective, plunging headlong and obsessively into challenges and finding solutions that were often cleverly innovative, bordering on genius. He had the respect of his peers, both socially and professionally. This filled him with pride and a deep sense of accomplishment that carried over into his marriage; he felt that his role as husband was totally fulfilled by his being such an outstanding breadwinner. He expected Gwen to cater to him, as he had been catered to and pampered by his mother and his doting spinster aunt through all his growing-up years.

Gwen had married Warren Davis while they were both undergraduates at West Virginia University in Morgantown. She was studying to be an elementary school teacher, and he, of course, was enrolled in the College of Engineering. They both got some monetary support from their parents and both had small academic scholarships, but to make ends meet they had to take out student loans and find summer employment. Gwen looked upon all this as part of the marriage partnership; her contribution was no less important than Warren's. But almost from the beginning he seemed to assume certain prerogatives, as if his studying, his education, and his eventual career took automatic precedence over hers. In the early days of love and togetherness she didn't bother to argue, telling herself she would stand up for her rights later if it became necessary. In the meantime she did most of the dishes, laundry, and other household chores and worked in her studying around these necessities, while Warren didn't have to contend with them. His grades were better than hers, and everyone knew that engineers made more money than teachers, so she stifled any nagging doubts she may have had and didn't question his assumed dominance.

She got pregnant not long after graduation and that put an end to her attempts to find a teaching position. Her daughter, Amy, was born the following spring. Warren was already working for Wheeling Steel, his drive in that area giving early evidence of becoming obsessive, if Gwen had only noticed the signs. But she was caught up in trying to be a wife and mother, even though, had she been able to admit the truth to herself, she would probably have preferred not to have her first child at this time. It was Warren who had wanted the pregnancy, and Gwen relinquished whatever ideas she may have entertained about going to work, earning a salary, and living the relatively care-free life-style of a young married woman unencumbered by children.

She loved Amy. That was not the problem. But more and more she began to see Warren as selfish, demanding, and overbearing. His pride in his work and his ability to earn recognition, praise, and advancements in her eyes began to take on the unattractive taint of smugness. The more he accomplished, the less he treated her as an equal. When these realizations first dawned on her, she fought against them . . . tried to submerge them in the rituals of shopping, housekeeping, entertaining friends, and taking care of Amy. Warren was an adequate father, giving his daughter much of his attention when he was home from work, but even this possible virtue became a fault when Gwen started to think her husband's attention to Amy could be his way of avoiding *her*. Or was she imagining it all? Was this the way married life inevitably turned out? Had she been too immature to take on the burden in the first place?

These self-doubts and dissatisfactions, never discussed openly between Gwen and Warren, festered insidiously and continued to poison their relationship. They said good night more often without making love or even holding each other tenderly. Warmth and cordiality degenerated to politeness. They talked a lot about Amy and the stages of her growing up, to avoid talking about themselves. When the divorce finally came, it shocked most of their friends, because outwardly the buildup had made barely a ripple. Inwardly, Gwen was devastated. They had been married six years. Amy was four. After all this time spent in inner turmoil—questioning herself, her motives, her worthiness as a wife, mother, and even as a person—Gwen's self-confidence was totally shattered. Yet, she had to go on being a mother to Amy, and had to make a career and a new life for herself.

About a year ago, after being divorced for seven months, she finally landed a job teaching fifth grade in a small West Virginia town not far from Wheeling. She had been called in to substitute when the regular teacher became sick, had gone on to finish out the term, and because of her excellent work had been rehired in the fall when another vacancy opened up. She had gone into her first day of teaching desperately trying to conceal from the class how scared she was. The first months had continued to be an enormously challenging struggle, till she saw that she could do the job, and, moreover, that she was good at it. The children, resentful at first because she had replaced their original teacher, eventually settled down, did what she told them, and even liked her. A milestone of her comeback from her divorce was the day

Johnny Adams, one of the toughest kids in the class, came in to her privately during recess and said he wanted to pass fifth grade, but if he failed it would be okay because he'd get to be with her another year, rather than with the meany in the next grade. "You mustn't call Mrs. Wilkes a meany, she's an excellent teacher," Gwen had said, but she couldn't help smiling over the compliment.

Warren had taken Amy over the Easter vacation so Gwen could spend some time with Sally, her younger sister, who was still in college. They had started out yesterday morning on a pleasant drive and picnic. Because of the new energy and self-confidence she had found, Gwen was able to discuss her marital problems and the divorce openly, even cheerfully, with Sally, and had hoped her sister might profit by her mistakes.

Now Sally was dead. And Gwen knew she had to try to stay alive and get back to Amy. She hoped that some of her grandfather's instincts for survival would have a resurgence in her as powerful as her love for her daughter.

Her eyes shut, but even in sleep she continued to sense the presence of the wire cage enveloping her like a coffin.

CHAPTER 9

Morgan Drey, the young anthropologist who had written *The Appeal of Witchcraft*, concluded his final lecture before Easter vacation to an evening class at New York City College:

"The thing that distinguishes man from the other animals, more than any other thing, is his ability to sublimate. His highly developed intellect can and does override his instincts. This has produced some of his noblest achievements and basest perversions.

"The animal called man can be noble or petty, comic, cowardly, pathetic, or brave. He has aspirations which are admirable, and some which are despicable. He can be taught, or misguided, to substitute the penetration of a dagger for the penetration of sex, the mindless unison of a Nazi goosestep for the subtler rhythms of poetry, the fleeting pleasure of orgasm for the deeper joy of sex in love. He is capable of perpetrating the worst cruelties and barbarities imaginable in the name of holy science, holy religion, or holy truth."

Morgan stopped and gazed at the class piercingly, to give his last sentence time to sink in. Then he said, "That's it for today, folks. Class dismissed ten minutes early, as I promised. Happy Easter." He started gathering up his books and papers.

A few class members lingered to ask a question or two, or to wish him a nice holiday. He was the last one to leave the room, and by that time he was crushingly lonely. No one was in the corridor, and all the classrooms were dark. His solitary footsteps reverberated in the hall.

Coming down the gray stone steps outside the building, he put his hand up and hailed a cab. He meant to tell the driver to take him home. But instead he said, "Washington Square." This was in Greenwich Village, near Cynthia's shop. He paid the cabbie and got out and walked . . . thinking about the intensely zealous, attractive young girl who had told him she never wanted to see him again. He had been unable to get her out of his mind. He remembered her lovely black hair and the vibrant glow of her black eyes.

The shop was closed, its panes of glass caged in and locked. A sign said: CLOSED FOR EASTER. But Morgan Drey lingered, trying to see if there might be someone inside taking inventory or something. Finally, he went into the bar next door and ordered a beer. Sipping it, he thought about Cynthia. He knew it was foolish of him to be so attracted to her, because on a rational level he had come to the conclusion that she was quite possibly mentally disturbed. But there was something about her that drew him like a magnet.

For the first time, ruefully, he admitted that he was infatuated; otherwise, he would heed the warning signs and back off. But he lacked the necessary good sense. His instincts were overriding his intellect. He wanted this girl even though she had all the earmarks of bad trouble.

Still, he might be able to help her. Her mind had been warped when she was younger, and he was the right fellow to unwarp it. Even if she got nothing else out of their relationship, that much would put her a bit ahead, wouldn't it?

He tossed down the remainder of his draft beer and gave the bartender his order for another.

Those services Cynthia had spoken of were supposed to take place over Easter. Morgan knew so little about her that he remembered just about every scrap of information she had let drop.

He recalled the name of a town she lived near: Cherry Hill. Rather than moping around over the long weekend, he could get himself a roadmap and drive there with his camera, telling her he had come to ask her to let him photograph the services. If she became enraged and turned him away, well, that would be the end of it; he'd turn around and drive home, swallowing his mortification. But if she accepted him and let him stay . . .

What in the world had come over him, for God's sake? He was coming on like a love-sick adolescent, hanging around the schoolyard for a glimpse of his secret heartthrob. He was certainly not comporting himself like a dignified twenty-eight-year-old anthropologist.

Tonight he'd get drunk. And in the morning the hangover might discourage him from going to Cherry Hill and making a fool of himself. In a wry frame of mind, he ordered a double shot of whisky to go with his third draft.

CHAPTER 10

Nancy awoke at four in the morning and could not sleep anymore. Gwen's supposedly upcoming escape attempt both tormented and tantalized her. If it only worked! But it wouldn't. Then, again, it might.

Locked inside the wire cage, Nancy couldn't picture herself free. The images had no tangibility. She had to fight against giving up. Her mind was mostly a blank. Her life wasn't passing in front of her. Maybe that meant she wasn't going to die.

Gwen was going to try to seduce the brothers, Luke and Abraham. Would such a thing be a mortal sin? If so, it would be on Gwen's soul, not Nancy's. Yet Nancy would benefit from it. She hoped. It made her feel guilty when she contemplated some of the saints her catechism classes taught her to revere: the ones who had allowed themselves to be butchered rather than giving in to sexual intercourse.

She had made a good confession, finally, after two years. She was in a state of grace, almost, providing stealing the groceries could be thought of as a venial sin. Maybe God had inspired her to get ready and purify her soul. But she was still scared to die, even knowing she would go to heaven.

She tried to think positively, as Gwen had urged. But in the confines of the cage this was difficult. Wild, panicky thoughts kept tumbling through her mind. Either the situation was truly hopeless, or else the numbness of fear made it seem so. Not one idea conducive to escape occurred to her.

Her ears perked up as she heard someone's footsteps on the stairs. Cynthia came into the living room and stopped in front of Nancy's cage, casually reaching out and resting her hand on the wire. Nancy's eyes widened. Cynthia was wearing a pink satin robe and appeared fresh and well rested, as if nothing disturbing was going on. She even smiled and then said, "Good morning."

"Good morning," Nancy replied, her voice breaking to a tiny croak as the automatic response issued from the depths of her conditioning, shaking her with a small shock wave of irony and dismay.

"Breakfast will be ready soon," said Cynthia quite pleasantly. With that, she strode through the dining room and into the kitchen and began banging pots and pans.

Gwen's sudden whisper startled Nancy. "Fucking bitch!" Gwen said under her breath.

"I didn't know you were awake," Nancy whispered back.

"In a little while you'll smell eggs, toast, and coffee," said Gwen. "But we won't get any. Luke, Cyrus, and Abraham will come down and they'll all have a nice hearty breakfast and a friendly chat. When they're done they'll give us some bread and cheese. Then they'll let us out to do our business. That's when our big chance will come. I was afraid to try it yesterday on my own. But now I have you to help. *One* of us might get away—or both of us, if we're lucky."

"I'm still scared," Nancy said. "I'm not sure what to do."

Gwen eyed her shrewdly, trying to instill confidence. "When the right moment comes, don't hesitate—make your move. Grab a stick or a rock. If you could play up to one of the brothers before-hand, that would double our chances of getting hold of a gun."

"I don't think I could stand to have them touch me," Nancy said.

"You're going to wait till they do worse?" Gwen challenged.

The three brothers clomped down the stairs. Luke and Abraham went directly into the dining room, but Cyrus lingered around the cages, leering and giggling and jabbing with his fingers—poking the girls from one side to another in their wire cells. Luckily, he didn't have his knife.

"Cyrus!" Cynthia called. "You come in and eat while it's hot!"

He gave a few final pokes, gleefully waddling around the side of Nancy's cage on his way into the dining room, where he dragged a chair across the carpet and sat down.

"Hotcakes instead of eggs today," Gwen said in a whisper. "How could anything that black-haired bitch touches smell so good?" Cursing was her way of boosting her courage.

Nancy lay flat on her back, staring up through wire mesh, trying to get over the stomach-churning anxiety of the recent torment from Cyrus. Turning toward Gwen, she asked, "Do they ever let the dumb one have the keys?"

"No, I'm afraid not. Why?"

"I guess he'd be the easiest one to trick."

"You know it and they know it," Gwen said.

A lively conversation ensued around the breakfast table. Nancy and Gwen could hear everything but could not see the participants because of the placement of their cages. They had to peer through the dining room archway on a sharp angle, the view further obstructed by their lowness to the floor and the intervening aspects of large pieces of furniture. Cynthia was giving instructions. When she spoke the three brothers listened.

"When you're done with the two in there, Luke and Abraham, you go on out and fetch a third one to keep them company. Mama expects there to be three. Cyrus, you needn't go along. You have your work to do, sweeping up the chapel and polishing the pews. Don't dawdle about it. People will be coming in tomorrow and expecting the usual thorough preparations. Most of them will be checked into motels in town. A few will stay here at the house. We've got to be congenial and accommodating at all times, just like Mama said."

"She wasn't mad at me last night," Luke said. "What happened with that other girl wasn't none of our fault."

"Be that as it may," said Cynthia, "we have got to have three, come hell or high water, tomorrow."

There was a racket of chairs being pushed back from the table, and then Luke and Abraham came into the living room. Cyrus pushed in behind them but Cynthia yelled for him to go on out the back door with his broom and get to work sweeping the chapel. Luke and Abraham both had the pistols they had taken from the deputies. Taking a ring of keys out of his pocket, Luke said, "Goin' to take you out in the field now to relieve yourselves. Don't want you lettin' go in here. Afterward, we'll lock you up again with somethin' to eat and drink. Behave yourselves now— or you don't have nothin' at all to eat."

"Why can't we go to the bathroom in here?" asked Nancy.

Gwen flashed a look at Nancy to tell her to shut up. If they didn't get outside, how were they ever going to escape?

"We ain't lettin' you into our bathroom, where there's stuff like glass and razor blades," said Luke. "You might get feisty, or you might try to slash your wrists." He unlocked the padlocks on the dog cages and let Nancy and Gwen out, keeping his pistol trained on them. Abraham backed him up, both brothers warily alert, not about to lose their captives and take flack from Cynthia and Mama.

Nancy and Gwen unbent slowly and stiffly, massaging and stretching their cramped muscles.

"Get a move on!" Abraham snapped. "This way. Out the back door."

Prodded in the back with the guns, Nancy and Gwen marched through the dining room with scraps of food still on the table, out through the large country kitchen and down off the back porch. Gwen looked at Nancy out of the corners of her eyes, signaling: Be brave and our chance will come.

It was a crisp spring morning with dew still on the grass. The two girls shivered and got goosebumps; they were wearing their underwear and nothing else. Barefoot, they stepped gingerly through the cold, wet grass. They were headed toward an outhouse adjacent to the cemetery and chapel across the field. The thought that Cyrus was out there filled Nancy with trepidation. "Where are we going?" she asked, playing dumb.

"Make any difference to you?" Abraham countered snidely.

"You can do your business right here where we can watch," said Luke, snickering.

"I can show you a better way to get some kicks," Gwen told the two brothers, stopping in her tracks and turning to face them seductively. "Why don't you let me and Nancy take the two of you into the woods for a while? Cynthia doesn't have to find out about it."

Luke chuckled derisively, but Abraham seemed interested. "If they already ain't virgins, what difference could it make?" he suggested to his brother.

"It's a trick," said Luke.

"But you both have guns," Gwen argued. "How could we get away with anything? Nancy and I talked about it last night, and we figured that if we were really nice to you, maybe you'd be nice to us."

"Maybe we would, at that," said Abraham shrewdly. "Why don't we have us some fun, Luke? Then we'll see if there's a way of helping the two girls."

"Well . . . maybe," Luke debated. His lusts were getting the better of him. He told himself that the risk would be minimal if the girls were willing to have sex in return for possible favors. Of course, the favors wouldn't ever be forthcoming, but they wouldn't have to know. It would be nice doing it with a pretty girl who was putting her all into it for a change, not having to be forced. "If you were real nice to us, maybe we'd let you go and capture two more," he said slyly.

Nancy was panicked. The way Gwen had talked, Nancy and Gwen both would have to give in to Luke and Abraham, or at least lead them on. What if it got out of control, and they never escaped at all? Or what if they were let loose and two other girls took their place? That would be a mortal sin for sure. Letting someone else die to save your own hide.

"I've got my mind made up to show you the best time you ever had," Gwen purred breathily, unsnapping her bra.

Abraham and Luke ogled her large, firm breasts. Following her lead, as if in a trance, Nancy took off her bra, too. The two brothers' eyes gleamed lecherously, darting back and forth, taking in first one girl, then the other. It was easy to believe that Nancy's wide-eyed stare was one of desire.

"Over there behind the trees," Luke said, gesturing with his gun. He had turned briefly, glancing over his shoulder, and when he turned back he was jolted by the sight of Abraham already fondling Gwen's breasts, his revolver stuck carelessly in his belt.

Luke felt he was moving in slow motion, as Gwen reached for the butt of Abraham's gun. But he got to her in time and smacked it out of her hand. Nancy saw it fall. Paralyzed for an instant, she was too late diving for it on the grass. Luke kicked it away, then gave her a savage chop behind the neck that sent her sprawling, nearly unconscious. By that time Abraham had recovered and was repeatedly slapping Gwen, beating her with his fists on her face and breasts, then punching her in the stomach, sending her writhing to the earth. She stayed down, moaning in pain, and Luke kicked her in the ribs. He picked up Abraham's pistol and handed it back.

"Filthy teases!" Luke snapped. "Tried to make blasted fools out of us, didn't they?"

Luke and Abraham dragged Nancy and Gwen to their feet and pushed them behind a clump of bushes and waited while they relieved themselves, then marched them back into the house, shoved them down into their cages, and locked them up. "Nothing to eat for you now!" Luke barked before stomping away. "They tried to escape," he told Cynthia, who was in the dining room cleaning up.

Gwen and Nancy lay on the bottoms of their cages, in pain and despair. Their escape attempt had failed miserably, and it was not likely they'd get another chance.

Out in the dining room, Cynthia was saying, "Tomorrow you

can take them down to the chapel, Luke. In the evening you'll be building a fire in there, and it will be warm enough so they won't die of pneumonia. Locked up in the chapel, they'll be hard put to give us any more trouble."

"I was under the impression you wanted only one down there at a time during the services, and only the one we're working with, at that," said Abraham.

"Put them in Uncle Sal's office," Cynthia instructed. "That way they won't see anything that's going on till we want them to. You understand, I mean for you to keep them in their cages."

"Yeah, I get the picture," growled Luke.

This last part of the discussion killed a ray of hope Gwen had been nurturing through the agony of her injuries. She had thought maybe they'd be locked up in a room, with more freedom of movement, rather than in the escape-proof wire cages. Now, that hope gone, she was overwhelmed by the knifing pain in her rib cage, which felt as if the whole side of her upper torso had been kicked in by Luke's heavy brown boot. More demoralized than ever, she gave in to thinking that maybe she never would see her daughter again.

Sitting back in her cage, wrapped in the ragged, musty blanket, Nancy began reciting a rosary. Luke and Abraham scoffed at her as they went out the front door. She heard them backing the van out of the garage at the side of the house; the garage door shut, a door slammed as one of the brothers hopped into the cab, and the van drove away. Cynthia came into the living room and stared down at the two girls in their cages. To Nancy she said, "Why do you pray? It will do you no good."

"Don't you believe in God?" Nancy inquired softly, after saying the amen at the end of a Hail Mary and then taking a deep breath before confronting Cynthia.

Cynthia smiled patronizingly. "You believe that your God is good and merciful, yet He has allowed such bad things to happen to you."

Nancy swallowed hard, her mouth and throat dry. She spoke

softly: "We're taught not to question His wisdom. He sent His only begotten Son to earth to suffer and die for our sins. Maybe He is asking me to suffer a little, too, so that I can be saved."

"Were you such a great and terrible sinner?" Cynthia said, amused.

Nancy lowered her eyes. Wrapped in her blanket and holding her ribs, Gwen gazed in open contempt at Cynthia's face.

"Some of your holy priests, even the ones you call saints, weren't so humbly able to accept pain as you are," Cynthia told Nancy. "Allow me to enlighten you. Have you ever been permitted to read eyewitness accounts of the bloody witch trials carried out in the name of your God? Fascinating, I assure you. For instance, in the 1500s a certain parish priest was condemned to be tortured until he should admit he had a pact with Satan—the inquisitors were convinced of his guilt merely because he was knowledgeable about some excellent herbal cures and had nursed some badly ill people in his village to total recovery. It was thought in those days that any unusual talent, beauty, or skill had to come from the Devil; in this way mediocrity and obedience were encouraged, while those with exceptional physical or mental attributes were put to death. So they hung the good priest on the rack and pulled his limbs from their sockets, and applied the thumbscrews till the blood spurted from the ends of his fingers, striking the wall five feet away, and all the while he kept praying to his God, as you have been doing now. He couldn't believe that this merciful God, who knew his innocence, would not intervene and put an end to his suffering. But no such intervention happened—the heavens did not open up; God did not descend in a ray of light—and the pious priest died horribly, his religious beliefs shattered along with his mind and body at the end when death finally took him. You see, there are times when evil will have its triumph, and nothing can change that fact. Evil is more powerful than good. Your God sits indifferently on His celestial throne, entertained by the agonized antics of His subjects, who writhe and jerk like dismembered puppets. Why are

you so vain as to imagine He cares a whit about you? Don't you
recall that even Jesus, the Son of God, cried out in His final
agony on the cross: Why hast Thou forsaken Me?"

Nancy could not answer. Her faith was not shaken by Cynthia's tirade. But she could not intellectualize her beliefs, especially not in the face of a challenge from someone who had
nothing to lose, whose life was not at stake. The rote memoriza-
tions of catechism class were of no use in such an existential argument.

"For now, you will pray mindlessly," Cynthia said. "But in the
end you'll know that your God has forsaken you and I am your
master."

"Get out of here, you bitch!" Gwen spat viciously, giving all
her energy to impotent hatred. Crying out so vehemently gave
her excruciating pain in her ribs.

Cynthia merely laughed and left the room, scornfully turning
her back on her victims.

In a little while, Nancy resumed praying her rosary, reciting it
from memory, keeping count of the Our Fathers and Hail Marys
by imagining herself fingering the beads.

CHAPTER 11

The sign still said Peterson's Country Store, although the place was not run anymore by Mr. Peterson, who had been driven away by grief ten years ago, after the mysterious disappearance of his young son and daughter. Now the owners were a nice elderly couple, Mr. and Mrs. Jamison; they used the few extra dollars they made in the store to supplement their Social Security. Sitting in a squeaky rocking chair behind the counter, Mrs. Jamison looked up from the red wool sweater she was knitting for her husband and watched fifteen-year-old Sharon Kennedy browsing among the aisles.

Sharon was always intrigued by the almost nonsensical variety of goods for sale, which included meat, poultry, coldcuts, and produce; fresh milk, eggs, and butter; dog collars, handkerchiefs, and shotgun shells; rifles, pistols, and handguns; fireworks, baby rattles, toys and games, and handbags; socks and underwear and toothpaste and non-prescription medicines. Just about anything and everything might be found in the country store—except sometimes just the thing you wanted.

"Got any Easter egg dye?" Sharon Kennedy called out.

"Let me see, now," said Mrs. Jamison, making the most of the opportunity for conversation, "I believe I saw some just the other day, when Mrs. Casper was in with her tribe of young ones. Oh, yes, Sharon, you look right over there on the third shelf, beside the toothpicks."

Delving and pulling out a packet, Sharon asked, "Do you think it's still good?" The package was so faded and old, having been in the store since God knew when; but the price was only twenty cents, which was typical of the sort of bargain that could be had sometimes in the country store if the goods hung around for years and years till just when you needed them.

"Oh, stuff like that never wears out!" exclaimed Mrs. Jamison.

Sharon began reading the directions so she could estimate how many packets she'd need to color eggs for her younger brothers and sisters. They weren't getting baskets this year because Daddy couldn't afford them, but at least Sharon could see to it that they each got a couple of Easter eggs. She would do the eggs at night after the younger children had gone to bed, so they'd be surprised on Sunday. She intended hiding the packets of dye in her jacket when she went into the house, bringing Daddy the aspirin he wanted for his cold. To buy the eggs and dye, she was using money one of her aunts had sent for her birthday.

"When the hell is she coming out?" Abraham mumbled impatiently under his breath. He and Luke had the van parked out in front of the country store, by the gasoline pumps. The store was located at a crossroads several miles from the Barnes estate.

The elderly Mr. Jamison, in bibbed coveralls and faded plaid shirt, finished pumping gasoline into the van and hung up the nozzle, then took his time screwing the gas cap back on. He hobbled around the side of the vehicle and spoke to Luke, the driver. "Some damn fine weather we're havin', ain't it? Old man winter can stay away for good, for all I care. Cold weather makes my bones ache. This here oughta make a real swell Easter."

"Yep," said Luke.

Chuckling as if a joke had been mutually enjoyed, Jamison said, "She didn't take a full tank. That'll be ten dollars."

Luke already had his wallet open, and he handed the old man a ten-dollar bill.

"Thank you kindly," said Mr. Jamison. "Have a nice day, now, y'all hear."

"Right, you old fart," said Abraham for Luke's ears only, barely moving his lips.

Luke took his time getting ready to pull out, slowly starting the engine and putting the van into gear. He and his brother watched Mr. Jamison limping toward the store. As the old man held the door open, Sharon stepped out with her bag of purchases.

Jamison smiled, saying, "Bye, now, Sharon. You tell your daddy me and Martha said hello, and hope he gets over his cold real soon."

"Thanks, Mr. Jamison. So long."

Sharon walked briskly across the gravel lot, turning left at the crossroads. From the van, Luke and Abraham watched, beguiled by her long brown hair and the youthful stride of her shapely legs and buttocks, encased in tight blue jeans.

Luke said, "This is the one, brother. Purty 'nough for ya?"

Abraham grinned lewdly. "Yup . . . this one's gonna make Mama real happy." In the cab of the van he leaned forward, tingling with anticipation of the cat-and-mouse game he and his brother would play with the girl before capturing her.

Luke pressed the gas pedal lightly, easing away from the pumps. The van crossed through the intersection, going in the same direction as Sharon and cruising slowly past her as she walked off the berm of the narrow, lonely blacktop road. She stopped, watching the van suspiciously, but felt relieved when the vehicle continued past her, going down a slight grade and disappearing around a bend in the distance.

"Thinks she's seen the last of us," Abraham chortled.

Luke found a suitable spot and pulled off to the side of the road. He turned the engine off and both brothers sat very still, watching and waiting for Sharon.

She was always frightened of walking alone, even in the daylight. The house where she lived with her widowed father and four little brothers and sisters was almost three miles from the country store. She was aware of the things that could happen to young girls like herself; the newspapers and TV were always full of stories of brutal rapes and murders. This was incomprehensible to her; it seemed too callous and unreal to believe in; yet she knew it happened, all too often. Her father was always admonishing her to be careful, not to trust anybody, even the boys or the teachers at school; he didn't even like her going to the store by herself, but she had done it to fetch him the aspirin.

When she rounded the bend and saw the white van parked less than fifty feet away, she stopped in her tracks. What could they be doing there? There were no houses around, and no other vehicles on the road. For an instant, Sharon considered turning around and going back and phoning her father to come get her at the store. But that would be silly. He was sick, and she shouldn't panic over nothing and make him get up out of bed. The two men in the van didn't seem to be paying her any mind. They were talking about something. Maybe they were lost and were waiting for her so they could ask directions. She resumed walking, picking up her pace so she could get past this white van as quickly as possible and be less scared.

But when she got closer the two men looked up, staring at her, steadfastly watching her approach. They both had disturbing grins on their faces; the looks they gave her were brazen, insulting, as though they were undressing her with their eyes. She lowered her gaze to the ground, feeling shrunken and frightened and demure. She clutched the brown bag she was carrying tightly to her breasts and walked in a mincing gait, wanting suddenly to seem as young and immature and unsexy as possible, so that maybe these two men would leave her alone.

When she was almost past the van, the horn blared loudly, shaking her so badly that she dropped her bag. She turned, expecting to be attacked. But the engine started up and the van peeled out, screeching and spraying clods of black dirt, and the man on the passenger's side turned around laughing at her as the vehicle sped down the road.

"Darn idiots!" she said aloud to exorcise her fear. She was

upset, but glad that the men had gone. The sun was bright in a
cloudless April sky, but that was not the only reason she was perspiring. She stooped and examined the carton of eggs she had
been carrying in her bag. Two eggs had broken when the bag hit
the asphalt at the side of the road. Smarting from the loss, she removed the good eggs temporarily and scraped the mess from the
broken ones out, then wiped her fingers on the grass. In a little
while she had the good eggs back in the carton and the carton
back in the bag. She started walking again, hurrying, her trip to
the store having become an ordeal.

Her anxiety increased when she approached a stretch where
the road was rather thickly wooded on both sides. But she had to
get past this if she expected to walk the rest of the way home. It
was here that Luke and Abraham leaped upon her, punching at
her and knocking her to the ground. They had concealed the van
in a narrow cul-de-sac some distance away so they could pounce
on the girl from cover, on foot. The sudden ferociousness of their
attack was overpowering, giving Sharon no chance to fight back
or flee. They stood back momentarily, leering at her, taking
sadistic enjoyment out of her feeble attempt to crawl away. Eggs
were smashed all over the blacktop pavement. Sharon's breath
was knocked out of her; she was badly hurt, nearly unconscious,
and terrified. Seeing her struggling to crawl on her hands and
knees, Abraham lashed out and kicked her in the ribs, sending
her sprawling on her face. With excruciating, blinding pain, her
right cheekbone smacked and scraped against the pavement.
Abraham drew back his boot to kick her again.

"Easy, now!" Luke shouted. "Don't want to kill this one, or
Mama will have her dander up for sure."

Abraham produced a coil of nylon rope from his hip pocket,
and he and Luke rolled Sharon over onto her back to get her
trussed up. In her delirium she continued to whimper and moan,
reduced to quavering helplessness from the punishment she had
taken. The two men tightly bound her wrists and ankles. Then
they carried her to the waiting van, the rear door wide open, a
wire-mesh dog cage inside. Luke and Abraham hoisted Sharon

by her wrists and ankles, as if she were trussed-up dead meat. Kneeling on the floor of the van, Luke gagged her by tying a large red bandanna over her mouth. Then she was put into her cage and the door was locked. She had no cognizance of this, for she had passed out.

Luke jumped into the cab of the van. Abraham closed the rear door, then hopped into the cab on the passenger's side. The van eased out of the cul-de-sac onto the narrow blacktop road and drove away.

"Should have raped her," Abraham said, the memory of his thwarted desire for Gwen and Nancy still fresh in his mind.

"Nope," Luke squelched. "This one could be a virgin, the kind Mama and Cynthia need."

"What about *us?*" said Abraham.

Luke didn't answer him but stepped on the gas and sped down the sunlit road.

CHAPTER 12

On Good Friday, Nancy, Gwen, and Sharon were moved out of the Barnes house. In their cages they were loaded into the van by Luke and Abraham, who then drove the vehicle across the field to the chapel, hoisted the caged girls out one at a time, and carried them into a roomy office that had been partitioned off from the main part of the church. Ten years ago when Uncle Sal used the chapel as his studio, the office was where he relaxed, met with some of his clients, or worked on his ledgers of accounts payable and receivable. Now the former office was crammed full of easels, palettes, and unfinished paintings of bygone Americana. Sal's large mahogany desk and tall black filing cabinets were pushed against one wall. Against another wall, Nancy and Gwen and Sharon were deposited in their cells of wire mesh. Huffing from exertion, Luke and Abraham went out, slamming the door and locking it behind them.

The girls examined their new surroundings. There was one window in the office, but the cages were too low to the floor for the prisoners to see out, except for a tantalizingly restrictive view of unbudded tree branches and clear blue sky. Since it was getting on toward noon, the sun beat down hard on the tarpaper roof, and motes of dust danced in yellow rays slanting through the solitary window. One of the white plaster walls had an outline drawn in chalk where Sal had intended to cut another window. The closed-in air was musty and hot. The three girls fidgeted and perspired, cramped in their cages, trying to find the best way to position themselves so their injuries wouldn't hurt so much. The discomfort of their prison added to their distress.

"What's going to happen to us?" Sharon asked. Like Nancy and Gwen, she had been stripped down to her underwear. Her ribs were bruised ugly shades of blue and yellow and her lower lip was split, caked with blood. Her left eye was black, swollen shut. She had remained unconscious all through the night and now had a frightful headache, which made her worry about the possibility of a concussion or skull fracture.

Gwen felt sorry for Sharon, and Nancy, too, for that matter. "We have to try to get out of here," Gwen said. The change of environment had rekindled in her the desperate hope of a new chance for escape; maybe there was something the Barnes brothers had overlooked.

"You must be losing your mind," said Nancy. "There's no way."

"We can't give up," Gwen insisted. Her eyes kept moving from side to side and up and down, trying to spot something that could be turned to their advantage. One factor that was against them was time. People had made miraculous escapes from prisons when they had years to dig secret tunnels or file through bars. But how much could be done in a day?

"Why are they keeping us here?" Sharon pleaded.

"They're going to kill us," Gwen said flatly. "That's why we have to escape. They murdered my sister and Nancy's two friends."

"Oh, God!" Sharon cried disbelievingly.

"They're not necessarily going to kill us," Nancy said. "After all, we don't really know what their rituals are like."

"Let me tell you something," Gwen said sternly. "My grandfather survived the Nazi concentration camps. Six million people were put to death, and most of them went passively to the gas chambers, willing to believe the lie that they were only going to take showers. They didn't want to face their deaths, and so they died without trying to resist, making it ridiculously easy for the SS butchers. Cynthia and her brothers mean to kill us after they've had their fun. Don't paralyze your will to survive by deluding yourself otherwise."

"*Why* is this happening?" cried Sharon, tears streaming down her cheeks from both eyes, even the blackened, swollen one, which had seemed puffed shut enough to lock the tears in.

"Because they're crazy," said Gwen. "No other reason. So try to think of a way out of here."

"God is punishing us," blurted Nancy.

Gwen looked at her in amazement.

"Jesus showed us that sins must be paid for in suffering," Nancy said feverently. "Going to confession seemed hard, but it was too easy. I thought my soul was cleansed. But a heavier penance was required. I understand that now, and I can accept it. I'm not going to be like that priest Cynthia told us about who renounced his faith in the end and went to hell."

"Oh, brother!" exclaimed Gwen. "Listen, Nancy. You probably weren't particularly religious before. Now you've succumbed to despair and you're clutching at anything that can make you believe your suffering has a purpose. It has none. Turning the other cheek won't help you—it will only make it easier for your enemies by blunting your instinct for survival. You're right where they want you—under their power!"

Nancy did not argue. Curled up on the floor of her cage, she turned her face to the wall to avoid further communication with Gwen, as if Gwen's ideas instead of the Barnes family were the enemies that might pollute her soul.

"Even some of the Nazi war criminals condemned at Nuremberg became religious before they were hanged for their atrocities," Gwen stated. "The sudden acquisition of deep faith is a common reaction of all sorts of people under stress. Charles Colson, for example."

"I'm religious, too," interjected Sharon, in case God was up there listening. "I'm not an atheist, like you seem to be, Gwen. But I'm not giving up, either. Maybe my daddy will come looking for me or call the sheriff or something. In the meantime, what can we do to help ourselves?"

"I don't know right off," Gwen admitted. "Look around for something in here that might give you an idea. Come on, Nancy—help out. I want to see my daughter Amy again. And your mother still loves you, doesn't she, despite your stepfather?"

But Nancy didn't respond. She had started praying another rosary, and rather than answering Gwen, she kept praying doggedly without moving her lips, saying the words to herself. The repetition of the familiar prayers almost took her mind off the feeling that she might as well die, anyway, because nobody in this world really cared about her. The shocks of the past few days had broken her spirit.

"Is that a palette knife under the desk chair?" asked Sharon, suddenly perking up.

She and Gwen leaned to one side of their cages and peered out anxiously. Nancy did not stir. "I believe it is," said Sharon, squinting at the knife out of her one good eye. Her cage was the closest one to it.

"Take your bra off," Gwen suggested. Seeing Sharon's puzzlement, she explained: "I'll take mine off, too, and pass it to you. By tying them together, maybe you can fish the knife out from under the chair and pull it close enough to grab it."

Sharon looked doubtful. "How far away is the knife?" she asked. "Looks like four or five feet to me, but my depth perception is not so hot because of my swollen eye."

"You're right," Gwen said dolefully. "About four feet. We'll never reach it without something long and stiff. Still, we may as well try. We've got nothing to lose."

The two girls took off their bras and Gwen managed to pass hers to Sharon, who tied the two together and made a loop at one end. But the gauge of the wire mesh was such that she could only stick her fingers out through the tiny steel bars. This prohibited her from getting enough finger or hand movement to fling the tied-together bras very far. She tried dropping them to the floor outside her cage and then crouching down and blowing hard at them in an attempt to force them out toward the knife. But the cloth material was too heavy, and no matter how hard she blew, it would barely budge. "Darn it!" she cried in exasperation, rocking back on her haunches, out of breath.

"Well, you tried," Gwen said consolingly, still trying to think of some way to make the attempt work.

Just then there was a loud ferocious rapping on the windowpane and Sharon looked up and screamed. Gwen stared, wide-eyed. Cyrus was out there, pressing his red beefy face against the glass, leering and giggling for all he was worth over his delicious eyeful of the nearly naked young girls. They covered themselves hastily with their ragged blankets. Cyrus stayed at the window for a long time, jabbering and pointing and carrying on, his nose and cheeks caked with window dirt he had rubbed away by pressing his face against the pane.

Gwen said, "He can't come in here . . . I don't think. He probably doesn't have a key."

Cyrus kept staring, spittle drooling from his thick, leering lips.

Nancy kept praying, stifling her terror. Through it all she hadn't made a move.

"He's so *creepy*," said Sharon, shuddering. She averted her good eye from Cyrus in the hopes that ignoring him would make him go away. Gwen did likewise, and eventually this seemed to work. When they no longer sensed his presence at the window, they turned and looked and saw with relief that he was gone.

Sharon passed Gwen's bra over to her and they both put their garments back on. Silently, they resumed checking out their prison, looking for a way to escape. Every now and then their eyes traveled to the out-of-reach palette knife, just a few feet away on the concrete floor. It was the only glimmer of something usable. But it might as well be on the moon. It wasn't much of a weapon, anyway, Sharon told herself ruefully. Gwen never had thought of it as a weapon, though. She figured that if they could get hold of it somehow, they could maybe jimmy the padlocks on their cages.

Outside, for the next couple of hours, there were sounds of hammering and sawing. Cyrus was hard at work, making three coffins.

CHAPTER 13

On Friday afternoon Morgan Drey drove through Cherry Hill slowly, looking for a place to eat and a place to stay. After a couple of futile stops, he found that the hotels were booked solid and other places of business, including restaurants, were closed from twelve till three, the hours during which Christ was crucified two thousand years ago. This was the Bible Belt. It was only two o'clock. Not many pedestrians were on the streets, but Morgan noticed quite a few parked cars with out-of-state license plates. Feeling strangely about it, he realized that Cynthia's prattle about a congregation must have a basis in reality; the booked-up hotels and out-of-state cars meant that a large number of people had materialized in this out-of-the-way West Virginia hamlet for the "services" Cynthia had talked about so proudly.

On the outskirts of town, Morgan spotted something called Bob and Dot's Motel, a row of ten plain yellow-brick units in no discernible architectural style, set back off the road in a gravel lot adjacent to Bob and Dot's Bar. There didn't appear to be a motel manager's office, so Morgan assumed that guests registered in the saloon. Six automobiles, four with out-of-state plates, were parked in the lot opposite six of the motel units, so maybe there was a vacancy. Morgan went into the saloon to find out. Glancing at his watch, he saw that he still had an hour to go till he could get a couple of hamburgers and some black coffee, unless Bob and Dot were radical enough not to observe Good Friday.

There was nobody in the saloon except the bartender, a grizzled, sour-faced old man in a Mickey Mouse T-shirt, who was hunching over the bar reading a newspaper. He looked up at the wall clock as Morgan walked in. "Can't serve you till three, Mister," he rasped disapprovingly, as if Morgan had committed a sacrilege by merely having food on his mind.

"I'd like a room in the motel," Morgan told him placatingly, not looking to get into an argument. "If possible."

The old man snorted. "Why in heaven's name wouldn't it be possible?" he said irritably. "Didn't you see the vacancy sign?" he smacked his hand on the bar belligerently.

"Yes, but that doesn't always mean there is one," said Morgan.

"Ten dollars a night, Mister. Take it or leave it."

"I'll take it," Morgan said. He paid in advance and without a word of thanks was handed a key to unit six. He didn't ask about the possibility of food and coffee later, not wanting to prolong his conversation with the feisty old man. He had noticed a menu of items such as chili, stew and Southern fried chicken posted above the bar and hoped these things would become available after three.

He parked his car in front of unit six and unlocked the door. Surprisingly, the accommodations weren't bad. The bedroom was clean and there was even a color TV. The bathroom had a glassed-in tub and shower, which was what Morgan was most interested in. After throwing his suitcase on the bed, he got undressed and took a long, hot shower. While the water beat against the nape of his neck, he thought about Cynthia. Now that he was this close to her, his trip to Cherry Hill seemed wildly foolish. Maybe he should get a good night's rest and drive back to New York, keeping it to himself that he had ever been so impetuous. Anybody who found out about this would laugh at him. Cynthia would probably laugh when he encountered her. What did he expect her to do—fall in love with him? Such things only happened in the movies. In real life these escapades ended in embarrassment and rejection, not in stealing the bride from the altar as Dustin Hoffman did in *The Graduate*. But Morgan knew he would not turn around and go home. Something inside him always made him see each misadventure through to its vainglorious conclusion. As an anthropologist he was scrupulously logical and rational, but his personal life was often ruled by a flamboyant, quixotic streak he had never been able to repress; sometimes he told himself this was what made him a human being, although a flawed one, rather than a cold, formidable, unapproachable scientist, like several of his more staid colleagues.

Two days ago he had gotten absurdly drunk in the Greenwich Village bar next door to Cynthia's shop, and had allowed himself to be picked up by a prostitute, on the theory that it would be good therapy. He had spent the night with her, falling asleep leadenly after a determined effort to blunt his passions and take the edge off his nutty impulse to hop in his car and drive six hundred miles to see Cynthia uninvited. When he awoke in a hotel room, the prostitute was gone and he was badly hung over. But he filled himself up with pancakes and coffee and drove all the way down through Pennsylvania in one day. Last night he had stayed in a hotel in Wheeling, West Virginia, and today he had driven the final two hundred miles to Cherry Hill. He was so tired his nerves were on edge, and he couldn't help having some severe trepidations about the outcome of all this. He still didn't know exactly where Cynthia lived. He had checked a telephone directory in one of the filled-up hotels where he had tried to get a room, but there was no listing under her last name. His idea was to freshen himself up, get some food into his stomach, and ask around town after three o'clock, when the merchants reopened their doors.

Lying on his bed in T-shirt and shorts, he fell asleep watching television, and when he awoke it was almost four o'clock. He got into a sweater and slacks and combed his hair, then crossed the parking lot to the bar and found it lively. He liked the smells of coffee, French fries, and chicken. The old man who had checked him in was nowhere in sight, and a much younger fellow was behind the bar, waiting on half a dozen customers. Several tables and booths were filled, too. Country and Western music blared from the jukebox.

Morgan sat on a barstool, purposely sandwiching himself between two men with whom he might be able to strike up a conversation. These men didn't look like Cherry Hill residents; instead, they might be out-of-towners here for Cynthia's services—part of her congregation. If so, they would know how to get to her place.

The bartender, a stocky, bald-headed man in gray work-clothes, took Morgan's order for chicken, French fries, cole slaw, and black coffee; it was more than he wanted to eat, but he figured that if he had a substantial meal to linger over it would give him more time to get something going with someone who had the information he was after. In the meantime, trying to be unobtrusive, he checked out the other patrons, who all appeared pretty normal considering the fact that at least some of them were probably indulging in fantasies of witchcraft, sorcery and related hocus-pocus. Maybe their idiosyncrasies were harmless. But Morgan didn't think so. To him they represented an aberration, a social retrogression that at best encouraged neurosis, and at worst led to schizophrenia. It might already be too late to rescue Cynthia from her delusions.

When the bartender brought his meal, he inquired loudly, wanting to be overheard: "Do you happen to know a young lady named Cynthia Barnes?"

"Why?"

The bartender's reply was natural and friendly enough, but Morgan had the feeling that conversations at the bar and at nearby tables had come to a halt. "I'm trying to get to her house," he said, keeping his volume up.

"There's not a Barnes family in town that I can think of," said the bartender. "Seems like there ought to be; it's a common enough name. But there ain't. If there was, I'd know about it. Not much escapes a fellow's attention in a town this small."

"How about in some of the outlying areas?"

"Could be, but I'm afraid I can't tell you for sure. Like me to freshen your coffee?"

Morgan nodded his head and the bartender poured from a full, steaming pot. The level of conversation in the place didn't quite seem to return to normal. It was hard for him to believe that his questions could have been this unsettling. Maybe it was his imagination. He was too keyed up to trust his perceptions. He spread butter on a hot home-baked roll and took a bite of it along with a forkful of delicious fried chicken.

"Pardon me, sir," the man on the barstool to his right said. "May I ask how you've come to know Cynthia Barnes?"

Turning, Morgan saw a slender little man with a handsome, weathered face, neat gray mustache, and slickly parted and combed gray hair worn just long enough to touch the tops of his ears. He was in white shoes, slacks, and shirt, with a powder-blue sport jacket, a gold bracelet on one wrist, a gold watch on the other. His clothes were stylish and expensive looking. He looked like an actor or a doctor, or an actor who might play a doctor on television. Morgan noticed his ring with an emblem of a skull, the eyes set with tiny rubies.

"I knew Cynthia in New York," Morgan said. "We dated, got to know each other, and she told me about some goings on down here. She invited me to come."

"How is it you don't have her address?" The man wore a smile but there was no humor in his question. The gentleman next to him was hunched forward on his stool, peering around him to scrutinize Morgan.

It seemed best to continue lying, now that he had already lied about being invited. "She gave me her address before she closed her store in Greenwich Village for the Easter holidays. I have no idea how I lost it, and she doesn't have a listed phone. But I drove down here, anyway. I didn't want to miss out on the things she described."

"You've been in the store?"

"Many times."

The man smiled. "Did you ever buy a witch's bottle?" he asked, giving the strange question an air of flippancy.

Morgan said, "Cynthia let me photograph some without buying them—for a book I was writing."

The man mulled this over. Finally, he stuck out his hand. "My name is Harvey Bronson. My friend here is John Logan. We are chiropractors from Columbus, Ohio."

"Morgan Drey. I'm an anthropologist. Pleased to meet you."

John Logan was short and stout, not fat but powerful looking, and as well dressed as Harvey Bronson. Shaking hands with Morgan, Logan said, "I hope you'll forgive us for being careful. Now that we understand you as a friend, we'll be happy to take you out to the Barnes estate with us. It's a pleasant drive, fifteen miles or so out into the countryside."

"If it's that far, I'd rather follow in my own car," said Morgan, thinking that he might have to leave by himself if Cynthia made him feel unwelcome.

"Yes, that would be better," Bronson agreed. He signaled the bartender for another round of cocktails and offered to buy Morgan a drink, but Morgan said no, thanks, coffee was all he wanted.

"Hung over?" Logan chortled.

"You guessed it," Morgan said, managing a dry chuckle.

The bartender brought two fresh cocktails and Bronson pulled out a wad of bills.

"Excuse me for a moment," Logan said, then hopped down off his barstool. He crossed the dance floor, in his half-waddling, short-legged gait, to a large circular booth on the far side of the dining area where a group of urbane-seeming men and women were eating and drinking. Morgan's attention remained briefly on Logan while Bronson was preoccupied with paying for the drinks he had ordered. Logan had approached a white-haired patriarchal gentleman, a commanding presence who must've weighed about three hundred pounds and seemed to be in charge of the people in the booth. After a nod of his head acknowledging

Logan's presence, the white-haired gentleman remained seated, listening intently while Logan talked to him, apparently imparting information, but they were too far away for Morgan to hear what was being said. When Logan got done talking, the white-haired man replied at some length, his eyes meeting Logan's piercingly, his lip movements clearly defined, as if issuing orders which must not be misunderstood. Morgan could make nothing out from the lip movements.

"Those people in the booth are friends, too," Harvey Bronson said. "But you can see that for yourself, Morgan." His eyes twinkled conspiratorially. "The man John is talking to is an extraordinary fellow. A mortician, Stanford Slater, from San Francisco. Perhaps you've heard of him."

"Can't say that I have," Morgan said, hoping the admission wasn't a *faux pas*. Bronson merely sipped his gin-and-tonic noncommittally while Logan waddled back across the dance floor and hopped up onto his stool.

It gave Morgan an eerie feeling to be surrounded by people who thought they were witches. He figured that the American Chiropractic Association would be as dismayed by Logan and Bronson and their dabbling in witchcraft as a group of nuclear physicists would be if one of their kind turned out to be an alchemist.

Morgan finished his chicken and French fries and his last sip of cold coffee. Turning to Bronson, he said, "What time are we leaving?"

"I'm ready now," Bronson said. "How about you, John?"

"Soon as I finish this," said Logan, gesturing with his drink.

Morgan glanced across the dance floor to the booth on the far side and saw that the patriarchal mortician Stanford Slater and his entourage were on the move, getting up from their table.

"Are they going out to Cynthia's, too?" asked Morgan.

"Yes, of course. We all are," Bronson replied cheerfully.

"Quite a crowd," Morgan said, making small talk.

Bronson eyed him appraisingly. "You really find all this a bit silly, don't you?"

It was both a question and an accusation, and Morgan did not know how to take it or what to say.

"Don't worry," said Bronson, smiling suddenly. "Some of the rest of us aren't totally serious about it, either. But it's fascinating, isn't it? It reminds me of primal-scream therapy—getting all the ugliness out of one's system in one weekend each year. We need outbursts like this, you see—at least some of us do—because our modern age requires us to be too rational, dignified, and restrained. Take me, for example. I can't tell you the number of patients I've had to be nice to, when I felt like twisting their necks the wrong way."

"I agree that it is fascinating," said Morgan, wondering just how wild things were going to get.

Logan said, "Of course, Cynthia thinks she's the high priestess and we're the followers. But really it's us egging her on, pushing her to new and greater excesses. It's something, though, how she's got those brothers of hers totally under her control."

"Some of us don't really believe in all the hocus-pocus," said Bronson. "But Cynthia does. So do most of the others. The rest of us recognize it as an excuse to do what we want to do, anyway. It's like a true-blue housewife getting drunk before she screws the milkman."

"I'll bet this weekend is going to be a corker," Logan enthused, getting up from his stool. "You can feel it in the air. I wouldn't miss it for anything."

"Where's your car, Morgan?" Bronson asked.

"In front of unit six."

"I suggest you check out and plan on staying with us at the house. Cynthia won't mind. Can you be ready in a half-hour?"

Morgan said that he could. Inwardly, he was elated at the invitation to stay at Cynthia's place and heartened by Logan's blithe assurance that Cynthia wouldn't mind. Maybe he had done the right thing in driving down here, after all. Even if his romantic aspirations were eventually thwarted, at least he was gathering good material for a book.

* * *

Following closely behind Harvey Bronson's silver Cadillac, Morgan Drey pulled into the long gravel driveway of the Barnes estate. Several late-model cars were parked there ahead of him. Slamming the door of his badly rusted green Plymouth, he took in the tree-shrouded view of the house with some surprise, finding it much more elegant than he had imagined, and Cynthia came out onto the front porch. She stood perfectly still, gazing at him in an unresponsive way, not glad to see him, not angry apparently, but lovely and remote in a spotless white hostess gown framed by two white pillars on the wide porch of the mansion. "Hello!" he called out tentatively, as if she were a beautiful but forbidden vision that could be frightened away by the sound of his voice.

"Morgan," she said, offering her slender white hand as he came closer, John Logan and Harvey Bronson close behind as he ascended the gray stone steps. Cynthia's hand briefly in Morgan's, he stood at her side in the coolness of evening and realized by a glimpse into the well-lighted living room that she must have known he was coming. Stanford Slater and his entourage were already there and, of course, had passed the word along so that Cynthia wouldn't be taken by surprise.

She shook hands with Logan and Bronson and said, "Do come in. Join the other guests and have some wine and relax."

Hoping it was his imagination, Morgan seemed to sense that she was much warmer toward the two chiropractors than she had been toward him.

Going past her on his way into the house, he let his eyes scan her face for some clue as to his degree of welcome, but she gave no such clue and his spirits sank. He felt that if she truly wanted him there, she'd show it more—unless she was merely going to make him suffer a bit, for having the gall to crash her party. She seemed regal, aloof, in total command of a setting in which she belonged and he did not. She didn't introduce him to anybody, either. But a tall, darkly handsome man in a three-piece blue suit came over to him and jauntily handed him a glass of red wine.

"I'm Luke Barnes," the man said, "Cynthia's brother."

"Pleased to meet you," Morgan said gratefully, shaking hands. "My name is Morgan Drey."

"You're the one who's in love with my sister," Luke said quite loudly, a brazen leer on his handsome but devilish face, as if he were an adolescent poking fun at another kid in the schoolyard at recess.

Stuck for a comeback, Morgan almost stammered, and Luke's impudent grin erupted into cruel, bucolic laughter.

Then Luke pivoted and walked away, leaving Morgan stranded in the middle of the room wondering how many of the guests had overheard Luke's taunting remark. Embarrassed and trying not to show it, he made his way to a straight-backed chair in a corner of the overly crowded living room, with its high beamed ceiling and heavy Victorian furniture. He downed half his wine in a series of rapid gulps, thinking that if he got a little loaded he might relax and enjoy himself and not get his feelings hurt so easily. Bronson and Logan seemed to know everybody at the party and moved about at their ease. Cynthia was carrying on a conversation across the room with the mortician, Stanford Slater, whose huge bulk reposed pontifically in a gigantic armchair upholstered in a gay, flowery pattern. The overall mood and chatter were reminiscent of any ordinary cocktail party, except for an ominous undercurrent Morgan could not quite put his finger on. Again, maybe it was his imagination. He felt an overpowering need to get Cynthia separated from the others somehow so he could talk to her.

Well, being a wallflower wasn't going to help. Making up his mind to socialize, he stood up, quaffed his wine, and took a decisive step or two in the direction of Cynthia Barnes and Stanford Slater, who were now surrounded by several others, but he was stopped by Harvey Bronson, who appeared tipsy.

"Isn't this rural environment wonderful!" Bronson exclaimed slurringly.

"Clean air," said Morgan, making himself agreeable.

"No, I don't mean the air," the chiropractor snapped back almost petulantly. "I'm referring to the absence of civilization. You can get away with murder out here. Morgan, allow me to refill your wineglass." He did so, pouring from a crystal decanter that he plucked from a nearby mahogany buffet, and then handed the full glass to Morgan before excusing himself and sidestepping toward an attractive but very sober-looking young woman who was now sitting in the straight-backed chair Morgan had vacated.

Morgan stood his ground for a moment, sipping wine and surveying the partyers. He wanted to shake his head in consternation when he thought of the common bond that had drawn them together in this out-of-the-way place, way off the beaten track, in the backwoods of West Virginia. These people who professed to be witches seemed middle- to upper-class for the most part. Well dressed, fashionable, reasonably educated, they were the sort whose jaded tastes might as easily have run to something like wife-swapping instead of to the kinkiness of witchcraft. Socializing with one another over drinks and cigarettes, they talked of politics, economics, travel, inflation, and so on. They didn't laugh much, though. And what laughter Morgan heard seemed tinny, forced, artificial, unless it was laughter like Luke's, coming at someone else's expense.

How to rescue Cynthia from this sort of existence?

As if thinking of her had drawn her toward him, he saw her disengaging herself from Stanford Slater and the others and making her way toward him with a smile on her face. He hoped that she had decided to forgive him for crashing her party. He wanted to be alone with her, but the best he could ask for in these surroundings was that nobody else would come over and horn in.

"I am sorry for being rude to you," she told him. "But I didn't invite you here. And I have no idea why you came."

"I wanted very much to see you. I had no plans for the holidays. And I thought you might let me take some photographs of the services you were so proud of." He grinned, trying his best to win her over.

"Mama would never allow it," she said soberly. "In fact, Morgan, I'm sure Mama would never approve of your being here. You don't believe as we do. Why do you wish to desecrate our ceremonies?"

"Desecrate?" He said it with more sarcasm than he intended.

Her expression went from haughtiness to anger. "Yes, desecrate!" she snapped.

He reached out, touching her arm, but she drew away from him instantly, her black eyes flashing. He fought down an impulse to scold her. But he could not hope to get close to her by lashing out, spitefully shattering her make-believe world. The only way to help her was to gain her confidence a little at a time, by pretending to go along with her to some extent and then eventually causing her to question her own beliefs. This did not seem impossible to Morgan. He knew about "deprogramming" and wished he could accomplish it in his own way with Cynthia.

"I'm sorry," he told her diplomatically. "I don't mean to always sound so smug and disapproving. Maybe I'd understand you better if I'd be more open-minded. I'm willing to try, if you'll give me a chance."

"It's not up to me. It's up to Mama," she said, still pouting.

"May I ask your mother's permission to stay and see the services?"

Cynthia thought it over for a long time. "I'll take you up to see her," she said finally.

Morgan allowed himself to be led through the throng of guests in the living room toward a long ascending staircase with a dark, curving banister. Many pairs of eyes watched him and Cynthia beginning to climb the stairs, and conversations halted. By the time Morgan and Cynthia reached the carpeted landing, it was as though no party was going on down in the living room. All Morgan heard was the muffled creaking of the floorboards as they climbed the stairs.

Cynthia had her hand on the doorknob and was pushing the door open. "Mama, a gentleman to see you," she said, motioning for Morgan to enter the bedroom.

When he stepped forward, his eyes went wide and he began

screaming. This was all the more frightening because he had never screamed before, never had encountered anything to tear that response from him. Simultaneously, he heard Cynthia laughing at him, as her brother Luke had laughed, loudly and maliciously, and her laughter was picked up and amplified by the crowds of people downstairs in the living room.

Meredith Barnes, Cynthia's mother, was dead. She was sitting in her rocking chair by the window, eyes wide open, embalmed. Morgan could not stop screaming. The revelation that Mama was dead was the equivalent of a true glimpse into the hell-ridden depths of Cynthia's insanity.

Footsteps came up the stairs toward Morgan and he choked off the gurgling scream in his throat and pivoted shakily, starting to gag, feeling sickened to the depths of his soul, brushing past Cynthia and the maniacal laughter distorting her face. Morgan would have bolted down the curving staircase and out of the house, out into the night. But he was seized roughly by the strong arms of Luke Barnes, and behind Luke were Abraham and Cyrus. Morgan tried to fight, lashing out wildly, but this only amused the three brothers. They pinned Morgan's arms behind his back and choked him into breathless helplessness while Cynthia continued to laugh shrilly.

The people from downstairs came up into the hallway, bemused looks on all their faces. Stanford Slater, breathing hard and sweating profusely from the effort of mounting the stairs, managed a thick-lipped, flaccid smile as he looked Morgan in the eyes. Morgan realized the embalming had been Slater's work. "You perverted bastard." Without a word, the mortician slapped Morgan hard in the face.

Harvey Bronson and John Logan, the two chiropractors, stood by leeringly, glasses of red wine in their hands. Bronson said boastfully, "I knew he wasn't supposed to be here when he didn't know the code. I asked him if he ever bought a witch's bottle, and I forget what he said,. but it wasn't the agreed-upon response."

"You see?" said Stanford Slater. "We played along with you

and got you here, where you said you wanted to be. Only now you're going to wish you never poked around where you weren't wanted."

Morgan felt Luke's hot breath on his neck as Luke tightened his full nelson. "Easy, now," Luke said, "and it'll be over painlessly almost before you know it."

John Logan, the short, muscular chiropractor, stepped forward. "Put him on the floor, flat on his stomach, and hold him down."

Morgan's legs were kicked out from under him and he fell, landing hard, as Cynthia's three brothers rolled him over and pinned him face down. The breath was knocked out of him and he ached all over but couldn't move, he had so much weight on his arms, legs, and back. The people in the hallway crowded in on him, and their hushed murmurs of expectancy were terrifying. With a rush of panic, Morgan wondered: Were they going to kill him? He couldn't see Cynthia; she was blocked from view.

John Logan set his half-empty wineglass on the floor by a banister post and knelt near Morgan's head. Morgan felt the strong, stubby hands of the chiropractor seizing him by the head and the back of the neck, and then his head and neck were twisted with a sharp, violent, agonizing pain that ended abruptly—very abruptly—and for a moment Morgan gave thanks that the pain was gone because it had been so excruciating that if it had lasted he could not have stood it at all and would certainly have passed out.

But now, he realized, he did not feel anything at all from the neck down.

He must be temporarily paralyzed. Luke and Cyrus and Abraham rolled him over onto his back and he saw all the people—Cynthia, Logan, Slater, Bronson, and all the others—staring down at him, grinning.

And then he truly panicked, so badly that he lost his mind. Adrenaline pumped through him, his thoughts became a wild, crazy jumble dashing everywhere at once and getting nowhere, while his body remained absolutely inert, like a heavy, useless sack of garbage.

Because he knew, even though he didn't want to believe it, that the paralysis caused by the chiropractor was not temporary at all, but final and permanent.

"Now Mama allows you to watch the services," Cynthia told him, in her softest and sweetest voice. "You can have a ringside seat, because we'll know you won't run away and tell on us afterward."

Morgan could feel the hot tears rolling down his cheeks, but he couldn't feel his arms, his legs, his toes, or his fingers.

CHAPTER 14

Just before sundown, Cyrus and Abraham went across the field to the chapel to start a fire. The main part of the old country church, where the services were to be held, was heated by a large black potbelly stove. A small electric heater was used to take the chill from Uncle Sal's former office, where Sharon, Gwen, and Nancy were being held prisoners.

Abraham was slightly drunk and anxious to get back to the party still in progress at the house. He unlocked the chapel door and Cyrus followed him in, trundling an armload of split wood. Cyrus stood in the doorway leering at the three caged girls as Abraham entered far enough to plug in the electric heater and adjust the dial.

"C'mon, Cyrus, I don't want to stay down here too long," Abraham said, clapping a hand on his brother's shoulder to get him moving out of his way and into the main part of the church, with its rows of varnished pews.

"What are they going to do?" Sharon whispered, still shaken by the appearance of Cyrus and Abraham in the chapel.

"Build a fire, it looks like," Gwen whispered back. "At least I hope so. I'm freezing."

Nancy didn't say a word. She wasn't asleep, though; she was too cold and scared to sleep and remained huddled in her blanket, knees drawn up in a fetal position on the floor of her cage. Gwen and Sharon were sitting facing each other, wrapped tightly in their blankets, too.

"I'm scared to death of the big dumb one," Sharon said.

The cast-iron door of the potbelly stove creaked on its rusty hinges as Abraham pulled it open. Cyrus dumped his armload of logs onto the hardwood floor and stooped to pick out choice pieces of kindling.

"Put it all in," Abraham said impatiently. "I ain't waitin' for the small stuff to catch. I'll get it all goin' at once with a few good squirts of charcoal lighter."

Abraham had the can of fluid in his hand and used it to saturate the wood that Cyrus obediently piled into the stove. When Abraham struck a wooden match and tossed it in, the whole works flared up into a roaring blaze, bathing the room in bright, flickering orange light. Abraham shifted his weight from one foot to the other, wishing the chore to be over so he could rejoin the party. Cyrus watched the fire contentedly.

Finally, Abraham said, "Cyrus, you stay here and make sure it catches good. The church has got to be good and warm by midnight. If the fire don't catch, come back up to the house and tell me. Otherwise, lock the padlock on the outside door and come on up yourself and have a good time. Can I trust you to do what I told you?"

Cyrus nodded his head with great solemnity, trying his best to look trustworthy.

"Okay," said Abraham. "Now, if you need to ask me for help, do it without letting Luke or Cynthia get wise. Understand me?"

Cyrus nodded his head up and down. Then he gave his attention to the blaze in the stove, till his brother Abraham went out the door. When he turned, his eyes gleamed as he thought about the girls in the other room.

Sharon screamed as soon as she saw Cyrus standing in the doorway, his thick lips wet with spittle.

"You get out of here!" Gwen snapped. "Out! Out!"

Cyrus was cowed momentarily, his beefy face slackening indecisively. Then something bright and shiny caught his eye on the floor beneath Uncle Sal's old chair. It was the palette knife. Exactly the kind of toy Cyrus liked. The lure of it was too much for him, and, giggling, he waddled into the room.

Horrified, Gwen and Sharon watched him getting on his fat knees, groping for the knife, grunting his satisfaction as he clutched it in his fat fingers.

"Get up, Nancy! Get *up*!" Gwen shrieked.

Nancy saw what was happening, scrambled frantically, and cringed in the farthest corner of her wire cage. Cyrus jabbed at her with the palette knife, then moved and jabbed again. Both times Nancy narrowly got out of the way.

Cyrus whirled for a try at Sharon, but the short, stubby blade of the knife spronged off the wires, twisting his wrist and making him scrape his knuckles. The knife fell into Sharon's cage. Cyrus jumped back, sucking on his skinned knuckles. Then he strode forward, moaning in rage and self-pity, and kicked Sharon's cage until she was jarred from one side to the other, banging and scraping against the wire mesh. When he was worn out, huffing for breath, Cyrus delivered a few last kicks at Nancy and Gwen, making their cages jump. After his tantrum, forgetting about the knife, he waddled out of the office with a pained look in his eyes.

The three girls listened with held breath for fear he might change his mind and return. They heard him slam the chapel door and snap the padlock. In a little while, Gwen regained her composure and said excitedly, "Sharon, we've got the knife!"

"Yes, but what good will it do?"

"What do you mean? We can use it to pry open the locks on our cages."

"And then what about the lock outside?"

Gwen sucked in her breath, struggling to keep hope and determination alive. "We have to take one step at a time, and we can't give up. If we get out of the cages, we may find a way out of the building. If nothing else, we can rush them next time they open the door."

"All right," said Sharon, whispering hoarsely in her desperation. "All right. I have the knife. I'll give it a try. "

"Pray for us, Nancy," Gwen said.

CHAPTER 15

In the office of Sheriff Wayne Cunningham in Cherry Hill, Bert Johnson and the sheriff shook hands. Sitting behind his old, battered wooden desk, Sheriff Cunningham told Bert to have a seat, pointing at a folding chair against the wall. Then he said, "What can I do for you, Mr. Johnson? I understand you're a lawman, too."

His voice was high and squeaky with a West Virginia twang. His hand had felt hard and calloused, as if his duties as a peace officer didn't prevent him from digging in the ground or pushing a plow. He was a short, wiry, straight-backed man with bushy black eyebrows and a brown mole on his chin, his black hair rumpled and streaked with gray.

"Yep, I'm a lawman," Bert said, glad of being able to establish a common bond. "Sheriff, I'm looking for my stepdaughter, Nancy. She's a runaway, seventeen years old. I'm afraid she might come to harm, and if so it'll be partly my fault. She left home because of a . . . misunderstanding . . . between the two of us. I want to find her and persuade her to come back. I've promised her mother to try and make things right."

The truth was, Harriet had been unbearable since Nancy's disappearance. Bert had not been able to bring himself to tell his wife the facts about what he had done. But Harriet sensed he was somehow to blame, and was holding it against him. He was in danger of losing her. In his misery, he entertained hopes of talking sense to Nancy, apologizing to her, even though she had led him on, and getting her to appreciate that it was in her best interests, as well as his, for her to go back to her mother and keep her mouth shut about what had driven her away.

Eyeing Bert, Sheriff Cunningham said, "Maybe you shouldn't blame yourself too much, Mr. Johnson. Lots of teen-agers go bad these days. And the parents or stepparents ain't always to blame."

Bert shrugged disconsolately, the picture of parental concern.

"What makes you think I can help you?" the sheriff asked. "You're not from this area, are you?"

"We make our home in Lewistown, in southwestern Pennsylvania. The day Nancy left home, three days ago, some buddies of mine in a patrol car saw her hitchhiking. They came around the block to talk to her, find out if everything was okay, but by that time she was being picked up by two young fellows in a white van. The cops in the patrol car got the license number. But they didn't follow. There was no reason to, as far as they were concerned."

The sheriff leaned forward, getting interested. "You tryin' to tell me you traced the van here? Lewistown is over two hundred miles away."

"That's right," Bert said. "I ran a check on the vehicle's license number, through the state police. It turns out your office has a bulletin out. Some teen-agers stole some groceries right here in town. They were riding in a white van, and the license plate tallies."

"How about that," the sheriff said appreciatively. "Good police work, Mr. Johnson."

"Thank you, Sheriff. Unfortunately, Nancy is going to have petty larceny hanging over her, if I do find her. She's never been in any bad trouble before. But she's undoubtedly one of the kids you're looking for."

The sheriff pursed his lips and leaned back, making his desk chair squeak. Soberly, he informed Bert, "I hate to tell you, but there's a chance she's in much worse trouble."

"Why?"

"That van you mentioned was pursued by two of my deputies, and they've dropped from sight. We found their squad car abandoned twenty miles out in the sticks. The radiator was smashed in. But we didn't find the deputies. We don't know what happened to them. I've got a shortage of men here, and the ones I can spare have been out trying to turn up a lead. But it's tough. The backwoods folks don't trust any agent of the law, and won't hardly cooperate. Lots of 'em run bootleg whisky, or distill it themselves in some of these old falling-down barns or abandoned coal mines. The Feds won't even come in to have a look around, 'cause they've had men go in and never be heard from again. That's just what has happened to my two deputies. So far we haven't had a bit of luck tracing them."

"Can I join the search?" Bert asked.

Thoughtfully, the sheriff fingered the mole on his chin. "I can't stop you, I reckon. In fact, I can prob'ly use your help. At least you're a lawman, instead of an inexperienced busybody. But you'd better be damn careful wandering around out in the boondocks by yourself. The only clue I can contribute is to show you on the county map the area where we found the abandoned squad car."

"That's all I can ask for. I appreciate it, Sheriff."

Both men stood up, and Bert came over to the map on the wall to have a closer look at where the sheriff was pointing.

CHAPTER 16

Sharon and Gwen had traded the palette knife back and forth for the past two hours, each having a try at jimmying the locks on their cages. The only light they had to work by was the faint illumination given off by the electric heater Abraham had plugged into the wall. Both girls had cut and skinned their fingers several times, but the locks wouldn't give.

They had to stop trying when they heard noises outside the church. The door was unlocked and people filed in, filling the pews. From where they were kept prisoners, the girls couldn't see what was happening. Sharon hid the palette knife under her ragged blanket. Gwen peered anxiously into the semi-darkness, trying for a glimpse of something through the doorway, but the angle was so sharp that she could see little. A large group of people was coming into the chapel, some of them were carrying candles and wearing black hooded robes. The coughs, whispered conversations, and restrained titters of laughter were reminiscent of any other congregation filing into a church.

Nancy sat up, moving to the rear of her cage, pressing her body backward against the wire mesh. From the depths of her soul, she had the apprehension that something awful was about to happen. Something sinful, revolting, and terrifying.

The congregation settled down. The silence was ominous.

Then Luke, Cyrus, and Abraham, wearing black robes, came into the office and unlocked Sharon's cage. "The last shall be first," Abraham said, chortling. Sharon backed away, wild-eyed, clutching the palette knife under her ratty blanket. "What's she got in her hand?" Luke demanded, as Cyrus reached in to pull her out. She made a stab with the knife, aiming for the meaty part of Cyrus' forearm but missing by inches. The big man jumped back, banging his knuckles on the top of the cage, roaring in pain and anger.

"Look out!" Luke yelled.

Sharon scrambled out of her cage, swishing the knife through the air, trying to carve a path through the three men. Abraham tripped her and she went down, sprawling. Luke smacked her over the head with the butt of his revolver, which he had drawn from beneath his robe. She flattened out, unconscious, and the palette knife dropped from her grasp. Luke picked it up and put it in his pocket. "Who the hell let her get hold of a knife?" he snapped, glowering straight at Cyrus.

The big man whimpered, sucking his sore knuckles.

"Serves you right," said Abraham. "Don't try to wheedle any pity."

While Nancy and Gwen watched fearfully, Luke and Abraham hauled Sharon limply to her feet and dragged her out to the main part of the church and the waiting congregation. Cyrus waddled behind them, after a mean, accusing glance back at the two girls cringing in their cages.

"What are they going to do to Sharon?" Nancy asked, her voice weak and trembly.

Gwen refrained from saying the awful answer that came immediately to mind. She strained to hear what was going on out in the church. The congregation had hushed. Footsteps and dragging sounds could be heard plainly. There were murmurs of excitement and someone said: "I commend you, Cynthia, on the youthful beauty of our honored guest!" The dragging sounds stopped and there were other noises—titters of laughter and subdued commentary all blurred together. Through the bars of her cage, Gwen looked over at Nancy, whose eyes were wide and glittering like a trapped animal's, her body quivering under her soiled blanket.

From out in the church came Cynthia's high, keening voice: "Lucifer, we ask you to accept the sacrifice of this child we now offer to you in return for your blessings. Bless our deeds, that we perform in your almighty name. Consecrate the blood we offer you, the blood that we drink in holy communion with you, the Lord of hell."

Still trembling violently, Nancy pressed her palms and fingers together till they were white, making a spire pointing upward through the bars of her cage, toward heaven. She began to pray fervently. "Oh, my God, I am heartily sorry for having offended Thee, and I renounce all my sins because I dread the loss of heaven and the pain of hell. But most of all I renounce . . ."

"Praying's not going to do any good!" Gwen blurted. "Oh! You're as bad as the ones out there!"

Suddenly there came a shattering, blood-curdling scream. The screaming didn't stop, but went on and on, rising and falling, reverberating in the small room where Nancy and Gwen were caged. Gwen shuddered, realizing the screams were coming from Sharon. Maybe it would have been better, Gwen thought, if Sharon had never regained consciousness.

Nancy continued praying desperately, her palms pressed tightly together as if they were pressed on her ears, shutting out the screams. "I renounce them because they offend Thee, my Lord, who are all good and deserving of all my love . . ."

The horrible screams kept resounding over and over, making Gwen want to throw up . . . or to hurl herself against the bars of her cage. She stuck her fingers in her ears but it didn't help. If it kept up she thought she'd go mad. When she unplugged her ears, once again she heard Cynthia's rantingly shrill voice, carrying over Sharon's weakening screams: "Oh, mighty Lord Satan, we worship you with all our hearts and humbly submit to your

desires and commandments. We believe, with everlasting conviction, that you are our creator, our benefactor, our lord and master . . ."

Nancy raised her voice, trying to drown out Cynthia, trying to
counteract one kind of prayer with another. "Our Father who art
in heaven, hallowed be Thy Name. Thy kingdom come, Thy
will be done, on earth as it is in heaven . . ."

Sharon's screams weakened still more and became dry, husky
moans. She had probably ruptured her larynx. Gwen wrapped
herself tightly in the dirty blanket in her cage and pressed her
body against the wire bars, numbed and horrified, unable to
comprehend why some of the people in the congregation would
not be moved to mercy and pity. Were they not human? How
could they *all* be such demented lunatics? In the face of such
evil, Nancy's prayers seemed futile and pathetic, overwhelmed
by Cynthia's depraved incantations: "Lucifer, we ask you to bless
her, the source of our communion. May her blood give us
strength to do your bidding. Amen."

There was an eerie, expectant silence out in the church that
lasted for long moments. Then Sharon emitted one last pitiful
scream, lacking in volume, which was cut short . . . and became
transformed into a bubbly, gurgling sound. The congregation
started moaning and squealing ecstatically while the gurgling
continued . . . and finally stopped. From the evil ones out there, a
great cry went up, almost a sound of unanimous orgasm.

"Oh, my God!" Gwen wailed. "They've killed her! They've
killed her!" She threw herself onto the floor of her cage, sobbing
hysterically.

CHAPTER 17

On Saturday morning, Holy Saturday, Bert Johnson drove slowly on a dirt road near the area where Sheriff Cunningham had said the missing deputies had abandoned their squad car. Bert kept glancing left, then right, checking out everything, hoping to be lucky enough to spot the white van or maybe some other clue, if one existed. He didn't really expect his search to yield results. The van was probably long gone from this part of the United States. Why would the kids stick around, especially if they had had something to do with the disappearance of the deputies?

Bert's heart jumped into his throat when he rounded a sharp bend and saw exactly what he did not expect to see: a white van up ahead on a stretch of straight, narrow road, obscured by a cloud of dust. It would probably never turn out to be the right van. But Bert stepped on the gas to catch up and have a look at the license plate. Then on second thought he decided he'd better drop back a little, so as to not panic whoever he was following.

After a couple of miles, the van slowed down, as if the driver was looking for a place to turn off. Bert allowed himself to come up closer—an impatient motorist not wanting to slacken speed. Now he could read the license number, and it was the one Sheriff Cunningham had given him. When the van turned off onto a narrow weed-grown road in the surrounding woods, Bert didn't pursue. Instead, he nonchalantly drove past, keeping his eyes straight ahead. He was able to note that there were two men in the cab of the van.

Going slowly over the ruts in what was little more than a cowpath, branches on either side swatting the windshield, Luke said to Abraham, "Was that sucker following us?"

"Naw. I don't think so. Why should he? Let's not be jumpy. Let's finish up and get back."

They came out of the woods into a grassy clearing. Out in the middle of the clearing, Cyrus, in his bibbed coveralls, was just finishing digging a deep grave. The big man grinned when he saw his brothers approaching and used the sleeve of his workshirt to wipe sweat from his broad forehead.

"Shit!" said Luke. "I told you to have him dig back among the trees, not out in the open."

"I know. I showed him right where to do it. He seems to be gettin' dumber lately, know what I mean?"

"Don't I ever."

"Well, it'll be okay. Nobody comes around here, anyhow."

"Maybe we ought to fill it in and go someplace else."

"Naw. That'd take hours."

Having parked his car in a cul-de-sac that offered some concealment, Bert Johnson took his service revolver out of the glove compartment and tucked it in his belt, under his jacket. He got out and, began walking, keeping to cover as much as possible, picking his way back toward the place where the van had entered the woods.

Luke and Abraham opened the rear door of the van and lifted out Sharon Kennedy's body, wrapped in a blood-soaked blanket which had been on the floor of her cage. They dumped the corpse into the hole as if disposing of garbage, and Cyrus began shoveling in dirt.

Bert Johnson watched, hiding at the edge of the clearing. He saw the two who had arrived in the van take spades from the back of the vehicle and help with the shoveling. In a while, the grave was filled in. The men covered the evidence of their work with leaves and brush, taking their time, doing a thorough job. When they finally piled into the van and the engine started up, from the distance away that Bert was hiding he could hardly make out where the ground had been disturbed.

He stayed hidden, gripping his revolver as he watched the van drive off. He wondered who had been buried. One thing that occurred to Bert was: if it was Nancy, she'd never be coming home to cause him any further trouble with Harriet.

Creeping out of his hiding place, he stayed close enough to the departing van to make it out through the trees. When it humped onto the dirt road, it turned left, headed back in the direction it had come from.

Bert walked back to his car and got in, pulled out of the cul-de-sac, and drove slowly in pursuit of the van, not wanting to catch up so quickly that he got himself spotted. When he rounded a bend obscured by trees, he just caught a glimpse of the van making a right turn. So he crept up and made the right, also.

There was the van, about a quarter-mile ahead on a straightaway, making an abrupt left. Bert took a chance and picked up some speed, figuring to make the left, too, but when he got there he saw that it was a gravel driveway and the van was just pulling into a garage, several late-model cars parked to one side. Adjacent to the garage was a large red-brick house with white pillars. Startled to have come up on the place like that, Bert made a snap decision to just cruise on by, hoping he didn't call undue attention to himself.

Several hundred yards down the road, he pulled over and waited for a good long while, the engine idling and his pistol in his hand in case somebody came after him. Nobody came. He turned the ignition off and got out, looking all around. Then he made his way back toward the house with the white pillars, keeping to the cover of woods on the left side of the road. When he got within viewing distance, he hid in a clump of weeds and peered out. The three grave-diggers had come out of the garage and were talking, near enough for Bert to hear.

"I think we ought to get rid of the van," Luke said. "It could be somebody will eventually come lookin' for the owners."

"Tomorrow," said Abraham. "We'll drive it a good ways off and ditch it. Strip it and set it on fire."

Luke clapped Cyrus on his brawny shoulder. "You can come and watch, brother," Luke said merrily. "You'd get a kick out of that, wouldn't you?"

"Fire," Cyrus said, grinning.

"You two get on in the house and see if Cynthia needs anything," Luke ordered. "I'm goin' over to the chapel to make sure the two girls are comfy and not up to any tricks. That incident with the palette knife wasn't a damn bit funny."

"It wasn't *my* fault," Abraham said. "Let me go with ya to help ya fool with the girls."

"I ain't gonna be foolin' with 'em," Luke snapped. "Get in the house like I told you. Both of you. Pronto!"

"Aw, shit, Luke, you always get to have all the fun," Abraham grumped, but he and Cyrus got moving while Luke glowered after them, making sure they obeyed. They went into the house, slamming the door.

Bert stayed in his hiding place, watching Luke cut between the house and the garage. He appeared to be headed toward some kind of church out back, about a hundred yards away, across a freshly mowed field. Bert waited till Luke unlocked the door and went inside. Then he skirted along the edge of the road, keeping to cover till he could cross out of sight of the house. Then, circling wide of the route Luke had taken, he cut across the field toward the church. He came up in back of the church and hid behind a large boulder at the foot of a hillside. It took him a while to catch his breath. Just when he was wondering what his next move should be—should he try to creep up closer to the church, or not?—he was startled by the sound of a door opening.

Edging his paunchy body around the side of the boulder, gun ready, Bert heard a door slam, followed by a metallic scrape and click. His diagonal view of the church entrance did not enable him to actually see Luke till he had gotten thirty or forty strides out into the field, on his way back. Bert stayed put, waiting for Luke to walk to the house and go in by the back porch.

A light went on, then off, and the rear of the house was dark. It didn't seem as though Luke would come back out. Bert came around the side of the boulder and crept as softly as he could to the back wall of the church, ducking under a window. This was a regular window in the corner, while all the rest were stained glass. Bert raised his head slowly and peeked in. He saw Nancy in some kind of cage, talking to another girl who was also caged. Nancy looked gaunt, disheveled, beaten up. So did the other girl. Bert couldn't hear what they were saying; the way their lips were moving, they seemed to be whispering—could be they were arguing. The other girl had the last word and then turned away, a wild desperate look about her. Nancy tugged on some kind of ratty blanket she had around her, and Bert got a glimpse of her bra strap. When her head turned abruptly in his direction, he ducked down out of sight.

He sneaked away from the window, cutting a wide swath around the field, out of sight of the house, till he was able to cross the road again. On his way back to his car, he kept to the woods at the edge of the road, glancing back over his shoulder frequently to make sure no one was coming after him.

He opened the car door and got in, laying his service revolver on the seat right beside him. He was breathing hard and perspiring, badly shaken; his mouth twitched; his hands trembled as he unlocked the glove compartment. He took out a pint of whisky, uncapped it frantically, and swigged down a third of it. He wiped his mouth with the back of his hand, then turned the bottle up and drank again. Laying the bottle on the car seat beside the gun, he turned the key in the ignition, scaring himself by the noise of the engine starting up. He took a long look back in the direction of the place where Nancy and the other girl were imprisoned. Then he put the car into gear and drove away.

CHAPTER 18

On Holy Saturday, near midnight, Luke and Abraham came for Gwen. They had their robes on. The rest of the congregation had already filed into the church.

"No! Take *me* instead!" Nancy pleaded when Luke began unlocking Gwen's cage.

"Nope. Got to save you for Easter," Luke said. "You should feel honored."

"You bastards!" Gwen hissed, fearful and helpless as a wild animal in a wire trap.

"Heh-heh-heh!" Abraham chortled. "Don't give us any trouble now. Come on out of there!"

Gwen scrambled out fast, taking Luke by surprise, tackling his ankles and bringing him down. He hit hard, grunting his pain, flailing clumsily in his loose-fitting black robe, as Gwen got halfway up in a mad dash for the door. Abraham stumbled over Luke but made a diving lunge for Gwen, slashing her naked shoulder with his nails. His fingers momentarily clutched her bra strap, but it came unsnapped. Luke yelled for help. Gwen yanked the door open and ran straight into Cyrus, bouncing off his chest. His big heavy right arm came at her in a lumbering roundhouse swat, clubbing her on the ear and batting her sideways so hard that she staggered and fell. Fighting to stay conscious, she tried to crawl, but Cyrus stomped on her spine and ground in the heel of his boot, giggling while she wriggled and screamed.

Abraham and Luke were outside now and so were several other robed figures carrying lighted candles, casting long, eerie shadows into the dark night. Roughly, Abraham and Cyrus yanked Gwen to her feet.

"Back inside!" Luke shouted. "Stinking bitch!"

The people with the candles preceded Luke, Gwen, Cyrus, and Abraham into the church, and Abraham slammed the door. Nancy was praying, trying to ignore everything that was going on. Gwen tried feebly to resist as she was dragged past Nancy's cage, but Abraham punched her in the stomach, knocking the last remainder of resistance out of her. She sagged limply in the arms of her captors, who dragged her down the center aisle toward the front of the church. Her ears were ringing and she was so dizzy she wanted to throw up. Through her pain and nausea, the congregation filling the pews was an amorphpus blur of leering faces and black velvet, unearthly in a haze of incense and flickering candlelight. Her head swam and for a moment she lost consciousness.

When she came to, she raised her head to see Cynthia standing before her, less than two feet away, robed in white. Cynthia's attitude was regal, her features ghostly, her pupils dilated. "Welcome!" she intoned solemnly. "Tonight you shall be our guest of honor." There were excited whispers and murmurs of approval from the congregation.

"You insane bitch!" Gwen said, squeaking it out with all the defiance she could muster. Abraham smacked her in the chest with his open hand, knocking the wind out of her, and as her knees went all rubbery the brothers twisted her around and shoved her down onto a solid wooden chair similar to an electric chair in size and construction. Quickly they encircled her wrists and ankles with leather straps, buckling them tight, and strapped her head back so it was held rigidly upright against a vertical post that was part of the chair, preventing any sort of movement.

"Undress her completely!" Cynthia commanded, and Luke took a knife from under his robe and sliced away Gwen's panties, tearing the tatters of the filmy garment away rudely, leaving her totally naked and vulnerable.

Cynthia stepped aside and Gwen shrieked when she saw she was sitting across from an elderly woman who was dead and mummified. "Meet my mother," said Cynthia.

Gwen once more lost consciousness, she was so weak from the beatings she had taken. Her vision blurred, as her eyes went shut. Her body relaxed, her head pulling downward against the leather strap.

Audible spasms of lust stirred among the congregation, under-the-breath sighs and throaty groans of arousal. Beneath their black robes, the witches were nude, coarse folds of fabric teasing their groins and nipples. Some reached hands under their own robes or the robes of others in the pews, to fondle and caress aroused and moistening flesh.

The door of the church opened and Morgan Drey was wheeled in by the two chiropractors, Harvey Bronson and John Logan. Behind them Stanford Slater shut the door then followed the procession up the aisle. Morgan was tied with coils of rope to a cushioned chaise longue with a redwood frame. He could feel nothing from the neck down, as Logan, the man who had made him a paraplegic, propelled him helplessly down the aisle of the church by lifting one end of the longue and rolling it along on its wooden wheels.

Luke, Cyrus, Abraham, Cynthia, and their deceased mother were seated around an altar, which was in the shape of a large, five-pointed star. Their faces appeared grotesque, demented, in the wildly flickering candlelight. At each point of the star stood a human skull and each skull supported a tall red candle, bloodlike rivulets of wax running down over the skulls' foreheads and dripping like tears from their eyesockets. The centerpiece of the altar was a huge black-and-red sculpture of an evil-looking goat-god with wild, curving horns and a pair of claw-like hands made to hold a silver dagger and an ornate silver chalice. On the wall behind the altar, above the mummified Mrs. Barnes, was an upside-down crucifix illuminated by candles in silver sconces.

Morgan stared as he was dollied nearer to the altar and the chiropractor brought him to a halt a few feet away. "A ringside seat like we promised," said Slater.

Rolling his head to one side, Morgan saw the tortured, unconscious girl in the executioner's chair. He felt sorry for her, and sorrier for himself. He didn't want to go on living as a cripple. His worst fear now was that maybe they wouldn't kill him. Cynthia's face, her very presence, the mocking memory of his infatuation with her, were nightmarish aspects of the overall nightmare of what had been done to him. He looked up at Cynthia, her perverse beauty looming over him, her lips curled in an evil, triumphant smile.

Suddenly Morgan thought he heard someone praying and he couldn't believe his ears. It was coming from somewhere inside the church: "Our Father. who art in heaven, hallowed be Thy name . . ."

Immediately the congregation began chanting in unison, drowning out the Lord's Prayer, overriding it with Latin or Greek that Morgan didn't understand. Cynthia stood in solemn majesty, lifted the altar's silver chalice in her two hands, and began her own incantation in a high, shrill voice that carried above the congregation's chant.

"Lucifer, we beg you to accept the sacrifice of this child whom we now offer to you, so that we may receive your blessings. Bless our deeds, that we perform in your almighty name. Consecrate the blood that we have come to offer you, the blood we drink to show our oneness with you, the Lord of hell."

All that Morgan had read and written about witchcraft and its obscenities was no match for what he was experiencing now. Helpless as he was, he wanted to get up and run, fleeing from the mindless chanting and the revolting ugliness of Cynthia's prayer.

"Oh, mighty Lord Satan, we worship you with all our hearts and humbly submit to your desires and commandments. We believe, with everlasting conviction, that you are our creator, our benefactor, our lord and master. We renounce Jehovah, his son Jesus Christ, and all their works. And we declare to you, Lord Satan, that we have no other wish but to belong to you for all eternity."

The chanting stopped. An air of expectancy filled the church. Once again Morgan heard a girl's voice, praying from somewhere: ". . . hallowed be Thy Name, Thy kingdom come, Thy will be done . . ."

It sounded like a young girl, praying energetically, perhaps being held prisoner. Instead of praying, Morgan thought, why didn't she try to escape? Probably her situation was as utterly hopeless as his. Prayer was all she had left. Her voice rang out in the clear: "Give us this day our daily bread and forgive us our trespasses, as we forgive those who trespass against us."

An uneven trade, thought Morgan. What trespasses could the young girl have committed that could even begin to stack up against what these monsters were going to do to her?

CHAPTER 19

Bert Johnson entered his home by the front door and was greeted in the living room by his wife, Harriet. Bert hung his head, looking tired and defeated. By his demeanor, Harriet knew right away that he had had no luck in his search for Nancy, and the hope in her eyes faded.

Bert merely said, "I'm sorry, honey."

"Oh, Bert!" Harriet wailed, throwing herself into his arms, burying her tears on his shoulder.

"I'm afraid she's run away for good," Bert offered. "If she isn't with Terri out in California, or doesn't show up there, I have no idea where to look next."

Harriet clung to him, her face streaked with tears. If she was going to lose Nancy, she didn't want to lose Bert, too. It would be unbearable.

Bert tried to be soothing, holding out hope. "Nancy will be all right, honey. She's old enough to take care of herself, after all. You and I did our best to raise her properly. If she runs out of money or gets sick or lonely, she'll come home some night with her tail between her legs, full of apologies, as if that could make up for how much she's hurt us. Then it will be up to us to forgive her and start over."

"Oh, Bert!" Harriet wailed, trembling against him.

CHAPTER 20

As if she had a subconscious awareness that something important was about to happen to her, Gwen suddenly came to, her eyes snapping open, her tear-streaked face contorting in agony as she once again knew where she was and felt the pain of her injuries. She moaned weakly, strapped in the chair. And her eyes flickered as she heard Nancy's distant praying: ". . . and lead us not into temptation, but deliver us from evil . . ."

Luke arose, taking from the altar a pair of crossed human bones and placing them in front of Gwen's throat, as a priest uses crossed candles to bless the throats of Catholics on Ash Wednesday. Gwen screamed, her voice hoarse. Abraham took the silver dagger from the altar and moved in close so that he and Luke flanked Gwen on either side.

The congregation began chanting again, drowning out the distant sound of the Lord's Prayer. Cynthia prayed: "Lucifer, we ask you to bless her, the source of our communion. May her blood give us strength to do your bidding."

Luke replaced the human bones on the altar. Cynthia handed him the silver chalice. Abraham laid his dagger across Gwen's throat, ready to slice the jugular vein so that Luke could use the chalice to collect her blood. Gwen emitted one last horrible scream, which was cut short by the slicing dagger as her life gurgled out of her . . . and her blood was collected.

For an instant the Lord's Prayer rang out. "For Thine is the kingdom and the power and the glory . . ." But it was drowned out by great moans of sadistic ecstasy that poured forth from the congregation. They looked on in lurid fascination, overwhelmed by the intensity of Cynthia's services, anxious to see blood spilled again and again.

In her cage Nancy prayed, trying to make herself heard above the din: "May her soul and all the souls of the faithful departed, through the mercy of God, rest in peace. And may perpetual light shine upon her."

At the altar, Gwen was dead and ghostly white, her life drained from her, trickles of blood dripping from her breasts to the floor. Most members of the congregation were sexually aroused. Stanford Slater, the old, obese mortician, had himself climaxed watching Gwen die. In the frenzy of it, many of the witches had stripped off their black robes and were naked in the pews, sweating and breathing hard, anxious to give themselves over to the orgy which would follow.

Unable to control his bladder, Morgan Drey lay in a puddle of urine which he was unable to feel.

Nancy shouted from the confines of her cage. "Forgive them, Father, for they know not what they do!"

Having collected Gwen's blood, Luke handed the chalice to Cynthia, who took it in her hands and held it skyward.

"By this blood, grant our beloved mother eternal life, Lord Satan! So that she, your faithful servant, may dwell among us forever!"

Morgan Drey watched in horror, as Cynthia approached the embalmed corpse of Meredith Barnes and put the chalice to the corpse's lips, making her "drink." Blood ran down Meredith's chin.

Morgan looked up at Cynthia as she came toward him, the bloody silver dagger in her hand. "Thank you," he whispered as the dagger came downward, stabbing into him. He couldn't feel it, only heard it punching into his groin, and he knew he must be bleeding, but he wasn't dead. And he wanted to be. *I thanked her prematurely,* he thought. And then the blade came at him again, flashing from behind Cynthia's demonic face, and still he didn't die, not till the third time, when she thrust the dagger upward on an angle, through his solar plexus and into his heart.

Standing over him with the dagger, Cynthia sliced his jugular vein. An approving gasp came from the congregation. They watched the chalice being filled, Cynthia collecting the sacrificial blood. She drank.

Stanford Slater stepped up and took the chalice from her and raised it to his lips. And other witches clamored to drink, too, crowding around.

Cynthia took off her bloodspattered white robe, her nipples erect, her sex tingling with excitement. Her brothers ogled her sheer, wanton, voluptuous beauty. And then, with Morgan dead and Gwen dead, in the presence of their corpses the orgy commenced, building to a frenzy.

Locked in her wire cage, enveloped by cries and moans and insane laughter of the witches in the throes of their depraved passions, Nancy prayed from the depths of her soul: "I believe in God, the Father Almighty. Creator of heaven and earth. I will put no false gods before Him . . ."

Her voice rang-out clear and unafraid, imbued with holy conviction. She did not feel the confines of her cage. Death held no terror for her. Her spirit was exulted. Her palms and fingers were pressed tightly together, making a spire that pointed the way toward heaven.